THE JOGGER

J.J. SPENCER

For Jimmy
the author of all my happy endings.

*"**Morning without you is a dwindled dawn.**"*
Emily Dickinson

CHAPTER 1

MUD AND FLOWERS

The hour was ungodly. Kate's sweet slumber rousted by a devilish itch. She struggled against the dreamy web distorting reality and blinked once, twice, three times into the dark room. Beneath the heavy covers, Danny's body heat afflicted all her senses. It was comfy, sedate, and safe. But she fought against her husband's familiar pull and forced her legs to move. Bolting out of bed into the still coolness of the house was a shock and exactly what she needed. Kate was done sleeping.

After hurrying through her morning routine, Kate skipped outside the backdoor and inhaled sharply. The air was heavy with moisture. The sky still peppered with stars. It was her favorite time of day. Too early for the earliest early bird and too late for the latest night owl. The predawn quiet of her suburban neighborhood gave her peace, soothed her restless spirit, and it made her glad. Happy with the knowledge that all it cost was a couple of hours of sleep.

Kate signaled her cold muscles awake with a few gentle stretches. She placed her palms on the side of her house and leaned her hips forward while keeping her heels flat. Grasping her ankle, she pulled the sole of her shoe to her butt and stretched. Before switching legs, she flicked on her safety light, a Christmas gift from her eldest son, Peter. Intended for a small dog, the lighted collar fit loosely around her wrist and blinked red. It was the sort of gift Kate appreciated most. Thoughtful, practical, and very useful.

Jogging down the driveway, she kept her eyes forward and breathed through her nose. The smell of spring was a savory combination of mud and flowering buds, a tender reminder of home. Kate's mother loved the changing seasons, and spring was a favorite on the farm.

Kate's muscles loosened when her shoes hit the exercise trail. Green parks and athletic fields were overly abundant in the Chicago suburbs, but Wheaton's Little League Park was a rare gem. Its exercise trail wove in and out of hilly valleys, providing scenic views and a challenging work out. Pushing the limits of her body, she quickened her pace and concentrated on the steady beat of her own footfalls.

It was a relief. Being present. Being one. Singular in the park. But it didn't last long. Kate's thoughts veered off the path after spotting his silhouette. He was running at her through the haze. Like always, his posture struck her hard. His stride was confident, proud, and masterly. The cool morning air burned inside her chest stalling her heart. It wasn't fear. It was something else.

Kate sped up—sped towards him. The jogger's hand brushed against hers—pounding feet stopped short—no words. They weren't necessary. The jogger climbed the steep grass embankment off the path and looked back only once. Switching off her safety light, Kate tucked the band into her jacket pocket and scurried through the wet grass.

The jogger was breathing heavily—one hand on his hip—and looking down at the fingertips of his dangling hand when she came flying over the small hill. Knocking the hat off his head, she ran fingers through his thick hair—pressing her face next to his.

She wanted to taste him—to burn his spicy scent into her memory. The delicate skin around her mouth stung from rubbing roughly against his unshaven face and neck. Ignoring the burn warning, she nuzzled further into his neck—licking—sucking—one hand twisted into his hair and the other gripped his ass.

Kate heard sporadic car traffic but remained undeterred. They were safely hidden in the narrow valley between the road and jogging path. Practiced at finding secluded spots in the park, she worried more about timing. Kate did not waste minutes on talk or foreplay. Her husband was at home sleeping in their warm bed, and all three boys needed to rise and ready themselves for school. Cringing, she pushed thoughts of her responsibilities to the corners of her mind. For a few stolen minutes, Kate was alone——alone with the jogger.

The jogger's eyes were almost black and deeply set with lashes lush and dark. He was asking with a look—pleading silently—pained, desperate need—very seductive. Sliding her hand beneath the waistband of his shorts, she smiled when he clenched his eyes shut. Stroking his erection, she waited for his raven eyes to open and gasped when they finally did.

"More, please," she answered his unspoken question in a whisper.

His eyes flashed. The jogger spun her—never releasing his hold—and ripped at her running shorts. Reaching around, he slid stiff fingers between her legs and hissed into the hair tucked behind her ear. Kate shuddered—his fingers strong—persistent. The pressure softened her bones—liquefied her internal organs. And then—she was on her knees—hands pressed into the wet grass.

"Spread your legs wider."

His cock thrust deep, and she could not stop the impulse—she cried out. It hurt to be penetrated so quickly from behind. His hands gripped her hips as he found his rhythm. They were perfectly proportionate—a seamless fit. It was exhilarating—letting go—no fear—no pretense. Just Kate. Kate alone. The jogger pounded against her ass—harder and harder. He was so new—so foreign—and so very dangerous. Adrenalin burned inside her

3

veins. She wanted to scream but bit it back—clenched jaw—eyes shut.

The moment cut like the blade of a searing hot knife. It was hopelessly accidental—shockingly thrilling—and over too quickly. Shuddering, she climaxed and nearly collapsed into the spongy grass. But he wasn't finished. Holding her weight in his grip, he continued his climb. Kate kept her eyes closed to the light of the breaking sun—lost in the sensation of being used—her body the object of desire—so deliciously sinful—so very wrong.

"More. You want more," he groaned.

Hot and slick with the jogger's sweat, she begged quietly for his release, "Please, please, please."

He growled low—deep—menacing, and climaxed. His lean, muscular body rigid—her own body soft, wet, and wasted. Still in his clutches, she did not move—relishing the subtle moan beneath his raspy breath. The thundering behind her ears faded and then it was over.

Standing, the jogger quickly pulled at his shorts. Without a word and without looking back, he climbed out of the grassy hideaway. He always left first.

With wobbly knees, Kate took a minute to situate her clothes and hair. The jogger wore a wedding ring. Definitely married, she knew little else about him. It didn't matter. Using her mind's eye, Kate closed the door and began her trek home.

When she turned into her neighborhood, the sun was officially up. Kate's bones were fortified with new starch. Her insides pumped with enriched blood, and she broke into an exhilarating sprint.

Molly was out early walking her yappy, little dog. Unable to ignore her neighbor without being rude, Kate waved with a long arm.

"I think it is going to be a beautiful day," Molly called.

Kate wasn't expected to stop and chat when she was clearly out of breath and concluding her daily jog. For once, the smile on her face felt genuine.

So Kate graciously nodded at Molly and sped up her driveway.

CHAPTER 2

MINE

The beard was new, and Danny fussed over it. He wasn't the type of man who spent a lot of time in front of the mirror, but the facial hair forced him to take extra time in the morning. Threats to shave it off were empty and meant to tease his wife. Kate considered the beard community property. She liked the way he used his soft whiskers to apply just the right amount of friction.

He could hear her rustling in the kitchen getting the boys' lunches ready. Cafeteria food wasn't real food according to Kate. Shaking his head, he stepped out of their master bathroom and into his closet. Danny had designed and built the first floor master suite onto their home after their youngest, Joey, was born. He needed Kate to get some distance from the boys, and she didn't protest.

"Why are you up so early?" she asked, rushing past him to make their bed.

"I'm catching the 7:15 train. I have a breakfast meeting." He smiled at her through the reflection of the dresser mirror as he knotted his tie. "Good run?"

"Does that mean you'll be home early?" she asked avoiding his question.

"Nope. I've got meetings all day."

Danny turned away from the mirror just as his wife pulled off her workout clothes. Modesty was not a virtue Kate valued. It drew him to her when they were young, and it made him a different man. Nakedness, his and hers, was something he got comfortable with very early on in their relationship. Kate made him unashamed. She loved his body, and she didn't care about his eyes on hers.

Tossing her clothes into the hamper, she made no effort at conversation and jumped into the shower without letting the water warm up. Danny followed her into the bathroom. He guessed her mood was the result of a long to-do list. She was a regimented housewife, and it wasn't fun teasing her about it anymore. Kate was unapologetic about the way she ran their household.

Danny frowned at the steam clouding the shower stall door. Watching her long hair darken with wetness, Danny felt a familiar tidal wave of emotion. "*Mine,*'" he repeated in an internal mantra. "*All mine.*"

"I don't like you running alone in the dark, Katie. It's time to get a dog."

"Another mouth to feed. No thanks."

She scrubbed herself pink with a soapy nylon sponge and did not meet his gaze.

"I wish I could join you." Danny glanced at his watch and put his large hand against the glass shower door. "Get on out of there. I want a kiss before I go."

Smiling, his wife stepped out of the shower and took the towel from his outstretched hand. Danny stuffed his hands into his pockets and watched with downcast eyes as she carefully dried off.

"You're cutting it close, Coach," Kate said.

Danny checked his watch before pulling his naked wife in for a hug.

"You make leaving the house difficult." He kissed her solidly on the mouth before adding, "I'll call and check in this afternoon."

Danny liked to keep tabs on her mood. Walking into the house unaware of the day's events was dangerous for any family man.

"These meetings you'll be in all day…will you be cracking skulls or selling something?"

Wet hair dripped down her bare shoulders, and the towel did nothing as a cover up. Naked on the bathroom rug, Kate wanted to talk. Danny pursed his lips to exaggerate the amount of thought he put into his answer. "I'll be doing a bit of both, I think."

"You'll leave them laying on the ice dazed and bleeding, I'm sure," Kate said confidently. "One way or another, you always get your way. Doesn't matter if you're checking them into the boards or flashing that sexy smile."

Conversation would require him to use more than a fraction of his brain, and he barely registered her ice hockey reference. Danny was eyeing the contour of her slim waist against the dramatic curve of her hips. Pregnancy drew a permanent line on Kate's body, and he viewed it as a good thing. It was easy to get a grip on her now.

Kate's body shivered, but she didn't reach for the robe hanging next the shower door. Danny drew his eyes over the muscles in her stomach and across the tips of her rosy, hard nipples. Finally, his gaze settled on her hazel eyes, and he was surprised. They were unfamiliar. Unreadable.

"I love you, Danny." Her voice broke on his name, and it gave him pause. But his thoughts flew to the train he needed to catch.

"And I love Trouble." It was his standard response, but her face fell. Danny could easily identify the emotion now...sadness.

Checking his watch for the third time, he frowned. Danny didn't have time to deal with problems. He was gonna have to hustle if he wanted to hit the coffee shop before boarding the train to Chicago.

"What is it?" His tone was sharper than he intended. Kate turned quickly and grabbed her robe. She shook her head and tied it shut.

"What's the matter, baby?"

Kate recovered with a smile. "We'll be waiting for you when you come home."

It was exactly what he needed to hear. After a quick peck good-bye, Danny left for work untroubled.

CHAPTER 3

ACTIONS HAVE CONSEQUENCES

Afternoons in the Maller household were quiet endeavors. Wiped out from his morning at pre-school, Joey needed time with his beloved blanket to recharge. Rolling around at Kate's feet, he sucked his thumb while she clipped and filed coupons.

The shrill ring of the kitchen phone made Joey jump, and Kate dropped her scissors. She hated answering the phone. Kate abused caller ID and often let her voicemail pick up her messages. The small screen on her remote phone read *Wheaton School District*.

"Hello? This is Kathryn Maller."

"Hello, Mrs. Maller. This is Mr. Burns over at Lark Elementary."

Frowning, Kate set her coupons on the counter and put her hand on her hip. "Is Billy okay?"

"He was using his skateboard to launch himself off the stairs leading to the faculty parking lot."

Kate was frustrated, but it wasn't directed at Billy. It was directed at Mr. Burns.

"Mrs. Maller, we don't mind the kids riding skateboards to school as long as they refrain from skating on school property. I believe I've made this policy clear to both you and Billy."

Kate rolled her eyes. Mr. Burns was a self-important ass. "Put him on the phone."

"Excuse me?" he asked.

"I want to speak with Bill," Kate reiterated with an impatient sigh.

"Sorry, Mom."

"Apologize to Mr. Burns. Promise it won't happen again and get your sorry butt home."

"Okay," Bill agreed quickly and handed the phone back to the vice-principal.

Hanging up the phone, Kate cursed under her breath. Now, she would have to punish him. Both Peter and Billy skateboarded during ice hockey's off-season, but her middle son liked to push the limits with his antics. Phone calls from the police were common. Fortunately, Billy was a polite kid who instinctually used his boyish charms with local law enforcement. He usually got off with just a parent phone call and a stern warning. Mr. Burns was a different story. The vice-principal was gunning for her son.

"Billy is in trouble again, little man."

Joey rolled over to look up at his mom. His eyes were sleepy, but his concern for his favorite brother made them wide with worry. "Skateboarding?" he asked without taking the thumb out of his mouth.

"Yep."

Kate nodded her head and began lining up the ingredients for their dinner on the kitchen counter. Joey watched her for a bit and then pushed himself off the floor. He went to the porch. It was the best place to wait for his big brothers. Kate found her youngest son sitting on the porch swing with his blanket draped over shoulders like a cape.

"Are you going to take away Billy's skateboard," he asked never tearing his eyes away from the street corner.

"Yep, and he loses the computer for the week."

Kate was tired of talking to Mr. Burns. Billy was going to be on foot during school hours. Dandelions were sprouting in the flower bed bordering the front walk, so Kate climbed down the stairs to yank them out by the root. Gardening was a favorite pastime, and flowers bloomed throughout her yard. Danny liked to remark to admiring neighbors that his wife's passion for yard work was the Wisconsin farm girl rebelling in the Chicago suburbs. But Kate just really loved digging in the dirt. It made her feel close to her mom. Her mother loved growing all sorts of things and sold produce from a stand at the end of their driveway in the late summer. Kate's fondest memories were of her mother wearing a funny hat underneath a bright sky.

Rounding the corner, Peter waved good-bye to a group of giggling girls. Built like his father, Peter had yet to reach his full height but was already taller than all his classmates. He had a head of wheat-gold hair like his mother, but people compared him to Danny because of his wide shoulders and gray eyes.

Speeding past Peter, Bill glided up the driveway on his skateboard. When he spotted his mother in front of the house, he hopped off the board and walked it over to her. He knew his fate and was prepared for its confiscation. Grateful for the lack of argument, Kate took the skateboard with a sympathetic smile.

"So tell me—what did Mr. Burns dish out as penance?" she asked.

Billy rolled his eyes, "I have to write a three hundred word essay on helmet safety."

Kate laughed and smacked him on the bottom with his skateboard.

"I'm sure that will be an adequate deterrent," she teased and then quickly decided the essay was punishment enough.

"I wasn't the only one skating. But of course, Mr. Burns picked me to haul inside," Billy complained.

"You've got a bad reputation. Keep that in mind when you start middle school next year. Establish yourself as a rule breaker from the get go, and you'll be pinned as a troublemaker."

Kate knew her son wasn't listening. Getting caught breaking rules only bothered him during hockey season when his skates could be taken away.

"Actions have consequences," she added mussing up Billy's hair as she herded the boys inside. "Don't ever forget that."

CHAPTER 4

LOCK DOWN

Danny couldn't rest until his family was safely tucked under his roof. Switching off lights, he ambled through his house checking and then double checking the locks on the doors and windows.

His stocking feet slid over the re-finished wood floor as he made his way to the stairs. Looking in on his sleeping sons was the last chore before joining Kate in bed. Kate was enjoying the quiet by reading. She could have fallen asleep, but Danny would wake her if necessary. His wife was a rare creature. He liked to think he was responsible, but he knew the truth. Kate loved sex. She loved it before they met and loved it still.

They had met at a house party their junior year at Madison. His buddy, Conner, was pre-law like Kate and was so terrified of her it was laughable. Conner called her trouble and filled Danny in on her man-eater status. Nothing Conner said made any difference. Kate was a corn-fed beauty in a flowered prairie skirt and faded jean jacket. When she took Danny's hand and pulled him into the kitchen pantry, he was awestruck. She carried condoms in the inside pocket of her jean jacket and ripped the stiff packaging open with her teeth. He ignored her sexual history and fucked her from behind because that was what she asked for. His first encounter with Kate in the pantry was by far the best sex he'd ever experienced, and he was hooked—completely hooked for twenty years.

Since becoming a mother, clues to her sexual prowess became less distinct. Danny was glad—relieved mostly—to see how easily she fell into the role of suburban housewife. They were an ordinary family. He kept his mouth shut, and no one was the wiser.

But lately, Kate's eyes shifted away from him and the boys. He recognized the look. It was the same dangerous glint that had him chasing her around Madison's campus. Love-making was out the window. Kate wanted to be fucked.

It had him rushing through his day—counting the hours—the minutes—until he could be alone with her. Danny hurried towards the cracked door of their bedroom.

Kate moved quickly to her bedside lamp and switched it off just as Danny stepped in the doorway. He took a moment to admire the way the dim light coming from their master bathroom framed her face. When she smiled and lifted her eyebrows, Danny dove for the bed.

She laughed, but then quickly frowned when he flopped over to look at her. "You're gonna break the bed one of these days."

"I'm surprised this thing has lasted as long as it has," he bounced so the headboard rattled against the wall.

"You won't think it's so funny when you have to write a check for new furniture."

"There's no budget for the bedroom, Trouble. You know that." Danny's eyes flashed with humor. "Maybe our next bed should have a canopy with a retractable mirror."

"Mirrors?" Kate shook her head slightly. "I was hoping for a handcuff friendly headboard."

Danny rolled on top of his wife and brushed the hair away from her face. "Too tempting," he murmured. "I might not ever let you loose."

"The handcuffs are for you, Coach," Kate said running her hands beneath the cotton of his white undershirt. "For once, I'd like to make you cry."

Danny made a contented noise from deep within his chest. Closing his eyes, he lowered his face to hers. "Tell me you love me," he murmured as his lips moved across her cheekbone and down her throat.

"I love you." Her answer was automatic, and he knew it was true. Of course, she loved him. Clutching at his back, she tried to pull him closer, but he propped his weight on his elbows leaving inches of space between them.

"Why?" he asked nuzzling behind her ear. "Why do you love me?"

Sighing patiently, she released her grip on him and sank back into the depths of their bed covers. The muscles in her body relaxed as she stroked his face.

"You don't judge," she murmured. "I can ask you for anything."

Using all her strength, she shoved Danny onto his back and straddled his hips. Her fingers slowly ran down the buttons of her night shirt. She caught his hands as they reached for her breasts and moved them so quickly to her ass that they landed on her flesh with a resounding smack.

"Ask me then," he growled. His lips pulled up into a wry smile when he felt her body thrill at his tone. He knew what she wanted. She wanted something new— and she wanted it so bad, it was good.

Leaning in, her hair fell over his face and she whispered in his ear. "Danny, please, I need to feel your hands on my ass. Make it hurt."

With a groan, he roughly threw her weight off and rose. He didn't look at her as he rounded the bed and clicked the lock in their door.

"Take your top off, but I want your panties on," he ordered as he removed his clothes.

Kate complied with watchful eyes and scooted herself off the bed when Danny sat in the overstuffed chair in the corner of their bedroom. She stood, letting the cool night air harden her nipples. He held her gaze until she shivered. Opening his arms, he invited her into his warm embrace.

She smiled, kneeled before him, laid her face against his belly, and kicked the ottoman out from behind her. Danny directed his eyes at the ceiling as he rubbed her naked shoulders, stoking the fire of desire smoldering beneath her cool flesh.

"Suck it," he murmured.

Holding his erection in his right hand, he inhaled sharply as she dragged her open mouth slowly down his belly. Kate was anxious to please. He could feel it in the way her body purred. Nuzzling into him, she began at the bottom of his shaft and ran her tongue along the length listening as he exhaled slowly. Danny kept his eyes on his wife's ass as she rocked back and forth. Occasionally, he would mumble her name, coaching her with throaty whispers. "You're so good, baby."

She looked up into his eyes without removing her mouth and moaned softly. Danny stopped her abruptly by laying hands on both sides of her face.

"No," he breathed. "I want to fuck you. Turn around."

Kate laid herself over the ottoman, and he dropped to his knees. Stroking the cotton of her panties, he made her wait. "Do you want me to spank you?"

"Yes," she gasped, squirming beneath his hands.

Growling, he roughly tore at her panties, pulling at them until her pale ass was bare. His breathing hitched when she adjusted her weight directing her ass up, inviting his full attention. Clenching his jaw, he smacked her squarely on the ass, closing his eyes when she cried out.

"More?" he asked, stroking her ass.

"Yes, Danny," she whined. "Please."

He groaned again and used the palm of his hand to pepper her bottom with one noisy slap after another. Kate threw her head back, crying every time his palm made contact. Finally, she pulled away. He let her weight collapse on the ottoman. Spreading her now pinked ass cheeks with both hands, he pressed his erection against her puckered asshole.

"Are you a bad girl?" he asked quietly.

"Yes," she whined clutching the ottoman beneath her. "Fuck me, Danny."

He resisted the urge to continue her punishment. Danny wanted so much to fuck her ass—but was afraid—afraid to ask—afraid to cross the line. Instead, he kicked open her legs and let his cock slide down to her wet spot. "Ready to be fucked?"

"Yes," she pleaded into the night. "Yes. I need it."

The sound of her voice propelled him forward, and he thrust into her welcoming flesh. He watched as his cock slipped in and out. Reaching, he locked onto her right wrist and tugged.

"Rub your clit, baby. Make yourself cum."

Kate did as she was told. Under his command, she was sopping wet, and so completely into it. Kate loved it—loved being fucked. Danny quickened his pace when he sensed Kate's excitement mounting.

Smacking her one last time with his open palm, he sent her flying over the cliff into climax. Her cries and shudders sent his body charging after—Danny climaxed with a triumphant groan. Slowly, he came back to his senses, counted his lucky stars, and ran a gentle hand over the marks on her ass.

Danny helped Kate to her feet and tucked her beneath their soft blankets. Stumbling to his side of the bed, he left his pajamas in a heap on the floor.

"Was I too rough on you, baby?" he asked as he punched his head into a pillow.

"No," she said returning his gentle gaze. "I like it. You don't mind, do you?"

"Don't worry about me." Danny pushed the hair out of her eyes and ran his fingers along the side of her face. "It's hot. So hot it scares me. Promise me, Katie. Promise to stop me if I hurt you too much."

Closing her eyes, Kate nodded her head and sighed. Danny closed his eyes too and drifted off to sleep.

CHAPTER 5

DISCOVERY

Their last sexual encounter was two mornings ago. The novelty of chance had worn off. He wanted her every morning. Problem. Dawn was breaking earlier with the approach of summer making private interludes difficult. He hoped if he rose to beat the rising sun, she would also. But she did not. Or maybe she was jogging a new route. Or skipping her jog all together. He didn't know, and it was making him crazy.

No longer able to concentrate at work or home, he decided to take action to remedy his miserable condition and stake out the park. He knew where she entered and exited the jogging path but nothing else. If she was still running her usual route, he was going to catch her and follow her home. It was 6:06 a.m.

Finally, from within the safety of his SUV, he saw her exit the park and turn north. Immediately his hand flew to the ignition, but he stopped. Patience. He let her get a proper lead and then carefully followed. It worked. He managed to trail her home undetected. Parking two houses down, he watched as the lights inside her home switched on.

Because of her neighborhood's coveted location near Wheaton's downtown and Chicago's Metra train line, property was expensive. He guessed the house was worth nearly half of a million. Not bad. But compared to the rest of the homes in the neighborhood, relatively modest.

Wealthier families bought existing homes, knocked them down, and rebuilt. Residents with average incomes remodeled, thereby sacrificing yard for square footage. Original from the front with its perched porch and leaded windows, it was easy to identify the additions made to her home.

The house was sunshine yellow with white trim. Curb appeal. Her yard was small but exceptionally well kept. It overflowed with spring flowers, shrubbery, and decorative trees. She had a green thumb. Or her husband did.

His hands clenched the steering wheel. Not knowing even the littlest things about her was driving him mad. Picking up his iPhone, he punched in her address and emailed his assistant. He wanted a detailed report researching the property and its owner on his desk by 10:00 a.m. He would finally know her name.

The neighborhood was waking up. People were letting out dogs, retrieving newspapers, and opening garages. He was drawing attention. Sitting alone in his SUV. No need for concern. His outward appearance was not suspicious. Avoiding eye contact with the droll neighbors, he scrolled through the directory on his iPhone. Waiting.

Finally, 7:15. The backdoor flew open, and the husband skipped out of the house. Shit. The man was a mountain. His hands fumbled with the zipper on the nylon briefcase slung across his barrel-like chest.

And then sweet heaven. She chased after him. Damp hair. Fresh faced. Her gray sweatshirt and loose fitting jeans did nothing to accent her nubile body, but she lit up with a happy smile. Pretty in an unassuming way. Holding out a cell phone, she called out. He could hear deep laughter as the husband turned back up the driveway and met her at the side of the house. Son of a bitch.

She leaned into him. Looked up into his eyes. And slid the phone into the front pocket of his slacks. She was average height, but next to the husband, she was miniscule. Shit. Six foot four. At least. Built, too. The man must work out. Damn. It wasn't even a fair fight.

Rage surged in his chest when he caught sight of her hands moving across the husband's colossal body. They landed on his ass. The husband laughed again. Son of a bitch. And pulled away. Idiot. No longer rushing, his walk had a new swagger to it. Asshole. The idiot had no idea his adoring wife was screwing around.

Hatred spurned his next move. Acting on instinct, he followed the husband. A commuter. How generic. Walking to the train like the other cattle. Probably middle management. Rubber-soled shoes. No suit coat. Just a button down shirt and tie. A cog in someone else's machine. Unimpressive. She was bored. That's why she was screwing around.

Town was buzzing with both foot and street traffic, and he circled three times before finding a parking spot across from the train station. The husband was on the platform sipping coffee from a paper cup. One of many. Lined up. Waiting for the inevitable train to carry him and his fellow cattle into the big city. How trite.

He gagged with disgust. Smug with the knowledge that his rival was unexceptional, he moved to disengage. His thoughts went to the office. But as he was about to pull away, he spotted a woman. She was beautiful. Shiny blond hair. Very leggy in a professional pant suit. And she was trying, quite successfully, to flirt with the husband.

Hah! Unthinkingly, he leapt out of his vehicle and jogged across the street for a better look. Was the husband a cheater? Is that why his wife was screwing around? Revenge. It made sense.

But as he milled among the commuters, getting closer and closer to his target, he lost enthusiasm. The blonde was obviously attracted. The husband was good looking, after all, in a lumberjack kind of way. And amiable. Joking and smiling.

Although the husband's behavior was gracious, it was not inappropriate. The cog kept a considerable distance. Stepping discreetly away when the blonde got too close. Huh. The husband wasn't fucking around. At least, not yet.

Suddenly, he felt a kinship with the blond woman. Smiling at the back of her head, he sent her his silent well-wishes and turned away. Best of luck. He wasn't alone in his designs against a deceivingly happy marriage. It only made the task that much more intriguing. So many players. So many outcomes.

He climbed into his SUV and sighed with satisfaction. Chasing the fox out of the park was not keeping with the game.

But he was changing the rules.

CHAPTER 6

IGNORING THE FLIGHT REFLEX

Kate woke to the warning click of her alarm clock. Left unchecked, the clock was set to startle Danny awake. Fighting the shadows of slumber, Kate felt her way over to the clock and then allowed thoughts of the jogger to pull her out of bed.

Ducking into the half-bath next to the kitchen, Kate washed herself with a warm cloth before brushing her teeth and pulling her hair into a tight ponytail. Her running shorts fit loosely, and the elastic waist slid off easily. Adding a zipped sweatshirt, she was out the back door and hurrying through her morning stretches.

Earphones were not a part of her morning regiment. Instead, Kate listened to the echoes of the empty street. It was how the jogger entered her routine. She heard his footfalls tracing her own on the jogging path circling the park.

For weeks, he stayed at a reasonable distance. Their strides kept a steady rhythm as they ran together in the park. When the trail curved, she stole glances of him. He was built like a runner with long legs and a lean torso. Holding himself ramrod straight, he pumped his arms as he ran. The jogger seldom wore anything heavier than a T-shirt and running shorts, and if it was wet, he wore a hat with Vanderbilt University's emblem on it.

He would have remained a stranger, but her shoelace broke. Instead of running past, he stopped and stood over her as she struggled with her shoe. The intimacy between the two loners was palpable. She felt recognition in the glassy darkness of his eyes and returned his gaze. He lowered himself to examine the broken lace. Eye to eye, they fell upon each other quickly. Her instincts simply took over.

It wasn't easy to think about. So, she deliberately chose not to. Acknowledging the ease in which she fell into the arms of another man was impossible. Kate shoved the memory to the corner of her mind and refocused her energy on the present.

The houses in her neighborhood were dark. The gas lamp-lights were still lit, and the morning haze wrapped around Kate like a damp blanket. The sidewalk was dark with moisture, and she pounded it with her feet. When she arrived at Winfield Road, her body was warm and ready to sprint across the empty intersection.

Most of the trees had their leaves, and the tulips and daffodils stood at attention as Kate jogged past. The fragrance of hydrangeas was thick in the air, and she breathed in their scent.

The jogging path wove in and out of the park's rolling hills, and new homes surrounded the north and west ends of the park. The little league diamonds were at the top of what once was a huge dirt mound. Her sons visited the fish pond located at the park's lowest point, and Kate liked to take Joey to the playground adjacent to the baseball diamonds. The park was a tribute to the town and provided recreation for every age group.

Looking up at the sky, Kate cursed the arriving sun. Dawn was beginning to break, and the haze was burning off. Daylight was arriving earlier and earlier, and she dreaded the inevitable. Soon, her encounters with the jogger would become impossible.

Concentrating on her breathing, Kate approached the parking lot and spotted the jogger. He was perched above the path near the entrance of the baseball diamond. Kate knew he had been standing watch for a while.

The jogger abruptly turned and ran towards the baseball diamond. He wanted her to follow. Veering off the path, she crossed the parking lot and climbed the hill. He was no longer out in the open. Quickly assessing the situation, Kate jogged over to one of the outbuildings surrounding the field. The outbuildings were used to sell concessions during baseball games and were locked to fend of vandalism. There was access, however, at the front of the building where someone had the foresight to build an overhang and counter.

Stepping into the enclosure, she sensed his presence immediately. The jogger stood in the shadows of the corner furthermost from the entrance. Taking two steps forward, her heart pounded in anticipation.

"I want to see your tits," he said.

His request was frightening, and blood rushed to her legs and feet. Usually, they were upon each other so quickly she didn't have time to think about her actions. But he wanted something different. Ignoring her flight reflex, she unzipped her sweatshirt and let it drop to the cement floor.

"Step out of the corner," she said. "I can't see you."

He took two long strides towards her. The jogger directed his attention at her cleavage. Sweat pooled between her tightly held breasts, and it bled through the dark fabric of her running tank.

Watching his eyes, Kate moved the left shoulder strap down and pulled her arm through slowly. Next, she moved to the right shoulder. She lowered the top over her breasts hoping to prolong his anticipation, but they sprang free from the constraints of the tight fabric. Looking down, she noticed her nipples were tight and hardened against the cool morning breeze. Deliberately, Kate cupped each breast and ran her thumbs over the tips. When she lifted her head, he was there.

He lifted her easily off the ground and placed her on the wood counter. His hands were soft and cool as they ran over her shoulders and down her front. He teased her nipples with a feather-like touch, and she arched her back hoping to tempt him into taking her into his mouth. Instead, he flicked the tip of her nipple with his index finger, and she gasped at the sharp sensation.

Moving his face to her left breast, he nibbled as his right hand traveled to her sweet spot. The jogger edged her forward, so she was hanging slightly off the counter. Slipping into her shorts, she shuddered when he rotated his hand and came into her pussy with his palm side up. His fingers delved deep inside as he sucked on her tits.

Groaning, she bucked against his hand. He kept her firmly in position on the counter by leaning his weight into her. His hand play was torture, and Kate resisted—pleading to be fucked. The jogger ignored her and savagely sucked and pulled on her nipples.

"I can't take it," she pleaded.

Relentless, he continued to force his hand up inside of her. "I want to feel you cum on my hand," he murmured.

Moving his mouth to the right nipple, he took her between his teeth and increased the speed and pressure on her pussy. She surrendered. Giving herself over completely to the sensation of his hand, his mouth, and his low murmurs. She cried out into the dawn. Using his left hand to cover her mouth, he continued to finger her with his right hand, encouraging her release. When he lowered her off the counter, she felt wilted—unable to stand up straight.

The jogger pushed her towards the dark corner of the out-building. Bending her over the windowless ledge, he worked her shorts off while she hung onto the ledge for support. Hastily, he pulled her hips until her torso was parallel with the floor. She laid her face against the rough surface of the outbuilding and waited breathlessly—helplessly. Hanging onto her hips, he slammed his cock into her sopping wet pussy. Their bodies slapped together with each thrust. Kate was swollen from cumming so hard, and each penetration split her apart.

"You're so wet," he moaned digging his fingers into her flesh.

Letting out a guttural moan, the jogger pulled out and spilled his cum onto her ass. Still breathing heavily, he used both hands to spread his own release over Kate's ass cheeks.

Neither one of them moved. Dawn broke through, and the shadows surrounding the outbuilding began to lift. The jogger deliberately backed away from her—leaving her alone—fully exposed.

She took a deep breath and tried to steady herself. Picking up her discarded sweatshirt, she draped it over her shoulders as she gingerly walked out of the concession stand.

Kate still had to get herself home. Readjusting her ponytail, she walked away and let her body pick up speed as she made her way down the hill. Once again on the jogging path, she didn't have to think.

Her feet just carried her home.

CHAPTER 7

SUBURBAN HELL

Kate needed coffee. She felt like a wet noodle, and she was sore from her early morning jaunt. Dropping Joey off at preschool expended the last of her energy. Grateful to have a quiet house to gather her senses, Kate left the disaster in the kitchen and opted to take a few minutes outside on her deck to relax with her cup of coffee.

Settling herself in a cedar Adirondack chair, she rested her head against the tall back and looked up at billowy clouds rushing across the spring sky. Stroking the wide arm of the chair, Kate contemplated staining the chairs white. It was a project Joey could help her with after school.

Kate soon realized sitting outside was a mistake. Molly was negotiating with her little dog in the adjacent yard. Too tired to have a conversation, she closed her eyes feigning sleep.

"Kathryn," Molly cried out. "I'm so glad to see you."

Opening her eyes, Kate plastered a smile and watched Molly crossing the invisible boundary between their two yards. "Good morning, Molly. How are you?"

Molly climbed the stairs of the deck and plopped herself into the match of Kate's chair.

"Would you like some coffee?" Kate asked holding up her own steaming cup.

"Oh, Lordee, no," Molly said with a laugh. "I've already had three cups. I just came over to give you this."

Digging into her cardigan pocket, Molly pulled out a neatly folded piece of paper. "I ran into a friend of yours," she said, watching Kate open the note.

Written in familiar handwriting was a cry for help. It read, *Save me. I'm in suburban hell,* and it was signed, *Sharon,* with a phone number and smiley face.

Embarrassed, Kate covered her grin with her hand and read the note again.

"Sharon Hilliard," Molly said. "I met her this morning in the principal's office at St. Ann's. She was registering her kids for school next fall. Were you very good friends?"

Nodding her head, Kate re-folded the note and slipped it into her back pocket. "I know her as Sharon Wodushek. Danny used to call her Woody. We were college roommates."

"That's how I made the connection. She moved here from Atlanta. When I asked what made her move to Illinios, she said she's been itching to get her family back to the midwest. She chose Wheaton because of friends from college who settled here. As soon as she said Madison, I thought of you and Dan. She was thrilled to find out we were neighbors. Said it would save her the trouble of tracking you down."

The last time Kate had contact with Sharon was years back after receiving a Christmas card. It included a photo of three girls wearing matching velvet dresses. It stuck in Kate's memory because the two older girls were smiling sweetly while their baby sister wailed red-faced for the camera.

"I can't remember the ages of her girls," Kate said.

"Eight, seven, and the little one is five. She'll be starting kindergarten next year. There is no place better to start kindergarten than St. Ann's. We have the greatest K5 teacher."

Kate masked her impatience with a weak smile. Molly never passed up an opportunity to sing the praises of her kids' parish school. Property taxes in Wheaton paid for the public school system, and Kate thought it ridiculous to write a check for a private school. But it was one of many opinions she kept to herself.

"Her husband, John, is a teacher in a Catholic elementary school."

"Not anymore," Molly said raising her eyebrows. "He's a Mr. Mom. Sharon said he has been for five years."

"Well, good for Sharon," Kate said looking away from Molly's disapproving eyes. "She must be doing well for herself. Last I heard she was working for an international corporation in Atlanta. I know her job required her to travel."

"She's got a new job now," Molly said. "She's a bigwig. Left her husband with the kids in Atlanta. They'll move up in the summer after finishing out school. Ya want to know the kicker?"

Kate tilted her head to indicate she was still listening.

"She bought one of those new houses off Geneva Road. Lives there all by herself. She said it's all but empty except for a mattress on the bedroom floor." Molly pursed her lips and shook her head slightly. "Imagine that. Living all alone in an empty house—I could never do that."

"Being separated from your family is never easy, but it sounds like she did it for the kids. Didn't want to disrupt their lives. And it's only temporary."

Kate took a sip of her coffee and looked over the rim of the cup at Molly. Her neighbor had a bad habit of comparing herself to other moms. Kate had a long list of things Molly would never do.

"Well, I should run," Molly said pushing herself out of the chair. "Got a hair appointment."

Molly didn't look like she needed a haircut, but Kate knew that was on purpose. Women like her neighbor got their hair cut every few weeks, and Kate was pretty sure Molly's little dog did too.

"Thanks a lot, Molly. I can't wait to call and reconnect."

"Oh, I was glad to be of help. Bye, bye."

Kate remained seated and watched Molly unchain her little dog and carry it back into the house. Shifting her weight, she pulled Sharon's note out of her pocket and read it again.

They met freshman year at the dorms. The circumstances of living on the same floor and not knowing anyone else made

31

them friends. Both Sharon and Kate were raised on farms in rural Wisconsin, but they had little else in common. Sharon was quiet, scholarly, and pious. She never missed Sunday morning mass despite late night partying. Kate, on the other hand, used college as an excuse to live like there was no tomorrow.

Smoothing out the creases in Sharon's note, Kate's heart warmed at the thought of seeing her again. They used to be close. Both girls changed majors junior year and were forced to go to school an extra year before graduating. They lived together in a small apartment off campus. It was pretty tame in comparison to their earlier college days. Kate was heavily involved with Danny by then, and Sharon was overloaded with classwork and studying for the CPA exam.

Kate pushed herself out of her chair and headed inside to answer the call for help. Friendship wasn't work when it came to Sharon.

CHAPTER 8

RE-INTRODUCING THE FEMININE

Danny was famous for grilling out on Sunday evenings. He did it no matter the weather. The grill had wheels, and he used them. If it was raining or snowing, he rolled it over to the garage. The neighborhood men knew his habit and often times walked over to share a beer while he tended the meat cooking over the hot coals.

The night Sharon was due to join them for their Sunday meal, he was warming up the grill while supervising the construction of Billy's skateboard ramp. Billy didn't want any help, but the noise he generated attracted the attention of both his brothers. All three boys were involved in the project with Danny supervising and refereeing the fights.

Kate was left alone to fret in the kitchen. She wasn't good at receiving company outside of her own family, and she was worried about not inviting Molly to join their party. Maneuvering around awkward social situations did not come naturally, and she hoped Molly would decide to stay inside for the evening.

"She's here, Dad," Joey shouted in obvious excitement.

When Kate stepped outside, Sharon was already introducing herself to the youngest Maller. "Oh my goodness, you look just like your Momma."

Kate shared her friend's warm smile. Sharon looked older, but in a good way. Her hair was trimmed short, framing her heart-shaped face and gentle blue eyes. She was wearing fitted khaki capris with an expensive looking belt and a pink oxford. Looking down at her own clothes, Kate felt like a slob. She didn't think to dress up and was wearing her usual housewife attire. Old Levis, a washed-out cotton polo, and Birkenstock sandals.

Danny gave Kate's hand an encouraging tug before greeting Sharon. "Lookee here," he said with gray eyes twinkling. "Woody's moved to town. Let the party get started."

Sharon gave Danny an affectionate smile. Pulling him into a hug, she let go of him abruptly and gave him a thorough once over. "Where's your face? Danny, you look like a bear. What are you thinking with this beard? Your strong jaw line was always your most attractive feature."

"Don't knock the beard, Sharon," Kate warned. "It has a very practical purpose."

Sharon rubbed the side of Danny's face and raised her eyebrows. "Okay. I get it now," she said. Capturing Kate's gaze, Sharon's eyes softened. "Katie, I can't express how great it is to see you again."

Kate walked into Sharon's hug. She was soft and her smell was distinctively feminine. Like vanilla mixed with baby powder. Kate's eyes welled with tears. Surprised and confused by her reaction, Kate broke the hug.

Quickly taking Sharon's hand, she pulled her friend up the deck stairs, "Come inside. I'll show you the house."

"I love the yellow," Sharon gushed. "In Atlanta, it's one beige model home right after another."

"I picked the color, Woody," Danny called out from the side of the garage. "Katie wanted all white. It was a fight."

Sharon dismissed Danny with a wave of her hand and followed Kate through the patio door. Plopping her designer purse onto the floor next to Danny's reading chair, Sharon sighed.

"You look just the same, Katie. It's so unfair. Why hasn't your ass gotten as big as mine? What are you doing so differently?"

"Maybe I look the same to you because I haven't changed my hairstyle and fashion sense in fifteen years." Kate was embarrassed by the compliment. "You, on the other hand, look fabulous. Like a woman with real style."

Turning away from her friend, Kate walked into her kitchen and opened the refrigerator. "Can I get you something to drink? I made sun tea this morning."

"That sounds good," Sharon said as she eased herself into the worn leather cushions of Danny's chair. "So," she said, giving her friend a knowing smile. "Danny looks great. Lucky you, Katie."

"Yes," Kate said, laughing to herself. Sharon was consistent. She had always had a thing for Danny. "Coaching the boys' hockey teams keeps him in shape. And his looks have stood the test of time."

"My God, that's an understatement. The man is getting better-looking with age," Sharon said, glancing out the sliding glass door at Kate's husband. "How long have you two been together now?"

"Well, I guess it must be just about nineteen years," Kate said after making a quick calculation.

"And to think, you almost broke up with him."

Kate nodded her head as she handed Sharon the cold glass of ice tea. Three months into their young romance, Danny had proclaimed his love. It spooked her, and she decided it was time to end it. All of her friends were upset when she confided her decision, but Sharon was angry. Danny was a prince, and Kate a fool for even considering tossing him aside. There was nothing anyone could say to change her mind. Kate was resolute. She was preparing for law school, and Danny's love was not in the plan. Until the phone call.

Looking into her friend's gentle blue eyes, Kate was unafraid of the earth-shattering memory. Because Sharon had lived it too. It was Sharon who handed Kate the phone. It was Sharon who witnessed Kate stoically receive the news of her mother's sudden death. And it was Sharon who knew enough to summon Danny.

35

Kate was tearing around their college apartment throwing things into a duffle bag, cursing about bus schedules, and didn't hear the door. Danny arrived breathless from running at top clip across campus. The surprise of seeing his young face aged by the depth of his love and concern yanked Kate out of her tunnel of numbness. She broke—sobbing uncontrollably for what seemed like forever.

It was Danny who put her back together. From that moment on, it was only Danny.

CHAPTER 9

THE POLITICS OF FRIENDSHIP

After dinner, Danny steered the boys outside and left the two friends alone. Kate usually attacked kitchen clean-up like a lone soldier. Having Sharon comfortably next to her, sharing her chores was lovely, and Kate felt giddy with happiness.

"Would you look at that?" Kate walked quickly over to the sliding glass doors.

Bill was getting ready to send Joey down the driveway in oversized rollerblades without a helmet.

"They're gonna kill the little guy one of these day." Kate moved her hand to the door handle and gave it a firm tug but stopped when she spotted Molly enjoying a glass of wine in her backyard. "Oh shit."

Next, she spied Molly's husband, Tom, in the driveway talking to Danny while the Ibner boys were busy pulling out the toys stored in the garage bins.

"What is it?" Sharon asked stepping away from the counter to glance out the window.

"It's Molly Ibner." Kate flinched and tossed her head in the direction of the backyard. "She's outside with her little dog."

"So. What's the big deal?"

"That's her husband, Tom. Her boys are in the garage."

"Let's invite her over. I want to thank her for relaying my message."

"No." Kate blocked the door. "I don't want you going down memory lane. I've got a reputation as a soft-spoken hockey mom. I don't want you messing with it."

"Soft-spoken hockey mom? That's a bunch of crap!" Sharon laughed. "Since when do you care what people think? Come on, Molly is nice."

"You think everyone is nice. I use Molly for information about the neighborhood, but the information highway runs two ways. She's got a big mouth."

"You're being paranoid." Sharon shoved Kate away with a sharp elbow and tugged the door open. "Molly, we're in here."

Waving back, Molly picked up the wine glass next to her patio chair and skipped through the yard.

"Shit, she's coming over." Quickly turning away, Kate ran a dishcloth over the counter and glanced nervously at the half-cleaned kitchen.

Sharon looked amused. "Just relax. Geez."

It was Sharon who welcomed Molly into Kate's house.

"I'm so glad you two found each other." Looking around, Molly lifted her eyebrows in approval. "Kathryn, I love the paint colors. And the countertops. Are they granite? Did you and Dan do the remodel yourself?"

"You've never been in here?" Sharon was surprised again.

"I guess we've never had the opportunity." Kate was trying not to sound defensive. "We usually talk in the yard."

"Kathryn spends most of the spring and summer outside in her garden."

"I've never heard anyone but your father call you Kathryn." Sharon couldn't hide her disapproval.

"Only Dan calls her Katie. I thought it was a husband-wife thing." Molly turned to look at Kate inquisitively.

38

"No, Danny calls her Trouble. Has since they started dating. Friends call her Kate."

"Oh please," Kate said leering at Sharon. "What does it matter? Kathryn, Kate, Katie? Besides, I know you didn't introduce yourself to Molly as Woody."

Sharon shrugged and gave Molly a reassuring smile. "Danny has a knack for nicknames."

"Molly, sit down." Kate directed her neighbor to Danny's chair. "Would you like something to drink?"

Molly was holding a glass of wine, but Kate knew it was protocol to offer guests refreshment.

"Oh, this girl came prepared," she said tipping her wine glass.

"Do you have any wine, Katie?" Sharon asked. "We should join her."

"I think I have some in the pantry."

Helping herself, Sharon pulled open the pantry door and stepped back in awe. "Whoa, Katie. You have to come to my house and organize my cabinets."

Pushing past her, Kate reached up to the top shelf and pulled down a bottle of red wine.

"Molly, come check this out. She's got floor-to-ceiling shelving complete with wicker baskets and see-through plastic containers."

"Cut it out," Kate closed the door.

"How old is this bottle?" Sharon asked as she dramatically dusted it off. "You never used to let booze lay around."

"College is over, Sharon. I don't make a habit of getting wasted around my boys."

Opening Kate's cabinets one at a time, Sharon blindly searched for glasses. She was perfectly comfortable nosing around, and Kate was glad Molly was there to witness it. It was obvious their friendship went beyond the typical uncomfortable social bullshit.

Smiling in triumph, Sharon reached for two wine glasses. "Corkscrew?"

Pulling out a corkscrew from a bottom drawer, Kate handed it over. She wasn't going to embarrass herself by attempting to open it. Sharon popped the bottle open easily, poured two glasses, and walked over to Molly.

39

Handing a glass to Kate, she held up her own. "Should we toast? To old and new friends."

Kate clinked glasses with a blank smile. She came from a long line of beer drinkers and clinking crystal was not a comfortable custom. Following Sharon's lead, Kate pulled a chair away from the kitchen table and sat next to the two women. Talking freely around Molly wasn't an option, so she tried to keep a smile on her face while they gracefully ran through the usual small talk.

Kate woke up when Molly pointed out the window. "I see you planted your tomatoes in pots this year."

"I'm trying to make room in my vegetable patch for cucumbers and lettuce."

"My husband, John, loves to grow fresh vegetables. It's his new hobby." Sharon added.

"You know, Kathryn, there is a group of us moms from St. Ann's that are petitioning the Village Board. We want the empty lot across from the library to become a community garden." Molly peered over glass and waited for a response.

"What exactly do you mean by *community garden*?" Kate was picturing wildflowers with a flagstone path.

"We have a community garden in Atlanta." Sharon nodded her head in understanding. "Our yard doesn't have enough sun, so John leases out a parcel and grows our vegetables there."

"Exactly. We've got petitions, and so far, people are very receptive to the idea." Molly set her glass down and spoke with her hands. "Most people in Wheaton don't have very big yards. The little yard we have is taken up by the play set. I would love to grow vegetables like Kathryn."

No one else in their neighborhood grew vegetables. It was a surprise to hear Molly's admiration.

"You said next to the library. Where exactly is that?" Sharon asked.

"The old library was in town, but the Village passed a referendum funding a new library a couple years ago. It's on the western edge of town near Winfield. It's not far from here."

"The empty lot is next to the park at the opposite end of the library parking lot. Joey likes to play there after we check out new books. It's always empty. But it won't be if there is garden. Kids can play while their parents work."

"We want to fit that into our proposal, but we don't know exactly how to do it. None of us have any real experience with this kind of thing." Molly frowned and picked up her glass. "We were thinking the village could divide the empty lot into six by twelve foot parcels. Label each parcel with a number and then open it up to the community. We haven't figured how much the village would charge, but we know they'll have to run some kind of watering system out there."

"I could help you with a cost analysis," Sharon offered. "I do stuff like that every day."

"You should highlight the benefits of the garden but also include an analysis of the negative. Initial costs to the Village and maintenance fees are a good place to start. But the members of the board will naturally think about the negative pushback from constituents. If you include an analysis of the negative—like the impact of car traffic and the effect on surrounding neighborhoods—they'll know how to weigh their decision." Kate stopped when she realized Molly was shocked by her tone and interest.

"The village board is less likely to turn away a complete analysis. That's all I meant to say," she quickly added to clarify her point.

"Katie interned at Wisconsin's capitol the summer before junior year. She knows politics." Sharon smiled proudly at her friend. "She was pre-law before changing her major to education."

"Education? I thought you worked in human resources before Peter was born."

Kate shrugged. "I taught high school history and government. Thankfully, it was a temporary position. Teaching was not my calling. When we moved to Chicago, a favorite professor of mine used his connections to help me land a job in human resources at a Chicago-based construction company. My educational background in contracts and labor law got me the job."

"Her GPA got her the job," Sharon corrected. "Katie is a gifted negotiator. The corporate suits liked her just as much as the union hacks," she added proudly.

"That was a long time ago," Kate said dismissively.

41

Pointing a finger at Kate, Molly's eyes sparked with purpose. "Why don't you two come to our meeting on Wednesday evening? We're meeting at 7:00 in a room at the library."

When Kate dropped her gaze, Molly added. "We could really use your help. The Village Board meets the first Tuesday of every month, and we'd like to get on the May docket, which means we only have a week to prepare something credible."

"You said Wednesday night?" Sharon pulled out her Blackberry. "I'm there."

They both looked to Kate. Hesitant to get involved, she weighed her decision against her experience as a hockey mom. Sitting in the stands with other parents making small talk was more difficult to endure than the temperature in the rink. The politics of the hockey association was Danny's domain. Working in a committee was something Kate was no longer practiced at. Her life was deliberately built, so she was accountable only to her family.

"Yeah, okay. I'll be there," she said despite herself.

CHAPTER 10

GOOD THING GOING

Sharon had given her red wine, and Danny wasn't there to stop it. Red wine gave Kate headaches. He knew she had a whopper coming on by the tense way her neck was holding up her head. After waving goodbye to Sharon in the driveway, Kate closed her eyes and pressed her face into his chest.

"Sharon said you looked great," she mumbled into his shirt.

Danny kissed her hair and rubbed her back. "She said I looked like a bear."

Pushing off the length of his body, Kate looked into his eyes, "Don't go thinking about shaving it off. The beard is as much mine as it is yours."

"Maybe it's time for a change," he teased, scratching his beard. "I can switch up my technique. Try something new with my mouth. Maybe incorporate a little teeth."

"Danny, we've got a good thing going. Don't mess with it because Sharon made a joke."

Wrapping an arm around her shoulders, he guided her up the deck steps. "I was watching you. You had a good time."

"I was surprised. It was emotional seeing her again. Molly wore me out though. I'm not used to so much talk." Gesturing with her hands, Kate fell into Danny's reading chair with a sigh. "School, church, hair. Blah, blah, blah." Kate winced and covered her face with her hands. "Sharon's got me roped into this garden committee thing and somehow that turned into a shopping date with her and Molly. Molly Ibner. Danny, I'm gonna crack. I know it. I'll make a smartass remark and hurt her feelings forever."

Danny disregarded his wife's concerns and went straight to his own. "Shopping with Molly and Sharon?"

Kate moaned before slinking back into the leather chair with a dramatic shrug. Danny turned on his heels and headed to the kitchen cabinet, which housed their supply of ibuprofen.

"Take it," he said, handing her a large glass of water and presenting the pills in his open palm. "And drink the whole glass."

He stood over her, waiting with hands on his hips while she chugged the water.

"Thank you," she said sheepishly, handing him the empty glass.

"Uh huh." He was thinking of his game. The Blackhawks were playing the Redwings. He was done for the night and wanted to sit.

"Joey is filthy," he said walking to the patio door to call the boys inside. "He needs a bath. I had him all day while you were busy getting stuff ready for Sharon. You'll have to handle bedtime. My game is on."

Kate pushed herself out of the chair and caught Joey as he jumped into her arms.

"Daddy says you're filthy," she said, examining his face. "You don't look too bad to me."

"Check his hands."

"Yikes," Kate said with mock horror as she headed up the stairs with Joey in her arms. "Were you digging for potatoes out back?"

Danny landed with a humph in his recliner and turned on the television. Bill wandered after and plopped on the couch. He was sucking noisily on a popsicle. Kate wouldn't want popsicles in the family room, but Danny decided to ignore his middle son as he scrolled through the television's directory. Baseball flickered across the screen, and he remembered that Kate's father had phoned earlier that day.

"Damn," he said hoisting himself out of his chair. "Kate," he boomed.

Listening to her tired footsteps on the hardwood floor upstairs, he waited.

"Yes?" she shouted over Joey's chatter.

"I forgot. Your dad called while you were at the store this morning. Says you're supposed to call your brother."

"Walt or Roger?"

"Walt."

"Did he say why?" she asked.

"Nope."

He didn't bother to remember the details. It was bound to lead to more questions, and Danny didn't want to talk anymore. He'd spent the evening talking. Danny wanted to watch his game. When he turned for the family room, he ran into Peter.

"I poured you a beer, Dad," he said holding the frosted mug Kate kept in the freezer.

Taking the beer, Danny glared at the boy. Waiting for the rest.

"Could you sign this for me?" he asked holding out a blue slip and a pen. "It's from my teacher."

"Peter, what the hell? Don't lay stuff like this on me on a Sunday night."

Crap. A blue slip couldn't be good news. Danny had two options. Grant Peter his sweetest fantasy, sign the paper, and enjoy his game. Or—"What's it say?" Danny asked, backing away warily.

"I didn't complete an assignment. Nothing big. I've got it in my backpack. I can finish it in study hall tomorrow. I don't have English until final period."

Too many details.

"Kate," Danny bellowed.

Peter covered his head with his arms and groaned.

"Peter's got something for you to sign," he yelled. Danny patted his eldest son on the shoulder as he passed by. "Go talk to your mother."

CHAPTER 11

FEIGNING INTEREST

It was a long weekend. The office was a relief. He didn't have to play house. He could relax. Be himself. It was amazing, really. The more he pulled away from home. The more he gloried in the tendencies of his own nature. The more successful he became at work. It was noticeable. Not only to him but to his colleagues. He was a force. Raking in the dollars.

Avoiding the wife and kids was becoming habit. But it was early. She wouldn't be expecting him. There wouldn't be questions. No reason for suspicion if he arrived home in another hour or so.

Surveillance was tricky. His white SUV was becoming too regular on her street, so he parked on the next one over. Good fortune. There was an empty home for sale. He could pass as a realtor. Waiting for potential buyers. From where he sat, he had a slightly skewed view of her backyard.

He carried the information file with him as a token. It was stowed in his briefcase. He didn't need to look at it. Total recall. Daniel and Kathryn Maller. Kathryn. He liked to say it aloud. It felt good on his

47

tongue. Mostly consonants. The y disguising itself as a vowel. How poetic. Kathryn. Mother of three. Housewife. Joint tax return for sixteen years. A vowel-less existence disguised as the American dream.

The husband was a mechanical engineer. It was almost laughable. Working at the same company for twelve years, Daniel's job title changed corresponding to the steady increase in pay. His criminal record was insignificant and confined to the college years. He was ticketed for serving liquor to minors, and the assault charge never went to court. Drunken brawl most likely. Nice to know regardless. Daniel Maller was no stranger to violent behavior.

Sighing, he admired their home. He couldn't help but be impressed. Daniel managed to afford a respectable piece of property on a standard paycheck. The man was responsible. No outstanding debt except for the home mortgage. Truth be told, Daniel had more equity in the home than he did. No doubt, it was the result of living a life within his means. A practical man. Shameful. Daniel went out of his depth when he married a woman like Kathryn. Practical men should know better than to overreach. He couldn't make himself feel sorry for the cog.

It wasn't smart to linger. He longed to see her in the flesh. But, alas, it wasn't to be. Circling one last time, he hid behind his sunglasses and peered into the lifeless windows of the sunshine yellow house. Was she home? Tomorrow, Kathryn.

In comparison to the Maller home, his home was palatial. Driving into the cavernous four-car garage used to give him a deep sense of satisfaction, but it meant nothing to him now. He stayed in the vehicle longer than he should have. His wife was growing suspicious of his moods and abnormal behavior. Forever on the lookout, her wide eyes and hypersensitive ears missed nothing. But she was a coward. Instead of confrontation, she simply tried harder. It was heartbreaking. Being near her was unbearable.

Slipping out of the leather seat of his SUV, he dragged his feet across the garage floor and stepped reluctantly into his home.

"Daddy," his wife called in her lilted voice. "Is that you?"

"Yes," he said tossing his car keys onto the mudroom counter. "It's me."

She greeted him in the kitchen. Her appearance almost made him cringe. She wore his favorite color. Lavender. And the jeans were freshly pressed. She knew his preference for high-heeled shoes and wore them despite the lack of occasion. Hair heavy with product glistened under the kitchen lighting and her face was flawlessly applied. Lip liner included. If she still possessed any natural beauty, it was effectively hidden beneath store-bought enhancements.

"You look nice," he said with as much emotion as he could muster.

"Thank you."

She kissed his cheek and then folded him into an embrace. He didn't pull away. It wasn't her fault that her soft, compliant body was repellant to him now. Whenever she ventured to touch him, his mind went to Kathryn. The true object of his desires. Comparisons were unavoidable.

His wife was a plump, juicy rabbit munching absentmindedly in a field of wild flowers. Cotton-tailed and egg shaped, she was prey on constant alert. In contrast, Kathryn was a bushy-tailed fox. Quick, intelligent, and cunning, she was hard to catch. Adapting well, but never quite fitting in with cultivated suburban living. Kathryn was an opportunistic feeder ready to pounce. His wife was nothing more than a nibbler. Squeezing her to his chest, his heart wrenched. He never meant to hurt her.

"How was your day?" he asked, feigning interest as he released her.

"I've got a surprise," she said, pulling on his elbow. "I made us dinner."

The dining room was set for two. Romantic. Flowers, candles, an open bottle of wine. He knew she spent more time dressing the table than preparing the meal. Picking dinner up at Whole Foods constituted home cooking to his wife.

"The kids?" he asked. Reaching for the bottle of wine, he poured himself a glass but remained standing.

"I got a sitter," she said, very pleased with herself. "They're in the playroom doing crafts."

He managed a smile before grabbing the bottle and turning away from her. Standing in front of the picture window framing their wooded backyard, he sipped his wine and tightly gripped the mouth of the bottle. It felt heavy as it dangled against his leg. Good. There was plenty. Getting drunk was a necessity. Perhaps, if he drank fast enough, he would pass out and be unable to meet her expectations. Performing was a horrible hardship.

"Kathryn?" he thought as he peered into the shadow falling across his yard. "Do you feel it too?"

CHAPTER 12

WARNING CLICK

Kate threw her feet out of bed and quietly went to freshen up and change into her running clothes. The skylight in the master bathroom was drumming an uneven rhythm as fat raindrops fell reluctantly from the dark sky.

While chugging down a bottle of water, she dug around the hall closet for a waterproof windbreaker. She was counting on the hood to shield her from the elements. Because she worried about injuring herself in the cold, dreary weather, Kate took her time stretching in the kitchen before heading out the door.

"Crap." In two long strides, she reached the pen and notepad she kept next to the phone and made a quick note to herself.

Kate meant to call her little brother yesterday but forgot. Why he wanted to talk to her was a mystery. Walt only called Danny, and the conversation was usually sports related.

Once outside, Kate's mood got a lift. The rain was now merely a drizzle. She switched on her safety light and pulled at the hood of her jacket until it rode low over her eyes. The hood provided cover and muffled sound. Blood whooshed behind her ears and reminded her of swimming in the ocean. Joey had yet to lay eyes on a real beach. Florida was slated as their next summer vacation.

Danny found a rental home on Sanibel Island, and he was nearly ready to make a deposit for a weeklong reservation.

Once across Winfield Road, Kate allowed her thoughts to drift to the jogger. The weather made a chance meeting unlikely. She felt a sharp jab in her heart at the prospect of missing him again, but relief quickly overrode the pain of disappointment. Pushing thoughts of their last thrilling encounter to the back of her mind, Kate concentrated on the feel of the ground beneath her feet.

The mist dampened her shorts and her socks were wet from running through puddles. Kate's hands were cold, so she tugged the sleeves of her long sleeve T-shirt out from under her wind-breaker and used them as mittens. Kate's mother feared the damp more than Wisconsin's brutal winters and would not approve of running in the rain. According to her mother, water bred sickness and weakened the flesh.

Kate's eyes lifted automatically to the spot where she saw the jogger last. Across from the parking lot, at the top of the hill next to the baseball diamonds, in the exact same spot where the jogger stood last Friday, was a lonesome dog. It reminded Kate of a Labrador, but its legs were too short. It was yellow with a square block head that was slightly darker than the rest of its body. Its ears were alert and stood straight up, but the tips folded down, giving the dog an almost comical air. It looked at Kate with curious eyes as she ran by, but it did not move. Glancing backwards, Kate returned the dog's stare and hoped its owner was nearby.

Her thoughts were about the dog as she concluded her run. Before stepping off the jogging path, she glanced behind, hoping to spy the dog with its owner. But instead, the jogger filled her vision. He was sprinting directly at her.

Kate's feet stopped immediately. She was still in the park. Turning to meet him, she waited. He was wearing a jacket similar to her own, but instead of a hood, he wore a baseball cap with Vanderbilt University's emblem on it. The hat had a youthful effect, and Kate liked the way his dark locks peeked out from underneath it. He stopped short and peered at Kate. His breathing was hard and his eyes were near panic.

"I wasn't sure—" he uttered, pausing unsteadily to take a deep breath. "I'm so sorry. I had to see you."

The depth of emotion under his tone was obvious. But Kate chose to focus on the reflective light sparking off the blackness of his pupils.

"I couldn't stop thinking of you. All weekend..." he tried again to make a connection. He was trying to impart something important.

Taking control, she switched off her safety light and reached for his hand. It was cold, so she rubbed it with her own, relaying her warmth to him. After looking quickly around, she led him off the path and into a clump of trees bordering someone's backyard. There was a thick hedge at the property line, and she headed towards it, towing the jogger through dense brush. They stumbled over roots and fallen limbs, but they never faltered. Both eager to be hidden safely off the path.

When they reached the hedge, she pushed him until his back was against the trunk of a tall, but narrow tree. The darkness of the morning and the thickness of the brush allowed them more than enough cover. Carelessly, she tossed his hat to the ground. Kate bit her bottom lip before braiding the fingers of both hands through his thick, silky hair. He closed his eyes in response, so she lingered—pulling the damp curls away from his face.

"Please," he murmured. "I need to know..."

Kate shushed him into silence before leaning into kiss him— making talk impossible. While she tasted his mouth, delicately running the tip of her tongue along his lower lip, his tight grip on her waist loosened. In a deliberate move, he pulled away her hood, and she shivered when both his cold hands cradled the sides of her face. His touch was gentle and full of longing. The jogger was in no hurry. It was Kate who finally broke the kiss.

"I want to see it," she whispered, sliding her hands down his torso to the waistband of his shorts.

She pulled at the shorts, and he helped by kicking them off. Kate wrapped a warm hand around his erection. The jogger moaned and closed his eyes.

The canopy of trees protected them from the drizzle, but the air was still thick with moisture. The smell of decomposing leaves and sticks was strangely erotic. As a small town farm girl, Kate had spent years rolling around in haystacks. Exploring with a neighbor boy, she tested the limits with one ear keenly listening for her mother's call. The memory fueled her desire, and Kate stroked the jogger harder—relishing the difference between farm girl and woman.

"Do you want me to suck it?" she asked.

His eyes opened wide, and he nodded his head in desperation. "Yes. God, yes."

Kate released the jogger and unzipped her jacket. She spread it like a blanket at his feet and kneeled down before he could fully comprehend what she was doing. His breathing became labored. Trying to control his excitement, she guessed. Placing both hands on his tight ass, she flicked her tongue over the tip of his cock, tasting his scent for the first time. Moaning in pleasure, Kate's body quivered with the thrill of discovery. He was so new—so foreign—so dangerous.

"Yes…" the jogger hissed as he thrust his cock towards her swollen lips. "Yes. More. Take it."

Kate steadied him by firmly gripping his ass. Slowly, she savored his entire length, reaching the base of his shaft. The jogger groaned as she pulled back, sliding her tongue over and around his cock as she withdrew her mouth.

Clutching at her hair with both hands, he pleaded. "Faster. Please. Faster."

Answering his pleas and cries, she worked his cock with her tongue. Randomly turning to nuzzle underneath—tugging gently on one ball and then the other. She took her fill of him—milking his release. The jogger shook violently before cumming into her open mouth. Kate looked up into his eyes, letting his cum spill over her lips. Their gaze held. His breathing finally quieted, and she rose off her knees. He remained leaning against the tree, looking up into the branches. Absentmindedly, he ran his hands through his hair. Kate shook out her jacket before shrugging it back on.

The jogger was wobbly when he shoved off the tree. He was not having an easy time locating his shorts and hat. It was still dark. She helped by finding his hat and held it out to him after he pulled on his shorts. Kate avoided his eyes and began to maneuver her way out of the woods. The jogger followed. Before leaving the cover of their tiny woodland, Kate peered into the dim light of the park, making sure they were still alone.

He always left first, and she waited. When he failed to lead, Kate took a deep breath and stepped out onto the jogging path. She felt uneasy—not liking the change.

"Do you ever think about leaving them?" he asked.

She whirled to meet his gaze. "No," she answered decisively. "Never."

The jogger lowered his head and ran in the opposite direction. Kate watched as he disappeared into the haze. The rain was coming down a little harder, so she pulled the hood back over her head. Enjoying the anonymity and the silence, Kate headed home.

All thoughts of the jogger were left in the park.

CHAPTER 13

COLD STOVE

"Whyda park so far away?" Joey asked. "The library's way over there."

Kate shifted her van into park and frowned at the windshield wipers moving across her view of the potential garden site.

"We're not going to the library today, little man," she said tugging at the clipboard hidden beneath Joey's backpack and snack box. "This is our last stop. I promise. We'll go home right after."

"Why are we here?" he asked, searching the empty parking lot bordering the grassy field.

"I need to check and see if this field is good for growing vegetables."

"Can I go to the park?" he asked, pointing to the childless playground equipment.

"Sure," Kate agreed. Joey was still wearing the rubber boots and bright red firefighter raincoat he wore to school. "Just be careful climbing. It's going to be slippery."

Excited by the prospect of playing at the park in the rain, Joey jumped loose of his car seat restraints.

"We can't stay long. Peter and Bill are home from school by now, and I need to start dinner," Kate called as Joey ran towards the park.

The ground in the field was slightly elevated above the parking lot and there were a few sad trees haphazardly placed at either end. Kate stepped out of her van gripping her clipboard and pencil. The grass was green and long, and the ground was hard beneath her rain boots. The dirt in the field was probably rocky fill removed to make the new library's basement. Money could be saved raising the garden beds with railroad ties and bringing in good dirt. Running a water source out to the lot would be the most expensive aspect of developing the community garden, but Kate made note of the fire hydrant positioned at the corner of the empty parking lot.

Along the back of the field was a fence with thick woods behind it. When Kate looked through the fence, she could see into the backyards of two homes. The homes were huge, even by Wheaton's standards, and very new. After taking a few measurements, Kate drew a quick diagram of how she would lay the garden parcels out. Satisfied with the information gathered, she felt confident and ready to go home.

"Joey," she called. "Time to go, little man."

Joey's back was turned as he struggled to climb up the wet slide. Kate watched as he clambered to the top and applauded when he finally turned around and held his arms up in triumph.

"Good job. You're no quitter," she laughed. Using both hands, she waved him back to the van. "Let's go, little man. I've got to start dinner."

Joey's music on the van radio kept him distracted while Kate drove through the neighborhood adjacent to the potential garden site. The neighborhood was well hidden off Lambert Road. Each lot was at least two acres and most were wooded. With so much property buffeting the homes, Kate could not imagine any negative pushback concerning the garden.

Kate signaled right and turned sharply onto Naperville Road. Thoughts of her two older boys home alone had her breaking the speed limit. Homework was probably still in backpacks.

When Kate opened the backdoor, she was surprised to find Danny in the hallway. His hair was wet, and he was already changed out of his work clothes. Kate winced. She usually picked him up at the train when it rained.

"Danny," she started. "I wasn't expecting you home."

"My meeting got canceled." His eyes were cold, and he ignored Joey as the boy tumbled through the door loaded down with his backpack. "Why are you soaking wet?" he demanded. "I tried your cell, but you didn't pick up."

"Oh, I'm sorry. I left it in the van." Kate began to peel Joey's wet clothes off.

"I got you the phone so I could get a hold of you. Why do I keep paying the bill if you refuse to answer the damn thing?"

"I forget, Danny. I only get calls from you."

"Where were you? I got drenched walking home."

"I'm sorry. I took Joey with me to the library to look at the empty lot for the community garden."

"For godsakes, Kate, it's raining. Did you have to go today?"

"The meeting with Molly's friends is tomorrow night. I wanted to have something prepared," she said holding up the clipboard as she brushed past him.

"So I suppose we won't be having dinner tomorrow night either." Danny waved his arms at the cold stove.

"No," Kate answered calmly. "I'm going to make dinner. Just give me thirty minutes. How does beef stew sound?"

Kate moved quickly to the stove and put on a large pot of water to boil for rice. She turned on the oven and pulled out a batch of refrigerator biscuits.

"The boys were fighting when I walked in the door." Danny's tone was still accusing. "I had to pull Peter off of Bill. He was pummeling him in the arm."

"Why were they fighting?" Kate asked as she put a container of homemade beef stew into the microwave to defrost.

"Something about the remote control," he answered.

"Did you punish them?" With all the testosterone in the house, Kate kept a firm lid on the violent outbursts. Broken rules were always met with consequences.

"I sent them to their rooms," Danny's outrage was finally dying out.

"I'll take care of it," Kate said with a smile. She wanted Danny to cool down. "Joey, why don't you go watch television until dinner is ready."

Their son was still standing in the back hallway, listening wide-eyed.

"Peter hit Billy?" he asked.

"Don't worry, little man," Kate promised. "I'll make them say sorry." She put her hands on his little shoulders and ushered him into the family room.

When she returned to the kitchen, she found Danny sitting cross-legged in his reading chair. He was running his right hand over his beard, staring blankly out into the backyard while his left hand massaged his iPhone. Kate assumed he was thinking about work and quickly walked past. Pouring a beer into a frosted mug, she watched her husband from the corner of her eye.

Wordlessly, she handed him the beer and returned quickly to the stove to finish dinner.

CHAPTER 14

DROP BY

The dinner table was unusually quiet. Peter and Bill were still mad at each other despite the forced apologies. Danny didn't know what Kate handed down as punishment for fighting, but whatever it was, it had both boys slumping in their chairs. Joey was the only one who felt like chatting. He wanted to hunt earthworms after dinner. Uncle Walt had schooled the boys on the habits of night crawlers, and Joey wanted to see how many he could catch out of their holes after the big rain.

Kate was careful. She herded the boys away from Danny, giving him a lot of space. He was grateful and didn't think to make excuses for his bad temper. If he wanted to talk, he would. Danny kept his iPhone close by. He was used to getting hit on by women. But Natalie Bell-Charles was no hockey mom looking for attention. She was gorgeous and confident, and she was making an aggressive play for him. It was the reason he took an earlier train. Physically avoiding Natalie was easy. Keeping her out of his thoughts was another thing entirely and not something he felt that guilty about. It wasn't like he was gonna fuck her.

Danny checked his e-mail again. Natalie Bell-Charles. Kate never thought twice about giving up her maiden name. Danny wouldn't have cared if she wanted to hyphenate Selbach. But Kate was different from Natalie. Natalie was young, from a new generation of independent career woman. Newly married, she was disillusioned with the institution. She wanted to know the key to a happy marriage. When Danny had playfully answered sex, her reaction was the opposite of what he expected. Natalie gave him a close-lipped smile and stroked his arm with a manicured finger. It was electric, and it scared the shit out of him. But Danny kept checking his e-mail anyway, re-reading her flirty messages.

After tucking Joey into bed, Kate walked past Danny and the boys in the family room and closed the door to the master bedroom. He thought about following. Asking about her day. Maybe retrieving the kiss he forfeited when she arrived home late. But he didn't. Hockey playoffs occupied his thoughts, and it was a welcome distraction.

The soft knocking on the front door confused Danny and the boys. No one dropped by this late on a school night. Kate stepped out of the bedroom in a robe and slippers with the same look of confusion on her face.

"Was that the door?" she asked Danny.

Danny put the game on pause and pushed himself out of the recliner. Kate followed hesitantly.

"Geez, Sharon," Danny sighed after opening the door. "You scared the crap out of us. Why didn't you just ring the bell?"

"I figured Joey was sleeping."

Sharon was clutching her trench coat tightly to her chest. She was cold. Kate shoved Danny aside and opened the door wide.

"Come in. Have you eaten?" she asked.

"No," Sharon admitted. "I was working. No reason to hurry home to an empty house."

Neither Sharon or Kate looked in Danny's direction as they stepped away and hurried to the kitchen. He frowned when Kate helped Sharon off with her coat. She was fussing. Happy to be of help to her friend.

"Dad," Peter complained from the couch. "The game."

Danny returned to the family room and turned the game back on, but instead of his recliner, he sat on the edge of the couch. He could hear Kate in the kitchen, reheating leftovers from dinner, while Sharon complained about a problem at work.

"Thank you, Katie, this smells great," Sharon said with a sigh. "I didn't drop by hoping you would feed me, honestly."

"I don't care why you dropped by," Kate answered. "I'm just glad you did."

A kitchen chair scrapped across the floor as Kate sat next to her friend.

"My car just kinda found its way over here. I needed to see a friendly face. My empty house was too much tonight."

"Missing the kids?"

"And John," Sharon said. The sadness in her voice was obvious even to Danny, and he glanced into the kitchen to see her pull out her Blackberry and show the screen to Kate. "He emailed me a photo. Sophie went on a field trip to the zoo."

"Oh Sharon," Kate gushed. "She's so beautiful."

Danny's heart twisted in his chest. A daughter was all Kate ever truly wanted, a namesake for her mom. She begged for a third child, and he finally gave in. The pregnancy was easy but resulted in a C-section. The baby was not only breech but also the wrong sex. Joey was supposed to be Margaret. Kate never expressed any disappointment, but Danny could see the sadness in her eyes when she nodded her consent. Tubal ligation would prevent further heartbreak. Danny wouldn't make the gamble again.

"I sympathize, Sharon, but you're doing the right thing. Let them finish out the school year. It's hard now, but summer is just around the corner."

"I know it," Sharon agreed. "I'm flying home this weekend," she added, cheered by the prospect.

"Do you need a ride to the airport?"

Danny grimaced. Kate must be offering his services. She never drove to the airport.

"Thanks, but no. I park my car at the airport. It's a piece of cake. The company's private jet flies in and out of Naperville. Letting me use the jet was part of the deal when I came aboard as CFO. The airport is convenient, and it was one of the reasons we chose Wheaton. I'd hate to have to fly out of O'Hare. God, that would be such a nightmare."

Private jets. Danny couldn't even afford to fly coach to Florida. They were packing up the van and road-tripping it. He tried not to resent his wife's friend, but the feelings crept in anyways.

Sharon waved goodbye from the front door after making arrangements to meet up with Kate and drive to Molly's meeting together. Kate stood on the porch in her robe and watched as Sharon pulled away. She kept her eyes downcast when she came back into the house. Danny couldn't gauge her mood.

Danny stayed up to channel surf before venturing into the master bedroom. Standing next to his side of the bed, he removed his watch and double checked his alarm clock. She had gone to sleep without him. Not a good sign.

The sheets were cold, and he reached for her automatically. Kate purred and nudged her body closer when he pulled her in to spoon. Danny buried his face into the thick hair laying across her shoulder and breathed in her warm scent. She curled. Pulling the blanket tightly around them. They were snug, his body easily enveloped Kate.

Danny pushed at the heavy blanket freeing his left hand. Starting at her knee, he drew his hand over her thigh and stopped at her hip. Kate sighed. Waking up, she rolled over and pushed her face close to his. She wasn't allowing any space between them. He wasn't surprised. Kate never stayed mad long, if she was even mad in the first place.

Danny kissed her then. Slowly, he delved deep. He didn't stop the kiss until he felt her hands on his back, clawing at his flesh, tugging him closer. She whimpered when he pulled away. He waited until her breathing slowed, waited until she opened her eyes.

"What time is it?" she murmured.

"It's not that late."

Kate rolled away and stretched, arching her back she threw her arms over her head. Danny took the opportunity to lie on top of her, pinning her to the mattress.

"Do you think people can tell?" he asked as he lined her collarbone with kisses. "You know, can tell how much we love sex?"

Kate moaned and threw her pelvis into his, searching and then grinding into his erection.

"Do you think we attract attention?" he asked again.

"I know how sexy you make me feel," Kate whispered, exposing her neck so he could rub his beard against it. "Maybe other people see it. I don't really care if they do."

Danny propped his weight on his elbow and began unbuttoning her night shirt. "Do you think Sharon sees it?" he whispered.

"Yes," Kate answered. "Sharon sees it. It makes her miss John."

Cupping her right breast in his hand, Danny ran a thumb over the nipple, playing with the tip as he watched it darken and tighten in the dim light of their bedroom. Kate whined again and arched her back into his touch.

"Did you ever think about keeping your maiden name?" he murmured as he continued to tease her. "Maybe hyphenate. Selbach-Maller?"

Kate's body fell back into the mattress, and she rolled onto her side. Danny felt her eyes peering at him through the darkness.

"Who is she?"

Danny froze. He sometimes forgot that his wife was smarter than he was.

"Who is she, Danny? This woman who can smell sex on you—the one you are comparing me to. Miss Hyphenated?"

"Someone on the train. She is a newlywed. Goes by both her maiden and married name." Danny stuck to the truth but then dropped a lie. "I'm not comparing. Just asking."

Kate's eyebrows were cocked. "She's coming onto you."

It was a statement of fact, not an accusation or a question.

Danny nodded. "Maybe a little."

Even he could tell his tone was nervous. He hoped it would pass as embarrassment. Kate responded by pushing him onto his back and straddling his hips in one lithe movement.

"Do I need to talk to her?" she asked. "Tell her to back off my man."

Danny chuckled and shook his head. "I think I can handle it."

"It's kinda sexy, you know," Kate murmured as she ran her hands over his naked chest.

"Sexy?"

"Knowing someone wants to fuck you. It's a turn-on."

Danny's body shuddered when she reached for his erection, dragging her thumb expertly over the bottom.

"Just so we're clear," he gasped. "I don't find it sexy."

Kate kissed his lips before pressing her tongue and front teeth along his neck. Danny steeled himself against her attentions and forced the words out in a sure voice.

"The thought of another guy wanting to fuck you pisses me off. It's the complete opposite of a turn-on."

Kate ignored him. She repositioned her hips and slammed herself down onto his cock.

Conversation over.

CHAPTER 15

LIGHTNING STRIKE

He was not sleeping well. Waking up earlier than usual, he fled his house and ran to the park. His habit was to keep circling. Waiting. Hoping Kathryn would appear.

The jogging trail was lit by soft gas lanterns, but he could not see very far ahead. The mist lay low in the valleys. Not to worry. Her little red blinking light was a beacon. Like Pavlov's dog, her light produced a conditioned bodily response. Heaven. Those first seconds after he spotted her. Absolute heaven.

He slowed his pace to a walk as he stared down at the pond. The lowest point in the park. Stopping on the path, he searched through the fog looking for the fishing pier. The fog lay heavily over the water, obstructing his view. Exiting the path, he walked through the wet grass and smiled. Frogs, hidden in the swampy grass next to the water, were croaking. Creating a noisy cacophony. Frogs. Leaping out of spring.

There were no frogs at the pond that first morning. That first morning, it was cold, quiet, and very still. The ice skating shed was where they first sought shelter. Set back from the fishing pier, its slanted roof was easy to spot today. But that first morning, it felt very private. Looking at the shed in the breaking dawn, he realized it was entirely exposed from the front. It faced the pond and the homes perched on the bordering hill. It certainly was not private. Not like he remembered.

Oh, how he longed to get her alone. To sit, to look into her sharp eyes, to talk, and to be private. To just be with her. His heart's desire. Kathryn. It would be ecstasy. There was a time when he believed she was a dream. Their trysts. The wild imaginings of a trapped man. But Kathryn was no dream.

As he approached the pond, he saw her standing on the fishing pier. Yes. Kathryn was very real. He stopped in his tracks. Afraid to breathe, he watched as she dropped down to one knee. Her attention focused. A dog. The same yellow dog he'd seen for the last week. A stray. Someone's unwanted burden. Abandoned in the park.

Kathryn was cautious. Examining the dog as it examined her. When the dog cocked its head, Kathryn did also. Her long po-nytail swishing to the side. And then she spoke. So low, he could not make out the words. Anxious to hear her voice, he stepped forward. The dog, alerted to his presence, turned and locked eyes. Even through the haze of the early morning, he could read the distrust. It darted off and disappeared into the trees.

"Making friends?" he asked. His tone light as he walked towards her. Hands on his hips.

"I think she's a stray," she said looking wistfully after the animal.

He walked slowly, deliberately, and stopped when he reached the mouth of the pier. Blocking her exit. Kathryn rose to her feet. She avoided his eyes and brushed quickly past. Trying to escape, he guessed. But she could not. He did not need to reach for her. The skin of his bare arm brushed her hand. He knew what she felt because he felt it too. It burned. She stopped. Struck, like he was. Like lightning. 380 kilovolts. It was lightning every time.

His body was still under the influence of the strike when he stumbled towards her. Limbs numb. Brain function inhibited. He fell upon her. His skin scorched. Their lips fused. Heat permeated the air between them.

Somehow, they made their way to the skating shed. The skating shed. Again. He had her crushed against the raw lumber of the interior wall. He sought her skin. Her tender flesh. So very responsive to his touch. Kathryn unleashed. Kathryn the vixen.

Moving his right hand to the back of her neck, he pulled at the red band holding her hair. He tore away from her lips and watched as the golden tresses fell loosely around her shoulders. Running both hands through her locks, he marveled at the texture. So vibrant. So healthy. So natural. Kathryn exuded sensuality. It came from a deep place and poured out. The gait of her jog. The glint of her eyes. The glow of her skin. The shimmer of hair. Her hair. Falling into her eyes. Tipping her head back, he pushed his face into her hair and breathed.

"No," she whispered.

No? Stepping back, his flesh singed. Bristled. Shredded at her rejection. Helpless, he reached out. Palms open. Surrender.

Relief. Her mouth pulled up into a crooked smile. Kathryn's eyes glinted with mischief. Was she teasing? Kathryn's hands, strong with purpose, pressed against his stomach pushing him back. Blindly, he let her guide. He felt the bench hit the back of his knees and sat. Looking up into her eyes, he savored the moment. The moment when she straddled his legs and pressed her cleavage beneath his nose. His hands flew along the flesh of her thigh and up into the loose fabric of her running shorts. Her ass taut beneath his grip. Her skin damp and cool from the morning chill.

The bench was wide and offered little comfort. It was merely there as a brace. Laying prone, he watched. Engrossed by her single-minded determination. Kathryn pulled down his shorts. His erection sprung free, and she positioned herself over it. He reached for her again. Clutching at her hips, he tried to pull her down. But she resisted. Kathryn held his gaze with utter confidence. Pulling the crotch of her shorts to the side, she sunk her hand into her pussy. Boldly, she slid her own fingers in and out.

No longer desperate. He was mesmerized. Watching her pleasure herself. Abruptly, she pulled her fingers out, and he groaned as she slid them between his lips.

"Taste me," she murmured, inviting him to suck her fingers clean.

"Put me inside," his voice thick, heavy with longing. "I need to be buried inside you."

"I know." Kathryn growled the words as she slowly came down on his erection. Engulfing his senses.

She was hot, surely hotter than 98.7. And wet. So wet. He slid easily into her. No resistance. Just utter abandon.

Kathryn was ruthless. He tried to hold out. Prolong the moment. But she made it impossible. Grinding into him, she thought only of herself. He was an object. Something hard to rub against. When she erupted, violently throwing herself against his chest, he climaxed along with her. Unwillingly. He answered her passionate cry with his own.

In a shockingly intimate gesture, she touched her nose to his and sighed heavily. He was still inside of her. Heaven. Her hair fell over his face. Blinding his peripheral vision. Forcing his stare. When their breathing quieted, he took her face in both hands. Held her in position.

And he finally asked, "What's your name? Tell me. I want you to tell me."

Kathryn's eyes hardened. She ripped away. Angry. Just as he expected. Her hair was wild, and she yanked at it. Searching the ground, she huffed in frustration. The ponytail holder lost.

After situating his own clothes, he took a deep breath. Strengthening his resolve. He touched her elbow, and she jumped. Eyes ablaze.

"One day," he said. "Outside the park, we will be introduced. I'll wait, but not forever."

Turning his back, he ran up the hill to the jogging trail. Leaving was agony. But he took solace.

When lightning strikes, it always leaves a mark.

CHAPTER 16

UNCLE WALT

When the phone rang, Kate answered without looking at the caller ID. She was on autopilot. Hurrying through her chores with her thoughts in a muddle. The jogger wanted to know her name.

"Hello?" she barked, waiting impatiently for an answer.

"Are you pissed at me or somethin'?" the voice asked. "Is that why you ain't calling me back?"

"Walter," she sighed, her mood shifting. It was always nice to hear her brother's voice. "I called," she said. "I left a message."

"Ahh, hell. I guess I gotta learn how to use the goddamn voice-mail. Dad always did that."

"What?"

"Dad's moved out, Katie. Left me the house."

"Hold on a second. I just talked to Dad on Sunday. He didn't say anything."

"The old man's been keepin' secrets. Bought a condo at that retirement complex. You know the one. Over in Bishop's Woods. Bought it awhile ago. Been sittin' on it. Bidin' his time I guess. Waitin' to pull the trigger."

"Dad left you the farm. He just moved out?" Kate's voice sounded shrill.

71

She didn't like feeling confused. Why would Dad move out? He had an ideal arrangement. Walter took care of the property and was good company. Her little brother was a rougher version of Dad's younger self.

"I'm getting married, Katie. I guess that's why he figured it was time."

Kate fell into Danny's reading chair and tried to make sense of the information. Walter was getting married.

"I didn't even know you were dating. What the hell is going on? We were just up there three weeks ago." Kate didn't hide the hurt in her voice. "You and dad are just the same. You never tell me anything."

"She's a great gal, Katie. She's a payroll clerk at the office. Has a little boy, raising him all by herself. But she ain't a whore," he vehemently added. "Not like the last chic I got tangled up with."

"She's got a son?"

"He's ten. Fifth grade like Bill. He was givin' her a hard time. So, I figured, what the hell, I got the uncle gig down pat. Why not help her out? Take the kid fishin'. Give him a little man time. Maybe straighten him out a bit."

Kate was no longer mad; she was amused. "So that's it? You take the kid fishing and then decide to marry his mom."

"I knocked her up."

Kate was laughing now. Walter was never one to sugarcoat things.

"You got her pregnant," she said. The words making her smile wider.

"It's a love child, Katie. This here's the real deal. The wedding is this weekend. I know it's short notice, but you know, I figured we ought to make it legit. The sooner, the better. Don't want Cody gettin' wrong ideas."

"Cody?"

"Yep. At first, I thought he was a pain in the ass, but I like him all right now. Plays little league. He's got one hell of an arm. Can't hit worth shit, but I'm workin' with him."

"This weekend? Geez, Walt, you didn't give me much notice."

"Well, you're due for a visit. The freezer is empty. Ahh hell, I never figured on you not cooking for me anymore. I suppose since I'm gettin' married and all, it wouldn't be right."

"She doesn't cook?" Kate asked and then quickly shook her head. First things first. "Walt, I don't even know her name."

"Rosemary. And she does cook, but not as good as you. Tries hard, you know. I don't say nothin'. But, damn, Katie, I'm gonna miss your chicken pot pie."

"I'll teach Rosemary the recipe," Kate promised.

"That would be awful nice of you. Like I said, she tries hard. Wants to learn."

"Well," Kate sighed. "I'm happy for you. You got yourself a readymade family. Little Walter is finally becoming a man."

"Knock it off with the Little Walter shit. I told Roger the same thing. The fellas from work will be at the wedding, and I don't want them picking up on that dumbass nickname. It's embarrassing."

"Roger?"

Their older brother lived in Alaska with his two sons and his wife, Ruth. They seldom visited. The boys, Kevin and Brandon, were in high school. Kate sent them birthday presents but had only met them once before.

"Count us in for sure then. If Roger can travel down to the lower forty-eight, then we can certainly drive two hours."

"We're gettin' married at the house on Saturday. Nothing fancy. About forty folks, mostly from work. Rosemary doesn't have much of a family. None worth speaking about anyways. Poor thing. She's had it rough. Done well for herself considering the plate that she was handed."

"I can't wait to meet her, Walt." Kate's heart warmed. "Can I do anything for you? Bring anything?"

"Mom's potato salad," he said quickly.

"Okay. You got it," Kate said mentally adding the ingredients to her shopping list. "Call if you need anything else."

"Sounds good."

Walt was ready to say good-bye. He was probably exhausted from talking so much.

"Walt?" Kate added quickly before he could hang up.

"Yeah?"

"Congratulations. And tell Rosemary and Cody that Aunt Katie said welcome to the family."

"Thanks," he said with real heart. "I'll be sure to do that. Gotta go now. Making a call. Hospital. Damn, I hate hospitals. Ya never know what you're gonna pull out the pipe."

Kate could hear the cringe in her brother's voice, and she smiled as she hung up the phone. Walt was a plumber like their dad. But unlike his dad, he preferred to punch a clock and refused to take over their family plumbing outfit.

Walter's greatest strength was knowing exactly who he was. He was a working stiff who lived for the weekend. Hunting, fishing, and a cold beer at the bar after work. Until now. Rosemary, a stepson, and a new baby. When Walter decided to take the plunge, he did it with style.

Sitting quietly with a thin smile on her lips, Kate stared down at the phone and tried to identify the ache in her chest. She should be happy. Her brother was getting married. Shoving the sadness to the corner of her mind, Kate took a deep breath and dialed Danny's office. Danny loved Walter as much as she did.

Today was a good day.

CHAPTER 17

SECRET EXCHANGE

Sharon was starving after the committee meeting and commandeered Kate and Molly to join her at La Cocina, the local Mexican restaurant. Kate was only drinking iced tea, but she was tired of being sober and thinking seriously about ordering a margarita. It was taking all her patience not to get angry at her friends.

Molly and Sharon entertained each other by making fun of Kate's clothes, hair, and makeup. After Molly's description of Kate's gardening hat and overalls, Sharon was doubled over rocking the table with her laughter.

"Bitches," Kate said, looking away again in search of the waitress.

"Katie never cared about clothes," Sharon said wiping away the tears of laughter on her apple cheeks. "Not that she needs to care. She could look sexy in a flour sack."

"Shut up," Kate gave Sharon a warning look, but it was ignored.

"What?" Sharon demanded. "It's true. Molly, you've seen the way she walks around."

Sharon's posture slouched, and she did a poor impression of her friend, peering around the restaurant with her eyes half closed.

"What was that?" Kate asked with a snort. "I don't do that."

"I can't imitate you. Believe me, I've tried," Sharon said with a shrug. "I can't do it. It's just not in my genetic makeup. But you," she pointed at Kate, "You're all up in your body."

Kate laughed when Sharon felt herself up with open palms.

"You know what I mean. It's confidence. You wear it like a skin. It makes you sexy."

Molly nodded in agreement, but her smile was teasing. "Imagine if she wore jeans that actually fit. Not many women can pull sexy off with the crotch of their pants hanging down to their knees."

Sharon snorted margarita out her nose. It took awhile for the laughter to die down after that. Kate was getting ready to walk to the bar and order a margarita herself when the waitress finally appeared.

"Katie, seriously," Sharon sobered and pointed a finger at her friend. "Friday, we're gonna buy you a pair of high-heeled shoes."

"No."

"Yes, we are. How old are those ugly things?" Sharon asked, looking disgustedly at Kate's Birkenstocks. "Yuck. I know their original color wasn't dirt."

"I hate high heels. They hurt my feet."

"True," Molly said, holding out her foot to display the black heeled pump peeking out of the wide leg of her jeans. "But they're so pretty."

Kate looked down her nose at Molly's feet and shook her head. "No way."

Sharon raised her eyebrows. "Come on. Do it for Danny."

"Tom loves high heel shoes," Molly said, sipping her drink. "He likes me to wear them to bed."

"Molly!" Kate couldn't help but shout. She was shocked. She couldn't believe Molly had sex, let alone sex in high heels.

"Well," Molly shrugged. "There's no harm in it as long as I'm the one wearing them."

The waitress returned with Kate's margarita. Interrupting their laughter, she took Sharon's empty dinner plate and slipped away again.

Sharon drew a finger over her margarita glass and looked wistfully at the table. "The things we do for our men."

"What?" Kate asked, her curiosity piqued. If Molly wore high heels to bed, what was Sharon doing? "What have you done, Sharon?"

Leaning over the table, Sharon looked around at the other restaurant patrons. "I got a tattoo," she whispered a little too loudly.

"You did not!" Kate was shouting again, but this time in outrage. "How could you? You said tattoos were trashy, and you threw a fit when I tried to get one."

"You wanted a tattoo?" Molly asked with a crooked smile. "When?"

"Spring break, sophomore year," Sharon's eyes lit up as she began the story. "Katie wandered into a tattoo parlor after a long night partying. She wanted a butterfly on her ankle."

"Sharon was so upset," Kate interrupted. "She almost started crying."

"I stopped her from getting the tat but couldn't stop her from bungee jumping."

"Bungee jumping?" Molly's mouth fell open.

"Sharon, enough already." Kate hid her face behind the wide brim of her margarita glass.

"It was awful," Sharon continued. "I started hyperventilating when they took her up in this scary, rattling, metal contraption. Katie walked right to the edge of the crane and did a swan dive." Sharon put her hands up in demonstration. "I screamed so loud, I swear to God, I almost threw up. And I was on the ground watching."

"Where was Danny?" Molly asked still wide-eyed with shock.

"We weren't going out at the time," Kate said, shaking her head. "It wasn't that big of a deal. It only cost thirty dollars. They were running a special down at the beach."

"Bungee jumping," Molly said in disbelief. "I'm sorry, Kathryn. I can't imagine you doing something like that."

"She was always doing crazy stuff like that," Sharon added. "I stood back and watched. I lived vicariously. Way too chicken to climb up on the bar and dance."

"Hey, I'm not the one with a tattoo," Kate said, shifting the conversation away from herself. "Where is it and what is it?"

Sharon leaned over the table and pulled the collar of her blouse down exposing the cleavage of her left breast.

"Baby chicks?" Kate smiled warmly at her friend. It wasn't nearly as naughty as she had imagined. They were actually kind of cute.

"I've got three of them. One for each baby." Sharon leaned back in her chair and smoothed out the wrinkles in her blouse. "John calls me Henny."

"Well," Kate said, slamming down her empty margarita glass. "That's a hell of a lot better than Woody. I've got to tell Danny he's been outdone."

Signaling for the waitress, Kate smiled widely and relaxed into her chair. The laughter and chatter filled her up with bubbly enthusiasm—like a newfound effervescence. Trusting Sharon and Molly was strangely liberating. And the evening was still young. It didn't have to end.

Kate ordered another round of margaritas.

CHAPTER 18

STIRRING THE POT

Danny got the boys into bed and went outside to wait for Kate on the front porch. She was out of the house after dark. It wasn't the first time, but this time it felt different. Sharing Kate with the kids and their extra-curricular activities never bothered him.

But, Kate was at a restaurant, a restaurant with a bar. Taking in a ragged breath, he checked his watch again. When she called him after the garden committee meeting, he didn't think to ask when to expect her home. Next time she went out with Sharon, he would definitely ask.

The night breeze blowing through the trees that lined their quiet neighborhood was suddenly filled with girlish laughter. They were on foot. Ready to spring, he positioned himself on the top step of the porch with his arms folded across his chest.

Sharon spotted him first. She ducked her face into Kate's hair and whispered. Kate stumbled and gave him a timid wave. Both Molly and Sharon giggled, and it pissed him off.

"Hey," Kate called from the sidewalk. "You sure look sexy up there."

Stopping in front of the house, she examined his face. Danny controlled his expression.

"I left the van in town," she began. "I think I might be drunk."

Molly and Sharon broke into another fit of giggles. Kate shuffled carefully across the lawn. When she reached the bottom of the porch stairs, she gripped the railing and looked up at him with exhausted eyes. Kate looked ready to collapse. Danny was at her side before she could blink.

"I've gotcha, baby," he murmured.

Danny got her into the house by supporting most of her weight. She whispered her apologies and excuses as he sat her on the bed and took her shoes off.

"It's okay," he repeated.

He was practiced at getting her clothes off but fumbled with thick fingers when he fastened the buttons of her night shirt. She was sleeping when he returned from the bathroom with ibuprofen and water, and he shook her awake to force down the medicine.

Relieved to have her safely in bed, he sat down on the edge of the mattress and smoothed the hair away from her face. Her cheeks were still flushed from her walk home. Running the back of his hand along her cheekbone, he waited for her skin to cool beneath his touch. The anxiety that was held so tightly in his chest finally dissipated. She was home. Danny kissed her good night and shut off the light.

Sharon was in the family room fingering the family photographs Kate displayed on the sofa table.

"Katie's one helluva housekeeper," she said, her voice full of mock admiration. "There's not one speck of dust anywhere."

Danny's posture was more relaxed now that his wife was home, but he didn't have any smiles for Sharon.

"I need a ride," she said. "Katie and I drove together."

He stomped towards the back hallway. Sharon followed closely behind and didn't say anything until they were pulling out of the driveway in his car.

"She only had two margaritas, Dan."

Danny clenched the steering wheel in restraint. Sharon's tone was condescending, and he called on all his years of coaching adolescent boys to keep himself from exploding.

"Kate doesn't drink anymore," he said, impressed by his own calm. "She's very careful about her diet."

Sharon snorted. "A few drinks isn't gonna kill her."

"Sharon, her mother was forty-eight years old when she died. Kate exercises every day and watches her sugar, because she is terrified of getting diabetes."

"Her mother had a heart attack." Sharon corrected.

"Congestive heart failure," Danny snapped. "Brought on by untreated diabetes. Don't tell me about Kate's family, Sharon. I know her better than you. I know her better than anyone."

Sharon was silent as they drove through downtown Wheaton, but Danny knew she was fuming. When she turned to face him, he gritted his teeth in anticipation.

"What happened to her?" she asked with narrow eyes. "She's different, Danny."

"She grew up," Danny said, cutting Sharon a warning glance, daring her to continue.

"That's not what I mean," she said, thoughtful now as she looked out at the lights streaming past the car window. "She's so guarded. I miss the old Kate. The fearless one. The one who never cared what people were thinking."

Danny smiled. "The old Kate still comes out now and then. It's just underneath the surface."

Sharon's blue eyes sharpened and her mouth tightened into a line.

"What?" Danny asked. "She's not in college anymore. She's a mother with three kids, a damn good mother. I like you, Sharon, but don't mess with my family. I can see what you're doing. You're stirring the pot, and I don't appreciate it."

When Danny pulled into Sharon's driveway, she was still quiet, deep in thought.

"I'm going to offer her a job."

Danny's mouth fell open. When she glanced over at him, he closed his jaw with an audible snap.

"I need her help," she said. "The job is a perfect fit for both of us."

"No, Sharon." Danny was too upset to disguise his anger.

"Joey is five years old. It's time for Kate to go back to work."

"Is your husband going back to work? Your littlest one is starting kindergarten next year too."

"John is a different kind of animal. He's not like Katie. He's content at home."

"What makes you think she's not content?" he shouted.

Sharon said nothing and waited while he calmed down.

"Everyone thinks it was me, but it wasn't." Danny was defensive now. "I encouraged her to go to law school. Told her I would follow. She didn't want it anymore."

"I know, Danny." Sharon's voice was low, but it throbbed with sincerity.

"Even after we were married," Danny's words poured out in a rush. "We were working in Chicago. Young professionals. We were both on our way up. She was climbing, just got a big promotion. She was making more money than me, Sharon. But, she wanted a baby, a family. It was her choice."

When Danny glimpsed at the passenger seat, he found Sharon relaxed, her hands folded serenely in her lap.

"Staying home was her choice," he repeated.

"I'm telling you for a reason. You and I both know Katie won't take the job without your support. So now it's your choice." Sharon put her hand on Danny's arm, but he yanked it away.

"You've got a lot of goddamn nerve, Sharon."

"What are you so afraid of?" Her voice was soft, soothing.

"I'm not afraid," Danny snapped.

"I recognize it, Dan. I know how a man behaves when he feels threatened."

"Don't patronize me," he said, rolling his eyes.

"I love her too. And, I owe her."

When Danny raised his eyebrows, she shrugged her shoulders. "I borrowed her backbone for so long, I finally grew one myself. Without Katie, I never would have changed my major from English to Accounting. And I never would have left home to take that job in Atlanta."

Sharon climbed out of the car, but instead of closing the door, she held it open and leaned in for one last look in his eyes.

"I'm sorry, Danny. I am stirring the pot. Your wife's been set on the stove too goddamn long. Just think about it. This is good for you too."

Nothing coherent went through Danny's thoughts as he sped home. Weaving a string of curse words together, he spun a web of hatred so tangled he couldn't recognize the source of his anger. He didn't want to.

Think about it. The wretched bitch from Kate's past left him no other choice.

CHAPTER 19

OFF SCHEDULE

The fact that she was lying next to him, sleeping peacefully, did little to calm his nerves. The sleep he did get was the restless kind, the kind that bordered on conscious thought and nightmare. He got out of bed early. The house was quiet, cool, and dark. Getting a glimpse of Kate's morning routine, Danny could not see the appeal. It was spooky. He would rather wake up to breaking sunshine, the smell of coffee, and the rattle of plates in the kitchen.

The kids woke up early, too. One by one, they came down the stairs and asked the same question.

"Where's Mom?"

It was especially difficult keeping Joey out of the master bedroom. He wanted to check on his mom, to make sure she was home. Finally, Danny relented. He followed Joey down the hall with a fresh cup of coffee. Barefoot in his Spiderman pajamas, Joey stood silently next to his mother.

Kate moaned softly and rolled over so her face was stuffed into the pillow. Danny set the coffee on the bedside table and ran a finger over her shoulder.

"Time to wake up, Trouble."

Kate propped herself off her pillow and squinted. When she saw both Joey and Danny standing next to the bed, she smiled widely.

"My goodness," she said opening both arms to Joey. "If I'm dreaming, please don't wake me."

Joey leapt into her arms. She held him close and looked up at Danny. Sharon was wrong. His wife was content.

"I brought you coffee," he said.

"Thank you," she said. "What time is it?"

"It's 6:30. You missed your run but don't worry. The boys are fed and upstairs getting dressed."

"Oh," Kate shoved herself and Joey to the side of the bed and sat up. "You better go get dressed too, little man. We have to walk to the train with Daddy. I left the van in town last night, and I need it to drive you to school."

"You left the van in town?" Joey asked.

"I did. It was such a nice night, I walked home with Mrs. Ibner and Mrs. Hilliard." Kate shuffled Joey out the bedroom door with a few instructions about appropriate school clothes.

Kate went to the bedside table. Going toe to toe with Danny, she gulped her coffee while running her free hand into the open fold of his bathrobe.

"How are you feeling?" Danny asked.

"I feel good," she said, before smiling wryly. "I kinda remember someone shoving ibuprofen down my throat before I passed out."

Danny nodded slightly but said nothing. They knew each other too well.

"I'm sorry about last night," she murmured. "Were you very worried? I probably should have called before leaving the restaurant."

"I was worried but don't be sorry," he said kissing her forehead. "I'm just not used to you going out with friends. Too possessive. It's unhealthy."

"I'm not used to it either," Kate said. "That's why I started drinking jumbo-sized margaritas."

She pulled away abruptly and set the coffee back on the table. Yanking at the covers, she transformed the tumble of blankets and pillows into an oasis of order and clean lines.

"How do you do that so quickly?" Danny asked.

"Years of practice," she said, tossing a decorative pillow onto the bed.

"Thank you," Danny said pulling her into a rough embrace. "For everything you do around here."

Squeezing her tightly, he nuzzled his beard into the delicate skin of her neck. "You are very appreciated," he whispered, firmly reinforcing his original statement.

Kate pushed herself away and examined his face. His sappy behavior was drawing suspicion, so he gave her an innocent smile. It worked. Kate dropped her eyes and headed to the bathroom.

"I'm gonna take a shower," she said as she disappeared behind the door.

Peter and Bill were in the process of making themselves lunches at the kitchen counter. It was a huge mess. The food they packed probably didn't meet Kate's standards of balanced nutrition, but Danny wasn't going to hover. The boys needed a lesson on self-sufficiency. Joey was still upstairs. Danny could hear him humming to himself.

"I'm gonna turn the television on for you, Joe. Your mom and I are getting dressed," he called up the stairs.

"I want Thomas Train," he called back.

Danny turned on the television and practically skipped to the master bedroom. Sex in the shower was rare during the school week. Kate was too busy. But she was running off schedule. Her night out was going to have at least one advantage.

Filling his lungs with the warm, moisture-laden air, Danny stood before the shower door and watched his wife rinse her soapy hair. She caught his lurking shape from the corner of her eye and reached to wipe the steam from the shower door.

"Are you comin' in?" she asked.

"Is there room?" he teased. Danny was already hanging up his robe.

Kate backed herself away from the water and waited with a crooked smile while Danny rinsed off in the hot stream of water. Danny focused on her face rather than her naked body. With her hair slicked back, he could appreciate the intelligent set of her eyes and the delicate line of her cheekbones. While he was admiring the seductive fullness of her lower lip, she stepped forward, rubbing her breasts against his chest, and reached for the nylon sponge.

Danny closed his eyes and got lost in the sensation of her gliding the soapy sponge across his body. He turned automatically, redirecting her attention to the tight muscles in his back.

"Tell me about the committee meeting," he prompted after sighing heavily.

"It was pretty much what you would expect. Women in khaki pants and strappy sandals. They weren't getting much done. Talking in circles mostly. I finally offered to write the proposal. Sharon's gonna come up with some numbers for me, so I can present it to the Village Planning Committee next Tuesday."

Danny spun around and faced her again. "Do you have time for that? We've got Walt's wedding this weekend."

She smiled before wrapping her arms around his neck. The fingers of her right hand pulled through his wet hair, and he threw his head back into the shower spray, enjoying her touch.

"I've got most of it written in my head already."

Kate ran her hands along his neck and across his shoulders. Biting her lip, she hitched her left leg around his hip, pressing herself into his erection.

"It's kinda fun," she murmured. "It's reassuring knowing I still have brain cells."

Dan hoisted her left thigh with a slippery hand and glided his erection into her. Her breathing hitched a little, but she quickly recovered. Adjusting her weight, she straddled him perfectly despite the fact that she was standing on the tiptoes of one leg.

"As long as you're having fun." His words came out in a growl, and she whimpered in the way she always did when his voice dropped an octave. Danny's right hand supported the thigh of the leg hitched around his waist, but his left hand was free to roam.

Kate's flesh felt different in the shower. It softened somehow. The muscles lining her legs and shoulders became supple, tender beneath the stream of hot water. But he was focused on her rosy, erect nipples. The beads of soap making her breasts slippery beneath his fingertips. Kate's gasps interrupted Danny's concentration. She locked her hands around his neck, anchored her weight, and leaned away. Kate arched like a bow directing her nipples to the ceiling.

Danny stumbled backwards taking her with him. He tightened his grip, unwilling to part for even the slightest moment. The hot water pounded his neck and shoulders, streamed down his chest like a waterfall, and pooled at their joined hips before raining down his legs.

Kate moved with urgency. Impatient, seduction already served. Grinding her hips in small circles she used Danny's thick thigh. Intent and completely focused on one goal, she sent his body into sensual overdrive. Danny's fingers dug into her heavy, wet hair. Cupping her face with his oversized hand, he locked onto her gaze and watched. Watched like the thousands of times before, watched as his wife worked her way towards climax.

She stiffened, the leg wrapped around his waist clenched, pulling him closer still. And then she cried. Her voice resonated within the tiled stall. Finally, she shuddered, her body releasing all tension. Danny breathed a sigh of relief. Her work complete, her goal accomplished, he was left with her compliant body.

Danny spun her around. With her palms flat against the shower wall, he yanked her hips. Impatient to be inside her again, he thrust with enough force to lift her off her toes, her face sliding against the steamy tile. Her ass reddened beneath his grip, leaving a mark, and his thoughts went there. Growling in restraint, his palm itched.

"Are you a bad girl?" he murmured as he pawed roughly at the fleshy pinked skin of her ass.

He waited, holding his breath in anticipation. Surely she would agree. She was bad. Kate was a bad girl.

"Yes," she whined.

Her answer actuating his trigger. Danny's open palm came down hard on her ass. The beads of water on her skin reverberated, and she cried again. Just as he suspected, his hand left a mark, his fingers distinct as the redness spread across her ass. He groaned and smacked her again, this time on the left cheek. Ignoring her cries, he continued to slam his cock into her. His handprints so vivid on her pale flesh. In one final thrust, he erupted, cumming inside her throbbing pussy.

"Kate," he gasped.

Clutched at her hips, he closed his eyes. Releasing Kate, he backed away until he felt the hot water of the shower hitting his neck and back. She pushed herself off the wall and turned. Holding out her arms, she fell, trusting him to catch her.

And he did.

CHAPTER 20

SNAPPING TURTLES

"Hey, little man, I have an idea. How would you feel about helping me with a homemade gift for Uncle Walt and Rosemary? It involves painting. Your brothers can put it together with Daddy's tools when they get home from school. That way, it'll be a gift from all of us."

"Painting?" Joey asked, wiping his mouth with the sleeve of shirt.

They were on the deck eating turkey sandwiches. Kate was a little manic from her crazy morning, but she was determined to get through her list of chores.

"Yeah, painting. When we were kids, we used to have a sign that read *Happy Day Farm* at the end of our driveway. Papa made it for your grandmother. It's what she used to call the farm."

Kate ran her finger along the rim of her milk glass and smiled at her son's cheeky face. He looked a lot like his Uncle Walter. "When Grandma died, Papa didn't care about the sign anymore. I don't know what happened to it. It disappeared one winter."

"Papa didn't care about it?" Joey's eyebrows pulled together and his brow furrowed with worry.

"Well, Grandma died very suddenly. The farm wasn't so happy without her around. But," Kate added, giving Joey a nudge, "now that Uncle Walt is getting married, there's gonna be a new family running the farm."

"It'll be happy again," Joey said.

"Right. So what do say? You want to help me?"

Joey nodded his head.

"Okay, but first, I've got to go for my run. I slept in this morning. Do you think you can keep up with me on your bike? I might have a surprise for you in the park."

"I can keep up," he promised.

Jumping up, he ran into the house. Kate piled the dishes into a stack and smiled as she turned towards the house.

Joey learned to ride a two-wheeler at three and half years old. At five years old, he was attempting wheelies. He kept up with Kate easily, but she didn't enjoy her run nearly as much as she did in the early morning. It felt different and not just because Joey was with her.

In the dawn, she felt like a lone soldier on patrol, braving the elements to explore the perimeter of her neighborhood. In the bright daylight, she felt like a spectacle, a housewife cliché. She especially hated running on the road. Cars followed closely behind as if they expected her to veer out wildly. Kate tried to avoid the road as much as possible by keeping herself and Joey on the sidewalk and was relieved when they finally reached the jogging trail.

"I'll meet you at the fishing pier," Kate called out to Joey.

She knew he was itching to take off. His front wheel wobbled a bit as he sped down the sharp embankment leading to the pond, but Kate didn't worry. Her conditioning as a mother of three boys made her nearly impossible to rattle. Even if Joey happened to fall from his bike, he would probably just roll a few times, shake off the dirt, and jump back on. The Mallers were tough. None of them, Kate included, were crybabies.

Breathing heavily, Kate stepped off the jogging path and walked down the grassy hill leading to the fishing pier. Joey's bike was carelessly tossed on the ground along with his helmet. Kate couldn't see him, but she assumed he was at the end of the pier hidden from view by the hedges lining the pond.

She ignored the ice skating shed and fingered the cellophane wrapped turkey breast in her jacket pocket. Kate couldn't stop thinking about the yellow dog. With Walt's wedding, the garden proposal, and her daily chores, she had more than enough on her plate to worry about. But still, she was fixated. The dog was nowhere to be seen. Kate stopped searching. The dog usually showed up on her own out of nowhere. Kate's plan was to make her presence known in the park and wait.

The thud of her footsteps on the seasoned wood of the pier reminded Kate of Wisconsin. When she was kid, she swam in the lakes and quarries around her home with her brothers. Joey was peering into the dark, green water and looked up when he heard his mother's approach.

"Turtles," he said pointing into the water.

"Really?" Kate hurried to the edge to take a look. "Well I'll be darned. In Wisconsin, we had snapping turtles. Mean, ornery creatures that could take your big toe off with one snap of their jaws."

Kate smiled at her wide-eyed son. "When it got really hot, Grandma would take me and your uncles to a quarry near our farm. We would run—tearing our clothes off as we went—to the cliff next to the water. Racing each other. But just as we took off, already flying in the air, we could hear Grandma screaming—'Watch out for snapping turtles!' Of course, it was too late by then. It was terrifying and thrilling at the same time. Snapping turtles." Kate shook her head and peered into the water. "We never did check the water before jumping."

"What's a quarry?"

"In Wisconsin, especially around Germantown, they mine rock. Lannon stone mostly. Like the stone Daddy used to make a path outside our back door." Joey nodded his head in understanding. "So they dig really deep, with huge machines. When they're all done, they abandon the quarry and let it fill up with spring water. It's not like swimming in a lake. It's surrounded by rocky cliffs. Great climbing. And it's very, very deep. The water is super cold. It feels great on a hot day."

"Will you take us sometime?"

"Sure," Kate said bumping him with her hip. "I'll ask Uncle Walt."

Both Kate and Joey stared down into the water. Searching the depths but seeing nothing—not even their reflections. When they looked up, they spotted a family of ducks swimming towards them.

"They think we have food," Kate said, pulling the turkey from her pocket. She waggled the food at the approaching ducks. "This isn't for you."

Before Joey could ask, the yellow dog made her appearance. She was sitting at the end of the pier. Her yellow eyes staring, waiting expectantly for Kate to make a move.

"Your surprise," Kate whispered to Joey. "Don't move too quickly. She's skittish."

Joey was a statue, not even breathing, as Kate walked slowly to the mouth of the pier.

"Hello, girl," she said holding out the cellophane wrapped turkey. "I brought you something."

When Kate stopped, the dog rose to her feet, ready to run. Dropping to one knee, Kate gave all her attention to unwrapping the turkey. She was careful not to make eye contact. The dog dropped her square head and tail and lowered herself to the ground. Smiling back at Joey, Kate held out the turkey. The dog crawled slowly over to Kate's outstretched hand and snatched the meat with her front teeth.

Joey walked over to Kate's side, and she put an arm around his tiny shoulders. The dog ran over to the ice skating shed. She dropped her prize in the grass and nibbled delicately at the crumbling portions.

Kate guided Joey towards the bench inside the shed. When they sat down, the dog lifted her head, but she didn't run. When she finished her food, she sat and licked her paws.

"Do you think she'll let me pet her?" Joey asked in whisper.

The dog abruptly stood and peered at Joey with her head cocked to the side.

"Let me try first." Kate got up from the bench and began her approach, but they got interrupted. The dog was alarmed by a pair of moms pushing strollers to the fishing pier, and she took off into the woods bordering the pond.

"Ahhh," Joey exclaimed.

"I'll keep trying," Kate said. "I think she likes me. Every time I'm in the park she shows up. She trusts me a little bit more each day."

"Do you think she likes kids?"

"I betcha she does," Kate said walking over to Joey's bike. "Tomorrow, when I run in the morning, the park won't be so crowded. We'll buy dog treats at the store. Maybe she'll let me come close enough to tie something around her neck."

"Do you think we can keep her?"

"I'm not making any promises," Kate said, securing Joey's helmet to his head. "But if she likes us, and we like her, I don't see why we couldn't keep her."

"I can't wait to tell Peter and Billy," Joey exclaimed as he hopped on his bike.

Kate gazed into the woods bordering the pond and searched without hope. She was gone. Tomorrow, Kate would try again.

CHAPTER 21

THE HAIRCUT

The boys were thrilled with the prospect of adopting a dog. Both Peter and Billy took off for the park after school, but they came home disappointed. Kate distracted them with Uncle Walt's project, and they retreated to the garage to prime and paint.

When Kate left for the train station to pick up Danny, all three boys were wearing their father's old button-down shirts and quietly painting together.

She was smiling. Happy and strumming her fingers to the country music on the radio as she drove to town. Danny wanted a ride. He was in a hurry to get home and catch sports coverage of the hockey playoffs.

Catering to the boys, Kate made man food. Tacos, black beans and rice, and nachos. She was hoping for some peace and quiet. Sharon emailed the garden numbers, and Kate was itching to get started on the proposal.

Still enjoying the music on the radio, Kate smiled at the pedestrians strolling past her parked van. She could see the train station and commuters flowing into the streets, but Danny wasn't among them. Finally, when the crowd thinned, she spotted him. He was trying to disentangle himself from a conversation with a professional looking blonde. Kate stared out the windshield. It had to be Miss Hyphenated.

The woman wore red high heels and a light gray pant suit. She was glittery from head to toe. Sparkling earrings dangled from her ears and shiny gold bangles hung from her wrists. Miss Hyphenated carried an oversized designer purse like Sharon, and she swung it back and forth as she flirted with Kate's husband. The woman couldn't stop touching herself. She concentrated mostly on the top button of her silk blouse, but eventually, as Danny pulled away, her fingers went to her hair.

Kate frowned. Sharon and Molly made fun of Kate's hair for a good ten minutes yesterday. The blond woman's hair was cut so it was wispy at the shoulders, but her blunt bangs framed her face. It made Kate ashamed. She'd let herself go. She dressed in work-out clothes most of the time and paid little attention to hair and makeup. Kate only really looked in the mirror once a day, and it usually involved brushing her teeth.

Finally, Danny got away. He must have said something funny, because the blond laughed hysterically before waving good-bye. Feeling inadequately dressed and under-groomed, Kate ran her fingers through her hair and moistened her lips by smacking them together. She needn't have bothered. Danny didn't pay her any attention. He climbed into the van and shut the music off. Kate sighed. Whenever Danny got in the van, he turned off the radio.

"Let's go," he said clapping his hands together. "I've been looking forward to this all day. Big game."

Kate fought her instincts and did not ask about Miss Hyphenated. Instead, she let him ramble about the importance of the big game. Kate's interest in hockey was limited to the teams her sons played on, but her disinterest did not deter Danny's enthusiasm.

"I'm thinking about getting my hair cut," Kate slipped into the conversation.

"Really?" Danny reached into the glove compartment and began ordering the contents.

Kate continued. "Sharon and Molly think a short haircut will make me look younger."

"Oh yeah?"

"I was afraid of the time commitment. I'd have to get my hair cut more frequently, but Sharon says short hair is easier to take care of. I'd save time on a daily basis."

"Well, then it sounds like a good idea." Danny fumbled with the window before finally looking at Kate.

"Do you think I'd look good with short hair?" she probed.

"Sure," he said quickly.

When Kate pulled into the driveway, the boys charged the van. They were excited with the dog news. Kate hung back and let the boys enter the house ahead of her. Loud and rambunctious, they were eager for the night's game to begin. Hockey.

Kate was so sick of hockey she wanted to puke.

Distracting herself with details of the garden proposal, she stepped into her noisy kitchen and went to work on serving dinner.

CHAPTER 22

SHADOW OF THE WOODS

He had made his wife cry. Wishing he could forget, he scanned the park again. The baseball diamond was the highest point. Best view. The morning was gray but streaks of sunlight were breaking in the west. Clear sky. No fog. No mist. No cover.

His back was stiff from sleeping in a chair, so he stretched. After arguing with his wife, he took refuge in his study. She wanted to take a trip. Just the two of them. Somewhere romantic. The thought was shockingly repulsive, and he snapped. Immediately afterwards, he was filled with guilt. Guilt so sickening that he paced the floor fighting the urge to wretch an apology from his burning stomach. But then, she called her father. Her daddy. Her hero. Her savior. After that, he felt nothing.

The rest of the evening was spent behind his desk compiling lists. Carefully crafting a plan. A call to action. The work gave him an outlet for his misery. Gave him hope. The decision was made. He was going to leave her. Time was all he needed. Just a week or so to move his monied assets. Make arrangements. He could be civil. Play along with her attempts to make him happy. Hurting his wife gave him no pleasure.

Kathryn. She was the prize. The key. And Kathryn was going to fight. She didn't want change. But he was going to force it. Anticipating her rejection, his response was prepared in advance.

There was sporadic traffic on the jogging trail. Mostly walkers. A few regulars. The fair weather drew them out. He kept count from his perch. At last, Kathryn strode into view. She was searching the park. His heart beat out of his chest, but he soon realized he was not the object of her hunt. She was scanning the woods as she ran on the path. Ducking her head. Searching the underbrush. The stray dog. She was leaving a trail. Enticing the animal with treats. It made him smile. A pet. Not an objectionable idea.

His feet flew. Adrenaline pumped through his veins. Kathryn the vixen. She was still a mystery. Discovering the unknown. Understanding the source of her emotion was the first step. Winning her affection, the ultimate goal.

Because he was familiar with her pace, he timed their meeting perfectly. The most poorly lit area of the jogging trail. Shadowed on one side by thick woods, the trail narrowed as it cut into the hill underneath the home run fence of the baseball diamond. The park district had constructed several tiered concrete walls up the incline to prevent erosion. Tall, bushy evergreens hid the lowest concrete ledge of the tiered overhang. It was safe. It was secluded, and it was part of his plan.

He surprised her. Kathryn actually jolted when he rounded the corner. Dropping his gaze, he slowed to the walk.

"I'm sorry," he said in a low voice. "Did I scare you?"

It sounded like teasing, and he knew it would stiffen her backbone.

"No," she corrected. "I was distracted."

"The yellow dog," he said eyeing the biscuit in her hand.

"Have you seen her?"

He smiled. He wished he had good news. "No, I haven't. Not today."

Kathryn's brow furrowed, and she tossed the treat into the darkened woods next to the jogging trail. She sighed as she watched the biscuit settle into green brush.

"I hope she's okay."

So sad. Unthinkingly, he took her hand. She was stunned. And he was, too, at the tenderness of his touch. Giving for once. Not selfish. Not wanting. Not hungry.

She stared down at their hands. Frozen. Undecided. And he took advantage of it while he could by picking up her other hand. Examining them for the first time. Strong and sturdy, these were not the hands of a pampered woman. Her nails were short and her fingers were nicked with old cuts. And there were fresh calluses on her right hand. Gardening? Stroking the rough patches with his thumb, he stepped closer.

"If you were mine, you would not have to work so hard," he murmured.

"I'm not yours," she warned as she yanked her hands away.

"True," he said pinching a wayward strand of hair and tucking it behind her ear. "But I think about it. Don't you? Think about leaving him?"

"No," she said.

"But you're not happy." Clear, concise, his strongest argument.

"You're wrong." Her tone did not waver. She was sure. "I am happy."

He repressed a smile. The rejection. Expected.

"Happy women don't cheat on their husbands with strange men in the park."

His retort was prepared, and he sounded smug despite his efforts at sincerity. Kathryn launched herself off the ground. Before he could blink, her right fist flashed before his eyes. Strong and sturdy, she landed a punch so powerful it blinded him. Tears and tiny shards of brilliant light disorientated him, and he stumbled backwards.

"Shit," he cursed as he cupped his enflamed cheek.

No one ever struck him. And it pissed him off. Kathryn stood defiantly. Both hands clenched at her sides. Daring him to react. For the second time in less than twenty-four hours, he had lashed out at a woman. Not with words this time. No. Kathryn was not scared of words. Feigning defeat, he slumped and kept his eyes on the path. His eyes would surely give him away. The anger. The fury.

Kathryn's fighting posture relaxed slightly, and he sprung. Gripping her wrists, he used the momentum of his charge to push her through the thick evergreens bordering the trail. He pinned her against the concrete ledge. Arms locked against her sides. When he looked into her eyes, they burned but not with hatred. It was same penetrating stare she gave him the first time they locked eyes. His reaction was involuntary. Just as it was then. She ground herself into his erection. Seduced, he let go of her wrists and roamed her body. Her thighs. Her ass. The curve of her hip.

Kathryn's hazel eyes darkened. She clawed at his neck with rough finger nails. When he flinched, she braided her fingers into his hair and pulled.

Looking him squarely in the eyes, she hissed, "My husband is off limits. Don't mention him again."

Kissing her deeply, he moved his right hand to her ponytail and released her hair. Catching her right wrist, he simultaneously moved his free hand and yanked her head back by grabbing a fistful of luxurious hair. Holding her there, he moved his lips to the warm, scented skin of her neck.

"No," he said defiantly as he sucked and licked.

She tried to wrench herself free, but he was stronger. Whining, Kathryn struggled against brute force. But then they heard approaching footfalls and froze. Their heavy breathing ceased. No one ever passed so closely.

Alone again, he peered into her smoldering eyes, and he was shocked with the realization. She did not call out. She did not want help.

"Aren't you afraid?" he asked relaxing his grip and giving her room to escape.

"No," she said. Her eyes sparked with lust. "Aren't you going to fuck me?"

Her shorts fell away as their hands tore at each other's clothing. His thoughts were violent. Alien and completely consuming. He didn't recognize the sounds rumbling from his chest. Kathryn responded in kind. Her growls subtly filled his consciousness. Overrode the fear. She liked it. Kathryn liked the fight. Longed for confrontation. Thrilled at domination.

His hands cupped her naked ass, and she leapt. Arms wrapped tightly around his neck. Her legs wound around his waist. Hoisting her up on the concrete ledge, his hands moved to her thighs. Tiny scratches torn into her flesh. The evergreens? The rough corners of the concrete wall?

Impatiently, she whined. Nudging her hips to the edge, she spread her legs wide.

"Fuck me," she gasped. "Now."

His head throbbed. Her words crashed. Reverberated in his ears. Somehow, she managed to kick his shorts down his legs. The muscles in her thighs tensed as she used her leg strength to draw him in. But he resisted. Resisted jumping into the fire.

Drawing his hands to her shoulders, he pushed her away. "Tell me your name."

Her eyes narrowed, and she shook her head violently. Groaning, she dove for his lips.

"Fuck me," she demanded into to his hot mouth.

"Your name first," he insisted before pressing his tongue deliciously into her supple lower lip.

She kissed back. Gingerly sucking on his upper lip, his body quivered. But then she came down hard. Snapping with her teeth. He cried out. Tasting blood, he wiped his mouth with the back of his hand. Kathryn had bitten him.

Her eyes were unapologetic. Her own lips drawn across her teeth in a tight line. She wanted to be fucked. So he gave in to the fury. He gave in to Kathryn.

It was strangely intoxicating. Abandoning all restraint. She welcomed it. Her flesh was hot and wet. Her fingers tore at his shirt and then at her own. Possessed, she pinched her own nipples. Writhing as he pounded into her.

"You love being fucked," he growled. "You like it rough. Such a dirty girl."

The words seemed to pierce her. She threw her hands into her hair. Covered her ears. Unacceptable.

Wrapping his hands around her wrists again, he pulled her hands away. Pinning them against the wall, he slammed his cock deep inside and leaned in to whisper.

"Is this what you like?" When she shook her head again. He growled. "To be fucked. Out in the open. Like an animal. Answer me."

"Yes," she cried as he delved deeper.

Grinding his hips. There was no space between them. Just friction so hot it was nearly intolerable.

Her body stiffened, and he felt her climax. The heat emanated from her core, and he could actually feel it. Feel the rush. Eruption. Sex poured out of her body. Thick, hot, and wet.

She shuddered and then sighed. "I. Love. It. Rough."

It was over quickly. Kathryn hung on. Her grip loose. Her body flayed as he took what he wanted. He got lost. Disorientated. And curse words, words he never used in the presence of a lady, poured out of his mouth in a steady stream. Kathryn's eyes closed. Her body bucked sporadically. Aftershocks. Clenching his teeth, he muffled the roar and climaxed. He came so hard he saw red. Flames.

Kathryn shifted her weight before letting her head fall against his shoulder. Her hair got in his mouth. Fell across his face and neck. Obscured his vision. They stayed that way longer than they should have. Their breathing leveled. The mood lifted.

Pulling away, he gently lowered her to the ground. She situated her jacket with shaky hands. It was endearing. Cute. After pulling up his own shorts, he bent and retrieved hers. Lifting one leg at a time, he clothed her. Her eyes were cloudy. Still recovering. So he took advantage and ran his fingers through her hair. Smoothing it away from her face. Her expression almost child-like.

"You've bewitched me," he said capturing her gaze. "I can think of little else. Just you. You in the park."

Kathryn swallowed before squaring her shoulders. But said nothing.

"You are the most fearsome creature I've ever beheld."

Embarrassed, she dropped her gaze.

"Listen to me," he said holding her by the elbows. "There is no one equal. You are not only beautiful but cunning. It's a wicked combination."

She scoffed. Kathryn was unaccustomed to receiving compliments.

"I've got to go," she said, brushing quickly past.

He followed closely behind and nearly ran into her frozen form on the jogging path. The yellow dog. It hunched low when it saw him. And it growled. Showing teeth. Kathryn gestured and shushed. She tried to soothe the beast, but it bolted into the woods.

"Damn it," she scowled in frustration.

"It's okay," he smiled. "You can try again tomorrow."

When she looked up at him, his smile widened. Kathryn loved danger. Another piece of her character discovered.

Sunshine broke around the curve of the path. Bruised, bloodied, and somewhat battered, he sprinted towards it. He left her behind in the shadow of the woods.

CHAPTER 23

FORGIVENESS

Oakbrook Mall was beautiful in the spring. Peculiar to the Chicago area, it was an outdoor mall with fountains and gardens. Tulips, daffodils, and hydrangeas were blooming, and the air was sweet with their scent.

Kate felt strange being out in the afternoon sun without her littlest companion. Joey went home with a friend from school so Kate could shop with Molly and Sharon. When she spotted Molly entering the mall, Kate did not flinch. Instead, she smiled and waved, and then smiled wider when Molly's quick step turned into a prance.

"Sharon just texted me," Molly said juggling her phone and purse with the same hand. "She is going to meet us at the restaurant."

Without Sharon, Kate was afraid things would be tense, but she was wrong. It was comfortable as they walked together.

The Greek restaurant they were meeting at had a terrace, so they found a table near the parking lot. Molly ordered white wine, but Kate drank iced tea. She had promised Danny no alcohol.

"Sharon," Molly called as she lifted herself out of her seat to wave. "Over here."

Sharon was wearing sunglasses and a light blue business suit. She was moving quickly through the parked cars and waved when she spotted them.

Sighing heavily, Sharon threw herself into the chair between Kate and Molly. "Ladies, I've been looking forward to this all week. Let's order right away." Sharon signaled the server impatiently. "I don't want to waste too much time eating. Kate needs major help."

After the server took their food orders, they all settled back into their seats and lifted their noses to the sun. Kate's restless mind wandered to the garden project. She knew Sharon had completed her assigned task, but she wondered about Molly and her friends from St. Ann's. They were supposed to canvas the neighborhood adjacent to the garden site.

"Any negative pushback on the garden?" Kate asked after the server delivered Sharon's drink.

"Yes," Molly groaned. "Her name is Ainsley Dixon. She has property bordering the empty lot and playground. Apparently, she made a lot of noise when the library was under construction. She is opposing the garden."

"Ainsley Dixon?" Kate asked. "I've never heard that name."

"She's new to Wheaton. Has two kids. Two-year-old boy and four-year-old girl," Molly suddenly became very serious. "Her husband might give us trouble. He's a big time attorney. When I spoke to her yesterday, she threatened to involve him if we didn't back off."

Kate laughed. "What's he gonna do? Sue us?"

Molly shook her head and grimaced. "Ainsley seemed to think his presence at the meeting would be enough to stop the garden."

"Molly," Sharon said, placing a hand on her arm. "Don't worry. You've never seen Kate in action. In Madison, she was captain of the Forensic Society. Queen of debate. She'll chew him up and spit him out."

Molly glanced at Kate. She was unconvinced, so Kate smiled confidently. "Ainsley?" Kate asked redirecting the conversation. "What kind of name is that?"

"Southern," Molly answered. "She's from Kentucky. Talks like Scarlett O'Hara."

"John and the kids have accents."

"Well, I suppose they would," Kate said, surprised at the notion. "Growing up in Georgia would lend itself to a southern drawl."

Sharon smiled eagerly and pulled out her computer-like phone. Scrolling though the index, she shared the latest photos of the girls.

"Is that John?" Molly asked lifting her eyebrows at the screen.

"Yes," Sharon sighed and gazed longingly at the photo. "I miss the big lug."

"He's cute." John's eyes were gentle like Sharon's but brown instead of blue.

"I've always been a sucker for a guy in a baseball cap," Kate added.

"He makes pretty babies anyways," Sharon said as she leaned away from the table to allow the server in with their lunch plates.

"Does John worry?" Kate asked keeping her eyes on her food. "You know, about you being out in the corporate world. Does he ever worry about you getting hit on by other men?"

"If he does, he's never said so." Sharon peered at Kate.

Kate read her friend easily. Sharon was curious about the intent behind the question.

"I was just wondering," Kate shrugged. "I saw Danny talking to a woman at the train station yesterday. She was coming on to him. And she was younger than me. A lot younger."

Molly's fork dropped on the table, but Sharon kept eating.

"What did you do?" Molly asked.

"Nothing. It's not new. I've seen it before. Moms from the hockey association love Danny." Kate rolled her eyes.

Molly's mouth remained hanging open.

Sharon dismissed Molly's concern with a wave of her hand. "Danny would never cheat on Kate. He's loyal like a dog. Definitely not the type."

Kate nodded her head in agreement and snorted. "Plus, he's a really bad liar. The stress of an extra-marital affair would have him sweating bullets. If he was fooling around, I would know it."

Molly sat stunned at Kate's cavalier reference to extra-marital affairs, but Kate refused to feel sorry for her comment. If they were going to be friends, Molly would have to be less of a prude.

"I could never tolerate another woman hitting on Tom," Molly said curtly. "And cheating is unforgivable. I'd throw him out."

Sharon exhaled loudly. "Molly, unless you're forced to be in the situation, it's impossible to say how you would react."

Molly bristled. Sharon's comment left the door wide open to questions she might not want to answer, so Kate interceded quickly.

"I need more iced tea," Kate called out to the server before turning to Molly. "Do you have Ainsley Dixon's number?"

"I don't," Molly answered. "But I can get it."

"Well…I was just thinking we should arrange a get-together. Something informal like coffee before the Village Board meeting on Tuesday. Maybe Monday afternoon? It would be helpful to understand her concerns before I stand up and make the proposal."

Molly's thoughts went immediately to her mission (as Kate knew they would), and she pulled out her phone.

"Monday. That's awfully soon. I better take care of it right away. I'll be right back," Molly said as she walked towards the restaurant entrance with her phone pressed to her ear.

Kate took the napkin off her lap and set it on the table. Staring at Sharon, she waited. Sharon pulled her sunglasses off and gave her friend a tight-lipped smile.

"I'm pretty sure John had an affair. It was a long time ago. Before Hannah was born." Sharon shrugged, picked up her fork, and took a big bite of her salad.

"Sharon, you can't drop something like that and not expect me to ask for details."

"He was talking about this woman a lot. You know, like too much," she said. "She was the mother of one of Sophie's girlfriends. I don't know if it was simply an emotional affair or sexual. But I know it ended. That's all that matters."

"How do you know it ended?"

"Right when the warning bells started going off—as soon as I got suspicious—the play dates ended, and he stopped talking about her. Then he was depressed for awhile." Sharon face fell just the tiniest bit, but then she shook her head. "I kept going on like nothing was wrong, and eventually he got over it."

"He got over it," Kate repeated. "But what about you?"

"I got over it too. He never stopped loving me, Katie. That I know for sure." Sharon shoved her food away and set both elbows firmly on the table. Her posture was defiant, but her tone was defensive.

"It was tough for him. I know it's no excuse, but still, you have no idea what it was like. I was traveling a lot, and he stayed home with the girls. Ballet, soccer, piano lessons. It was emasculating. It made him vulnerable. So," she added finally. "I forgave him."

"But you don't know for sure he was cheating."

"I don't want to know for sure," she answered quickly.

Sharon examined Kate's face, so she nodded her head in understanding.

Dropping her eyes, Sharon fingered the tablecloth. "Do you think less of me?"

"The opposite," Kate said assuredly. "It makes me love you even more."

Sharon scoffed. "I'm weak, Katie. I can't live without John."

Shaking her head in earnest, Kate laid her hand on Sharon's. "No. It's not weakness, Sharon. Focusing on the present and on the future instead of the past took a tremendous amount of strength. I'm proud of you."

Sharon gripped Kate's hand and squeezed. There was nothing superficial about their friendship. It wasn't merely margaritas, memory lane, and shopping trips. Their friendship survived distance and time and picked up right where it left off. Kate's heart brimmed over with emotion, and it took a moment for her to recognize it.

It was gratitude.

CHAPTER 24

CROSSING LINES

Kate was dehydrated and her head was buzzing. Shopping wore her out—too much sensory stimulation.

On the way home, she stopped at the local pizzeria and let Joey pick out the toppings. The pizza was warm in the oven, and the salad was made and waiting on the counter. Kate left her shopping bags on her bed, and left her little boy in front of the television. She needed a breather, so she went on the front porch with a large glass of ice water.

Setting herself in a rocking chair, she watched the corner for Peter and Billy. In the late afternoon sun, she imagined the carefully applied makeup on her face sweating off. Molly insisted they start their shopping exercise at the makeup counter. Kate spent forty-five minutes in a chrome high chair while two skinny sales ladies preached eye color, skin tone, and crow's feet. It was a learning experience.

All and all, it was a successful shopping trip. Kate even managed to run into Crate n' Barrel and purchase a set of beer mugs for Rosemary and Walt. The *Happy Day Farm* sign was complete, so all Kate needed to do was finish preparing ten pounds of wedding

115

potato salad. She could afford a couple minutes rocking on her front porch before packing for the trip to Wisconsin.

Kate set her water down when Billy rounded the corner alone. Peter was three steps behind with a group of fellow middle schoolers. Coasting up the block behind the boys was a conspicuous white SUV. It was shiny, foreign, and expensive.

Kate hopped out of her rocker and descended the steps of the porch. Shielding her eyes, she peered down the street. Billy looked briefly at the driver as the SUV slowly passed but didn't make any move to signal hello. Kate got a clear look. It was the jogger.

He kept his eyes on the road and stepped on the gas when his vehicle crossed over the property line. He looked different in a suit coat and tie and wore wire rimmed glasses, but there was no mistake. It was him. The jogger was making a move outside the park.

Swallowing down her anger, Kate greeted her sons. Focus and discipline kept her on task. She completed her afternoon chores and drove to the train station at five o'clock. Danny left a message on the machine while she was out shopping. He wanted a ride.

Once again, Kate was stuck in the van watching her husband wave good-bye to the blonde woman with a spray-on tan and acrylic fingernails. The anger she swallowed earlier welled at the back of her throat, and Kate tasted bile. She was prepared to confront Danny. But when he climbed in the van, the cheery disposition he had on display for Miss Hyphenated disappeared.

Snapping off the radio, he turned on Kate. "Do you have any idea how much money you spent today?"

Kate was rendered speechless. She was not used to being lectured about her spending practices and was so ashamed she couldn't look at Danny. Putting the car in drive, she tried to focus as she pulled out into traffic.

"I got an e-mail alert from the bank today, Kate. There was unusual activity on our account. Unusual," he scoffed. "I checked the total cost of your spending spree on line. I can't believe you were so irresponsible. What were you thinking?"

"I can take it back," Kate said, hating the defensive tone her voice. "It's still in shopping bags."

"Kate, I just put a deposit down on the beach house." Danny was waving his arms around, reminding Kate of the way he yelled at the boys on his hockey team after a poor performance. "I had insufficient funds in our account."

"You didn't tell me," Kate complained. "How was I supposed to know?"

"Sharon makes a hell of a lot more money than I do. We can't afford to live according to her tastes."

Kate didn't like Danny singling out Sharon for the blame. "It wasn't her fault. I got carried away. I'm not used to shopping with friends. I let them influence my judgment. It was fun."

"Next time you want to have fun with Sharon, go bowling," he huffed.

"Don't talk to me in that tone, Danny," Kate snapped. "I never buy clothes, and you know that. Molly and Sharon were trying to be helpful. They wanted me to look good."

"Hmmph," Danny mumbled. "I'll be sure to tell Peter and Bill that when they ask why we can't afford new skates next season. Their mother wanted to look good."

Swerving to the side of the road, Kate slammed the van into park. "Enough," she seethed. Looking straight ahead, she fired back. "Were you thinking about your family while you were flirting with Miss Hyphenated. I thought you were going to handle her, Danny. But I suppose you are too busy amusing yourself with idle comparisons to your wife. Is that what you are doing? Or are you enamored? Enjoying the attention of a younger woman?"

Danny was struck silent by Kate's accusations, but amusement replaced shock, and he laughed.

"Get out of the van," Kate demanded, pointing at the passenger door.

"No," Danny smirked. "You're crazy. I'm not getting out."

"Fine," Kate jerked the keys out of the ignition and climbed out the door.

"Where are you going?" Danny was out of the van peering over the roof.

Turning, Kate took aim and threw the keys at his head. But he was quick and ducked. They landed somewhere on the lawn behind him.

"The pizza is in the oven, and Peter has a paper due on Monday. Have a nice night," she said, never looking back.

"Katie, come on. Don't be ridiculous."

She heard cars slowing down to watch the scene and didn't care. He tried to call her back again, but she responded by flicking him off, so he stopped.

Kate kept her feet pointed towards the Little League Park. She didn't think. She just kept walking. Kate let her instincts take over. The park—she'd find herself in the park.

CHAPTER 25

CHEST PAINS

Danny occupied his twitchy hands by cleaning the kitchen. It was late. All the boys were tucked in for the night. He expected her home in time to put Joey to bed, but she didn't show. Then he waited expectantly for Peter and Billy's bedtime, but still no Kate. It wasn't like her, disappearing on the kids. *The kids were Kate's top priority.*

Again his eyes flashed to the phone. Sharon. He could call Sharon. But what would he say?

Stalling, he wiped the counter and moved to the kitchen table. The boys had left the milk jug out. It was warm. Frustrated, he turned abruptly for the refrigerator and yanked the door open. The interior light flashed, and Danny stood dumbstruck. He never noticed before. It sparkled. The shelves were neat and stacked with colorful healthy-looking food. Danny shoved the milk onto a shelf and slammed the door shut. But not before spying two large containers of fresh potato salad. Kate spent most of her day out of the house but still managed to make food for her brother's wedding.

Danny's hands came down hard on the counter top. He was an asshole. An asshole who tore into his hard-working wife for spending money. Worse, he was an asshole who flirted with women on the train.

When he heard the back door open, Danny fought the impulse to run to her side. He remained in the kitchen with both palms flat against the counter. Kate jerked herself upright when she saw him.

"Are the kids in bed?" she asked lightly.

She wasn't mad anymore. "Yes, but Billy and Peter are probably still awake."

"I should go check on them," she said.

Kate didn't move. She stood in the hallway and pulled the hair away from her face. Was she wearing make up?

"Are you hungry?" he asked. "I saved you a plate."

Something he said or did made her smile and relief cleared his anxious thoughts. Kate shook her head no and made her way to the stairs. The kids—*the kids were Kate's top priority*. Danny followed. He couldn't help himself. Kate tiptoed into Joey's room and sat on the edge of his bed. He stirred immediately.

"Momma?"

Kate ran her hands through his hair and shushed him.

"Where were you?" he asked, grabbing her wrist and holding her hand to his face.

"I'm sorry, little man. I went to the park."

"The dog," he said, his voice more alert now. "Did you find her?"

"No," Kate sighed. "But the park was very crowded. Night baseball. Marigold was probably hiding."

"Marigold?" he asked.

"I named her."

"Like the flower," Joey nodded.

Danny smiled into the darkened bedroom. Kate's five-year-old son was schooled on the names of flowers.

"It was Grandma's favorite." Kate kissed Joey's forehead and lifted herself off the bed. "Go to sleep. We've got an exciting day tomorrow. Uncle Walt is getting married."

"Good night," he mumbled before sticking his thumb back in his mouth.

"Good night, little man."

Kate didn't need to check on the big boys. They were waiting in the hallway. She made her excuses and gave each boy a big hug and a kiss. Like Danny, their postures changed as soon as she spoke. Kate righted their universe, made everything okay.

Danny shuffled behind as she made her way to their bedroom. The shopping bags were waiting, ominous, the source of all the trouble. Kate plopped down on the bed. Pulling one leg underneath her, she fingered the largest bag.

"I'll take it all back on Monday. I don't know what came over me."

"I'm sorry," he said, sitting next to her. "I overreacted. Next time you go shopping with the girls use credit instead of debit."

Kate twitched her nose before placing her hand lightly in his. "I don't think I'll go shopping with them again. It's too dangerous."

Danny tightened his hand around hers. "But you said it was fun."

Kate shook her head. She was sad. Danny had made his wife sad.

"I like that you've been spending time with Sharon and Molly. It's good for you." Danny was proud at how convincing he sounded, but Kate shook her head again.

"I don't know about that," she mumbled as she pressed her face into his arm.

It felt good having her there. Next to him on the bed, hanging onto his arm, using his body for comfort. Danny buried his nose in her hair.

"About the woman on the train, Katie, she sits next to me, not the other way around."

Kate pushed herself away and looked warily into his eyes. "She wants to fuck you, Danny."

A guilty smile crept across his face. "She has a husband."

"That means nothing."

Danny nodded his head sheepishly. "What do you want me to do?"

"Tell her you are happily married, and if that doesn't work, tell her your wife will kick her ass if she doesn't leave you alone."

"Okay," he said with a chuckle. "By the way, it's nice."

"What?"

"You being jealous. It's never happened before. I like it."

Kate rolled her eyes and got off the bed. She reached for the bags and piled them in a corner near the door.

"Aren't you gonna show me what you bought?"

"I'm taking everything back. What's the point?" Kate shrugged and turned for the bathroom, but Danny caught her hand.

"Show me," he smiled.

"It's late. I just want to go to sleep."

There was something stubbornly childish about the set of her chin, and it made Danny playful. Hopping up, he made a grab for the bags and began pulling items out.

"Danny, don't," Kate complained yanking the bags away. "I feel foolish."

"Foolish?" The word stopped Danny cold. Kate was never foolish.

"Yes, foolish. Who am I kidding? I am not and never will be a lady who lunches."

"What are you talking about?" Danny wasn't going to give any credence to her objections. He wanted to see what she was hiding. "You eat lunch all the time."

"That's not what I mean, and you know it."

She fought him, but he managed to get his hands on something soft. When he pulled it out of the bag, he saw it was a dress with tiny red flowers and girly ruffles.

"This is pretty," he said fanning it out against his own large frame.

"Knock it off." She wasn't giving in yet, but she was laughing.

"Give me a fashion show," he said shoving the dress into her arms. "It's the least you can do after nearly giving me a heart attack at work. Insufficient funds. I actually got chest pains."

Kate slouched and stomped into the bathroom with her goodies. It was an act. She was smiling. Her eyes were lit up again. Danny waited in the overstuffed chair in the corner. He wished for a beer but wouldn't leave her while she was happy.

"Holy shit." Danny's eyes actually popped out of his head when she waltzed out of the bathroom.

She was still wearing the same pale green polo, but the jeans were new and super sexy. Kate knew it too. She had a glint in her eye and her hands were stuffed in the front pockets. She was posing. Twirling around, she gave him a view of her ass.

"Do you like them?" she asked as she looked over shoulder at him.

"Um, yeah, I do," he said running a hand over his beard. "They make your legs look super long. And your ass, babe, I betcha I could bounce a quarter off it."

"Sharon said it was a crime for a woman with an ass like this not to own a pair of jeans like these."

"I have to agree with Woody on that one. You're keepin' the jeans."

"They cost two hundred dollars, Danny."

"I don't care, Trouble," he said, his thoughts still a bit blurry. "You're keepin' them, and I am gonna enjoy peeling them off every time you wear them."

It was fun watching her dive into the bags. She pulled out dainty looking panties and frilly bras and laughed as she told the story of how Molly and Sharon helped her pick them out.

The dress was last, and Danny could see how much she liked it by the way she handled it with delicate fingers. His heart was overwhelmed. He could afford her this. It was such a little thing. Kate wanted to look pretty. And she did. The dress wasn't tight like the jeans, but it flowed off her skin and gave her a breezy look. It landed just above the knees, showing off her strong legs. Kate stood in front of the mirror and adjusted the neckline.

"It's versatile," she said. "Watch this."

She shrugged, pulled at the dress, and it fell along her shoulders. Suddenly, the skin of her neck and the gentle line of her collarbone led to the curve of her breasts. She took his breath away.

"Wait," she said running for the bags. "You've got to see the dress with the boots."

Boots too. Christ. She was gonna kill him. Walking across the room, she stood in front of Danny with hands on her hips and held out her right foot.

"Yes?" she asked. "They make the outfit, don't they? Sharon and Molly tried to get me to buy high heeled shoes, but I couldn't do it. Not my style."

Style. His wife had style now. And it wasn't suburban chic or sporty hockey mom—it was smokin' frickin' hot. The chest pains returned. Getting out of his chair, he reached for her. Danny pulled her close, tried to absorb her into his body.

"Don't mess it up," she complained. "I still have to take the dress back."

"Oh, it's not going anywhere, baby," he said.

Lifting her face to his, he kissed her long and hard. The heat built and desire overrode his fears, his worries. The dress. He wanted his hands in it, under it. Kate melded to his strong frame. Standing on her tiptoes in red boots, she kissed him back.

"I want to fuck you in this dress," he moaned into her open mouth.

Kate pulled away and turned for the bedroom door. Clicking the lock, she leaned her weight against the door frame.

"And the boots?" she murmured, her voice full of sexy longing.

Danny lunged. The boots never left her feet.

CHAPTER 26

THE BEGINNING

Early Saturday mornings were desolate. Today especially. The emptiness surrounded him. His pounding feet echoed. Driving the barrenness into his consciousness. Into his heart. Kathryn. She would not show. He knew it. His empty heart thudded inside his chest. Bereft.

Kathryn was punishing him. Punishing herself. But he only did what was necessary. Did what she would not do herself. Spring had sprung. Darkness no longer a disguise. It was the summer sun that broke the morning. It was not his fault. Revealing himself was an act of courage. There was no turning back. Looking back was a waste of time. His feet left the jogging trail, and he flew. Kathryn the vixen would not escape so easily.

Her neighborhood was quiet. Still sleeping. He could breathe again. Filling his lungs with the crisp morning air, he shook the tension out of his arms and shoulders. His fingers warming. The blood reaching the tips. She was close. The morning no longer bleak. Prospects no longer stark.

Immediately, his eyes went to her charming yellow house. Drew across the porch. The windows. Surprisingly, her garage was open. The family van parked near the back door. Open from the rear.

Luggage, grocery bags, and food containers were piled in the driveway. They were going somewhere. She was going somewhere.

His jogging stride stuttered. Kathryn was in the backyard. Yanking at a garden hose, she was directing the spray of a water sprinkler. Gardening. The momentum of his feet kept him moving past. But then his pace slowed. Slowed until he stopped altogether. In four giant backward steps, he was at the end of her driveway. His heart racing. Breathing in through the nose. Exhaling through the mouth. He waited.

Kathryn wore faded cutoff shorts that rode low over her hips. Sexy and youthful. Almost collegiate. Her hair was loose and shimmered in the early light. It hung across her face like a curtain as she fussed with the sprinkler. The button-down shirt was flannel, oversized, and mannish. Belonging to the idiot husband most likely. It was as long as her shorts. And open. He could not see what she wore underneath. But he could wait. Patience.

She stood facing the garden. Her back to him. Examining her work. Finally, she turned. Eyes on her hands, she brushed them clean. Her face was soft. Her posture relaxed when she lifted her eyes and caught him standing at the end of her driveway. Heaven. Their gaze met and locked. He half-expected her to return to the house. That would have been the safe thing. But of course, Kathryn chose the dangerous.

Tossing her head, the hair flew away from her face, and she jogged. Kathryn jogged barefoot to the end of the driveway. She answered his dreams and wore a tight fitting tank top beneath Daniel's shirt. It rode slightly up her belly, and he could see skin. Rapturous, glorious skin.

It was disarming seeing her adorned with jewelry. A long gold chain hung around her neck. A thick decorative crucifix dangled next to her cleavage. How curious. His breathing slowed but his skin was slick with sweat. He wished he was showered. Clean. Fresh for once. Next time. Perhaps next time, he would be properly groomed.

"Good morning." There was no hint of anger in her greeting. Her eyes bright. Fresh faced, there was a light wash of color on her cheeks. Her lips sheen with color. Lipstick? Her skin looked moist, and he longed to touch it. Her scent was citrus. Tangy. Invigorating to the senses. He inhaled deeply. Taking her all in. Nirvana.

"Going on a trip?" His tone casual. Not expecting an answer.

"Yes," she said. "Home to Wisconsin."

Surprise. The wily fox actually answered. Repressing a grin, his body turned with hers, and she led him away from the house. Down the sidewalk. Out of view. They walked together.

"For how long?" he asked.

"Just one night. My brother is getting married."

"You have a brother," he nodded as he filed away the new information.

"Two actually. My older brother works on the pipeline in Alaska. He's flown in for the occasion."

"A reunion," he interjected.

"Yes. At the family farm," she sighed.

So forthcoming. How intriguing. A farmer's daughter. Wisconsin.

"I was at the park last night," she added suddenly.

She stopped at the corner. With her back to the street. She kept one eye on him and one eye on her house.

"If I had known, I would have met you," he said, deliberately apologetic.

She shook her head. "It was probably for the best. I was angry."

"Because I found you?"

"Yes. Because you found me," she stuffed her hands into her front pockets.

Her posture was still open. The opposite of what he expected.

"But you're not angry now," he smiled.

"No. I'm resigned. This," she said gesturing first to herself and then to him. "This thing between us. It's over."

"It doesn't have to be over, Kathryn."

Her name rolled off his tongue. Delicious. His body thrilled at the sound of it. Did she feel it too? The way he made her name drip with honey. It had to move her. But she remained serious. Poker-faced.

"It's over."

"Or just beginning," he countered.

127

She sighed and looked away. Her house. Kathryn's family still inside.

"I am not looking for romance," she said sternly. "I have it already with Danny. He's my lover."

She meant to hurt him, and she did. Jerking away, he clenched his jaw in restraint. Danny. How trite. The cog. Danny-boy. A sophomoric name for a mountainous man. His counter arguments were lost in the pain. In the agony. He struggled to recover. Grasping, his eyes drew away from her face and down her neck. Her cleavage. The necklace.

"I've never seen you wear jewelry," he said. "It's an unusual piece. An antique?"

"It was my mother's," she said, lifting it with careless fingers. Glancing at it, she let it drop quickly. "I thought I should wear it today. It will make my dad happy. She died when I was twenty."

"Oh," he said, stunned. "My mother died when I was twenty-two."

Kathryn pursed her lips. Any emotion she felt at his admission was carefully hidden. She was toying with him. Handing out information about herself like candy but showing no apparent interest in his personal offerings. But he couldn't help but be intrigued. Her mother wore a crucifix. A pious woman. That would explain the rebellious daughter.

"Was your mother very religious?" he asked.

Kathryn shook her head. Her chin set as if she was offended by the notion. "She described herself as a cafeteria Catholic. My mom had her own ideas."

"She was clever then," he said, smiling affectionately. "Like you."

Kathryn was wistful. But it lasted only for a second.

"You are especially beautiful today," he said, hoping to distract her from good-bye with his heartfelt words. "So luscious. Your skin is radiant. You look too young to be the mother of three. It's quite unfair outshining the bride."

Kathryn blinked a few times, but then her eyes narrowed with determination. "You need to go. It's over. I've closed the door."

Closed the door. How bleak. He could see she meant it. He could hear it in her voice. But it did not matter. He would force her out of the shallows. Kathryn belonged in deep water. She needed the dark depths. The dangerous lurking of the unknown.

"Aren't you curious?" he asked. When she raised her eyebrows, he smiled. "Don't you want to know my name?"

"I'd rather not," she pleaded. "My memories of the park…" she paused and her eyes flew to her house.

One of her sons appeared. He was searching blindly up the road. When he caught sight of Kathryn, he waved hesitantly. Kathryn waved back but dismissively.

"I have to go."

"First finish," he prodded. "Your memories?"

"Please understand. You've ruined everything. Don't tell me your name. It will make it worse."

Worse? Oh, how he longed for an opportunity to decipher the workings of her mind.

Kathryn stiffened and stepped away. Her son was moving closer. Coming down the sidewalk. He got a good look at the boy. His sandy brown hair was tousled and too long. His air devilish. A rebellious spirit. Even from a distance he could see the spark in the eyes. Like Kathryn. The boy was intelligent.

"Billy," she called. "Go back to the house. I'll be there in a minute."

Billy. An old-fashioned name. A namesake? The boy stopped but did not return to the house. He waited on the sidewalk. Suspicious. And rightly so.

"He looks like you," he said. "How old is he?"

"He's nearly eleven. My middle boy."

"You have three sons," he said. A statement of fact.

"Yes. Boys run in the family. My brother Roger has two sons as well. I'm hoping Walter will produce a baby girl. It would be a nice change."

Roger. Walter. Billy. So much information. Was she doing this on purpose? Was she trying to bore him with the details of her life? Didn't she know how he longed for this? How he hungered for information? Pursing his lips, he tried to hide his brimming amusement. Kathryn the fox. Trickery made her that much more seductive.

"I have a little girl," he added.

Why not? For every tidbit she offered, he would offer something in return.

"People say she resembles me but only in appearance. She's very theatrical. Loves to sing. Wants to be on *American Idol.* I can't carry a tune in a bucket."

Kathryn's attention shifted away from her son and returned to him. She was studying his face. Reading it. He stubbornly held onto the poker-face. A perfect mirror of her own expression.

Suddenly, with cobra like speed, she grabbed his arm. Poker-face abandoned, he stared into her eyes. The blackness of her pupils hypnotic. It actually hurt. Her touch too painful to bear, because he could not have her. He could not relieve the ache.

"Good-bye," she said.

The words throbbed with sincerity. Throbbed with emotion. And then she was gone. Her fiery touch leaving a mark. He did not watch her go. He willed his hollow legs to move. Move forward. Awed at his own strength, he jogged away.

Kathryn wanted to remain trapped in the present. But he could not allow it. A future with him was the only alternative. The husband provided a comfortable life. But comfort was not what Kathryn wanted. Not what she needed.

It was the truth. And living a lie, a curse. It was only a matter of time. Logic and truth were on his side. Patience.

It was just the beginning.

CHAPTER 27

HOME

Kate distracted herself on the drive to Germantown by silently reciting the names of the exits off I-94. The boys were quiet too. The drive was overly familiar. Seasoned travelers, the boys kept themselves amused by plugging into various portable electronic devices. Kate rested her head against her seat and closed her eyes. When Danny suddenly switched off the radio, she sat up and glanced in his direction.

"Do you ever think about going back to work?" he asked in a tone that was too casual.

Kate mouth twitched at the corners, and she smiled reluctantly. "I do sometimes. Why do you ask?"

"I was just thinking about that teaching job you had in Wisconsin. I wonder what it would take to get re-certified to teach in Illinios."

Kate scrunched her face up in distaste. "That job was temporary, and I hated it, Danny. You know that."

"But you were good at it," he reminded her. "The principal offered you a permanent position. If we hadn't gotten married, you might have stuck it out. Learned to like it."

131

"Doubtful," Kate said looking out the window at the rolling farm fields.

"You could teach history and government at St. Francis. The boys could attend high school tuition free. They have a top notch hockey program. And the coach has connections with major universities."

Kate stopped herself from rolling her eyes. Danny wanted the boys to play college hockey and even fantasized about them going pro.

"Your name alone is enough to get them noticed. You've taken more teams to state championships than any other coach in league history." Kate kept her eyes on the horizon and kept her tone muted.

Danny threw a backward glance at the boys. Satisfied they were occupied elsewhere, he leaned into whisper to Kate.

"Billy has a real shot," he said. When Kate failed to agree, he got defensive. "I'm serious. He's already faster than me, and he's smart. Smarter than any kid I've ever coached."

"Fine," Kate said, shrugging her shoulders. "But I can't see how me teaching at St. Francis is going to help him with his game. Besides, Wheaton has a great public high school."

Danny frowned at the road. When he looked in Kate's direction, she smiled and the frown immediately disappeared. His eyes went to her crossed legs. Reaching to her side of the vehicle, he wrapped a palm around her thigh.

"I can see your muscles," he said running his fingers possessively down her leg. "I'm gonna have to start kickin' up my workout. I won't be able to keep up with you pretty soon."

Kate uncrossed her legs and slouched into the seat. Spreading her legs, she gave him easy access underneath the wide legs of her cut offs.

"If you couldn't keep up," she teased. "I would just slow down, Coach. Keep pace with you."

"Mmm," he said smiling slyly. "I like the sound of that."

Danny kept his hand on her leg stroking her skin absentmindedly with his thumb.

"What would you want to do then?" he pressed. "It should be something you're interested in. Nutrition maybe. You could go back to school."

"Where is this coming from?" she asked suspiciously.

"Nowhere," he said removing his hand. "I just worry sometimes. Joey goes to school full time next year, and I know you, Trouble. You're gonna lose your mind sittin' at home."

"I'm not going back to school. Please," she said disgustedly. "Sitting in a classroom will make me crazier than sitting at home."

"As a licensed nutritionist, you could get a job at a clinic. Maybe work in a hospital."

Kate tried to seriously consider what he was proposing, but she couldn't. It was too funny.

"What?" he asked when she laughed.

"I don't have the temperament, Danny," she said. "I can't counsel people on nutrition. I don't have the patience."

Danny shook his head in disagreement. "That's not true. You are very patient and a fine role model, the picture of health and fitness."

"Sure, I might help a few people, but more often than not, my advice would be ignored," Kate sat up in her seat and kept her voice stern. "My mom died because she refused to take responsibility for her own health. I will always love her, but I will never forgive her for letting herself die."

Danny took Kate's hand. "Your mother was from a different era, Katie. She didn't know any better."

"My mom knew she was sick," Kate corrected. "And she did nothing. I can't be around people who won't help themselves."

"Okay," Danny said his tone soothing. "It was just a thought."

"If I go back to work, I would want a job that paid enough to be worthwhile. I'm not leaving home without some serious monetary compensation."

"It's not about the money," Danny pursed his lips in disapproval. "If you got a job, I would want it to make you happy."

"Like your job makes you happy," Kate teased.

"That's different."

"Not really." Kate stretched across the seat and kissed Danny on the cheek. "But I love you for saying so."

Danny sighed and switched on the music.

The Germantown in Kate's childhood memories was a small farming community with lots of wide open spaces. Today, it was a thriving Milwaukee suburb. Since exiting the expressway, Kate counted three superstores.

The two-lane highway that ran in front of the Selbach's farmhouse was now four lanes. Over the years, the highway encroached on the front yard, bringing the farm house closer to traffic. Kate's father sold off most of the farmland to finance her education. Only four acres remained, but it provided a nice buffer between the house and Germantown's sprawling neighborhood development.

Directly north of the farmhouse was a gigantic parking lot attached to a modern evangelical church. The first ten minutes of Kate's Sunday phone call with her dad were usually spent with her listening to him rant about the traffic lined up in front of the house.

"Welcome to the Happy Day Farm," Danny called out as the van pulled into the gravel driveway.

"Wow," Kate said. "Everything looks so nice."

The white clapboard house was adorned with snappy new red shutters, and the bay windows at the front sparkled in the late morning sun. Typical to rural Wisconsin, the front door was not at the front, but rather at the side facing the driveway. The porch and its thin white railings had a new coat of paint, and to Kate's amazement, her mother's deserted planters held purple and yellow pansies.

Billy and Joey wasted no time climbing out of the van. Off like shots from a gun, they disappeared around the barn before Danny pulled the key out of the ignition. Peter fiddled with his earphones, and Kate and Danny shared a look. Their oldest son was too mature for tire swings and haylofts. Lifting her eyes to the barn, Kate's smile widened at the sound of her brother's cackling laughter. Walter must have joined the boys at the tire swing. The creak of the screen door alerted Kate to her father's approach, and she leapt up the porch stairs, throwing herself into his outstretched arms.

"Dad, you look so handsome," she said, not bothering to let go of him as they descended the steps to the driveway.

He was freshly shaved and was looking very clean in a button-down shirt and ironed khakis.

"That brother of yours," he shook his head in disgust. "He's not finished with that damn wedding gazebo. I wore my good clothes thinkin' it was done. I can't pound a nail lookin' like this. All my work clothes are at the condo."

"Hello, Mr. Selbach," Danny said holding out his hand. "How are you, sir?"

Kate smiled and pressed her face into her father's sleeve. Danny never took to calling her dad Bill. But then again, Dad never invited him to do so.

"Do me a favor and go out back," Dad said after shaking Danny hand. "Check on that dumb ass's progress. Lend a hand if you have to, Dan. We only got a couple hours before folks start showin' up."

"Katie's got a bunch of stuff in the back," Danny said opening the van's hatch. "Let me unload first."

Dad caught Peter around the shoulders. "Me and this guy will do it," he said. "You go on back."

"My God, Pete," Dad said looking at Peter. "Am I shrinkin' or have you grown a foot since the last time I saw you?"

"I think it might be a bit a both, Papa," Peter teased.

"Hell, I know it," Dad sighed. "I'm shrinkin' at such a rate. Gonna hafta bury me in a shoebox."

Peter grabbed the heavy stuff out of the back before Dad had a chance. The questions began, and Peter answered them all as he followed his grandfather into the house.

Kate gave Danny's hand a tug as he brushed past. He stopped and smiled. The fine lines around his gray eyes crinkled, and he gave her hand a quick squeeze. Kate kissed him on the cheek and sent him off to help Walter.

As he walked away, Danny looked over his shoulder and winked.

CHAPTER 28

THE UNFORGIVABLE

"Ever think about moving back here?" Kate asked Roger. "Ruth told me she loves Wisconsin."

They were carrying trash to the end of the driveway. The wedding festivities died down after Walter and Rosemary left for their honeymoon night. Only family was left, and they were in the barn roughhousing and dancing to music. Roger was staying close to Kate, catching up on lost time.

"Shit, Katie, my boys would go into culture shock if we moved to the lower forty-eight."

"Your boys are almost grown," Kate reminded him. "They'll be off to college soon. Don't you ever think about retirement?"

"I've got a nice pension coming. And so does Ruth. But other than that, I don't think about it."

"Danny and I talk about Florida. I'd like to go south. I can't stand winter anymore."

"No ice hockey in Florida," Roger teased.

"Danny says the same thing," Kate laughed. "I told him he can take up beach volleyball."

"Some of us guys don't take to change very well," Roger warned.

"Yeah, but look at Dad," Kate said, giving her brother a nudge as they made their way back to the house. "He seems to have adjusted well to retirement. Loves his new condo."

"That's just because of the action he's gettin,'" Roger snorted. "The old man is charmin' the pants off the women at Bishop's Woods. Literally."

Kate's mouth fell open. "No," she shouted, swatting Roger's arm.

Roger nodded. "The boys and I helped him move the heavy stuff into his condo last week. He's got those ladies falling over themselves trying to get at him. He's not at all shy about it either. Tell's them straight out he's not looking for love, just a roll in the sack."

"Dad is a player?" Kate said in disbelief.

"I'm proud of him," Roger said puffing out his chest. "Bodes well for me, if you know what I mean. Nice to know the old man's equipment still works."

"Shut up, Roger. You're grossing me out."

Roger laughed. "Then I won't tell you what Dad said about the valuable properties of petroleum jelly."

Kate shuddered but then burst out in laughter. "I suppose it's good for him. At least he's getting exercise."

Roger pulled a bottle of beer out of the cooler near the back door. He leaned up against the stoop railing, and Kate sat at his feet on the stairs. They both looked into the bright lights of the evangelical church next door and watched as people trickled out and climbed into their cars. Most were smiling and talking in loud voices to one another.

"Busy place," Roger observed before taking a swig of beer.

"What do you suppose they were doing at church on a Saturday night?" Kate asked.

"Looking for hope. Or forgiveness maybe. One of the two."

"Forgiveness," Kate sighed. "I still haven't mastered that one."

"Most people don't deserve it," Roger scoffed. "Church folks are the worst kind of sinner, because they're all high and mighty. You gotta know, Katie, more than one of those bible thumpers is screwing around. Not many people walk their talk, and some things are unforgivable."

"Have you always been so cynical?" Kate teased.

"Yep," he said, chugging his beer.

"I've done some pretty unforgivable things," she conceded.

Roger laughed and sat down next to Kate. "Yeah, you were crazy reckless for awhile there. Truth is, I was surprised you never got yourself knocked up."

"I did, Roger," Kate said glancing at his face. When it froze in shock, she shrugged her shoulders. "I thought you knew."

"When?" he asked and then his eyes were fierce. "Who?"

"Seth Boyle."

"Shit, Katie, Seth Boyle?" he said, his face suddenly sad.

"My first," she said. "I was crazy about him."

"Well, sure," he said. "You two were a sweet couple. Student council brainiacs and all that."

"He wanted to get married. I was so in love, I probably would have done it. But then I went to Ma."

"Holy crap, the old lady knew?"

"She scheduled the abortion," Katie said.

She smiled grimly when Roger gasped. "It never came to that. I miscarried. Spent the whole night in the bathroom with Ma sitting on the edge of the bathtub shaking her head at me. She kept saying, 'I thought you were smarter, Kathryn.'"

Kate sighed before adding, "She took me for birth control pills the next day."

"Makes sense now," Roger's eyes gleamed with new understanding. "I figured you went wild out of revenge. I thought Seth broke your heart."

"He did. I was shattered." Kate shrugged. "Seth didn't believe me when I told him I lost the baby. Didn't matter anyways. I was going to have an abortion, and he couldn't love me after that." Kate gave her brother a nudge. "Unforgivable, remember?"

"You were just a kid. You can be forgiven. Ma, on the other hand, I'm not so sure. I can't believe she was so cold."

"Ma had high hopes. She wanted me to accomplish the things she never did. I know she'd be disappointed in me now."

"That's not true, Katie. She wanted you to go to school and be successful, but I don't think she would have denied you a happy marriage and children."

"Maybe Ma knew me better than I knew myself," Kate said looking up at the starry sky. "Maybe she knew I wasn't built for the domestic life."

"Ahh," Roger said pushing off the stairs to stand over her. "Now you're just talkin' stupid. You're a great mother, and Danny, shit Katie, Danny is a helluva guy."

"True," Kate smiled as she stood up. "Danny is the best thing about me."

They walked silently towards the barn together, but Kate knew her brother was upset by the way he was clenching and unclenching his jaw.

"That's a bunch of bullshit. Danny ain't the best thing about you," he finally concluded defiantly into the night air. "Women like you—like you and my Ruthie—don't need men to make them better. Danny knows it and so do I. If I croaked tomorrow, I know Ruth would be just fine. You both have it. You're tough."

"I used to be strong, but I'm not so sure anymore. Danny protects me in a lot different ways," Kate admitted. "You know me, Rog. I never could back away from a fight. But I've been so careful not making waves—avoiding conflict—I don't think I can do it anymore."

"Do what?"

Kate looked into her brother's eyes. "Finish a fight," Kate confessed.

Roger's laugh roared over the music pouring from the barn. "Hell, Katie," he snorted. "Just because you haven't picked a fight in awhile don't mean you can't win one if you had too. Don't kid yourself."

Kate smiled and ran a hand through her brother's arm. It was exactly what she needed to hear.

CHAPTER 29

1972 CHEVY TRUCK

Danny was leaning up against the barn door watching the festivities wind down when he saw his wife grip the loft ladder and throw one leg over the edge. She was completely at ease and comfortable in her surroundings. But Danny's eyes went to the swinging hem of her short dress. He was across the floor and up the ladder in seconds. Shielding her with his body, they descended one rung at time.

Danny wrapped two hands possessively around her waist when his feet hit the ground. Kate fell backwards into his arms. She was laughing. Giddy with happiness after a day with her brothers.

"Joey was asleep before I could zip up his sleeping bag."

"Do you think he'll be all right out here with the big boys?" Danny asked.

"I can't make him come inside, Danny." Kate lamented. "It would break his heart. Peter will keep an eye on him."

"Walter told me he is going finish the loft with bunks and run radiator heat up there. Doesn't want us to stop visiting."

"I know," Kate said, nodding her head. "He's got all sorts of plans. I don't think he realizes how busy he'll be after the baby is born."

"He's happy, and Rosemary is crazy about him."

Rosemary stood at least three inches taller than Walter, and she was built. Her wedding dress was modest but there was no hiding her assets. Her laugh was equally robust, and she sang Walter's praises the entire afternoon.

"She's very sweet," Kate added. "I promised to come up and help her this summer with the raspberry bushes. She wants to get the U-pickum business going again."

"Your dad will be pleased," Danny said. "The Happy Day Farm will be open for business again."

"It was a beautiful day," Kate unwrapped herself from Danny's arms and took his hand.

Tugging him along, she shouted over the music at her brother. "Rog," she called. "Could you make sure the boys shut down in the next hour or so? I want to show Danny something."

Roger waved effectively dismissing them both. Kate was nearly skipping as she pulled Danny into the shadows of the Walt's carefully kept workshop. It was a bachelor's paradise. Walter's motorcycle and fishing boat fit in either corner, and he mounted a television with satellite hook-up to the wall above his tool bench.

"Where are you taking me, Trouble?" Danny asked when she pulled a set of keys off the peg board next to the door.

Kate's eyes sparked, and he hurried to see what had her so excited. The security light outside the workshop door flashed, and Danny blinked in confusion at the sight of his wife stroking the hood of an old Chevy. The truck was blue, but by the looks of the chipped paint, it was once red.

"Walt is selling it for a friend." Kate crossed her booted feet and leaned her back up against the hood. She ran both hands across the truck until her arms were spread wide. The thick gold chain around her neck glowed in the bright light, but the pendant was hidden beneath the soft fabric of her dress.

"He stowed it back here for the wedding. Asked me to put it at the end of the drive when all the folks went home." She jingled the keys dangling at the end of her fingers. "You want to go for a ride, Coach?"

"Hell yeah." Danny tried to get a hand on her, but she was already around the hood and yanking the driver's side door open.

The interior of the cab smelled like a sour mix of Armor-all and Windex. The bench seat groaned under Danny's weight, and its springs tightened in protest. Kate's enthusiasm wasn't dampened by the creaking hinges, and she giggled when the engine roared to life.

"New motor," she said lovingly as she shifted the truck into drive.

He wanted to touch her, nuzzle into her hair, kiss her neck, run a hand into that Godforsaken dress—but he didn't. Kate was in her own world as the truck revved down the highway.

"How much do they want for it?" Danny asked.

"Walter said fifteen hundred bucks. His buddy's live-in girlfriend is forcing him to sell. He was only keeping it for sentimental reasons. It needs tires, but Walt said the bed liner is new."

"Are you thinkin' about trading in your van?"

Kate sighed happily. "No, I just wanted to see what it felt like to get behind the wheel. My first boyfriend had a truck like this. Almost identical. 1972 Chevy four by four."

Kate's romantic history was blurry to Danny, because he preferred it that way. But he never heard her refer to anyone but himself as a boyfriend, and it got his back up.

"I thought I was your first boyfriend," he said, controlling his tone.

Kate laughed. "Sorry, Coach. Seth Boyle was my first love. We were a hot couple for a year or so."

"You loved him?" Danny demanded. "Are you serious?"

"Well, I thought it was love," she amended. "He popped my cherry in the bed of his truck. When he broke up with me, it hurt so much I thought I was gonna die."

"He broke up with you?"

Danny knew he sounded like an idiot, but he couldn't help himself. He was in shock.

Kate smiled wickedly out the windshield. "I got him back though. I slept with the entire percussion section. Messed with his head. Poor Seth," she sighed. "He had to quit marching band."

Danny laughed—this was the Kate he knew. She pulled into a deserted parkway and drove beneath a canopy of trees. It was dark, but he could see the lights of a parking lot ahead. When the truck's headlights flashed across the carved stone of the park entrance, he realized they were at the quarry.

Kate parked the truck in the empty lot and pulled the key out of the ignition. They sat quietly for a minute and listened as the truck's engine popped and hissed.

Danny had come to the quarry with Kate years ago. They were still dating and needed a place to escape from Mr. Selbach's stare. It was different than he remembered. A twelve foot fence now forbade access. The gate was locked tight, but there was a spot along the fence where someone bent it up from the bottom. Kids. Kids like Seth and Kate. Danny winced. "What did Seth Boyle do to you in this truck?"

Kate slid across the bench seat and took his hand. "Nothing you haven't done to me."

It was dark, but the gas lamps near the gate cast enough light to catch the glint in her hazel eyes. Kate wore her wheat-gold hair down for the wedding but twisted the front back into a simple clip. It was falling out, so Danny pushed the hair away from her face.

"You looked beautiful today."

Her eyes dropped to her lap, and she fidgeted with the skirt of her dress. "You think so?" she asked.

Danny shook his head in disbelief. The admiring glances from Walter's buddies had him on edge all day. Forcing introductions as Walter's brother-in-law, Danny was acquainted with more plumbers than he ever thought possible.

"Don't pretend you don't know," he said as he picked up her hand and kissed it softly. "I know you can see it. It's written all over my face every time I look at you."

When he lifted his eyes to meet her gaze, he was surprised by what he saw. There was worry.

"What's the matter, baby?"

"I miss Roger," she murmured. "He's going back tomorrow. I don't want to say good-bye."

"We'll go visit," Danny said, wrapping an arm around her shoulders. "This time for real. Next summer."

Kate shook her head but then mumbled her agreement at his plan. It was as if his words had no weight. But suddenly, she came back to him. Her eyes clear and bright. Looking out the window, she searched the fence line.

"I promised Joey I would take him to see the quarry. He was curious, but I don't think we'll have time tomorrow."

"You can take him to the quarry in Naperville."

"Naperville?" Kate asked, stunned.

"Illinios has quarries too, Katie," he teased. "In Naperville, they have one that's been converted for recreation. It's surrounded by woods and trails. It has a nice area for families, and dogs are welcome."

"Really?"

"We'll go this summer." Danny smiled.

"With Marigold," Kate added looking wistfully out the window.

"I'm sure she's fine, Katie."

"You don't mind?" Kate asked. "Adopting a dog?"

"I'm happy you're finally listening to me. Running alone in the park is dangerous. A dog will give me some peace of mind."

Kate's mood shifted again. This time it was in a direction he understood. She held his gaze as she lifted herself off the vinyl seat of the truck. Her hands slid under her dress and before Danny could blink she was tossing her panties onto the floor. In two swift tugs, her boots joined the panties, and she straddled his lap, pantyless and barefoot.

"Tight quarters," she murmured before kissing his lips with an open mouth.

Danny glanced around the cab of the truck. He would have preferred a little more room to maneuver, but with Kate, he was always game. He kissed her back, searching the inside of her hot mouth with his tongue. She moaned and settled herself in his lap, grinding into his erection. The dress—goddamn it—it was so sheer, so soft, he needed to suppress the urge to rip it off.

Kate must have sensed his frustration. Pulling away from him, she tugged until the dress fell off her shoulders revealing the gilded crucifix and strapless bra beneath. The bra cut into her breasts, too bountiful for their lacy constraints. Kate shrugged, shoving her cleavage under his nose, and sighed when she freed herself from the bra. The sheer fabric of the dress barely covered her nipples.

Kate wrapped her hands around his neck and lifted herself off his lap. His beard. She liked to rub her tits on his beard. He lost all sense of his surroundings. He couldn't see. Danny could only smell, taste, and hear her soft whines as she forced him to suckle, moving her nipples across his face. Back and forth. Up and down. The precious metal of the crucifix scrapping his face—his lips, teeth, and tongue running across the cool surface of the pendant.

Danny's hands moved to her naked ass, her hips tilted forward, the strong muscles taut. He pulled at her flesh, separating her ass cheeks, and she cried. The kind of sharp cry that told him it hurt. But Kate didn't pull away. Instead, her breathing increasing to a pant and she clutched him tighter, his hot breath making her tits moist, making her dress wet.

Mine, Danny's own breathing grew heavy as he tried to get air. Oxygen. She was hunched, curled around his body and face, suffocating him. *Mine*. His thoughts jealous. Jealous of the boy Kate loved. Seth Boyle broke her heart. He wished he knew her then. Wished he knew the boy. The boy who stirred the devil inside Kate awake.

Lifting her roughly off his lap, he moved to the center of the bench seat. Without looking at her face, he pulled at her arms.

"Over my lap," he said shoving her face into the driver's seat. "I want you over my lap."

With her elbows tucked underneath, she lay on her belly, his erection rubbing against her hip. Her knees were bent and the tops of her narrow feet were pressed against the passenger window. Perfectly placed.

Danny slid his right hand slowly up the back of her thigh, lifting the dress. Kate—completely vulnerable—began to tense. Her body quivered, ready for the slap, ready for the sting. But Danny exhaled loudly, releasing the tension in his own body. Licking the fingers of his left hand, he moved the dress away with his right and slid the wet fingers down the crack of her ass.

"I love your ass, baby," he whispered, nudging ever so lightly, he encouraged her to spread her legs.

Danny smiled to himself when she complied immediately. Lifting her ass, she craved the attention. Slowly he moved his fingers into her pussy. It was dripping after his first penetration. Danny kept pressure on her sweet spot with his thumb as he slid his fingers and out. All the while, the fingers of his left hand clawed at her ass, spreading her cheeks apart, his concentration on her puckered asshole. So tight, how he longed to spread her wide and rip her apart. She wouldn't push him away. She belonged to him. Kate loved being fucked...trusted him enough to let it hurt.

Increasing the pressure with his right hand, he murmured encouragement, his own excitement mounted as she lifted herself off his lap, meeting every penetration of his fingers with a moan. Danny could feel the blood rushing to her core—the heat building beneath his fingers.

"Could Seth do this to you?" he asked, his clear voice breaking through the heavy panting within the closed space of the truck.

Danny pulled his wet fingers out of her pussy and dragged them across her asshole. Rubbing the tiny rosebud, he heard her gasp as he pushed his thick finger through. Kate cried out and tried to wrench free, but he held her down with his left arm and slowly delved deeper.

"Danny," she pleaded. "It hurts."

"Did Seth do this to you?" he asked again patiently moving his finger. He forced her tight ass open.

"No," she cried. "Danny, please."

Danny released her then but wouldn't let her rest. Before she could catch her breath, he shoved the fingers of his right hand into her drenched pussy. Ruthlessly, he went to work on her. It didn't take long. He knew it wouldn't. The sting of his forced intrusion still fresh in her memory, Kate's body stiffened in climax. Moaning softly into the dark, she collapsed onto his lap and shuddered when he withdrew his hand.

When she recovered, Danny slid out from underneath her weight. Opening the passenger door, he hopped out. The interior cab light made her cringe. Kate buried her face in her arms and whined.

He ignored her complaints and grabbed at her knees. Gripping her tightly, he pulled her belly down across the seat like a rag doll. Danny set her feet on the black top but shoved her shoulders back down on the seat when she tried to stand.

"I've wanted to fuck you like this all day," he said as he situated her dress over her ass.

Gently, he stroked it. Danny petted her with one hand and unzipped his fly with the other. Keeping the dress between his fingers and her skin, he waited until he felt her body relax beneath his touch. And then—without warning—he slammed his cock into her sopping wet pussy. Kate clawed at the seat, fought to brace herself against his pounding, but he was stronger. Danny pulled at her hips, forcing her to meet his thrust. Slapping against her backside, he rode her until she cried his name.

"You're so wet," he growled. "So wet, Katie."

She cried again, encouraging his release, but he held back. So close to the edge, his muscles tensed. Danny stopped the pounding and stroked the pinked flesh of her ass. His breathing was labored. Every muscle coiled. Ready to spring. Running a moistened finger down the crack of her ass, he found her asshole and pushed through again. Kate squirmed. And cried. A cry of agony.

"Isn't that what you like," he growled. Slapping her on the ass, he wouldn't let her wiggle away. His pulsing cock still deep inside her pussy. "Don't you like being fucked."

Kate's whole body shivered, thrilling at his words. She liked it. He moved his finger inside her ass. Her breath came out in a rhythmic pant. She was trying to control the pain.

"You're a bad girl," he reminded her as he spread her ass cheeks wide. "You know it's true. Answer me. Are you a bad girl?"

Kate nodded and gasped, "Yes, Danny."

Leaning into the truck, he whispered into her neck. "Tell me, baby."

"I'm bad."

"Yes," he murmured. "Where do you want it? Where do you want me to fuck you?"

"Fuck my pussy, Danny. Please."

Danny removed his finger slowly, and she moaned, in pleasure, this time.

Clawing her ass cheeks apart with her fingernails, she gave him a clear view of his cock, deep inside. It throbbed.

"Fuck me, Danny," she gasped. "Cum in my pussy."

Danny released a fierce growl. Rocking the truck with every long penetration, he showed no mercy, ripping her to shreds with his determination. With one final thrust, he climaxed. Crying out her name, he arched his back and spilt his cum. Laying claim, Danny breathed heavily into the night sky. *Mine, mine.*

The interior light of the cab clicked off, alerting both Kate and Danny to time and place. Slowly, he withdrew. He situated her dress before pulling up his own jeans. Kate lay wasted, still half inside the truck. Danny lifted her into his arms. He supported her limp body and rocked her back and forth.

"Are you okay, baby?"

Kate nodded into his chest. "Yes."

Relieved, Danny hugged her closer, enjoying the sweet smell of sweat on her neck. "I'm sorry. I don't know what came over me."

Kate patted his chest. "It's okay," she assured him. "I like it rough, too, you know."

"It was the dress."

"I hope you didn't ruin it," she laughed, swatting him in the arm.

The gold chain around her neck was tangled in her hair, and he pulled at it, his fingers too thick and clumsy to be of much help. Kate's slender fingers made quick work of it, and the necklace hung loose around her neck in seconds.

Looking up into his eyes, she was suddenly serious. "I think you'll have to drive us back to the farm."

Danny helped her into the truck and cringed again as she gingerly situated her panties and sat herself carefully on the seat.

"I'm so sorry, Katie," he said. "Was it too much? Did I hurt you?"

Reaching through the open door, Kate laid her right hand along the side of his face. "I'm okay. You're just too much man, Danny Maller," she sighed and leaned out of the truck to kiss him gently on the lips.

Too much man, he scoffed as he jogged to the driver side door. Everything he had in excess was because of Kate.

When the engine of the truck roared to life, Kate set her head on Danny's shoulder and sighed. "I love this truck."

Danny laughed as he put his foot down on the enormous gas pedal, "I think I love it too."

CHAPTER 30

MESS

It was easier being away from Kathryn. Knowing the reason for her absence gave him a feeling of proprietorship. Lightened his burden. She was still in his thoughts, but he was able to prioritize. Spend time with his children. Focus on making the last moments with his family pleasant.

Just as expected, his father-in-law called at the office. Voiced concerns. It was obvious the old man suspected he was cheating, but the accusation was never made. His father-in-law preferred to circumvent the topic and exulted the value of family. It was hard to listen. His thoughts too smug. The father-in-law too predictable.

But with Kathryn gone attending to family duties, he chose to follow his father-in-law's advice and focused on the children. They were not at fault. It was his mistake not theirs. Their mother, a poor choice.

Relating to young children was difficult but also very amusing. His own daughter was non-sensical. Too much like her mother, Brenna was flippant and prattled endlessly about characters he had trouble discerning as fictional or actual. He took her to the Cosley Farm, the local petting zoo, and she complained about the smell. It gave her happiness, however, spending time with him.

Daddy-time, Brenna called it. When he held her hand, it felt incredibly soft and his heart swelled. Perhaps that was the essence of fatherhood. The incredibly soft hand of a four-year-old placed trustingly in his own.

Branigan was another matter all together. The females of the household were sleeping, but the boy heard rustling in the kitchen and padded downstairs in his pajamas. Seated in the chair opposite his in the sunroom, Branigan watched his every move with sleepy eyes.

"Would you like some milk?"

The hair tumbled into Branigan's round face as he shook his head violently. "Pancakes," he demanded.

"Will you help?"

The boy hopped out of his chair and ran into the kitchen. An obvious yes. Following behind, he caught his son in front of the freezer holding a yellow box.

"Frozen pancakes," he said in disgust. "I don't think so, buddy. You and dad are going to make the real thing. From scratch."

Suspicious of the stool, Branigan remained on the floor and watched as he placed ingredients and cooking utensils on the counter. His son didn't help. Choosing instead to observe.

A new family tradition. When Branigan and Brenna came for a visit after the separation, they would make pancakes. It was perfectly quaint. The stuff childhood memories were made of. Perhaps Kathryn would join them. In her bare feet and fitted tank top, she could set the table. Pour the juice.

Kathryn's sons would be a good influence. Already too whiney, Branigan was also an overly cautious child weary of any kind of physical activity. Kathryn's children, on the other hand, propelled themselves on skateboards. Helmet-less more often than not. Their homemade ramp providing endless thrills. Appropriately rowdy. He already liked the Maller boys tremendously. Love was not too much of a leap.

He dreamed about bonding with Kathryn's sons in the mountains. Skiing and snowboarding. Natural sports for young men so infatuated with speed. It could be a common interest. A shared hobby. Christmas in Colorado.

"Ta dah," he said presenting his son with a plate of golden brown silver dollar pancakes.

"Sticky," Branigan complained and then yanked at his own hair in frustration.

Jerking the plate away, he stared down at his son. Sticky? Weren't pancakes by their very nature sticky? He set the offensive plate on the counter and lifted the boy onto a high stool.

"Just try," he encouraged holding up a petite fork with a Disney character on it. "They're daddy's specialty."

Branigan's eyes went from suspicion to anger. He slammed both fists down on the counter successfully flipping the plate.

Of course, his fatherly instinct was to soothe. But before he could reach for him, Branigan emitted an earsplitting screech.

Looking down at his pudgy hands in horror, his son screamed. "Sticky!"

His mother came running into the kitchen. Her robe flying open as she dashed to the sink and unwound a handful of paper towels.

"Shh," she repeated as she cleaned Branigan's hands.

It was disturbing to watch. The care in which she attended to their son was too focused. Too concentrated. And quite frankly, a waste of paper towels. The tears continued to spew even after Branigan's little paws were clean, and she pulled him in for a protective hug. Stroking his back. Placating his tantrum.

She was quick to excuse their son's inexcusable behavior. "He can't stand getting his hands dirty."

Her voice was unconcerned. She was simply sharing a fact. As if the behavioral characteristic wasn't completely bizarre and mildly psychotic.

"Oh," he said mutely.

Turning his back on his wife and child, he went about the business of cleaning up his mess.

Perhaps, Kathryn could help him with that as well.

CHAPTER 31

MARIGOLD

Steak and potatoes. The early dinner was Kate's idea. Since arriving home, she was impatient, bustling around the house. Dinner was her final chore, and she wanted it out of the way.

Kate set the table outside on the deck. When Danny brought the food from the grill, he laughed. She was at the sliding glass door in her running clothes with a pocket full of dog biscuits and a newly purchased collar and leash in her hand.

"What?" she demanded.

Danny fell into his chair signaling the boys to join him. "I give up," he said. "I can't keep up with you. How can you have energy to go jogging? I'm exhausted."

"You going to look for Marigold?" Peter asked as he forked his steak.

"I want to go too, Momma," Joey tugged on his mother's arm.

"That's not a good idea, little man," Kate said as she shuffled him towards his dinner. "Marigold is shy. If I do bring her home, you have to be very gentle and quiet."

Kate ran a hand across Danny's shoulders and then she was gone.

155

"I don't like the name," Billy complained. "Marigold. It's embarrassing."

"It was Grandma's favorite flower," Joey said in defense. "And she's yellow. Just like the flower."

"Mom plants marigolds around her vegetables," Peter added in a neutral tone. "She says it keeps out the rabbits. Their smell makes the critters stay away."

"Still stupid," Billy mumbled.

"Your mother found her, so she gets to name her," Danny playfully smacked Billy on the back of his head and then frowned. "You need a haircut."

"No," he shook his head vehemently. "Mom said it's okay as long as it doesn't go over my shoulders."

Danny shrugged. "Well, if mom is okay with you becoming a long-haired freak then I suppose I am too."

"Where did you guys go last night with that old truck Uncle Walt's trying to sell?" Billy asked.

Danny smiled. Like his mother, very little got past Billy. "Your mom wanted to go for a ride. We drove out to the quarry. Got busy under the stars. Made out."

Peter and Billy rolled their eyes in disgust, but Joey was upset. "The quarry? Mom was supposed to take me. Not you."

"It was late, Joe. But Mom did say she was planning on taking you to the quarry in Naperville."

"Quarry?"

Danny had the attention of both Billy and Peter now.

"Quarries are open pit mines. Mining companies dig for rock, gravel, and sand. It creates a man-made lake with no bottom."

"No bottom?"

"No bottom you can reach by holding your breath. It can be very dangerous. Some guy went missing a few years back in Naperville, and it was suspected he drowned in the quarry." Danny smiled at the faces of his wide-eyed sons, and he felt like teasing. "There's flooded mining equipment at the bottom. Left behind because there was no way to bring it up. I betcha dead bodies get caught up on it."

"Cool," Billy replied enthusiastically. "Can we go?"

"Too cold," Danny said taking a bite of his steak. "You have to wait for summer. The beach is not open yet, and they don't allow diving off the cliffs anymore. Too risky. It's easy to get hurt, and Naperville doesn't want to be liable."

"Well that sucks," Peter griped.

"Lawyers," Billy added. "Mom says they spoil all the fun. Calls them filthy bloodsuckers."

"Yep, your mother hates lawyers," Danny nodded happily, grateful it was true.

After dinner, Danny supervised the boys loading the dishwasher and then went to sit on the deck with a beer. He had neglected his e-mail the entire weekend. Taking a deep breath, he picked up his phone and scrolled through the directory. He got butterflies in his stomach when he saw her name. Natalie Bell-Charles.

Kate was right. Natalie wanted to fuck him—four messages, two of them photographs. He deleted them as soon as they flashed on the small screen. They were innocent enough. One of Natalie in a Redwing jersey, because she was from Michigan. And one of Natalie in biking gear, because she rode in a charity event over the weekend raising money for cancer research. Danny winced. He knew way too much about her.

It was a bad idea from the very beginning. Danny couldn't be friends with a woman. Especially not a good-looking woman who loved hockey and wanted to fuck him. Still, he hated to be rude and didn't like the idea of hurting Natalie's feelings. He replied to one message. His carefully crafted lines zoomed across the invisible communication highway, and a thrill went up his spine. Was she waiting for it?

Danny's heart nearly jumped out of his chest when his wife came jogging up the driveway. Dropping his phone, he rose to greet her. Smiling ear to ear, Kate presented him with Marigold.

The dog was a two-toned yellow and very dirty. Its head was square, and its legs were too short for its stout body. Very mutty. When Kate stopped, the dog sat and looked up with gold eyes so devoted and loving Danny couldn't help but feel affection for the odd looking animal.

"You found her." He was relieved.

"It was like she was waiting for me, Danny."

Kate got down on one knee and rubbed the dog behind the ears. The boys descended quickly. Marigold was shy but willing. Her long tail never stopped wagging.

A bowlful of borrowed kibble from Molly's little dog Max, a sudsy bath with the garden hose, one good brushing, and Marigold was officially a Maller. The black tips of the dog's ears flapped as she eagerly followed Peter around the yard. Their eldest son appointed himself trainer and was schooling Marigold on the property line. Leading her on a leash, he yanked her back into the yard every time she crossed the line.

"She's smart," Kate sighed.

"And she has a good temperament," Danny added, reaching across the arm of his deck chair to take Kate's hand.

Kate leaned her head back onto her own chair and smiled at him. "I'll call Molly's vet first thing tomorrow."

Danny nodded before looking up at the darkening sky. "We should get these guys inside. It's way past Joey's bedtime, and they have school tomorrow."

He worried the dog wasn't housebroken, but Marigold bound into the house after Kate and wasn't the least bit skittish. It was obvious who the dog favored, so there was no argument about where she was going to sleep. After Joey was tucked in, Marigold trailed Kate into their bedroom, and Danny planted himself in his recliner to catch up on sport news.

When he walked into the bedroom, he found his wife in no need of company. Marigold was curled up in a tight ball in the center of their bed.

Danny set his hands on his hips and shook his head disapprovingly. "I don't know how I feel about this. Should she be allowed on the bed?"

"She's so tired, Danny," Kate pleaded, laying a hand on the dog's back. "Please. Just for tonight. I'll buy her a doggie bed tomorrow."

Making a face, Danny stomped into the bathroom. Returning to the bed, Danny lifted the blankets and tried to slide the dog over. Marigold looked at him with her eyes half-closed, very female and very stubborn.

"Geez," he said scooting into his crowded bed. "Katie, come on, this is ridiculous."

"Just for tonight," Kate stretched to his side of the mattress and smacked his cheek with a noisy kiss. "She might be afraid."

Danny scoffed. "This dog is not afraid. She's movin' in on my woman. Tomorrow, Trouble," he said sternly. "Marigold is outta of the marital bed."

"I promise," Kate giggled.

Danny tried to remember why a dog was a good idea. Rolling over onto his side, he closed his eyes with a huff and his thoughts flashed on Natalie Bell-Charles. *Red.*

A rumble grew from his chest, and it slipped through his lips before he could catch it. Danny turned it into a cough and read-justed his face into the pillow. The thought of Natalie Bell-Charles in her red suit and matching high heeled shoes made his dick hard.

Natalie sometimes took her suit coat off and laid it across her lap. The delicate fabric of her blouse couldn't hide the lacy lines of her bra. Hard nipples shot out through the silk, screaming come and get me.

Can't be helped. Danny beat back his feelings of guilt. He was a man after all, and it wasn't like he was gonna fuck her.

CHAPTER 32

CHOICE

Sharon made a habit of calling Kate every day which was fine except today she threw out the unexpected. A job. In the carefully crafted proposition, Sharon called it an '*opportunity.*' And she was not playing around. Sharon seriously wanted Kate to work for her. The phone conversation was quick. *"Don't give me an answer now. Just think about it. We'll talk later."* Stunned, Kate hung up the phone and drove straight to Molly's house. They were carpooling to Cup of Java for coffee with Ainsley Dixon. More talk. Kate regretted suggesting it.

"What did the vet say?" Molly asked conversationally from the passenger seat.

Kate smiled nervously. Molly assumed Kate was distracted, because she was thinking about her new dog.

"He said from the look of her teeth she is somewhere between one and two years old."

"You're lucky," Molly said smiling. "Marigold is great with the kids, and she stays in the yard. I was worried she might run away on you."

"I know," Kate agreed. "But it's almost like she chose to adopt me, not the other way around."

Molly smiled in understanding. "Sorry about the timing of this meeting. I know you are usually making dinner around now, but it couldn't be helped. Ainsley Dixon's sitter couldn't do it any other time."

"No, it's not a problem. Danny called this afternoon. He's not coming home for dinner. Some kind of work thing. I'm just gonna make pancakes and sausage for the kids."

"Breakfast for dinner," Molly laughed. "That's a cute idea."

"Joey thinks it's fun," Kate shrugged. "He likes to do the flipping."

Kate slid into a free parking spot and pulled the key out of the ignition. She hurried to get out of the van but realized Molly was applying lip gloss and fixing her hair in the mirror on the passenger visor.

"You make me feel like a slob, Molly," Kate complained.

Molly dismissed her with a wave. "You look great."

Kate frowned at her button-down oxford and faded Levis. She wished she'd worn her new jeans. Molly was wearing some kind of outfit that was a cross between workout and lounge wear. Reaching across the seat, Kate fingered the soft fabric of Molly's slacks.

"These are nice," she said. "Casual but dressy at the same time."

"Elastic waist," Molly said wagging her eyebrows. "I got them for travel. We're taking the boys to visit Tom's parents in Texas when school gets out."

When they stepped up to the coffee shop's storefront, Molly pointed out Ainsley Dixon through the window. She was a pretty woman with a round face and over-styled hair. Her mouth was moving quickly in conversation with two other suburban looking housewives.

"She brought some of her neighbors," Molly sighed.

Molly gave the women a big smile as she stepped up to the small cluster of armchairs. She introduced herself with learned grace and then turned to Kate.

"Ladies," Molly said, gesturing like she was introducing a showcase prize. "I'd like you to meet Kathryn Maller."

Kate shook all three women's hands and quickly noted how they all wore flashy rings and bangles. Ainsley Dixon was meticulously

162

dressed. It was obvious she appreciated style. Ainsley used clothes to accentuate the positives and downplay the negatives of her figure. It was a skill Kate very much admired—a skill she herself did not have the patience to acquire.

"I'm going to get some tea," Kate said excusing herself. "Molly, can I get you something? Ladies? Does anyone need a refill?"

Molly asked for a café latte, and Kate made her way over to counter, but she kept a keen ear on the conversation she left behind. Ainsley and her neighbors complained about the library and the vicinity of the playground to their property. Car traffic was their most pressing concern which seemed silly to Kate since their subdivision entrance was off Lambert Road and nowhere near the library parking lot.

Kate repressed a grin as she walked back to group. Molly had lost control of the argument, and Ainsley was now worrying about lyme disease.

"You can't possibly believe that a community garden would result in a lyme disease epidemic," Molly's eyes were pleading for help as Kate handed her the coffee.

"Gardens attract deer, Molly. And deer carry lyme disease," Ainsley replied condescendingly.

Kate sat deeply into the armchair and patiently picked apart her scone. She ate and sipped her tea quietly as the arguments went round and round. Ainsley Dixon's accent was charming. Very feminine, she reminded Kate of a southern belle. She found herself swayed to Ainsley's point of view simply because her soft singsongy voice was pleasant to listen to.

Molly's body language was tense and her frown deepened as she tried to reason with Ainsley and her friends. When the conversation transitioned into uncomfortable silence, Kate decided it was time to interject.

Lifting her cup up to her lips, she blew on her hot tea. "I would have thought you ladies would prefer a community garden to a skatepark."

Kate sipped her tea and then set it carefully down on the table. The atmosphere around their circle was electric. Molly was visibly shocked by the news.

"Skatepark," Ainsley exclaimed. "Who said anything about a skatepark?"

"Your kids are littler than mine, so you probably don't run in quite the same circles as I do," Kate explained with a smile. "But parents of middle schoolers and high schoolers are fed up with Wheaton's Park System. Kids can't inline skate or ride skateboards on sidewalks. And, they get themselves in trouble at the parks by launching themselves off railings and playground equipment."

Molly composed herself enough to nod in agreement. "It's true. Wheaton Police are on constant lookout for violations of the No Skating Code. It's a real problem. Some parents are frustrated. They feel like their kids are getting unfairly picked on."

"Has it gone before the Village Board? I don't understand how something like a skatepark could be under consideration without notifying the community."

"Well, just like with the garden, there's a skatepark committee and a petition going around. I'm afraid Danny might have signed it, but I'm not sure. That's why the garden committee is in such a hurry to get our proposal before the Village Planning Committee. We're trying to beat them to the punch. Lay claim over the empty lot."

"Why the library site?" Ainsley asked. "Why can't they build a skateboard park in Village Square or at the Little League Park?"

"The lot behind the library is perfect," Kate shrugged. "It's right off Roosevelt Road which connects it with Glen Ellyn and Winfield. Or at least that's the talk at the ice rink. Danny and I are heavily involved with the DuPage County Ice Hockey Association. Hockey players are notorious inline skaters."

"You're right Kathryn," Molly nodded. "The library site is ideal for a skatepark. Communities from all around DuPage County would benefit."

"It gets me in trouble at home, but personally, I would much rather see the site developed as a garden. Just think about the added liability a skatepark will give the Village," Kate shook her head discouragingly.

"No one gets hurt gardening. At least not usually," Molly laughed.

Ainsley bit her lip. "I should talk to my husband. He's a lawyer and might have something valuable to add."

"A lawyer?" Kate said, leaning towards Ainsley. "What kind of law does he practice?"

Ainsley lifted her chin slightly in pride. "Corporate and tax law, but I'm sure he can decipher the local codes concerning parks and recreation."

They finished their coffee and tea in polite conversation. Kate and Molly excused themselves from the group and left after a friendly good-bye. Molly waited until they pulled out into traffic before she broke out into laughter.

"I underestimated you, Kathryn," Molly said. "You are a very good liar. I almost believed you myself. There's no skatepark."

"It was something they could hate more than a community garden," Kate explained. "Most of the time people just want to feel like they have control. So, I gave them a choice."

"You're diabolical," Molly snorted as Kate pulled into her driveway. "I love it."

"Hey Molly, before you go, could I ask for some advice?"

"Sure, doll," Molly said. "What is it?"

"I was thinking of cutting my hair," Kate pulled her hair out of its ponytail, and it fell dramatically onto her face. "Sharon thinks something short would be flattering on me."

Molly's face brightened at the prospect. "I can call my guy, Robert. He usually books five weeks ahead, but maybe he could get you in sooner."

"Will you come with me?" Kate asked. "I'll need help explaining what I want, and I might chicken out."

"Absolutely," Molly agreed wholeheartedly. "I'll call right away and let you know when he can fit you in."

"Thanks."

"No, thank you," Molly said. "You were great today."

Kate felt optimistic as she watched Molly skip into her house. She was finally getting a handle on her future. No longer standing still, she was making real changes.

New dog, new project, new job, new look—a new Kate.

CHAPTER 33

JOYRIDE

When Danny pulled onto the parkway, he spied Kate in the backyard with the boys. Her tomboy upbringing was on display. She was expertly hitting a ball with a bat. Marigold was acting as retriever. Danny smiled inwardly. Kate finally found someone who liked to play baseball.

The squeak of the brakes alerted Marigold, and she barked. Danny was impressed. She sounded viscous. His family stood hesitantly. All with the same look on their faces—confusion.

Reaching for his briefcase, Danny hopped out of the vehicle and grinned. He held the door open with his right arm and lifted his left to showboat his surprise.

"Daddy's home," he shouted.

Kate was the first to come to her senses. And to Danny's utter delight, she screamed. Jumping up and down, she screeched in reckless, girly abandon. The boys and Marigold chased her swishing ponytail down the driveway. Danny didn't have time to brace himself. Kate slammed into him so hard it knocked him backwards. Hurling herself off the ground, she wrapped her legs around his waist and peppered his face with kisses.

"Danny," she repeated over and over. "Thank you."

167

Hugging her close, he ignored the curious looks of their neighbors. Kate's reaction was worth the fifteen hundred bucks.

"I couldn't resist," he shrugged. "You looked eighteen years old behind the wheel. I thought, what the hell. Why not get a fun car for the summer. We can store it at Walt's during the winter."

Kate ripped the keys out of his hand, jumped into the truck, and slammed the door. She was giggling and eighteen again.

"I love it," she proclaimed, stroking the enormous steering wheel.

"I left work a little early and took the Amtrak train to Milwaukee. Your brother and dad met me. We traded papers, and I drove home. It was a rocky ride, but the truck had no problem on the expressway."

"You lied," Kate teased. "You said you had a dinner meeting."

"Forgive me, baby?" Danny asked holding his right hand over his heart insincerely.

The boys circled and examined their mother's new truck. Marigold jumped up on the passenger side door anxious to get a look at Kate.

"Let her in, Peter," Kate said as she turned the key in the ignition.

When the engine turned over in a noisy rumble, Kate's eyes danced with happiness. Marigold leapt into the cab of the truck, nosed Kate's cheek, and then settled herself into the passenger seat.

"Climb in the back, boys," Kate directed. "We'll go for a spin."

Shocked, the boys looked to Danny.

"Go ahead," he encouraged. "Just don't draw too much attention to yourselves."

The phrase "kids aren't cargo" passed through his brain as Peter, Billy, and Joey settled themselves into the bed of the truck, but he wasn't going to be the one to spoil their fun.

Alone in the driveway, he smiled as his wife backed out. Before shifting the truck into drive, she flipped on the radio and blasted the local country station. Kate blew him a kiss and sped away. He didn't turn to meet the footsteps approaching from behind. He was enjoying the view too much.

"A pick-up truck?" Molly asked delicately.

"Some women like diamonds," he laughed. "It just so happens my woman likes old beat-up Chevy trucks."

"Very nice, Danny," Tom said. "Is it some kind of anniversary? Or are you feeling guilty about something?"

Taken aback, Danny examined his neighbor's eyes but quickly concluded it was a joke.

"No special occasion, Tom," Danny replied. "Just wanted to raise the bar so high no other man could possibly breach it."

"Yeah," Tom snorted. "It's tough to top the *Dukes of Hazzard.* Didn't Cooter drive a truck like that?"

Danny's temper flared and not at Tom's snide comment. It was Kate's resemblance to Daisy Duke. It never occurred to him that behind the wheel of a pickup Kate's cornfed beauty might appeal to other men. And Danny was pissed, at himself.

"Shut up, Tom," Molly said, grabbing onto Danny's arm. "Dan knows how to make his wife happy. Maybe you should take some lessons."

"How 'bout it, Coach?" Tom leered. "Givin' out lessons?"

Danny backed away and headed towards the house. "My particular expertise is limited to one woman. Sorry, buddy, you're on your own."

Molly and Tom traced his steps as they made their way home. Before Danny could signal good-bye, Molly stopped short and caught his attention.

"You know, Dan," she said smugly. "Kathryn was pretty amazing this afternoon."

"Oh," Danny was confused. He couldn't remember Kate's plans for the day. "Is that right?"

"We had coffee with a few women who oppose the community garden," Molly clarified. "Kathryn threw a red herring at them. Completely diverted the argument. Those poor women didn't know what hit them."

"Yeah, I'm not surprised. Katie was a champion debater in Madison."

"That's what Sharon said," Molly nodded her head. "I had no idea, Dan."

When Danny shook his head indicating he did not understand her train of thought, Molly smiled.

"I had no idea she was so smart," she said.

"Of course she's smart," Tom said giving Danny a dig. "She married Mr. Wonderful, didn't she?"

Danny rolled his eyes with a chuckle for Tom's benefit and then waved good-bye to his neighbors. It was lonely walking into an empty house. He missed his family, and he was sorry he didn't think to join Kate's joyride.

Next time, he would.

CHAPTER 34

THE FUTURE

Kate examined her face in the mirror as she combed her wet hair back. Fine lines traced the corners of her eyes and mouth, but they didn't bother her. What she feared most—more than growing old—was growing stale. Kate needed to move forward. She needed to keep her mind on the future. Sharon's job offered her an outlet, but she was afraid. She couldn't move forward without Danny.

It was late. Later than her usual bedtime. The whole household was in an uproar from Danny's surprise gift, and it took awhile to settle down. Kate dropped the damp towel wrapped around her body and walked naked into their closet.

She wanted something sexy—something new that would attract Danny's attention. Fingering the long line of button-down shirts, her eyes went to the stack of hockey jerseys piled on the shelf. The softest one was Danny's old practice jersey from Madison. Faded, it was more tomato red than Badger red, and its neck and cuffs were white.

Kate stood in front of the mirror again. She yanked at the collar loosening the pull strings until the shirt fell open across her cleavage. Finally, she dug through her underwear drawer and located an ancient pair of black thong panties.

171

"Still sexy," she said to Marigold who was lying in her new but already beloved dog bed.

Thong panties were not practical for daily wear, but they could be fun on special occasions.

The dog stayed at her heels as she walked across the floor of her silent house. Marigold was a part of her now—her constant companion. She grabbed a bottle of beer from the refrigerator and headed out the front door. Marigold came with her and stood watch over the neighborhood from the top of the porch steps.

Danny was already there—hidden in the corner. It was very dark and all Kate could see was the rocking of his hulking shadow.

"Whatcha got goin' on there, Trouble?" he asked in a low husky voice.

"Do you like it?" she asked basking in the light coming from inside their house.

"You don't have much on underneath. I can see straight through that jersey from here."

"Maybe it was a mistake," she said stepping away from the light. "I'm feeling a little chilled."

"Your hair is wet. No wonder you're cold. Come on over." Danny held out his arms. "I'll keep you warm."

Kate jumped into his lap. Covering her hands with the long sleeves of the jersey, she took a sip of her beer.

"Are you drinking beer?" Danny asked. "What's come over you, Trouble?"

"It matches the truck," she teased before snuggling into his shoulder.

"Ahh," he grumbled. "Don't say that. I'm starting to have buyer's remorse. Maybe the truck wasn't such a good idea."

"No," Kate protested. "I love it. You can't take it away."

"Of course not." Danny kissed her forehead and stroked her back. "But it's not the typical vehicle for a married woman with three children."

Kate laughed. "Are you saying the truck is sexy?"

"It is with you driving it."

She laughed again, but Danny persisted. "I'm telling you Katie, men are gonna start crawling out of the woodwork. Please, just watch it. Don't talk to strangers and don't make eye contact with any guys who might be looking your way."

"Uh huh," Kate agreed. "Just like you did with Miss Hyphenated."

"Katie, please. Just promise you'll be extra careful."

Kate could sense the urgency in his tone and stopped teasing at once. "I promise, Coach. I'll be careful."

Danny smiled and hugged her closer. She was getting warmer in his strong arms. Kate relaxed and melded naturally into the contours of Danny's hard body.

"I've got to fix that light," Danny said pointing to the driveway lantern.

Kate nodded. That's why it was darker than usual. No lantern.

"Darkness has its advantages," Kate said as she set her beer onto the side table.

Danny continued to rock the chair back and forth as she ran her hand over his chest. She always followed the same pattern. Chest, shoulders, biceps, abs. Chest, shoulders, biceps, abs. He was so ample—so strong beneath her palm.

"You sure looked good when I pulled up this evening," he murmured into the night. "You were hitting the hell out of that ball. Maybe you should join a softball league."

Kate nuzzled her face into his neck and scoffed. "Softball? Danny, you know I won't play with anything other than a hardball. It's just not any fun scoring with something soft."

Danny sighed and leaned his head back into the chair. Kate sat up in his lap and moved her lips to his—enjoying the sensation of his beard rubbing against her face. She opened his mouth with her tongue and ignited the fire that was already smoldering deep inside her chest. She loved him. Danny was more than she deserved.

"First base," she said in between kisses.

Their breathing was growing heavy, but Danny's hands remained on the arms of the chair. He was letting her drive. Kate reached impatiently for his right hand and guided it up into the confines of his old jersey.

Placing his palm firmly around her breast, she sighed, "Second base."

She felt the corner of his lips pull up into a smile beneath her kiss.

"Slow down, slugger," he teased, letting his voice drop an octave. "You know the ball's going over that fence. There's no need to rush around the bases."

Kate's body surged with longing, and she twisted in his lap—searching for his erection. Like a desperate itch, she was compelled to scratch. Danny knew how to relieve the throbbing ache. He filled her up and set her loose. Alone in the shadows with Danny, she was almost whole. She needed to feel it. She needed to rub up against it. Danny groaned when she ground into him, and he pinned her to his chest. He held her still, and she whined in complaint.

"Third base," she begged.

Danny drew his right hand slowly down her belly and then along her hip. His fingers dug beneath the waistband of her panties, and she shifted her weight—spreading her legs instinctively. She held her breath. Waiting—waiting for Danny's strong fingers.

Marigold suddenly lurched to her feet and released a furious growl. Both Kate and Danny broke from their embrace and stared at the dog. The hair on her back was raised, and she snarled.

Danny threw his head back in frustration. "That dog and I are going to have serious problems."

Kate leapt off Danny's lap and reprimanded Marigold sharply. Her tail fell between her legs, and she followed Kate inside the door.

"I'll be coming to bed in a few minutes, sweet girl," she said as she closed the door on Marigold's worried gold eyes.

Prancing back to Danny, Kate pushed aside the rocker's ottoman and kneeled in between his legs. The clank of Danny's belt buckle echoed through her cloudy desirous thoughts, and she made fast work of his button fly. Kate pulled his T-shirt free and ran both hands up his torso. The coarse hair felt so familiar. It was a comfort, and she nuzzled her face into his belly.

She could feel Danny's eyes gazing down at her. A few cars drove past the house, and Danny raised his head in alarm. But Kate didn't worry—the porch was private. The manicured hedges around the perched landing provided cover as long as Kate stayed on her knees. Danny was the only one visible from the street, and it was very dark.

Kate wrapped a warm palm around Danny's erection and quickly went down on the shaft. He gasped and tried to pull away at the suddenness of her attack, but she stubbornly kept him at the back of her throat.

Kate moaned softly as she ran her tongue up his shaft before releasing him. She ripped the jersey over her head and pulled at the waistband of his jeans. Danny lifted himself off the seat, so Kate could slide his jeans and boxers down to his ankles.

When she looked up at him, Danny's attention was focused on her naked chest. Kate cupped a breast in each hand and fell back so she was sitting on her ankles. The wet hair was falling in her eyes, so she threw head back and looked at Danny from beneath her eyelashes. The watchful stare added to her excitement. His breathing caught as she ran her thumbs over the hard tips of her nipples. He liked it. Danny liked watching, and he slouched further into the chair—moving his hard cock closer to her mouth.

Emboldened, Kate let her mouth fall open slightly—tempting him—inviting him. The warm spring breeze carried the scent of lilacs as she relaxed under her own touch. Danny locked onto her gaze as she increased speed—flicking both nipples with the planed fingers of both hands.

Danny gripped the base of his cock with his right hand. "Rub your tits on it," he groaned as he spread his legs wide.

Kate lifted herself onto her knees and dove for his cock. Sucking noisily, she moistened his shaft. Danny cursed in restraint and then sighed when she enveloped his cock between her tits. Kate wrapped one arm around his waist and used the other hand to push her breasts together. Sliding his cock, she licked the tip every time it emerged from her cleavage.

Danny growled in frustration. His left hand crept across her shoulder and grabbed a fistful of wet hair. Yanking her head back, he cleared his view.

"Yes. I want to see it," he groaned. "Faster, baby."

Neighbors out for an evening stroll with their dog passed by the front of their house. Their conversation drifted to the porch, but Kate's attention was elsewhere. Danny was clenching his jaw in restraint. The muscles in his neck were taut, so she went down quickly on his cock. Daring him to come. His back arched, but Kate gripped his leg and refused to let go. Danny sucked in a deep breath and tensed.

Releasing him quickly, Kate threw her head back and pumped his cock with her right hand. Danny came on her tits, and she sighed—her whole body awash with satisfaction as she used both hands to spread his cum over breasts.

Danny gripped her shoulders roughly. "Turn around," he directed.

Bent over the ottoman, Kate let her head dangle and got lost in the sensation of Danny's hands petting her ass possessively—pulling at the coarse lace of her thong. His erection diminished slightly after climax, but he was still hard.. She could feel his cock pressed against her backside. Kicking her legs apart, he began with a long, penetrating rhythm that steadily rocked Kate back and forth.

"Rub your clit," he directed.

Reaching behind with her right hand, Kate did as she was told. Danny murmured encouragement into the shadows.

"You're such a bad girl. So wet. Rub that clit," he coached. "Give it to me."

"I want to feel you cum, baby," he whispered, increasing the intensity of his pounding.

Kate forgot to breathe. She was concentrating so hard—so lost in the sensation of being taken—taken from behind. The pressure of her fingers delivered an electric shock through her body, and she rubbed her clit under Danny's instruction. His deep husky voice spoke to her. Her name in his murmurings shook her to the core, and she stiffened in climax. Kate came hard and cried out his name. Her whole body rocked and then she collapsed into the deep cushion of the ottoman.

Danny soothed her with his soft, loving words. "You're so sexy."

When her breathing slowed, he stroked her ass possessively and chuckled softly.

"I want my name right here," he said running a thumb over her left cheek. "For my birthday, instead of a new shirt, how about my name tattooed forever on the best piece of ass in town."

Kate laughed as she shoved herself upright. She tried to clear her thoughts by pulling the damp hair away from her face.

"You better put this back on," Danny teased and then tossed her his old practice jersey. "You already gave the neighbors an earful. You don't need to give them an eyeful too."

Danny situated his clothes as Kate struggled with her own. She was suddenly very warm. Still a bit breathless, she plopped herself in the rocker next to Danny's and reached for the beer she left on the side table.

She took a swig and smiled. "Sharon has a tattoo."

"No," Danny exclaimed. "Where?"

Cupping her own left breast, Kate showcased her cleavage through his old jersey. "Three little yellow chicks. One for each baby—on her left breast."

"Nice," Danny lifted his eyebrows in approval. "I betcha Sharon screams like a banchee in the sack."

"You think?"

Danny nodded into the night. It was quiet, and Kate felt safe in her husband's company. Now was the time.

"Sharon offered me a job," she blurted.

Kate watched and waited for Danny's reaction. He surprised her. Instead of shock or disbelief, he pursed his lips and nodded once. Danny folded his hands in his lap and gave her a weak smile.

"What kind of job?" he asked.

Kate couldn't detect any displeasure in his tone.

"Her company is purchasing a manufacturing plant in Addison. It's been troubled with labor and safety issues, and Sharon wants me to act as an independent liaison between the union and the corporate office. She says my experience negotiating contracts will make me perfect for the job."

"It's been a long time," Danny warned.

Kate frowned. "I saved Katt Construction millions of dollars, Dan. I was negotiating contracts with Chicago labor unions my third year out of college. Human Resources was just a stepping stone. They offered me a management position before I got pregnant with Peter."

"That's not what I meant, Trouble," Danny's face broke into a grin. "I know you can do the job. What I meant was, it's been a long time since you've worked for someone else. Do you think you'll be able to answer to a boss? Put up with other people's bullshit?"

"I don't know," Kate shrugged. "But it's a temporary position, so it won't be the end of the world if I hate it. When the problems are resolved, I'll be on my way. Sharon said it's bound to lead to other opportunities, but for the short term, I'd be an outside consultant. I'd bill her for my time, so the hours would be somewhat flexible. Mostly early mornings at the factory, and afternoons at my home office communicating with corporate. Sharon won't need me until the end of August, so I'll have three months to get our house in order."

"Did she suggest how much you should charge as Kathryn Maller Esquire?"

"Ninety bucks an hour."

This time Danny reacted just as she expected. "Holy shit," he exclaimed. "Ninety bucks an hour?"

"Sharon said it's what other labor consultants charge."

"What are the drawbacks?" Danny asked in an objective tone.

"I'll be out of the house very early. I wouldn't be around to send the kids off to school."

"Is that the only negative? Because if this is something you really want to do, we can deal with that."

"I'd have a lot less time around the house, but I think I could handle it. I've always been pretty good at managing my time," Kate was thinking out loud. "And if things got too crazy, we could hire someone to come in once a week and clean. Lots of people do that."

Danny chuckled. "If you're making ninety bucks an hour, we'd definitely be able to afford a housekeeper."

"Tell me what you are really thinking, Dan," Kate said, reaching for his hand.

Danny folded her hand into his and squeezed. "I think you oughta do it."

"Really?"

"Yes," he said. "I've seen changes in you since you started spending more time outside of the house. As much as I'd like to keep you all to myself, I know it's selfish."

"I love you, Danny."

"I know," Danny kissed her hand. "Don't worry, baby. Change is scary for me, but I think I can smother my possessive nature for ninety bucks an hour."

"I want to put most of it in the bank for the boys," Kate said, her voice ripe with enthusiasm. "Save for college. Madison could be an option for them. We won't have to worry about the out-of-state tuition. And we should take a trip. Just the two of us."

"Just the two of us, Trouble," Danny sighed. "Sounds like heaven to me."

No longer afraid, Kate kept her mind on the future and moved forward with Danny.

CHAPTER 35

INTRODUCTION

"When I agreed to let you drive to the Village Board meeting, I didn't know we would be riding in a shitty blue pickup truck." Sharon's face was crumpled in distaste as she stood outside the passenger door.

"You look very pretty," Kate sang from the driver's seat.

Sharon was polished in tailored pants and a silk blouse. Punching the door handle, Kate's friend pulled the door open and eyed the seat.

"I'm wearing heels, Katie," she said, still unconvinced. "How the hell am I gonna climb up into this frickin' thing?"

"Come on. It'll be fun." Kate encouraged. Nothing could dampen her mood.

Kate laughed when Sharon dramatically tossed her designer bag onto the bench seat. Pulling at the leg of her left pant, Sharon set the toe of her high heeled shoe into the cab and anchored her weight to the door with her right hand. She made an audible heave and launched herself up onto the seat.

Sharon ignored Kate's giggles and smoothed out the creases of her blouse. "Why the hell is Danny turning you into a redneck?"

Sharon slammed the door shut and turned around to glance through the rear window. "Well," she sighed. "At least you don't have a mounted shot gun."

"No," Kate teased, "But I've got a mounted tool box. It's got a lock and everything."

Giving Sharon a huge grin, Kate reached for the radio and cranked country music.

Sharon shook her head. "Good Lord, Katie."

Kate tapped her fingers to the music. She felt Sharon's eyes studying her, and she laughed.

"You're glowing. Danny must know what he's doing."

Kate wagged her eyebrows in response.

"And the boots," Sharon added. "They go well with the truck."

"I'm wearing my new jeans too," Kate said.

"But the belt is old. I remember it. You used to wear it all the time," Sharon said with a glare. "I hate you, Katie. Your waist size hasn't changed since college."

"I thought you'd be proud of me," Kate said defensively. "I actually accessorized an outfit."

When Danny got home from work, she left the kitchen to take a few extra minutes to get dressed. Kate brushed out her hair until it crackled with static electricity and then secured it in a loose twist at her neck. She gave up trying to remember the cosmetic ladies' instructions and applied makeup according to her own modest standards.

Digging through her closet, she found a thin, soft gray cardigan sweater similar to the style Molly often wore. It was a forgotten Christmas gift from Danny's mother. Kate pulled it over a sexy white tank top. But when she stood in front of the mirror, she felt like she was going to a PTA meeting. The sweater was cropped but loose and too preppy. So Kate undid the pearl buttons, wrapped the sweater tightly, and bound it with a worn, black, leather belt that had hung forgotten behind her closet door for years.

The chunky beaded necklace Joey made for Mother's Day was the final touch. It slipped easily over her head. Joey had grown tired of the project, and the beads were slightly lopsided. But it spelled out his name in big block letters, and she loved it.

Sharon's cell phone buzzed, and she swore underneath her breath. She pressed a few buttons and shoved it roughly back into a pocket.

"What's the matter?" Kate asked.

"Nothing," Sharon said. "Just work. I have a short fuse today. My weekend sucked. Hannah wouldn't let go of me when I left for the airport."

Kate ran her hand across her friend's shoulder. "They'll be joining you in a few weeks."

"Meanwhile, the guilt is killing me."

"Trust me, Sharon," Kate said as she pulled her truck into City Hall. "Even if you were with them twenty-four hours a day, seven days a week, they would still find something to make you feel guilty about."

"It's the nature of motherhood, I suppose," Sharon sighed.

All of Kate's carefully prepared documents were neatly bundled, and she carried them into City Hall like a school girl. Kate's boots made a resounding clack in comparison to the sharp click of Sharon's spiked heels.

"There she is," Molly shouted, waving Kate and Sharon over to the gathered group.

Molly took the pile of stapled proposals out of Kate's arms and handed them to a clerk. Every Village Board member was going to have a copy of the garden proposal before Kate stood before them and asked to be heard.

"Ainsley Dixon brought her lawyer husband," Molly said as she pointed into the conference room.

Kate's eyes swept across the room. It was impressive. The wall opposite the entrance was paneled with finished wood. The Village Board sat in front of its audience on a slightly elevated platform that curved in a dramatic semi-circle. Each board member had an upholstered high back office chair, a microphone, and a prominent plaque with his or her name on it.

Ainsley and her husband were sitting in the first row with their backs to the door. Ainsley was nervously fidgeting with her fingernails while her husband sat quietly next to her. His legs were crossed and set in the aisle. Her lawyer husband had his back slightly turned, and Kate felt a pang of sympathy. Ainsley looked alone. The neighbors who accompanied her to the coffee shop were not there, and Kate hoped that signified they no longer objected to the garden.

"Ainsley's husband is super hot." Molly's girlish admiration was mirrored in the eyes of her gathered friends.

Kate shrugged. All lawyers looked the same to her. Ainsley's husband wore an expensive dark blue suit, and although she could not see his face, she could tell his hair was slicked back with some kind of hair product.

"Are you ready?" Molly asked as she searched for an empty seat.

"Piece of cake," Kate said confidently.

The garden committee was unable to sit together, but Sharon and Kate found two seats in the back row near the door. Soon after, the Village president called the meeting to order, and the secretary called roll.

Kate leaned over to Sharon, "This is going to take awhile. New business is never introduced until the end of these things."

Sharon's reaction to the meeting proceedings was the exact opposite of Kate's. Kate was sitting straight up in her chair listening intently. Sharon, on the other hand, was bored silly. She started amusing herself by cleaning out her purse. Eventually, she moved onto filing her fingernails, and finally, she ended up flipping through the directory on her Blackberry.

"I could use a margarita," she complained.

Kate waved her off as the Village president wrapped up the last bit of old business.

"The Board now welcomes new business to the floor."

Molly turned in her seat, and Sharon gave Kate a pat of encouragement as she stood.

"Good evening, gentleman and ladies," she said in a clear loud voice. "My name is Kathryn Maller, and I respectfully propose on the behalf of United Gardeners for an Edible Landscape, to the Director of Planning and Economic Development, Mr. James Kozak, that he would—along with the Village Environmental Improvement Commission—consider the construction of a community garden in the vacant lot adjacent to Wheaton's Public Library."

Kate frowned at Sharon when she applauded, but Molly and the other committee members quickly joined in and overrode her objections.

Smiling again, Kate squared her shoulders. "For your consideration, we have provided you and your fellow board members with a five-page document detailing our proposal and projected costs."

The board members began thumbing through the pile of papers placed in front of them. Ainsley Dixon nudged her husband who reluctantly stood and joined Kate in her address to the Village Board.

"Excuse me, ladies and gentlemen," he said. "My name is Jeff Dixon."

Before he could turn to face the Board, the wheels in Kate's brain screeched to a halt and then violently freeze-framed on the moment. It was the jogger. Her immediate recognition evoked a corresponding bodily response. Her heart stalled, and her knees locked in fright. The jogger—Jeff Dixon. They were introduced.

"I own a home bordering the proposed location of the garden," he continued, unaffected by their forced proximity to one another. "I would like to add an objection to Mrs. Maller's proposal."

Mrs. Maller—Kate blinked. He spoke her married name deliberately—letting it roll off his tongue—he caressed her from across the room.

Jeff Dixon turned his body, so he was now facing Kate. He wore dark wire-rimmed glasses that matched his eyes and hair. They were off-putting, and Kate tried to look past them. Placing one hand his pocket, the jogger—Jeff—used the other to direct attention towards her.

"What Mrs. Maller and her associates have failed to provide to the Board is a resolution to the parking problem their garden will impose on the library. Mrs. Maller," the jogger—Jeff—licked his lips lightly as he said her name. "Where do you suppose the overrun of automobiles visiting the library, the garden, and the adjacent playground will park?"

As he gestured with his left hand, Kate's eyes flashed on the red ponytail holder wound around his wrist. Kate's ponytail holder—a souvenir from the park—the fishing pier—the skating shed—the first time he asked for her name.

Kate stared at the jogger—Jeff Dixon—Ainsley Dixon's husband. She failed to feel the other eyes. The eyes of the audience, the Village Board, and her friends. Jeff Dixon's mouth twitched at the corners. He was withholding a grin, and his raven eyes glistened in approval. He was having fun. And his voice—his tone—*shit,* everything about him—was as sexy as hell.

Sharon smacked Kate's leg throwing her off balance. Kate stuttered before righting her posture.

"Mr. Dixon," she began—using the same deliberate articulation as he did with her name. "You obviously have not visited the public library. If you had, you would understand that the library has an overabundance of available parking. In fact, the Library Commission has issued concerns with this very Village Board. Since the relocation of the library facility, community usage has dropped considerably. The garden's proposed location will surely bolster library patronage, thereby promoting it as a valuable community asset."

Jeff Dixon was no longer able to withhold his grin. When it broke across his face, Kate was momentarily blinded by his beauty. White teeth—like a shark—she reminded herself—like a lawyer.

"Mrs. Maller," he said her name for the fourth time. "The Village Planning and Zoning Committee recommended the library parking lot allotment. Are you suggesting that they were incorrect in their assessment?"

"The Planning and Zoning Committee are not required to strictly adhere to any code, Mr. Dixon," Kate countered.

Did the rest of the audience feel the energy buzzing throughout their exchange? Kate didn't care. The jogger—Jeff Dixon—wore a tailored suit and tie. And he wore it well.

"United Gardeners for an Edible Landscape is not asking for the approval of garden construction at this time. We are, merely, at this time," she continued slowly, "asking for consideration. If the Village Board grants our request, I am sure the appropriate commissions will decide if parking availability is reasonable. Ultimately, our assertion, Mr. Dixon, is that a garden will substantially improve the appearance and function of the library site. A community garden will also enhance the character of our town. The Village of Wheaton is built on a citizenship committed to family values. The very family values a community garden will help foster."

Kate took a deep breath before tearing her gaze away from Jeff Dixon's panty-dropping smile and long, lean frame. He was so confident—so self-assured. It made the tips of her fingers tingle.

Addressing the Board directly, she forced a smile. "Full compliance with an obscure parking ordinance need not dismiss our proposal from consideration."

"Thank you, Mrs. Maller and Mr. Dixon," the Village President finally interjected. "Mrs. Maller's garden proposal will be added to the Village Downtown Design Review Board's agenda, and I will also suggest that the Village Environmental Improvement Commission take it under serious consideration. Is there any other new business?"

Ainsley's arm shot up from her seat, and she yanked her husband back down next to her. Kate tried to sit but couldn't. Instead, she flew out of the meeting room with Sharon stumbling to keep up.

Sharon's praise fell on deaf ears as Kate woodenly paced outside the conference room doors. Jeff Dixon said her name. Jeff Dixon wore her ponytail holder. Jeff Dixon's eyes glistened beneath thick lashes. Jeff Dixon's dark hair curled at the nape of his neck. Jeff Dixon was married. She was married. Danny.

The sound of the Village president's pounding gavel woke Kate out of her panic. The meeting was concluded.

Tugging on Sharon's arm, she attempted to tow her towards the exit. "Did you say something about a margarita?"

CHAPTER 36

CONGENIAL LIVING

He took it as a sign. The Village Board meeting an omen. His efforts to placate his wife were rewarded by the gods of karma. When Kathryn stood and introduced herself to the assembled crowd, he almost burst into flames. But amazingly, he managed to pull it together and made the fated introduction. It was good fortune. They were now acquainted. No need to explain their association. Serendipity brought Kathryn to him. It was a sign. A very good sign.

When the droll Board meeting concluded, he rose from his seat and discovered her missing. So unlike her. Running away. His spirits fell, but he capitulated his disappointment. And forced his wife to introduce him to Kathryn's fellow committee members. The United Gardeners for an Edible Landscape. Very clever.

Molly Ibner, Kathryn's neighbor, was a wellspring of information. Milling outside the conference room, he bided his time. Small talk. Fishing for clues. In no hurry to return home.

The gods of karma smiled again. Kathryn sprung out of the ladies room. Her face impatient, she held the door open for her friend. Like always, her appearance struck him like lightning. The jeans. A second skin. He had to tear his gaze away from her tight runner's ass. The desire in his eyes too obvious.

Instead, he dwelled on her fashion sense. A puzzle piece to her complex character. The cotton cardigan contradicted the red cowboy boots and black belt. The homemade necklace signifying her affection for children. A mother. The fiercest kind of mother. Like a fox, Kathryn loved her kits.

He stood feigning conversation. Partially concealed behind a pillar. He watched her in his peripheral vision. She was making a break for the door when the men converged. They wanted to shake her hand. Congratulate her. Her argument had already won with two male members of the Board. He would have thought them rivals, but Kathryn cringed at their approach and then only laughed mildly at their vapid jokes. She let her friend do the talking.

Kathryn's sharp eyes scanned the room. Unable to resist, he stepped out into the open. Her reaction priceless. Her eyes popped open, and she gripped her friend's arm for support. Lightning. Kathryn was fighting against it. Their attraction. Their natural chemistry. Stuffing the hands into his pockets, he let the smile creep across his face.

Kathryn's eyes narrowed. She let go of her friend, squared her shoulders, and drew her gaze away from his face and down his body. He was grateful. For once, he felt properly groomed. Ready for her appraisal.

Abruptly, she spun on her heels and strode for the door. Her friend hurried good-byes to the disappointed gentlemen.

"Molly," her friend called out before chasing Kathryn's long stride. "We're going for margaritas. Come meet us."

Margaritas? Suddenly, he was thirsty. Hurrying his own good-byes, he took his wife by the arm and ran after his heart's desire. Brushing past Kathryn's disappointed gentlemen, he choked back the laughter. They were also contemplating margaritas.

"Mrs. Maller," he called.

He liked to pronounce her name like a purr. Accentuate the r. "Mrs. Maller," he called again but louder this time.

He felt his wife's confused stare as he dragged her along. Ainsley wasn't used to moving quickly. Kathryn's friend stopped. Thwarting her escape. The setting sun backlit their silhouettes. Kathryn's skin glowed. Her hair shimmered.

The friend's blue eyes swept over him, and she cocked her eyebrows. Piercing. Intelligent. Of course Kathryn's friend was intelligent.

"May I speak with you for a moment please?" he called as he maneuvered through the parked cars.

He left Ainsley behind. Too slow. Kathryn dismissed the friend and handed over a set of keys.

"You go on ahead," she said. "I'll see what he has to say."

Kathryn turned and strode to meet him. She smiled, but it was not meant for him.

"Hi, Ainsley," she said, reaching a hand out to his breathless wife as she ran to catch up with him. "It's nice to see you again."

His wife greeted her warmly before latching herself to his arm. "This is my husband," she said through gasps of air. "Jeff, this is Kathryn."

Taking the keys out of his pocket, he handed them to his wife. "I'd like to speak to Mrs. Maller," he said softly. "Why don't you wait for me in the car? I'll only be a moment."

"Okay," she agreed. Always so trusting. "Good-bye, Kathryn."

They both watched as his wife casually strolled away from an exchange that was entirely un-casual. Dangerous, actually.

"I'm sorry," he began. "I did not know about your association with the garden. It was not my intention to surprise you in front of a group of people. If it will make you happy, I will withdraw my objection."

The tension around Kathryn's mouth relaxed. She seemed to believe him. "You're a lawyer," she said dryly.

"And you should have been."

Kathryn rolled her eyes. "I hate lawyers."

"Molly Ibner told me you were pre-law. A champion debater at Madison. She said you gave it all up for Danny."

"People believe what they want to believe," she shrugged.

"Then it's not true," he pressed.

"No, it's not. Danny encouraged me to go to law school. He forced me to take the LSATs. Offered to find a job near any school I chose, but I didn't want it anymore."

"Shame. You were very good," he smiled. "A natural. Your argument was clear, concise, and appealed to the emotions of the audience. I was impressed. As was everyone in the room."

"My friend is waiting," she said, tossing her head towards the truck. Her friend was leaning against the passenger door punching at her Blackberry. "What is it that you want, Jeff?"

It was the first time he heard his name in her voice, and he smiled. "How was Walter's wedding?"

She ignored his attempt at friendly conversation and scowled. "What's with the ponytail holder? You're creepin' me out, Jeff."

"Oh," he said, surprised. He'd forgotten he was wearing it. "A remembrance. Evidence that you do exist. It gets me through the day. Performing is such a hardship, don't you think?"

"Isn't Ainsley curious?" she asked, glancing towards his SUV. "Why would a lawyer in an eight hundred dollar suit wear a red elastic band around his wrist?"

He shrugged. "She's too afraid to ask. Denial is a powerful coping mechanism."

Kathryn's eyes were suddenly full of regret. "I wish you would let this go."

"I can't," he said reaching for his billfold. Unfolding it slowly, he pulled out a business card with his thumb. "I want you to call me. We need to meet. Talk privately."

Kathryn shook her head and crossed her arms. The door closed.

"Take the card, Kathryn," he said in an even tone. Forcing the door open.

She reached for it. Their fingers briefly shared a conduit. Electric. She was so close. Heaven. How he ached to touch her. Stroke her hair. Free it from its constraints. Gathered into a luxurious heap at her neck, the messy twist demonstrated a devil-may-care attitude. Her hair. Tangled and damp. Sticking to her face.

Hanging down into his. It was his most favorite thing about her. Caramel colored. Wild and unruly. Ecstasy.

"I won't call," she warned.

"Then I'll knock on your door."

"Are you stalking me, Jeff?" she hissed. "Are you some sort of psychotic maniac who won't take no for an answer?"

He chuckled. Because she wasn't far off the mark. He was stalking her. Creeping around her darkened house at night, he listened to her having sex with her cog husband on their front porch. The yellow dog nearly alerted her to his lurking presence. Stalker, yes. Psychotic maniac, no. He controlled his jealous rage quite well.

Daniel Maller was indeed her lover. Of course, he despised the idiot husband, but reason overrode passions, and he was grateful for the knowledge his snooping uncovered. He understood his rival better now. The husband was not sexually inept, but he was possessive and jealous. Like the selfish giant who guarded his golden goose. The cog kept Kathryn caged at home. Shackled with housework and children. Isolated. Alone.

"I only want to talk," he countered. "You owe me that, Kathryn. I promise to control myself. I am a gentleman. I've never forced myself on you."

Kathryn's eyes narrowed as she contemplated. She flicked his business card with her fingers and took a deep breath. Softening. "I'll meet you tomorrow morning in the park. At the fishing pier. 5:30."

"Thank you," he said, smiling widely.

"Make sure you wash that shit out of your hair," she quipped. "I hate that look on you."

"You don't like the suit?" he teased, straightening his lapels. "You prefer the jogging shorts and ball cap?"

"Yes," she said, nodding warily. "I do."

"I don't," he said. "I love seeing you out of your running gear. You have a flair for style not many women can pull off. You are more beautiful every time I see you."

She laughed then. Wholeheartedly. She did not believe him.

"It's true," he argued. "You were jaw-droppingly gorgeous this evening and so confident and at ease in front of an audience."

Unconvinced, she laughed again.

"Kathryn, every male in that conference room was enraptured. How could you not notice?"

The fox actually blushed pink. Shocking. His honest assessment of her performance flustered her confidence. Unpracticed at receiving compliments, she obviously struggled to come up with a response. Idiot husband. Undeserving. An ingrate. He drove her away by forcing her into a tedious lifestyle. Boredom the culprit. Domesticating Kathryn a losing battle. She prowled the park. Drawn to danger. The fox hunted thrills.

"Does Mr. Maller ever dress you up?" he asked knowingly treading on dangerous territory. Evoking her husband was forbidden. "Take you out. Show you off?"

He would. Take her out. A fine meal followed by slow dancing. Kathryn in his arms. What would she wear? Something sexy no doubt. Silk perhaps. Or leather. Kathryn's tight ass in a leather skirt. Heaven.

"What about Ainsley?" she snapped. "Do you dress her up? Show her off?"

"Don't worry about Ainsley," he soothed. "I made love to her last night, and she is finally content. It has been weeks since I've touched her willingly."

Kathryn's face dropped. Exactly the reaction he hoped for. His heart nearly leapt out of his chest in exultation.

Inspired by the idiot husband's love making skills, he returned home to his wife and spread her legs. It wasn't a complete re-enactment. Crude language upset her. He replaced the cog's graphic, intensely erotic murmurings with gentle, loving coaxing. It was work but good practice. And worth it. His wife was satiated. Ainsley's hyper-sensitivity mollified.

"How does that make you feel?" he probed. "Knowing I had sex with my wife?"

Kathryn shook her head violently. Unable to answer. Her hands tightly fisted as she crossed her arms across her chest.

"I'm sorry if I offended you," he said softly. "Poor Ainsley cannot compare. Every one of our morning trysts is burned in my memory. She is much more inhibited. My wife needs to feel loved.

Needs to feel coveted before she will relax and allow herself to orgasm. You are so much more wanton. So much more carnal. Ainsley has very girlish notions about romance."

Kathryn's chin set stubbornly. "I like romance."

He smiled knowingly and could not stop from touching her. He fingered the homemade necklace dangling around her neck. "Of course," he murmured. "Everyone likes romance."

He would have been happy to stay there forever, but her friend disturbed their tense sexual bubble. His eyes flew from Kathryn's face. Warning her of the friend's unwelcome approach. Kathryn jerked away. Night fell while they spoke. The parking lot's harsh lighting casted shadows.

Kathryn began by clearing her throat. "Sharon Hilliard, meet Jeff Dixon."

Sharon glowered. Suspicious. She carefully appraised his body language. "How do you do?" she said as she tightly gripped his hand and shook.

Confident. Sharon was no lamb.

"I was just telling Mrs. Maller how impressed I was by her argument. She is quite a force to be reckoned with."

"Yes," Sharon nodded. "She is. Her husband is very proud. If he wasn't at home attending to their three boys, he would have been at her side tonight. Danny never missed one of her debates in college. Loved watching her kick ass. I, other hand, preferred watching Danny kick ass. On the ice. Hockey is quite the blood sport, you know."

"You two went to school together?" he asked coyly. Ignoring her cloaked warning.

"All three of us went to school together," she corrected deliberately. "Katie, Katie's husband, Danny, and I graduated from the University of Wisconsin, Madison. Danny was there on a hockey scholarship. He was quite the campus star."

Katie? It was difficult to hide his distaste for the nickname. Kathryn was so *not* a Katie. How could Sharon not know this? How could her jock husband not know this? But most importantly, how could Kathryn not know this? He stared at Kathryn blankly. Searching for clues to the inner working of her mind.

195

"We should go," Kathryn said, alarmed at the approaching crowd of fellow gardeners. "We are meeting some friends for drinks."

"Have fun," he said as they turned to go. "It was a pleasure making your acquaintance."

Instead of moving away like he should, he lingered. Unwilling to part, he pulled his cell phone out and stalled. Straining to hear her conversation while pretending to check his messages.

"What did he want?" Sharon asked in a voice loud enough to be meant for his ears.

"He wanted to meet and talk about the garden," Kathryn murmured, showcasing his business card as evidence.

He smiled to himself when she slid the card into the rear pocket of her jeans. His name was plastered on the best piece of ass in town. Not the idiot husband.

"That's not all he wanted," Sharon sneered, throwing a threatening glance over her shoulder.

"You got that impression too, huh?" Kathryn snorted. "Thanks for coming to my rescue. Danny said the truck would have men crawlin' out of the woodwork."

Absurd. As if the decrepit truck could add to Kathryn's natural allure. Reluctantly, he pointed his feet towards his wife and moved.

Patience. Control. Logic. He used the gathered knowledge about her character to build a case. Winning, the only acceptable outcome. Failure, a tragedy.

Kathryn the vixen chaffed at the binds of congenial living. Setting her free was his heart's desire.

CHAPTER 37

WALLOWING

Margaritas at La Cocina was a distraction. Kate welcomed the meaningless talk and ordered iced tea. She wanted to keep a clear head. Her early morning meeting with Jeff Dixon remained in the back of her every thought. But, Kate managed to play along with Sharon's idea of lively conversation. The committee members were a surprisingly rowdy group. They got very loud, and no one cared that Kate remained sober.

After dropping Sharon off at her house, Kate drove home with her windows rolled down. The evening was cool, but she felt like she was suffocating. The smell of cigarette smoke and Mexican food permeated Kate's hair and clothes. She couldn't escape it.

When Sharon's chatter disappeared, the panic hit. Desperate to pull herself together, she thought through her options. Jeff Dixon was a lawyer, and she understood lawyers. Kate was going to reason with him.

Denying her attraction to Jeff Dixon was not helpful. But she couldn't face it. Not yet. Not tonight. Danny was foremost in her thoughts. Danny and the boys. Jeff Dixon was a threat. Ainsley Dixon was a victim.

Kate punished herself by visualizing Ainsley Dixon in her head. The woman was so naive and so very helpless. Even if Kate successfully drove Jeff Dixon away where would that leave poor Ainsley? Who would look after the wife's interests?

Kate wore her guilt like a leaden coat as she trudged up her driveway. She was so sorry. Wallowing in regret, she pushed open the door.

The sound of Marigold's nails on the ceramic tile in the back hall greeted her. The house was asleep. A soft glow came from the light above the kitchen sink, and Kate fell to her knees. Marigold whined. Her tail whacked Kate as she circled excitedly.

Kate smiled and shushed the animal. Taking her furry head into both hands, she looked into Marigold's loving gold eyes.

"Don't worry, sweet girl," she murmured. "I will always come home. I promise."

CHAPTER 38

FRENZY

Danny was startled awake by the breeze of shifting covers. She was naked. That was the first realization. The second, she was wet. Freshly showered. Kate smelled like soap.

"Baby," he sighed with a smile. "How was the Board meeting?"

Kate didn't answer. She fell on him. Her elbows pinned his shoulders to the mattress and her fingers braided roughly into his hair. Kate kissed him until the haze of sleep faded from his consciousness.

She was on her knees. Straddling his hips and pressing her chest into his. Danny ran his hands up her strong thighs and gripped her uplifted ass. He imagined her ass riding high. Exposed to the empty room and so tempting. He groaned beneath her persistent kiss and gripped her tighter. Spreading her ass cheeks apart, he imagined fucking it from behind. Tearing her apart. Making her cry out in agony.

Her cold, wet hair was a shock to his sleepy, warm skin, and he shuddered reflexively when she dragged her face down his naked chest. Sucking in a breath, he lifted his hips. Kate ripped his pajama bottoms off and dove for his cock.

It was too much. Waking up out of a dead sleep, her naked body on top of his, her mouth wrapped around his erection. Kate's forehead slammed into his abdomen as she sucked noisily. Her chilly right hand gripped the base of his shaft. It was too much.

He cursed before desperately clutching at the bedding. He yanked the pillow out from beneath his head and muffled his cries with it. It was sweet torture.

Kate's release was just as sudden as her attack, and it left him gasping. When she came down hard on his cock, he cried out again. She was ramming him. Impaling herself on his erection. Tearing the pillow away from his face, he looked up at her in utter disbelief.

"Kate," he moaned. "My God."

He tried to slow her down. Restraining her hips, he cursed again. She growled and smacked his hands away. Danny struggled to see her face, to read her eyes, but the wet hair, and the darkness of night made it impossible. Grasping, his hands moved to her face. He wanted to pull the hair away, look at his wife. But she cried out in frustration and gripped his wrists with strong tenacious fingers.

Danny gave up. Kate pinned his arms above his head and went to work. He focused on the glorious pull of gravity. Her tits rocked in rhythm with her ruthless fucking. He was afraid to move, afraid to disrupt her concentration. So, he opened his mouth and hoped her tits would graze his wet lips and very willing tongue. Danny was forgotten in her frenzy.

And it suited him fine.

CHAPTER 39

'PERSONAL JOURNEY'

Kate slept hard. The warning click of the alarm woke her, but Kate preferred to stay in the shadow of Danny's hulking body.

His hot breath caressed her neck, and his twitching hand lay possessively across her hip. Kate smiled sleepily at the sensation. Danny was alternately loosening and tightening his grip in his dreams. Kate also felt Marigold's stare. The dog sat sentry at the side of the bed. Knowing she would not have to brave Jeff Dixon alone, Kate summoned her courage and opened her eyes.

Marigold's enthusiasm for their morning run was enough to set her in motion. The streets were quiet, and she felt better—more like herself—as she ran with her dog through the neighborhood. Kate forgot her surroundings and autopilot steered her towards the park. Lulled into hypnotic concentration by the thud of her falling footsteps, she silently prepared for her confrontation.

Kate framed her argument around one key point. Their affair, like most extra-marital affairs, was doomed to failure. Convincing Jeff Dixon of this simple fact was her first task. Second, she needed to elicit his cooperation in containing the wreckage. Minimizing the damage to both their families was paramount.

Marigold's mood changed as soon as they set foot into the park. Her ears went back, and she lowered her tail. The dog's natural instincts were to follow, and she kept pace with her new owner. But Kate could sense the worry. The memory of abandonment still haunted Marigold, so Kate pulled the leash taut in reminder. Marigold belonged to her. Marigold could trust her new home.

The sun was breaking over the horizon, but the haze of the chilly night still clung in the steep valleys of the park. The cool air was moist and the perfect antidote to Kate's hot breath and thundering pulse. The sky was lit with threads of pale color forecasting a beautiful spring day. Kate allowed herself to be hopeful— allowed herself to be optimistic.

Jeff Dixon was at the fishing pier waiting. Leaning against the railing, he smiled at her from beneath his ball cap and waved. His posture was relaxed—non-combative. A good place to start.

Kate didn't slow down. Her feet left the jogging trail, and she flew down the grassy hill with Marigold faithfully at her side. Jeff Dixon's cheeks were a contrasting pink to the dark stubble of his morning beard. His mouth was pulled into a crooked grin and his raven eyes sparked—not with passion but with happiness. He was glad to see her.

Kate's stomach lurched—her task was daunting and fear crept into her thinking. Shoving her emotions to the side, she set her hands on her hips, kept her eyes downcast, and used her breathlessness as an excuse to remain silent.

"Good morning," he began. "I see you've got yourself a jogging partner."

"Marigold," Kate said, tugging on her leash.

The dog sat instantly. She looked up at Kate before turning her gaze on Jeff Dixon.

"She cleaned up nicely," he said, nodding with approval. "I bet your boys are enjoying her. How has she adapted? Has she assimilated into your household?"

Kate was confused by his genuine interest. Jeff Dixon's sincerity was disarming.

"Yes," Kate answered as she reached down to scratch Marigold behind the ears. "She's a part of the family now."

"Lucky girl," he said softly.

Marigold cocked her head and then wagged her tail reluctantly. They walked together to the end of the pier. Marigold was on high alert, searching for ducks and critters in the tall, swampy grass surrounding the perimeter of the pond. Kate let out the slack in Marigold's leash and leaned over the railing. Looking up at the dark houses on the hill opposite the fishing pier, she took a deep breath and began.

"I apologize if I've hurt you, Jeff," she said. "I take responsibility for my actions. It was reckless and stupid. But you must know—please try to understand—I will never leave Danny."

"Don't apologize, Kathryn," Jeff said as he peered at her profile. "You've saved my life. I'm grateful."

"I'm sorry," she said looking down at her hands. "I can't continue to see you. I've met your wife. I know the names of your children. It's over."

"It's not over," he said in a voice so soft it was almost inaudible. "Your journey has just begun. I'm further along, but you will catch up. I'm leaving my wife, Kathryn."

"Jeff," Kate was pleading. "Please don't do that. Not for me."

"I'm not doing it for you," he said. "I'm doing it for me and for Ainsley. I've re-evaluated my life, and I need to stop compartmentalizing. It's self-destructive and unfair. Unfair to Ainsley, most of all. She deserves a man who can honestly make her happy. It's not me. It's too much work. Being with Ainsley is like trying to fit a square peg in a round hole."

"So that's it?" Kate snapped. "You're going to break Ainsley's heart. And then what? Where do you think your personal journey will end? Because, I can tell you with certainty—this thing—this connection between you and I—will not lead to happily ever after."

"Do not misunderstand me," Jeff warned as he pushed himself upright. "I am not breezily overlooking the pain my leaving will cause my wife and kids. I understand the consequences of my actions. I'm not a bad man. I will always love Ainsley, and I intend to participate in the lives of our children. But our marriage is a festering wound. It will kill both of us. I've got to lance it. Let it bleed. Of course, it will hurt like hell, but it's the only way we get out of this situation alive."

Kate covered her face with her hands. "Poor Ainsley," she moaned.

"Ainsley will heal," he said. "She is a lot stronger than she looks. I will take all the blame. Assure her it was not her fault."

Standing upright, Kate looked Jeff squarely in the eyes. "The guilt for the part I've played in destroying her family is crushing. I can't bear it."

"I understand," Jeff said, smiling slightly. "But you will heal too. It will just take time."

Kate shook her head and locked onto his dark eyes. "I will never leave my family. I love Danny. I love my life."

Jeff raised one eyebrow. "No, Kathryn. People who love their lives do not have sex with strangers in the park. It was a diversion from the banal aspect of your daily life. It was the same for me. Escapism was how we coped. But I've decided to escape for real. And it's a relief, Kathryn."

Kate began carefully. "Wrecking two families will have consequences. The reality of those consequences will burden our relationship with disappointed expectations, guilt, and distrust."

A smile crept across Jeff's face. He looked at her in the same way he looked at her at the Village Board Meeting. He was impressed.

"I'm not asking you to leave your husband," he said. "For right now, I'm only asking you to give me a chance. I know you feel it too. You've already admitted to it. You call it 'this thing,' but I call it a soul connection. It's powerful. Like nothing I've ever experienced."

"You're confused," she said in an even tone. "What we have is great sex, and it's not a solid foundation for a future."

Jeff laughed before reaching out to stroke her arm. "Our physical connection is one part of the whole. Great sex is the product of our attraction—not the cause."

Kate gazed down at the fingers of his hand. His touch was tender. Not meant to seduce but to comfort. It still sent a thrill up her spine. She was ashamed to admit her weakness. She knew his name. She knew his wife. She knew the names of his children, yet she still craved his touch. Squaring her shoulders, she acknowledged the holes in her own character and faced them head on.

"I'm sorry, Jeff. It's over."

Sighing heavily, Jeff removed his hand. "I'm sorry, too."

He reached into the pocket of his shorts and pulled out his cell phone. Gazing down at the screen, he punched at the buttons.

"I wish you wouldn't make me do this," he said. "But you've given me no other choice."

Pursing his lips into a severe frown, he held the tiny screen out for Kate. The faces were unclear, but she recognized her own voice. The crying, the whines, the pleading, as Jeff Dixon spread her legs wide and delved his hand deep inside. The outbuilding. He fucked her with his hand first and then bent her over the windowless ledge overlooking the park.

Shocked and betrayed, she clenched her eyes shut and fought the urge to scream. Losing control would be a huge mistake. She needed time to think —time to plan.

"Tomorrow night," Jeff said. "Meet me here at 9:00. I'm going to take you somewhere. Somewhere private."

"Okay," Kate said—her knees weakened in surrender. "Tomorrow."

CHAPTER 40

THE GETAWAY

After printing off the boarding passes, he erased the hard drive on his home computer. He organized his family's itinerary in a file folder and collapsed in the chair behind his desk. His personal records and files were already packed. Stowed in his getaway car. All vital business taken care of. His relief was coupled with bitter sadness.

The children could sense something amiss. Their mother disappeared when he arrived home early from work. He made them dinner. Grilled cheese sandwiches with carrot sticks. They stayed close to him. Closer than usual. Normal behavior he reasoned. Their mother could not be trusted. Not at the moment. Her emotional state too erratic.

It broke his heart. With their mother wrecked in the bedroom, he felt unduly close to his children. Hurting them the final act. Necessary but still incredibly painful.

Picking up the file folder, he trudged upstairs. He walked down the narrow hallway alone. His children tucked in bed. The stories he read before kissing them good night rolled around in his head. The glow of their night lights reflected into the hall. Warding off bad dreams. The night lights illuminated his footsteps.

When he opened the door of their bedroom suite, he found his wife sprawled across the couch set beneath their window. Her cell phone pressed tightly to her ear. Still talking. Probably her sister. Her family too far away. It was a tragic scene. His wife's round face red and puffy. Tissues strewn on the carpet. He set himself on the bed and waited.

His wife snapped her phone shut and laid it across her soft stomach. Supporting her head with her arm, she searched their wooded backyard. It was dark. Nothing to see.

"Daddy told me to stay," she said keeping her eyes on the black glass of the window. Her weak reflection peered back helplessly. "He thinks I am giving up too soon."

"What do you want to do?" he asked.

"I want to go home," she gasped and fought tears. "My momma. My sister. They're all in Kentucky."

He nodded. There was nothing else to say. She knew. Her snooping uncovered the illicit sex video on his computer. He regretted leaving it there. It was stupid. The pain unnecessary. She needn't have known about his infidelity. But it was too late. His carelessness embarrassing.

"Do you think I should go?" she asked. Still not looking at him.

He exhaled loudly. He had told her the marriage was over. No need for professional counseling. It didn't work out. Time to move on. But still, she wanted his advice. Needed his approval. His counsel.

"I think you should take the kids and go home," he said as gently as could. "You will need your family. Ainsley, honey, please look at me."

Wiping the tears away, she kept her eyes downcast but at least turned her face towards his.

"You need to be strong," he said sternly. "The kids must be your priority. They need you. Are you listening to me? Honey, do you understand what I am saying?"

She nodded. "Yes. The children. My priorities."

"We will talk later about the conditions of our separation. Now is not a good time to be making big decisions about residence. I know you love your family but don't think about moving quite yet.

We'll give it some time. Let the sting wear off before we sort out the particularities of our eventual divorce. I won't fight you. This was my fault. I will do whatever you need."

"Jeff," she cried. More tears. "Are you sure?"

He moaned internally. This road again. It was done. The hysterics growing tiresome. Standing up, he walked over and sat on the edge of the chair next to the couch.

"I printed off your boarding passes," he said, handing her the folder. "I also put an itinerary inside. I've arranged for a car service to pick you and the kids up at 9:00 a.m. tomorrow. Ainsley, are you listening?"

She nodded weakly and opened the folder blindly.

"Check your bags with the porter at the airport. Tip him, Ainsley. Five dollars a bag. Do you have enough cash?"

Looking up at him, she blinked. Vacant. He reached into his back pocket and pulled out his billfold. Unfolding the money, he set it inside the folder.

"You will have to ask someone at the airport which gate the plane is departing from. Get through security as soon as you arrive. Don't dawdle."

"Thank you, Jeff," she said meekly.

"I e-mailed your flight information to your sister. She will meet you at the airport in Louisville and help you with the bags and children. Power up your cell phone overnight and make sure you turn it on as soon as you walk off the plane. It's a precaution. In case your sister can't find you."

He stood. It was too painful to look at her. He turned way. Gave her his back. He wanted to run. Get away from her. Patience. Responsibilities first.

"Is there anything else you need?" he asked, looking at the bedroom door. "Before I go?"

"Could you get the luggage from the basement?" she sniffled.

"Yes," he said already in motion. "Of course."

Checking his watch, he flew down the stairs. He still had an hour before picking up Kathryn at the park. Plenty of time to help his wife pack.

CHAPTER 41

TANGLED

Kate was restless. But Marigold was the only one who noticed. She scurried behind as Kate went room to room—picking up strewn shoes—wiping down already clean surfaces—sweeping the kitchen floor for the second time since dinner.

The boys were in bed. She checked. Peter was reading a book. Both Joey and Billy were asleep. It was time. She donned her running gear and strode to the back door. Danny was at the kitchen table paying bills on his laptop. He was muttering to himself.

"I'm going for a run," she called out. When Danny did not lift his head, she added her excuses. "I'm leaving Marigold. She's pretty worn out from playing ball in the backyard. I was busy today, and I think she needs a rest from trailing me."

Danny raised his hand and waved without looking in her direction. "Have a good run, babe."

She flew out the door before he could think to ask questions. Kate felt like her body was strung with thousands of tiny frayed wires. The closer she got to the park the more frazzled she became. She was strangely emotional. Vacillating wildly, she wanted to scream in outrage one minute, and then wanted to wail in despair the next. She imagined killing him more than once—a crime of passion. It wasn't smart, and she reasoned her way out—vowed to take one day at time, to dig herself out of the hole she created.

He wasn't at the pier. The baseball diamonds were lit, and the parking lot was crowded. Noise from the little league games drifted down to the pond. Kate paced a length of grass in front of the ice skating shed. She wasn't alone at the pier. There were high school kids kidding around and climbing on the railings. Kate decided to wait on the jogging trail. The laughter the kids were generating was too grating.

She saw him coming over the hill from the direction of the baseball diamonds. He was walking on the jogging trail. His hands loosely stuffed in the front pockets of his jeans. The breeze shifted, and the hair blew away from his face. Jeff's loose-fitting button-down flowed against the clean line of his shoulders. He wore glasses. The same ones he had worn at the Village Board Meeting. His frame was distinctively v-shaped. Wide shoulders and a narrow runner's waist—lean and muscular—lovely.

Kate jogged to meet him—unwilling to watch his approach.

"I'm sorry," he began. "Have you been waiting long?"

"No," she said curtly. "There were kids at the pier."

"I brought my car," he said, turning on his heel he directed her towards the parking lot with a long arm.

"Where are you taking me?"

"Well," he said looking up at the stars. "I was actually thinking about getting some ice cream. Mint chocolate chip. It's my drug of choice. I had a hard day. Ainsley went through my computer files and found the video of you and me."

Kate gripped his arm in horror, but he kept moving forward—dragging her along. "No, Jeff," she cried.

"Don't worry," he said, patting her hand. "She doesn't know it was you. The picture was distorted, and the lighting was poor. My filmmaking abilities are very rudimentary. I don't know why I was keeping it. It was stupid. I erased it off the hard drive. I never meant for anyone else to see it."

"What did you tell her? Is she okay? Oh God, I'm so sorry."

"I slept in the guest room last night. I was tired and didn't have the patience to deal with her needy pawing. My moodiness finally pushed her over the edge. She spent the night fishing through my desk. She caught me before I left for work. She was screeching. It was difficult to understand her at first, but I got the gist after a few incoherent minutes," he chuckled bitterly.

"I told her the affair was over. Assured her it had been for weeks. I apologized for hurting her. She seemed to believe me. Not that it really matters. Our marriage is over. I checked into a hotel close to work, but it's just for the night. She is taking the kids and going home to Kentucky. I doubt she will ever come back to Chicago. She never wanted to leave her family in the first place."

Jeff stopped at the passenger door of his SUV. He held the door open for Kate and smiled weakly. The sight of his tired, sad eyes struck her hard. She was sympathetic. And not for Ainsley. Kate quickly reminded herself that she was being blackmailed. *She hated him.*

Narrowing her eyes, she frowned before climbing into the SUV. "I'm not going for ice cream, Jeff. This is not a date."

He sighed. "Fine."

Kate adjusted herself in the soft leather seat, and Jeff gently closed the door behind her. He jogged around the front of the vehicle. He was graceful—his stride was loping and casual. Danny didn't jog. He ran and always like he was wearing skates on his feet.

When Jeff turned the key in the ignition, classic rock blared from the radio, and he quickly switched the music off. His hands moved to the gear shift between the seats, and he glided the SUV out of the parking lot. Her red ponytail holder was no longer on his wrist. It was around the gear shift. She stared at it warily as they drove past the bright lights of Roosevelt Road. Jeff signaled, and they were suddenly absorbed into the freeway traffic. Speeding up, Jeff kept his left hand on the wheel and his right hand set loosely on top of the gear shift. She had never noticed his fingers before. They were long and lean like his frame, and the nails were neatly filed—the hands of a lawyer.

"What are you thinking?" he asked, glancing carefully in her direction.

"I'm thinking about how much I hate you," she replied coolly.

"I understand. You have a lot reasons to hate me," he said but then added quietly—more to himself than to her. "Hate us."

After fifteen minutes of stubborn silence, he exited the freeway and pulled into a residence suites hotel. Kate froze in her seat—overwhelmed with panic. Jeff parked the SUV. He pulled the keys out of the ignition and turned to smile patiently at her.

"Kathryn," he said, his brow furrowed with worry. "Are you all right?"

"Please," she begged.

Kate gripped the leather seat. The lights of the dash slowly faded as did the automatic headlights of Jeff's fancy SUV, and her stomach sank. Inhaling in a quick pant, she shook her head from side to side. Her ponytail violently whipped her face. Jeff wrapped his warm palm around her neck. He stroked at the tension—shushing her like a baby.

"I can't do it," she gasped pleading with her eyes. "Don't make me go inside. Jeff, please, I can't. No, please."

Kate gulped—swallowing down a mouthful of air. A hotel—long hallways—beds. Lying down with Jeff Dixon. Finally naked—tangled in blankets.

She shook her head again and whined. No. Her pulse thundered through her veins. She was losing it—losing control. *Danny. Jeff.* Her thoughts flashed like a strobe light. The thick mist of predawn—the park. The bedroom. Danny—cool sheets. Danny's warm breath. Danny's hand twitched—her naked hip. Naked. *Danny. Jeff.* The touch of bare skin.

"Kathryn, calm down," Jeff soothed. He put the key back in the ignition and started the SUV. "I brought you here because it's private. I didn't mean to offend you."

Kate nodded and loosened her grip on the seat. She closed her eyes and shoved her fears to the back of her thoughts. *Danny. She loved Danny.*

"My office is close by," he said staring out the windshield. "It's empty. Is that okay?"

Kate nodded her consent, and they were off again.

"Thank you, Jeff," she said not intending to weight the words with so much sincerity.

"I hate upsetting you, Kathryn," he said, reaching over to tuck a loose strand of hair behind her ear.

His finger tip grazed her neck, and she sucked in a breath. Her nerves were so raw—she thrilled at the sensation. She felt everything and ached. Looking at his strong profile from beneath her eyelashes, the heat built. Not panic—a slow burn seeped down her spine—settled between her legs. She wanted him. She needed to satisfy the craving—the unbearable thirst—the hunger. Get him out of her system. Purge the need. Reason would return. But first, she needed to fuck him. And not on a bed.

"How much further?" she demanded.

Jeff reached for her hand and pulled it into his lap—held it against his thigh. He felt it too. It was burning in the glassy black pools of his eyes. He accelerated. The powerful engine purred, hurling them past slower traffic.

"Not long now," he murmured. "Ten minutes, Kathryn."

"Ten minutes," she repeated.

Kate stared at her hand—enveloped warmly in his soft grip. She thought about pulling away. But she was afraid. If she freed her hand, it might find its way to the hair curling at his neck—maybe to the soft fabric of his cotton shirt—maybe to his waistband. The thought of touching him without restraint made her heart stutter. So her hand remained where it was, and she watched the clock.

Ten minutes.

CHAPTER 42

STRIDE FOR STRIDE

He released her hand to shift the vehicle into park, and she leapt. In one swift movement, she was outside. Kathryn the fox. Rounding the hood. Her figure drew mysteriously across the hollow parking structure. He took his glasses off and hurried to join her. She was alone. They were alone. The empty space echoed.

He gripped her hand. Familiar now. It folded easily into his. The elevator. He lengthened his stride. Prepared to tow her if necessary. But she kept pace. Of course. Kathryn met him stride for stride. The doors opened immediately.

They both exhaled in relief and jumped over the threshold. He punched the number of his office floor. The doors barely had time to close. She was on him that quickly. Pressed up against the paneled wall of the elevator, he struggled against the temptation. Lightning. The burn. Kathryn's breath was heavy. Her hands searching. She tore at his shirt. Freed it from his waistband.

He caught her by the wrists and shushed her. Kathryn whined. Impatient. She strained. Fighting. Overpowering her, he pushed at her stubborn weight. Like two magnets. Only brute force could separate them. Keeping her at arm's length, he walked her to the opposite wall. Staring into her hazel eyes. Not green. Not brown. They made their own color. He pinned her wrists to sides of her face. Her breathing slowed. Her pouty mouth fell open slightly. And he dove.

The elevator shot to the twenty-ninth floor, but he dove down. Into the depths of her mouth. So hot. Locked together, their mouths sealed. Her lips so full. So luscious. She sucked the air from his mouth. No escape. He felt the thrill of breathlessness.

The elevator doors slid open, and they stumbled through. Their lips still locked. Fused. Scorched. Her hips pressed against his erection. She sought it out. Their forward motion slammed into the glass entryway of his firm.

"Fuck," he cursed.

His keycard. He unwound his arms from around her waist and searched blindly for his billfold. Kathryn hung on. Her hands clawed at his neck. She kissed his bottom lip. Pulled at it. Ran her tongue along it.

Their bodies swung in with the door. It was dark. Too dark, and he lurched for the light panel. Taking Kathryn with him. His lips desperate for hers. He pounded on the switch. Lights went on randomly throughout the floor.

He led her towards his office. Like a dance. They never broke their embrace. Kathryn kicked off her running shoes. A moan escaped from his lips. Her clothes. He couldn't wait and stopped their progress. The jacket had to go. Pressing his forehead to hers, he sighed and drew the zipper down with careful fingers. A running tank. A deep blue running tank. Her breasts crushed beneath the tight fabric. Her hard nipples. Straining.

"Kathryn," he moaned into her mouth.

She gasped and jerked backwards. The slightest pressure. So delicious. Her tits between his thumbs and forefingers.

"You like that," he sighed as he pushed her backwards.

"Yes," she whined. "God, yes."

A desk. Someone's desk acted as an anchor. Papers scattered to the floor. Yanking at her jacket, he drew it across her naked shoulders and down her arms.

"Let's have it off," he demanded as he tossed it to the floor. "All of it, Kathryn."

She blinked. But quickly righted herself. Looking him squarely in the eyes, she moved her hands to the hem of her tank. And then it was gone. Her breasts fell away. Free. She set one hand on his shoulder and picked up her leg. One at a time, she tugged off her socks. Barefoot. Kathryn's natural state. And he smiled.

Hair escaped her ponytail. So he smoothed it back before gently kissing her lips. He knew how to release her unruly locks. And he did so. Jubilantly.

"So beautiful," he whispered as he buried his face into her neck.

Her scent tangy. Like citrus. Maybe lemon or grapefruit. Lotion. Not perfume. Kathryn shimmied off her running shorts. And she was naked. Beneath his hands she was totally exposed. His eyes flew to his office door. It was a short distance. They could make it.

Pulling her into his arms, he held her close. Breathing in her scent. Luxuriating in her hair. He directed backwards. She went willingly. Letting him guide, she concentrated her attention on the buttons of his shirt. He helped by shrugging it off. But she wasn't satisfied.

She pulled at his undershirt and grunted. "Off."

It joined his discarded cotton oxford. The palms of her hands stroked his chest. Ran over the muscles of his arms and shoulders. Taut from holding her so close. He groaned and looked up at the ceiling tiles when they slammed into the door of his office. Forged together. Melded. Her hips ground into his. Small, elegant, circular motions. Her right hand moved between her legs. And she stroked his erection before moving to the fly of his jeans.

"Kathryn," he moaned again as he kicked off his shoes. "I want you."

"Yes," she agreed.

Her hand moved inside his jeans. Along the waist. Beneath the elastic of his boxers. She gripped his bare ass. Welded together this way, he searched the front pocket of his jeans and pulled out his keys. Fumbling through the haze of desire, he found it. The keys clanked against the glass door. And they burst through.

Somehow his jeans found their way to his ankles. Impeding his movement. He kicked them off. Sighing with relief, he ran his hands over the bare skin of her back. And she did the same. Connected at the hips, their naked bodies formed a perfect union. Two forms carved from a single stone. Like a marble statue. Sculpted lovers. They kissed openmouthed. Her tongue flicked his. And played chase. Back and forth. They sought each other out.

Tired of the game, Kathryn whined impatiently and wrenched herself free. Her sharp eyes flew across the shadowy office and landed on the leather couch. She pushed him. Until he was seated in the deep cushions. Kathryn climbed on top. Straddling his hips with her knees, she positioned herself over his erection. She came down with a huff. So wet. So hot. His heart's desire. Kathryn the vixen. Inside Kathryn. Her throbbing hot flesh.

"Fuck me," he encouraged. Gripping her ass.

The pupils of her eyes widened. Her brow furrowed. And she rocked. She rode him. The air between them became thick with the smell of sex. Her scent. Rich and sweet. He groaned. He could taste it. The sensual fragrance. So very potent.

He sucked in a breath. Shored his strength. He wanted to take his time. He was determined to hold back. He concentrated on her flushed cheeks. The curve of her collarbone. The line of her shoulders. Kathryn's arms went to the back of the couch. She got a firm grip and used her upper body strength to grind herself roughly into his lap.

"Kathryn," he groaned again.

"Suck them," she ordered as she shoved her tits into his mouth. "Like before. Pinch me. Harder."

He closed his eyes in restraint. She wasn't making it easy. His whole body was overcome. Ready to burst, he obeyed her order. Concentrated on her ascent. Focused on her pleasure. She increased her speed. The intensity never faltered. And finally, she stiffened. Arched beneath his hands. Her flesh quivered. Release. Sweet release. She whimpered quietly as he stroked her back.

"Shh, Kathryn," he soothed.

He kissed her eyelids. Her little nose. Her pinked cheeks. Holding her face between his hands, he touched his forehead to hers when her breathing quieted.

"Say my name," he murmured.

She pulled away. Her chin set.

"Say my name," he said firmly.

"No."

Fury raged in his chest. Kathryn. So stubborn. She would not relent. Would not make the slightest concession. He shoved her off his lap. And she fell. But Kathryn did not stay down. She was up again before he could stand. Taking her by the shoulders, he looked deeply into her hazel eyes.

"Kathryn," he warned.

"No." She defiantly shook her head.

He flew at her. His polished wood desk was their pyre. His work papers scattered. Kathryn's flailing arms knocked everything that got in the way to the floor. His desk lamp crashed. It was fuel. The chaotic noise fed the fire. He pulled at her hips until she was hanging over the edge. Kathryn moved her feet to the desk. She spread herself wide. She reached for him with tenacious fingers. Vixen. She wanted more.

He pounded into her flesh. She cried out when he fell upon her. Buried his face into her neck. A love bite. A mark. For the idiot husband. He wrapped his mouth around the tender skin and sucked mercilessly. Kathryn squirmed and wrenched free.

"No," she cried. She yanked at his hair.

"Aaah!" Licking his lips, he stared down into her desperate eyes. "Say it." He wrapped his hands around her wrists and pinned them above her head. "Say my name. Say. It. Now."

Kathryn took a tiny breath. "Jeff," she whispered.

It was enough. He loosened his grip. His touch gentled, and he cupped her breasts in each hand. Running a thumb over the hard tips, he made love to her.

Kathryn hands lay loosely over his forearms. The fight gone. Surrender. She kept her eyes open. Her face soft.

And she whispered. Over and over. *Jeff, Jeff.* Faster. More urgently as she began to climb again. He kept rhythm. Never stopped. Never quickened. Slow, long strokes into her luscious body. Kathryn the fox came apart at the seams and exploded beneath his own hands. Under his command. Twice. He made her cum twice.

Ecstasy. Kathryn gave him what he wanted. What he needed. His name. Whispered so deliciously. She gave it up. Finally. *Jeff.* And he came soon after. His scent. Her scent. Intermingled. He breathed it in. Filled his lungs.

"Kathryn," he moaned.

"Jeff," she answered.

Heaven.

CHAPTER 43

HITTING HOME

She had crossed a dangerous line. Lying prone—spread—on his desk, she closed her eyes after she came—after he came—he stroked her skin. It was tender and intimate. She lay still—eyes shut—calculating.

Her appetite for everything Jeff Dixon was weakness. She knew how to discipline weakness, and that was how she would beat him. She would beat him like a bad habit.

"You're bleeding," Jeff said.

His hands stroked her inner thighs as he gently withdrew himself from her. Mortified, her eyes flew open.

"It's okay," Jeff reassured her. "It doesn't bother me."

He was not the least bit perturbed—the nature of womanhood inoffensive. Giving her a hand, he helped her to a sitting position.

His dark eyes searched her own. "How do you feel? You look a little dazed."

Kate didn't answer. Instead, she hopped off the desk. Jeff steadied her wobbling legs before walking with her towards a narrow door.

"The bathroom," he said. "Go ahead and freshen up. I'll run to the ladies room. I'm sure we have supplies."

Jeff flicked on the bathroom light, and they both cringed. It was bright, and their reflexes were not yet quick enough to tolerate the suddenness of change. Kate peeked at him through a veil of messy hair. She was still embarrassed, but Jeff wasn't, and it made it easier.

"Thank you," she said.

She stepped off the thick carpeting and onto the cold ceramic tile. The temperature was a shock. Kate folded in on herself and jumped on her tip toes. When she looked up, she caught Jeff's smile before he could turn his back.

Running a hand absentmindedly through his hair, he gazed at the wreckage of his office. The look on his face made him appear younger than his years. For a split second, Kate felt it too. The trilling of youthful abandon sang through her veins. But quickly—before she could register her emotions—she shut the door.

Kate avoided the mirror. Ducking her head, she washed her face with harsh soap and rinsed with cold water. She was naked and alone in Jeff Dixon's private bathroom. She knew—at the very least—he was a partner in this obviously prestigious law firm. It was so ironic she laughed. But his quiet knock quickly wiped the smile off her face.

"Kathryn?"

Reaching a long arm through the crack of the door, she snatched the pile of feminine sanitary products from his hand. Two tampons and a plastic-wrapped pad. Before she could close the door, he leaned into the bathroom and set her clothes on the edge of the sink. They were neatly folded in a pile.

"I thought you might be cold," he said before disappearing.

He was considerate. It meant nothing, and she shoved her feelings of gratitude aside. She gave up a little of herself tonight. He couldn't deny it. It was time he gave her something in return.

When she stepped back into the office, Kate was sure she was strong enough to face him. But she wasn't. Jeff Dixon was barefoot and bare-chested as he picked up the mess off the floor. His beauty assaulted her sensibilities, and she was struck silent. Streamlined and sleek, the tightly knit muscles of his back and shoulders were not overworked. They were contoured by consistent jogging and nothing else. Lean, trim, and perfectly masculine, the sight of him sent an ice cold bullet through Kate's heart.

Before he could turn his raven eyes on her, Kate strode past his desk and to the wall of windows facing east. The lights of Chicago's distant skyline blinked on the horizon. The night was a dangerous blue-black, and she was shocked to see bolts of lightning in the distance. Still far off, she could not hear thunder. But the storm was approaching, and her thoughts went to home.

"Lightning," she said quietly.

Jeff walked up from behind and gazed out the window. "They were predicting thundershowers."

Kate dropped her gaze from the horizon to the wood credenza behind Jeff's desk. Chrome picture frames in an assortment of sizes lined the polished wood. She picked up the largest. Tilting it towards the indirect light coming from the bathroom, she examined the photograph. Ainsley and Jeff were dressed in formal attire and posing with the governor of Illinios. Kate dragged her admiring eyes away from Jeff Dixon in a fitted black tuxedo, and focused on Ainsley. She wore a floor length, lavender gown. Complete with sparkling diamonds, she was the elegant wife of an important man.

"Ainsley is beautiful," Kate said, holding out the photograph as evidence.

Jeff was smart enough to say nothing. He lifted his eyebrows and waited.

"I could never compete," she added.

At this, he snorted a curt laugh. "I don't want you to."

"What do you want then?" Kate asked, peering into the dark depths of his eyes.

"I want you to sit down next to me. Let's talk." Jeff walked over to his leather couch and plopped into the cushions with an exaggerated sigh.

"I have to get home," Kate warned.

He pulled his phone out of the front pocket of his jeans and waved it enticingly at her. "Give me a couple minutes."

Frowning, Kate snatched the white T-shirt draped carelessly over his desk chair and tossed it at him.

"Get dressed first," she negotiated stubbornly.

Jeff's face broke into a wide grin. "Why? Am I making you uncomfortable?"

Clenching her teeth, Kate breathed through her nose. She weighted her words with hostility. "I could lie, but what's the use? Obviously, I'm attracted. Obviously, I can't resist you," Kate rolled her eyes. "So, please, put your shirt on."

He laughed. It was the throaty laugh of a serious man. He threw the T-shirt over his head before shrugging on his oxford. He left it open. Like his jeans, his shirt was left unbuttoned. Kate yanked the hair away from her face, took a deep breath, and sat on the couch.

Jeff held out his phone. "Take it."

Kate took the phone with hesitant fingers. It wasn't familiar technology and not really a phone. It was a handheld computer with a beach scene as a screensaver.

"The Cayman Islands," he said when he noticed her interest. "Have you ever been?"

"Nope," Kate said, keeping her eyes on the miniature screen. "It looks beautiful."

"I travel there for work," he said, throwing an arm along the back of the couch. "It's my favorite beach."

Kate snorted. "I can't imagine having a favorite beach. I love them all."

She felt his eyes examining her face. But she didn't look at him. Frowning at the device in her palm, she pursed her lips and pressed the only visible button. Flashy icons blossomed across the screen.

Jeff leaned his head over her shoulder. "Camera," he directed.

Kate looked up into his eyes.

"Touch the icon with your finger," he added. "I'd do it, but I thought you'd prefer to erase the file yourself."

Kate accessed the file by following his directions and sighed with relief after hitting delete. Jeff was right. The picture quality was very poor, but it was her voice, her moans and cries, and she was glad to be rid of the concrete evidence.

"Do you have other copies?" she asked, handing him the phone.

"No," he replied. "You have no reason to believe me. I betrayed your trust, and I am sorry, Kathryn. It was wrong. Very ungentlemanly. But at the time, I was desperately gathering evidence to prove you were not a fantasy. Please accept my apology."

"You pride yourself on being a gentleman," Kate challenged.

"Yes, I do," he said defensively.

"You forced me here, Jeff," Kate reminded him sternly. "Is blackmail the act of a gentleman?"

"I suppose you've got me on that one," he said softly.

Drawing gentle fingers through the hair falling around her face, he smoothed out the tangled mess. Kate tried to implore him with her eyes. But she was ignored. He was concentrating intently as he tidied her appearance with delicate fingers.

"Can I ask you a question?" he asked—his face suddenly playful.

Kate nodded. She was too distracted by the sensation of his hands in her hair to speak.

"What is that scent you are wearing?" he asked. "I can't pick it out, and it's driving me crazy."

Kate sighed at the easiness of the inquiry. "My lotion?" she smiled. "Citrus Mistress."

Jeff laughed his throaty laugh, and Kate smiled back warily.

"It smells like vacation," she shrugged.

"I like it," he said—nuzzling his nose into her neck. Inhaling deeply, he made a contented noise. "It's subtle. And natural. Very organic. Like you."

"I wish you wouldn't say things like that," Kate said, cringing and moving away.

"Like what?"

"Things that make it sound like you know me," Kate let her head fall against the back of the couch. "You don't."

Jeff mirrored her movements. His head fell back, and he gazed at her from beneath thick, jet black eyelashes. He was so relaxed—so casual.

"Oh, I think you'd be surprised at how well I know you, Mrs. Maller," he smirked.

Kate righted herself and turned towards him. Pulling one leg beneath her, she made an inviting gesture.

"Surprise me, Mr. Dixon," she challenged.

"It might scare you," he warned. His eyes glinted with mischief, and Kate's pulse raced. He was pulling her in again. Seducing her into the dark depths of his eyes. Steeling her backbone, she gestured again.

"I'm waiting," she taunted.

Jeff shook his head and gave her a worried glance.

Taking a deep breath, he began, "A farm girl…you've never outgrown your working class roots. You always do your best and pride yourself on being useful. Able to juggle many things at once, you are a very good housewife and mother. But the tedious nature of your work leaves you dissatisfied. You are very smart. Smarter than most people, and it makes you impatient. You don't suffer fools. And because of this, you come across as stand-offish, aloof, and stuck up. But it doesn't bother you because you are unwilling to become a member of the herd. You are not a pack animal. Kathryn—you are a loner. You crave independence. You love your children and are fiercely protective, but at the same time, you resent them."

Jeff stopped his analysis. His eyes swept over her face. He was gauging her reaction. Kate blinked. She couldn't hold her poker-face.

His voice softened. "You hate that you can't be happy. You hate a lot things about yourself."

Kate pushed herself off the couch and looked down at him warily. She was tired. "Will you take me home now?" she asked.

"Of course."

Jeff led her out of the office—shutting off lights and locking doors behind them. Once in the elevator, he let her put distance between them. Jeff gave her space.

"I want to see you again," he said, directing his words to the floor. "You'll need rest and time to think things through. But the day after next—and from then on—we'll meet at the entrance of the park. 5:30 a.m. We'll jog together and see where it goes from there."

"I can't meet your expectations, Jeff," she sighed. "The excitement will wear off. We can't escape. You spoke of my personality traits—my defects—I'll carry those forward. Only it will be worse.

The self-loathing—the lack of self-respect—it will poison the future."

"I don't agree, Kathryn," he said, shaking his head as he held the elevator doors open for her. "Because I know the source of your misery. You are pretending to be something you're not. You compartmentalize your feelings—your needs—your desires. But no one can live like that. Sooner or later, those feelings, needs, and desires will collide."

Jeff walked over to the passenger door of his SUV and held it open for her. When she was settled in her seat, he smiled at her gently.

"I've learned that abiding by my own nature is the only path to happiness. It's the same for you. It's the same for everyone, Kathryn," he said softly. "I won't apologize for recognizing myself in you. I like what I see. And you should too."

Jeff jogged around the hood and slid into the driver's seat. He set his glasses back on and pulled out of the parking garage. They were on the empty expressway before he spoke again.

"I never needed the video to blackmail you," he murmured. "You must realize that."

Kate nodded. "If you hurt my family, I will never forgive you. I'll hate you forever."

"I know," he sighed. "Please, don't make me do it."

Fat droplets of rain pelted the windshield. Jeff switched on the wipers, and Kate was grateful for the calming effect of the rhythmic noise.

"You are underestimating my feelings for Danny. I love him."

"Okay. I will concede to that fact if you will at least consider my proposition." Jeff glanced over at her with arched eyebrows. "Love is an emotion and emotions can vary in degrees and intensity."

"I knew who Danny was when I married him. My life with him is the life I very deliberately chose," Kate snapped. "I've betrayed him, I know. I've committed an unforgivable sin. But he makes me a better person, and I'll fight for him. I'm warning you, Jeff. You don't want to test my devotion. I will protect Danny."

The soft green glow from the dashboard lights was dim, but Kate could see the emotions as they ripped across Jeff's face. Clenching and unclenching the steering wheel, he directed the SUV off the expressway and raced past the lights of Roosevelt Road. She was nearly home.

After composing himself, he began slowly. "I spied on you. Please forgive me, but you can understand that I was naturally curious. I can recognize your husband," he shrugged. "I take the train into Chicago occasionally for work."

Kate froze in her seat. She didn't like the direction of the conversation.

"I spotted him on the platform," he said. His lips pulled into a tight smile. "You have to admit, he's hard to miss. I sat behind the two of them and eavesdropped. I didn't find her conversation interesting, but she's beautiful, Kathryn. Very leggy and artificially blond. An account executive for an advertising firm. Her name is Natalie."

Kate shuddered before cramming her eyes shut. It was useless. She knew who Jeff was talking about. She could picture the woman in her head. Natalie.

"Have you ever checked his e-mail?" Jeff asked. "His computer? It's how Ainsley confirmed her suspicions. Online infidelity oftentimes leads to real time sex."

"Danny is not cheating on me," Kate seethed.

"Maybe not in the technical sense," Jeff admitted before coasting to a stop. "But he's definitely screwing around."

Kate kept her eyes on her hands. The powerful flurry of emotions was confusing, but rage won out. Her rage thundered in unison with the real life storm lighting up the sky.

"God help me if it ever comes to fisticuffs," Jeff muttered. "How tall is he anyways? Six foot five?"

Her eyes flew automatically to her house. Kate's posture stiffened. *He had brought her home.* Marigold was standing next to Danny on the porch. They were both peering at the strange vehicle. Through the rain and prevailing darkness, she read her husband's body language. Danny was worried. He would be relieved to see her, but it wouldn't last long.

"You did this on purpose," Kate snarled.

She leapt out of the SUV and slammed the passenger door shut with as much force as she could muster. Strong winds gusted through the trees and shrubs surrounding her house. Kate put her head down and charged through the freezing cold rain. It was too late to dodge raindrops.

The thunderstorm already hit home.

CHAPTER 44

HOWLING INTO THE WIND

Danny recognized her as soon as she threw her legs out of the SUV. Relief washed through him, but it was quickly chased down by anger. He tried to catch a glimpse of the driver, but the glare of the street light obstructed his view. It was too dark. Too dark and too late for his wife to be driving around in a strange German SUV.

Danny didn't have time to blink. Kate was on the porch in a flash. Marigold was the first to greet Kate. Soaking wet and shivering, Kate dropped to one knee and gave the nervous dog all of her attention. Danny kept an eye on the foreign vehicle and caught the shadow of a wave; he waved back automatically. It took a second to register the ghostly shape behind the wheel. Danny froze. It was distinctively male, a man had driven Kate home.

"Who the fuck?" he bellowed as the SUV pulled away. "Kate, what the hell?"

He was waving the portable phone clutched in his hand.

"Come on, sweet girl," Kate said. Leaping to her feet, she ignored his blustering and flew into the house with the dog close to her side. "I'm freezing."

He followed his wife. Slamming the front door closed, he secured the dead bolt and charged after her.

"Kate," he tried harder to complete a sentence. "Who the fuck was that?"

She was already peeling off her wet clothes and tossing them in the clothes hamper. "Keep your voice down," she admonished. "It's late. You'll wake the boys."

"Don't tell me to keep it down," he yelled. "Where have you been?"

He realized he was still clutching the phone in his hand. Disgusted, he hurled it across the room. It landed in the overstuffed chair in the corner. Marigold's ears went back and her wagging tail went between her legs.

Kate wrapped Danny's flannel robe around her naked body and crouched over the scared dog. "Knock it off, Danny. You're behaving like an overgrown child."

She still hadn't answered his question. He wanted to shake it out of her, but instead, he ground his teeth and lifted her off the floor by the elbows. Kate didn't fight him. She didn't even get mad when he tossed her onto the bed. Readjusting the robe around her body, she gave herself a hug. She was cold and still very wet.

"You went out for a jog over two hours ago, Kate," he yelled. "Who was the driver of the fucking SUV?"

He set his hands on his hips and stared into her eyes. They were tired and apologetic.

"I'm sorry," she said. Marigold set her head on the bed next to her, and Kate scratched the dog behind the ears. "I thought about calling, but the whole situation was weird."

"Weird?"

"I went for a jog to the library," she explained. "I wanted to check out the parking situation again. While I was there, I tried to peek at the backyards bordering the garden site. It was dark. I couldn't see much, so I thought I'd run through the neighborhood. Get a better sense of the proximity of the homes to the site. Ainsley was outside, and she waved me down. I was caught off guard. I wasn't expecting a confrontation. But she was actually really nice. She gave me a tour of her backyard and invited me inside."

"Ainsley?"

"She's the woman who opposes the garden. I told you all about this, Dan. Molly and I had coffee with her on Monday." Kate was using her mom tone on him.

"If she was so nice, why didn't she let you use the phone?" he snapped.

"I didn't want to ask. It was an uncomfortable situation. I got my period." Kate pushed herself off the bed and strode over to the laundry basket. Reaching into the pocket of her jacket, she pulled out a tampon for his inspection. He took a step backwards.

"It was awkward. Her husband was there. I got the impression they were fighting. I felt bad for her. She seemed desperate for company."

Walking into the bathroom, Kate turned the water on in the shower stall. Danny strode in but stopped cold in the doorway. She was standing in the middle of floor holding the tampon in her right hand like a loaded weapon.

"She didn't want me to go," she added. "And I kind of owed her for saving me. I was embarrassed, Danny. I got caught running past her house and then I had to ask her for help. She let me clean up and gave me supplies."

Kate walked over to the toilet and set the tampon on the lid. Marigold squeezed past Danny in the doorway—she didn't want to let Kate out of her sight. Danny stayed frozen. Frozen on the bathroom's threshold, he could not see Kate, but he could hear her contented groan as the hot water hit her chilled body. Frustrated, he strode out of the room. The garden project was taking up too much of her time.

It was ridiculous. He was too angry to look at her, but he couldn't stay away from her either. He charged back into the bathroom and tripped over the dog.

"God damn it," he cursed.

"Danny, watch where you're going," Kate wiped the moisture off the shower door and gave him a dirty look.

"I've been tripping over this damn dog for the last hour," he yelled. "Marigold was as nervous as I was. Why did you leave her behind? I only agreed to a dog, because I didn't want you running alone in the dark."

"I'm sorry," Kate said as she shut the water off. "Next time I'll take her."

"Next time," Danny sneered.

She stepped out of the shower and reached for a towel. He was trapped by her naked body. Danny kept his eyes on the floor. He always gave her a lot of space when she got her period. He didn't like to think of her as frail or weak. In his head, Kate was unbreakable, a force of nature. When she bled, it weakened his heart. It made him vulnerable too. So he left the bathroom again and gave her privacy.

"There's not going to be a next time," he shouted as he paced outside the bathroom's doorway. "I'm sick of the community garden. I don't want you running around at night, and I don't want you taking rides from strangers."

Danny walked over to their window and peeked outside. The street was empty. The thunder and lightning had passed over, but the rain was still coming down in sheets. The streetlight in front of their house lit the rain's slanted path. It pounded the pavement and rolled like a river towards the sewer grates.

"Who drove you home?" he asked.

"Jeff Dixon," Kate replied.

Danny let the window shade crash against the glass. "Who the fuck is Jeff Dixon?"

Stomping into the bathroom, he caught Kate in the middle of brushing her teeth.

"Ainsley Dixon's husband," she spit—her mouth was full of foamy paste.

"Whose husband?"

"Ainsley Dixon," she sighed. "The woman who opposes the garden."

Kate actually had the nerve to roll her eyes at him. Her attitude was pissing him off even more. Danny leaned up against the doorway and eyed the toilet. The tampon was gone. Folding his arms across his chest, he growled.

"I'm sorry I worried you, Danny," Kate said after rinsing her mouth.

"I don't like you driving around with strange men," he snapped. Waving his arms, he turned his back on her. "What did you say his name was?"

"Jeff Dixon," she called over her shoulder. "He's a lawyer."

He could hear the disgust in her voice, but it didn't make him feel better.

"Ainsley insisted he drive me home," she said.

Kate walked past him and opened her dresser drawer. She pulled out a ratty pair of underwear reserved for this time of month. Underwear meant no sex. Kate only wore them to bed when she was menstruating. Danny covered his face with his hands and took a deep breath. She kept talking as she put on her pajamas.

"It was raining," she added. "I think she felt guilty for keeping me so late."

"Was he good looking?" Danny asked. His brain wasn't ready to downshift out of anger. He was still at war. He just didn't know with whom or with what he was at war.

"Good looking?" she asked.

She was so nonchalant. It made his blood boil. Couldn't she see how upset he was?

"The lawyer," he shouted. Danny forgot his name again. "Was he good looking?"

"I guess," Kate laughed as she pulled the covers of the bed back. "Danny what is wrong with you? He gave me a ride for Christ's sake."

"I don't like it. My wife should not be alone with a strange man late at night." Danny shook his head and paced.

"Don't start," Kate sneered as she climbed into bed.

He watched in disbelief as she snuggled under the covers and closed her eyes.

"What is that hell is that supposed to mean?" he demanded. "You're the one who started this. You're the one who went missing in the middle of the night."

Kate shot up in bed and pointed a finger at him. "I think you're projecting your feelings of guilt onto me."

Glaring at her finger, he took a step forward. "Projecting?"

"Yeah," she nodded. "Miss Hyphenated from the train. You're looking for a reason to deflect your guilt. You're the one who is flirting with people of the opposite sex. Not me."

"I'm not flirting," he stumbled to keep up. "She sits next to me. Not the other way around. And she knows I'm married."

"Whatever you say, Dan," Kate retorted before punching her head into the pillows. "I don't want to talk about it. I'm too tired to waste energy on Miss Hyphenated."

"No more jogging at night. You jog in the morning, Kate," he shouted. "I can't take all these changes. You've got me spinning."

"You can't impose a curfew on me. I needed to get out of this goddamn house. Why is that so hard to understand?" She spoke at the ceiling in a tone too close to a shout, and she was waving her arms stiffly above the covers.

"I was walking around like a caged animal. I know you were too busy to notice Dan, but I had a really long day with the kids. I tucked them all into bed, and I didn't ask for help." Kate's arms slapped against the bed before going rigid.

Her voice quieted but instead of a shout, it came out in a hiss. "No, of course not, I would never ask for help. I would never ask you to read Joey his bedtime story. God forbid you shut ESPN off for twenty minutes to share sweet talk with your little boy."

He was shocked by the nasty tone of her sarcasm. Kate's hands flew to the sides of her face. Pursing her lips, she breathed through her nose. Danny couldn't remember Kate's mood before she left the house. He hadn't been paying attention. But he did remember the moment when he realized she was gone. It was when he decided to compose a witty reply to Natalie Bell-Charles's e-mail.

"I don't want to talk about this anymore," she said between gritted teeth. "I took care of the kids and then took some time for myself and went for jog."

Kate took a deep breath before continuing her rant. "I got caught up in conversation as I tried to make friends with an enemy of the community garden. I know the garden has nothing at all to do with hockey, but regardless, it is a project I care very much about. I'm sorry I worried you. I've apologized at least four times. I feel like shit, okay? Are you trying to make me feel worse on purpose?"

Maybe he was projecting. He did feel like an asshole. Kate was entitled to alone time, and the time she did take for herself never interfered with the kids. *The kids were Kate's top priority.* It was probably a good time for his own apology, but he was still mad. Not at Kate. But at the situation. He was an unwilling passenger on an emotional carousel. He wanted to get off the carnival ride and go sulk for awhile.

"Can I get you something?" he asked in a voice that came out wrong. He tried to sound more genuine. "Do you need an ibuprofen?"

He knew she used it for muscle pain. It probably worked for all that female stuff too.

"No," she sighed, rolling back over onto her side. "Just shut the lights off and close the door."

Danny flipped the lights off as he stepped into the hall. "Next time call," he said sternly before closing the door.

His worry morphed into anger, and the anger fizzled into guilt. Danny was exhausted, but his gut was churning with excess energy. He moved instinctively around his home, making his rounds for the second time. He felt compelled to double check the locks on his doors and windows. He finished his inspection at the front door.

Unbolting the lock, he stepped onto the porch. Beneath the sheltering eaves, he was safe and dry from the rain. Any other night he would have taken comfort from his advantage. But the storm was a menace distorting his perception of reality. Puffing his chest out, he stood watch. Ready to frighten away attackers, Danny wanted to howl into the wind but didn't.

Slumping his shoulders, he turned on his heels and went back into the house. He needed to check his e-mail before going to bed. Natalie Bell-Charles might have responded to his message in the interim of his emotional meltdown.

Danny didn't question his own motives as he scanned through the inbox directory. It was simply routine before plugging his iPhone into the charger, and routine was exactly what he needed to ease his troubled mind.

CHAPTER 45

SOFT EARTH

Kate woke up sick. Stumbling out of bed, she went to the medicine cabinet. Normally, she would jog the ache out of her head. Endorphins combated her menstrual symptoms better than any over-the-counter medication. But Kate would endure the pain. It was punishment. The physical culmination of her lies and deceit. The pounding in her head was a bitter reminder. Her worlds were colliding.

Joey was late for school. After arguing about the nutritional value of sugar cereal, he pranced outside with his backpack loosely hanging from his shoulders. Kate was digging through her purse, looking for a breath mint when she walked into him. Joey stood frozen on the edge of the driveway.

"Get in the truck, Joe," Kate said pushing him gently forward.

Marigold was already waiting next to the driver's side door. Whenever possible, Kate took Marigold along on her errands.

"Mom," Joey shouted. "Don't step on them."

Joey threw his body in front of Kate. Worms littered the black-top of the driveway. The rain chased them out of their holes. A few were flattened already, some were drowned in shallow puddles, but most were struggling to find soft earth.

Kate ran tense fingers through her hair—massaging her tight scalp. "We're late already, little man. We don't have time to rescue earthworms."

Joey tossed his backpack onto the wet grass and made a dash for the weed bucket. She watched helplessly as her son tiptoed his way down the driveway. The teacher would have to accept her apologies. Joey was all heart. Murdering innocent worms was a sin she couldn't commit.

She threw her purse into the truck and commanded Marigold to sit. The dog watched with curious eyes as Kate and Joey stooped over the driveway—picking worms into the bucket. Kate lost track of time. Her neck and shoulders were stiff when they dumped the squirming worms into the vegetable patch.

On any other day, she would have been happy to participate in Joey's rescue mission. Not today—today, it was a chore. Joey got to school twenty minutes late, and Kate pretended not to notice his grime-encrusted fingernails as she kissed him goodbye.

She spent the rest of her morning doing housework. Her head wasn't pounding anymore. The medicine did its work, but it couldn't alleviate the strain of the tight muscles in her shoulders, neck, and scalp. Sharp and dull at the same time, the pressure kept her in a bad mood.

After picking Joey up from school, she fed him lunch and turned on a cartoon television network she never let him watch. Shuffling into her bedroom, she pulled the window shades and lay down. Kate closed her eyes—she closed her eyes on everything.

Hours later, her rest was disturbed. Kate opened one eye and discovered Peter standing over her. He was eating an apple. Marigold was standing next to him. Wagging her tail, the dog gazed lovingly at Peter.

"Are you sick?" Peter asked. "Do you want me to call Dad?"

Kate pushed herself to a sit. "No, I'm just tired, honey."

"Can I have a pop, Mom?" Billy was leaning into her bedroom by hanging onto the door frame. "It's Friday, and I haven't had one all week."

Normally, she would use his request as leverage to get homework finished or his room cleaned, but her head was pounding. She was too weak to hold negotiations.

"Yes," she said on her way to the medicine cabinet.

"I want one too," Peter whined.

"Fine, but take Marigold for walk first." Marigold liked this idea and left Kate's side to follow Peter.

When Kate passed the family room on her way to the kitchen, she found Joey on the rug still watching television. He made the most of his lack of supervision. Sofa pillows were scattered and an empty cracker box lay on the coffee table.

"Nice work, Joe," she mumbled.

Joey never tore his eyes away from the cartoon mayhem on Danny's big screen. Kate picked up the garbage and trudged into the kitchen to make dinner. She had forgotten to take the pork chops out of the freezer, so she was forced to put them in the microwave to defrost.

"Can I download some music?" Billy asked in between chugs of his Coke.

"Is your homework done?" Kate already knew the answer to her question.

"I finished it at school," he said as predicted.

"Mom, Billy took his iPod to school. He was listening to it on the walk home," Peter called from the back hall.

Billy gave his brother a dirty look before throwing his empty can into the recycle bin.

"I thought I told you to take Marigold for a walk," she reminded her older son in hopes of diffusing a conflict.

Kate heard the click of the dog leash. "He's gonna lose it, Mom. And then he'll want to borrow mine."

"You're such a narc, Pete," Billy leered.

Peter was in the middle of responding to his brother when the microwave beeped. Kate let the pork chops go too long, and the sides of the meat were grey and bubbly. Dinner was going to be tough to chew.

Peter threw some nasty words at Billy and slammed the back door on his way out, jolting his mother's already frazzled nervous system. Kate set a large sauté pan on the stove to heat up olive oil with crushed garlic. As the garlic sizzled, she coated the chops with bread crumbs and parmesan cheese. The phone rang after the chops were in the pan.

"Mom," Billy yelled from the top of the stairs. "It's Mrs. Hilliard."

Kate picked up the extension in the kitchen. "Hello, Sharon."

"Where the hell have you been? I left messages."

"I'm sorry. I forgot to call you back," Kate mumbled into the phone. She had ignored the phone all day. In truth, Kate never checked her messages.

"I need your help. The painter is coming on Monday. He dropped off a bunch of color fans. I don't know what the hell I'm doing. Can you come by tomorrow morning and help me? He wants to go out and buy supplies and is nagging me to make a decision."

"Tomorrow is Saturday, Sharon."

"Yeah, so?"

"Shit," Kate shouted after catching the smell of smoke and scorched meat. She burnt her hand removing the pan from the stove. "Shit, shit, shit."

"What?" Sharon asked.

"I forgot to turn the burner down," Kate complained. "I just ruined dinner."

"God forbid your boys eat fast food, right?" Sharon teased.

"I give up," Kate said, dumping the sad-looking pork chops into the garbage. "French fries it is."

"So, can you help me?" Sharon asked.

"Help with what?"

"Geez, Katie, help me pick out paint colors. Can you come over at around 9:30 tomorrow morning?"

"Sure," Kate said, examining her injured hand. "Tomorrow."

Kate let the crusty pan soak and herded her confused boys out the back door.

"What's burning?" Peter asked.

"Dinner. We're going out. But first, we've got to pick up Daddy at the train."

Marigold got good-bye kisses from all the boys and tried to squeeze past Kate. "Sorry, girl," Kate said. "I'll bring you a doggie bag."

"Where are we going to eat?" Joey asked after he was buckled into the van.

Kate looked down at her clothes. They weren't really weather appropriate—the running shorts especially. But the spring chill felt good on her sticky skin, so she didn't bother with a jacket. She managed to pull her hair into a messy ponytail before leaving the house, but she wore no make-up.

If Jeff was spying today, he would not regard her as beautiful or intriguing. None of the things he called her before applied. Tired and haggard were more suitable. Would he be repulsed? Or would he want to take her away? Rescue her? Kate gasped. The memory was painful. Jeff Dixon's mischievous smile—tousled hair—and thick eyelashes. It made her heart wrench. Quickly, she shoved him to the corner of her mind. Joey was waiting for an answer to his question.

"Somewhere fast," she said curtly.

Kate parked across from the station. She had a few minutes, so she left the boys and ran into Danny's dry cleaner. Loaded down with laundered shirts, she jogged back to the van—cringing at the scream of a braking train. The crossing gates were down. Warning bells were ringing and lights were flashing as passengers burst forth—anxious to get home—most people kept their heads down and their feet moving. The kids added to the headbanger atmosphere. Bickering assaulted her when she opened the rear hatch of the van.

"Boys," Kate shouted over the racket. "Knock it off."

"There's Daddy," Joey called out from his seat.

Kate was having a hard time. There were too many shirts for the short hook in the rear of the van. She ground her teeth together—preventing the curse words swirling in her head from escaping.

"Whoa," Peter said admiringly. "Who's that?"

"She's pretty," Joey added.

Kate's eyes lifted from the tangle of wire hangers and plastic wrap. She caught sight of Billy first. He was turned in his seat.

Staring at his mother, he lifted his eyebrows, and pointed discreetly in the direction of the train station.

Miss Hyphenated. That bitch. Natalie.

The blaring noise and lights from the train tracks faded to the background. Kate's brain got very roomy. Crystalline. She was hyper-aware of her surroundings. The foot traffic pouring out of the station and onto the sidewalks of town became picturesque. Flat. Like a moving mural.

She could feel the energy of people in her peripheral vision, but her concentration was elsewhere. Her boys scrambled inside the van—following her with their eyes as she took off down the sidewalk. The cars. She knew which car was going to turn—which car was going to stop—and she dodged them half-aware as she zipped across Main Street.

Kate's breath was steady. The spring air was still crisp and fresh from the cleansing rain. It tasted good on her tongue—on her lips. Her blood flowed easily. Her tense muscles finally loose. It was a relief. Her headache gone. She struggled no more. She was on soft earth again.

Her mind's eye focused like a microscope. *Natalie.* Danny. He knew she was coming—his face panic stricken—caught. But he was immaterial. Insubstantial. Flat in her view scope. *Natalie.* Kate evaluated her target. Every detail of the young woman shone in vivid color. *Natalie.* In a red suit. An account executive. Advertising.

Her mind and body operated in perfect harmony. It was heaven. Feeling strong. Feeling powerful. The physical and mental surge was exhilarating.

Smiling, Kate pounced.

CHAPTER 46

TURN-ON

It was scariest moment of his life. Danny felt like he was caught in the middle of a video game. His wife shot across the street like she was being directed by remote control. *Stop. Pause.* He screamed inside his head.

Natalie Bell-Charles kept chatting, tossing her hair, fingering the gold charm hanging at her neck. She had no idea what was coming, so he tore away from her. Springing down the station's steps, he tried to protect her. He tried to catch Kate.

His first swipe caught nothing but air. Kate flew past him. She took the stairs three at time. Lunging, he managed to get a grip on her wrist. Kate looked then, not at him, but at his hand—the thing stopping her progress.

"Kate," he began in reasonable tone.

He was looking up at her, pleading with his eyes from the bottom step, but she wasn't listening. Kate extended her right arm and gripped the metal hand rail, her powerful legs planted. Both knees bent, her right foot was on the top step, her left one step below. The muscles in her calves and thighs were taut. The veins in her wrist prominent as she anchored herself. *My God, when did she get so strong?*

247

Using the advantage of position, she jerked herself free. Danny stumbled backwards. His heavy briefcase slipped from his shoulder, his laptop. He tried to catch the briefcase before it slammed into the concrete wall but only succeeded in dumping it over. His files and his papers landed on the sidewalk.

He was at a complete loss—confused. The importance of saving his work clashed with the severity of the moment. Kate was already confronting Natalie, her posture casual.

"Hello," she said cordially.

Danny bent over his briefcase while keeping an eye on Kate. She was too cool, and he knew her too well. His wife was setting Natalie up on a butcher block before cleaving her head off.

"I'm Kathryn Maller."

Smiling, Kate held her hand out. *No.* Danny shook his head. *Don't.*

"Natalie Bell-Charles." Natalie took Kate's hand. She smiled politely, but she was embarrassed. The awkwardness of the situation was not lost on her. Nervous, her free hand fidgeted.

Kate laughed, but not in a way that would put Natalie at ease. "Yes," Kate nodded. "Miss Hyphenated. That's what I call you. Danny never gave me your actual name, so I made one up."

Shit. Danny abandoned his briefcase. They were holding up traffic, blocking the stairs leading to the sidewalk. People were watching and listening. Familiar people. Fellow commuters. Witnesses who knew him, knew Natalie, and recognized them together.

Danny stood between the two women. He tried to shuffle them out of the way, to free the stairs. But no one, not even the crowd, was moving.

Natalie gave Danny a confused look. "Miss Hyphenated?"

"Yes, princess," Kate said. "We laugh at you."

Fuck. Kate moved so fast it was a blur. Natalie's left hand was suddenly in Kate's right. Holding Natalie's ring under her nose, she examined the diamond.

"It's beautiful," she smiled. "Two karats? I wonder how Prince Charming would feel about you eye-fucking my husband."

Natalie tried to rip her hand away, but Kate wasn't letting go. Danny heard snickering from the crowd loosely gathered behind him, and it added to his fear, his dread, his overwhelming desire to throw his wife over his shoulder and run.

"I'm sorry?" Natalie mumbled weakly, tugging at Kate's grip. "We were just talking."

Danny's moved to restrain his wife, but she cut him down with a glare, and he froze. He was scared—scared shitless. Leaning into Natalie's personal space, Kate breathed in deeply. She was taking in her scent, deciding if Natalie was good enough to eat.

"I'm going to do you a favor and answer your late-night musings," she whispered loudly into Natalie's ear. "Your wildest fantasies—they're all true. He is as good as he looks. And princess, his cock is enormous."

"Shit," Danny dove in between them, breaking Kate's vice-like grip on Natalie's hand.

Run. Danny silently pled with Natalie. *Run.* Kate was too nimble, too agile. He tried in vain to get a good grip on her. She was dodging, fighting him off, but her eyes never left Natalie.

"That's right, princess," Kate yelled. "You'd never survive the pounding. Danny would snap you in half."

"Jesus," he cried.

Finally, he got his arms wrapped around her. Natalie was a good ten feet away, but not safe yet. Kate used the ground to leverage her leg strength, and she strained against Danny's superior brawn. Finally, he lifted her off the ground, giving her nowhere to go.

"I won't tolerate Briefcase Barbie making a play for my man," Kate shouted after Natalie.

His wife's voice rang over the train's chug, the thrum of traffic. Every word was precisely articulated.

"Before you make another run at Danny, you better load up on carbs, princess! Kicking your skinny ass will be way too easy."

Again, laughter from his fellow commuters. He needed her to stop. She had crossed the line.

"Kate," he admonished. "The kids."

Kate clenched her fists and in complete frustration, roared until she had no breath in her lungs. Natalie glanced behind her shoulder, her eyes full of fear, and made it around the corner.

Run, he thought. *Run home.* Natalie was safely out of view, and Kate finally stopped struggling.

"The kids are watching," he reminded before setting Kate back on her feet.

The kids were Kate's top priority, always the kids. Kate's eyes flew to the van parked across the street. All three boys had their faces pressed to the windshield. Danny was breathing heavily—his heart hammering—but Kate's breathing was even, unaffected by their wrestling match. She backed away from him, her eyes full of disgust.

The crowd was beginning to disperse, but Danny could feel the stares, the disapproval, and it wasn't directed at Kate. It was directed at him. Two women actually had the nerve to pat Kate on the shoulder as they brushed past. Kate didn't take notice.

"Really, Dan?" she asked shaking her head. "Is that what gets you off these days? Fake eyelashes and ultra-white teeth. That woman reeked of plastic."

"I'm not talking about this right now," he said, turning on his heels.

Kate followed closely behind. She stood and watched with her arms crossed as he retrieved his files and briefcase.

"How ya doin' there, Dan?"

Danny closed his eyes and cursed underneath his breath. *Randy DeVrees.* Of course, Randy wanted to give him a hard time.

"Looks like you can use a little help," Randy's tone was condescending. Not at all helpful.

"No, I'm fine," Danny directing his comment to his briefcase.

"Hello, my name is Randy DeVrees."

Shit. Danny looked up hesitantly. Randy was extending a hand to Kate.

"Go fuck yourself, Randy," Kate replied.

Danny rose to his feet and shot Randy a warning look. It was ignored. In suit and tie, Randy swung his briefcase back and forth with his left hand while his right was stuffed deep inside his pant pocket. Randy's eyebrows shot up in surprise, but he was amused—not afraid like he should have been. *Fucking idiot. Never poke a rattlesnake.*

"I'm sorry," Randy apologized insincerely. "I only meant to offer my assistance."

Kate's eyes swept down from Randy's face and landed on the hand twitching inside his pant pocket. "I know exactly what you meant to do, Mr. Stiffy," she replied, cool as ice. "Take that needle dick you're fingering and go home. The show is over. You'll have to rub one off on your own."

Danny groaned and took Kate by the elbow. She gave him a dirty look but walked with him as they crossed Main Street.

"What is wrong with you?" he hissed. "I see those people every fucking day."

"I know, Dan," she sneered. "And what do you suppose those people think about you and Miss Hyphenated? I betcha they think it's strictly platonic. Two buddies shootin' the shit."

"You overreacted and made yourself look ridiculous."

His grip on her elbow tightened automatically, and Kate reacted violently. She wrenched her arm loose and shoved. Kate ran—she ran away from him.

"If anyone is ridiculous, it's you," she shouted over her shoulder. "Natalie Bell-Charles. Give me a fucking break."

Kate was picking up speed. The boys were still glued to the windshield, their eyes wide. Kate pointed a finger at them as she sped past. "Get back in your seats," she shouted.

Danny ran after her. She wasn't going to stop, and he couldn't lose her. "Katie," he called. "Please, baby."

Danny glimpsed Joey's face. The boy was terrified. His mother didn't stop. His mother ran past him. Danny felt Joey's pain, and it hurt like hell. Kate was angry. Angry enough to take off on her boys, and it was his fucking fault. Throwing his briefcase into the van's open hatch, he freed his arms and pumped. *Shit.* He was out of shape.

"Baby, please," Danny begged. "I'm sorry. You're right. It's my fault."

She slowed to a walk, and he caught up. Danny tried to pull her into an embrace, but she wasn't ready. Kate didn't want to be touched.

"I'm sorry," he repeated after he caught his breath.

Kate nodded but kept her eyes on her feet. He gave her a minute. She needed to think, to calm down. Kate did not stay mad long.

"I have never had sex with her," he finally added. "I would never do that to you...to us."

She looked up then, not angry but sad. He read her eyes, the turn of her mouth, the set of her chin. Kate nodded her head once—decisively—she still believed in him.

"I know you wouldn't." Ducking her head, she walked into his embrace.

Danny pulled her in, held her snug into his chest. She fit beautifully, and he sighed. It was where she belonged.

"Damn," Danny snorted as they walked back to the van with arms wrapped around each. "It was like the good ol' days. I haven't seen you that pissed in a long while."

"I snapped," Kate shrugged.

"You sure did," Danny laughed. "Baby, you still got it. Katie Selbach will forever be badass."

"I didn't intend to embarrass you, Danny. I was aiming for Miss Hyphenated."

"It's okay," he said kissing her on the head. "I can't help but be a little flattered."

"Momma," Joey was out of his seat with his arms outstretched.

"It's okay, Joey," she said after pulling him into a hug. "I lost my temper, but I feel better now."

Peter's eyes were darting back and forth between Danny and Kate—reading the mood and fighting back laughter. After Kate buckled Joey into his seat, Peter's face broke into an excited grin.

"That was totally awesome, Mom," he blurted. "The coolest thing you've ever done."

"That's enough, Pete," Danny warned as he held the passenger door open for Kate.

"She was defending your honor, Dad," Peter laughed. "Mom coulda kicked that blonde lady's butt."

"You're way prettier than her, Momma," Joey exclaimed.

"Thank you for saying so, little man."

252

"It was a misunderstanding," Danny explained. "Your mother thought that woman was being too flirty, and I agreed. I won't be friends with her anymore."

"Doesn't matter now...does it?" Billy asked quietly from the back seat.

Kate turned in her seat to look at her middle son, and they locked eyes.

"Mom took care of it," Billy added for good measure. His tone was even and without emotion.

Kate nodded at Billy—the apple of her eye, her pride and joy— they were bookends of each other. "That's right, Bill. Mom took care of it," she promised in an equally even and emotionless tone.

Danny chuckled to himself as he rounded the van. Natalie Bell-Charles wasn't worth the energy. He imagined her at home cowering in her husband's arms...looking for gentle reassurances. Women like Natalie needed to be stroked, to be looked after. His wife was badass. And he was surprised at how much it still turned him on.

CHAPTER 47

911 PORSCHE TURBO

He arrived first, and he was tired of it. The night before, Kathryn waited for him. He caught her pacing on the jogging path. Anxious. And it was nice. He liked how it made him feel. Controlled. Sovereign. Dominant. One day. One day soon, Kathryn would admit her true feelings, and she would wait. Wait for him.

Heaven. Kathryn in red running shorts. The cropped gray hooded sweatshirt was an obvious afterthought. Zipped halfway. It hung loosely around her shoulders. Kathryn's breasts were held tightly in place by a white jogging tank. Her cleavage exposed. Her breasts heaved with her forward progress. The wily fox. Maybe her wardrobe choice was not such an obvious afterthought. He couldn't help it. He smiled.

Her ponytail swished from side to side. Cheeks flushed from exertion. She was running hard. Her yellow dog keeping stride. Marigold. The sun was very nearly over the horizon, and she no longer needed her blinking safety light. His days of desperately searching the haze for her beacon were over.

He stretched. Jogged in place. Warmed his cool muscles. He was ready when she set foot on the trail. Kathryn and her dog. He ran parallel. The dog gave him a sideway glance, but it was focused. Focused on Kathryn.

They fell into an easy rhythm. Natural. How it was so supposed to be. Partners. Jogging through the park together. They were not alone, but they could have been a married couple exercising on a Saturday morning. No one was the wiser. And it was glorious.

The pond. The fishing pier. He directed them off the trail and down the steep embankment. Time alone. Time to talk. Breathless they walked to the end of the pier. Eyes on their feet. The air was too cool to be humid but damp enough to capture the scent of swamp. He could taste the green on his tongue.

Marigold was excited. Searching for ducklings, the dog tugged on her leash. Kathryn leaned over the railing and peered into the thick water. He examined her face. It was soft. So he took a deep breath and waded in. Time to broach the inevitable subject. The idiot husband who waited impatiently on the porch of Kathryn's charming yellow house.

"Was Danny very angry?" he asked.

"Yes," she sighed. "But I handled it."

"You lied."

"Of course," she said cooly. "Isn't that what you wanted? I am officially a cheater and killing my marriage one lie at a time."

"Kathryn," he began slowly. "You are such a fascinating creature. Did you not think you were cheating before? How does lying change anything?"

"It's conscious now," she said with words full of venom. "I love Danny. I hate manipulating him. I don't like making him into a fool."

He turned his face away to hide his amusement. Her reasoning was flawed. She actually believed the deceit began with the lies. But he expected her resistance. The denial. The lies took her into deeper waters, and she didn't like it. Kathryn was struggling to maintain her footing.

"I know this is hard," he said finally. "I wish I could make things easier for you."

Kathryn looked up at him. Her hazel eyes full of stubborn tears. It pained him to see her so distressed. Reaching out, he took her hand. It was cold. Much colder than his. He rubbed the flesh of her hand. Warming her.

"I can't keep seeing you," she whispered. "Please, leave me alone."

Holding her hand in his, he examined it. Strong and sturdy. The practical hands of a volatile woman. His heart skipped. "What's this?" he demanded as he ran a thumb over her palm.

"I burned myself making dinner," she shrugged.

Ahh. She worked too hard. Her life was riddled with chores. Gently, he folded her hand into his and brought it up for a kiss. She didn't pull away. Instead, Kathryn took a deep breath. His touch made her shiver. He held her hand to his face, and she moved it deliberately to his neck. Unconsciously, he leaned into her. Luxuriating in the sensation of her fingers threading through his hair. Her eyes were pained. Battling her inner demons, he guessed. He couldn't allow her to dwell long in the shadows. Pressing her against the railing, his hands cradled her face.

"Kathryn," he whispered in between kisses. "Kathryn. So lovely. How I've longed to see you. Touch you."

She answered him with small cries of her own. So reluctant. So torn. Her whines gave her away. She was enjoying it. Enjoying him.

"Please," she begged. Kathryn stared into his eyes. "Please, Jeff, leave me alone."

He ran his hands down her arms. Her wrists. So delicate. He pushed at the sleeves of her sweatshirt. Wanting to feel more of her flesh, but not wanting to cross the line of desire. Restraint. Control.

He closed his eyes and set his forehead to hers. "I can't. You don't belong with him. Kathryn, you know it's true."

She stiffened slightly beneath his hands, and he lifted his eyes. For the briefest of seconds, he saw a flash. The sadness gone. Kathryn's eyes ablaze. The fox. She was playing him. Drawing on his sympathies. No doubt her pain was real. But she was using it. Using it as a weapon against him. Such a fearsome creature. He was overwhelmed with longing.

257

Moaning, he abandoned all restraint. All control. And dove for her mouth. Wrapping himself around her body, he enveloped her with his warmth. It was so easy. Like two corresponding pieces, their souls made a resounding click. They belonged together. How could she deny this simple truth?

Finally, he released her, and she gasped. He chuckled and held her face close. Their breathing ragged. The limits of desire tested. He ran his hands down her arms once more. She was warm now. The sunlight shone in between them. It was like a spot light on her marked skin. Bruises.

Alarmed, he took a step away and roughly shoved at her sweatshirt. Kathryn stood limply as he examined her arms. "Did your husband do this to you?" he asked between clenched teeth.

"Not intentionally," she said smiling wryly. "He was trying to restrain me. I lost my temper."

"Kathryn," he swallowed down the rage burning a path up his stomach and through his chest. "Is this because of me? Were you fighting because of us?"

"Jeff," she chuckled. "What did you expect? Directly or indirectly, every spat, every disagreement, every tussle is because of you. It's not just Danny. My friends. My kids. The rude attendant at the gas station. This thing between us is affecting my life."

Stepping away, he turned abruptly and gave her his back. Perhaps, he should let her go. Let her be. He could not allow her to be hurt. It was agony. Pacing, he tried to let reason prevail. His passions were ruling him now. It was so unfair.

Kathryn. His heart's desire. Did loving her mean forcing her to face the painful truth? Or did loving her mean letting go? Leaving her alone. He shook his head. Leaving her alone was unimaginable. Intolerable. And utterly selfish. How was he different than the husband? The cog kept Kathryn trapped at home. If he had Kathryn to himself, would he do the same?

"I have to go," she said tugging at Marigold's leash. "Are we going to finish our jog, or have you decided leaving me alone is the only gentlemanly thing to do?"

"Kathryn, my fox," he teased. "I always finish what I begin."

258

They proceeded through the park at a steady pace. Their breathing easy. The silence lonely. He needed distraction. His thoughts too negative. "Tell me about the truck," he said lightly.

"A gift from Danny," she said smugly. "He knew I loved it, so he bought it for me."

"You love a rust bucket that gets ten miles to the gallon and disturbs the peace every time the engine rolls over?"

"Yes," she said. "For all of those reasons, I love it."

"Kathryn," he said as they climbed the trail behind the baseball diamond. "If I could, I would buy you a red 911 Porsche Turbo."

"Hah," she snorted. "Maybe you don't know me as well as you think."

"No," he contradicted. "The truck is Kathryn the farm girl. The van is Kathryn the dutiful mother. And the Porsche is Kathryn the fox."

"I don't have enough room in my garage," she teased.

"Admit it," he probed. "You belong behind the wheel of a flaming red Porsche."

"I will not admit it," she said stubbornly, but then quickly added. "Not red anyways. Too flashy. Not my style."

Jeff pondered for a minute and then nudged her playfully as they rounded the trail into a small clearing. "Black then."

Kathryn lifted her eyebrows and smiled. It wasn't a yes. But it wasn't a no either. He lengthened his stride in jubilation. His excitement was difficult to conceal. The wily fox could not resist. A black 911 Porsche Turbo.

Kathryn gave him a maybe.

CHAPTER 48

FAITH

Kate walked around Sharon's empty house examining color wheels—discerning shades of blue, green, and pink. It was hard to concentrate. Her early morning jog with Jeff Dixon was jarring to her confidence. It wasn't about the sex anymore. They were connecting on a completely different level. Kate's thoughts kept going to the fishing pier—to the park. But Sharon's chatter echoed through the expansive rooms, holding her prisoner in the present.

"I should have brought Danny," Kate complained after comparing samples of fabric. "He's the one who is good at this. Not me."

"Are you serious?" Sharon asked. "Danny decorated your house?"

Kate laughed. "Yeah, he did, and he finds it offensive when people assume it was me who masterminded the design. You'd think he'd be embarrassed, but he's not. He's proud of his affinity for bold, contrasting colors. He says the world has too much beige and gray."

"You've got quite a man, Katie-girl," Sharon sighed. "Don't ever take him for granted."

Setting the color wheels on the kitchen counter, Kate pulled at a yellow legal pad and began numbering the rooms of the house. Their chore was nearly done.

"You've always had a crush on Danny," Kate teased.

"Absolutely," Sharon exclaimed. "I'll admit it. I've been crushin' on Danny from the very beginning, and if it wasn't for me, you never would have given him a chance."

Kate ran her hands through her hair and exhaled loudly. Sharon's gentle blue eyes crumbled her defenses. Her stomach trembled. "I've done something terrible," Kate confessed.

Sharon leaned against the kitchen counter and folded her arms across her chest. "Okay," she said hesitantly. "This should be interesting."

"Do you remember Jeff Dixon?" Kate asked.

Sharon's gentle blue eyes widened in horror. Immediately, Kate backpedaled. She did not question Sharon's loyalty, but she could never forget her friend loved Danny too.

"I ran into Ainsley Dixon," Kate began, repeating the lie she told the night before. "She invited me into her house. We got to talking and lost track of time. It got late, and it was raining, so Jeff drove me home."

"And?" Sharon asked warily.

"He's very smart, Sharon," Kate shrugged. "And very good looking."

"Yes, he is," Sharon agreed dryly. "Did you have sex with him?"

Kate shook her head no and sighed when her friend's lips pulled up into a tight smile.

"I saw it in his eyes at the Village Board Meeting. He came onto you?"

Kate nodded. "Yes, and I liked it, Sharon. Encouraged it even. I lost control of the conversation."

"Ahh, Katie," Sharon warned. "You've got to be careful with a man like Jeff Dixon. He's sexy but also dangerous. He doesn't strike me as someone who plays games."

"He told me his marriage is over."

Sharon gasped, and Kate's heart wrenched. The truth was horrific. Sharon's reaction was justified.

"He said being married to Ainsley was like shoving a square peg into a round hole."

"And let me guess…he believes your hole is square?" Sharon laughed.

"Don't laugh," Kate cried. "It was an awful thing to say, and I could relate. I understood what he meant."

"Messing around with Jeff Dixon is a huge mistake," she snapped.

"I know that," Kate whined. "I do. But when he looks at me, I feel something. It's very seductive."

"He's dangerous," Sharon said firmly. "That's why he's seductive."

"Maybe at first," Kate shrugged. "But after talking to him, it feels like much more. I recognize myself in his eyes. It's exciting just talking to him. I love Danny—of course I do—but being married to him has made me less than…"

"Katie, who do you think you're talking to?" Sharon interrupted. "I've seen you with Danny. You two are still hot for each other. And you can't fake that kind of chemistry."

"But outside of the house, I'm someone else. Someone's mom. Someone's wife. And I've been fine with that. Honestly fine. Until now." Kate threw her hands up in surrender. "Obviously, I am fooling myself. If I am truly happy, why would I be tempted to jump into the arms of Jeff Dixon?"

"Listen to yourself for a second, Katie," Sharon said calmly. "Because I can't believe my ears. Jeff Dixon is not the key to your happiness, and neither is Danny, for that matter. Only you can make yourself happy. You are the captain of your ship. You can sail into the sunset or right over a cliff. The choice is yours."

Groaning, Kate covered her face with her hands. "I'm a bad person. How could I even look at another man? I don't deserve Danny. He's too good for me."

"Good Lord," Sharon snorted. "Now you sound like that asshole, whatshisname. That roommate of Danny's. The one who hated you."

"Conner Trask," Kate mumbled.

"That's right. He absolutely hated the idea of you and Danny together. The guy did everything he could to keep Danny away from you. And it didn't work." Sharon smiled widely, but Kate failed to see the humor.

"Danny should have listened. Conner was right. I am trouble."

"Danny knew exactly what he was doing, and he loves you. No one knows you better. Katie, you never lied about who you were— not to Danny anyways. Maybe you've been lying to the Molly Ibners of the world but that's easy enough to fix. Just stop caring so much about what other people think."

"But what should I do about Jeff Dixon?" Kate whined.

"I can't answer that," Sharon shrugged. "As much as I would like to tell you what to do, I can't. It's your life, Katie, and ultimately, you're responsible for the choices you make."

"Will you still love me if I choose wrong?"

"You won't choose wrong." Sharon wrapped her soft arms around Kate.

It was a very motherly gesture, and Kate couldn't stop herself. The dam broke, and the tears would not stop falling. Sharon simply held her close and wasn't at all alarmed by her collapse.

"Katie, have some faith," Sharon said after the cries became sniffles. "You are a strong, determined woman who won't stay down long."

Kate was running low on faith but was willing to borrow some of Sharon's.

"Thank you," she nodded. "I feel better."

It was a lie, but she did feel better saying it. Stepping out of Sharon's embrace, Kate made a promise to herself. She promised to keep lying until the lies became the truth. It wasn't the kind of faith Sharon was calling for, but it was the only kind of faith Kate could muster.

CHAPTER 49

NO CONTACT

Danny spent Saturday morning working in the yard. Kate was out with Sharon, and he was with the boys trimming back perennials and edging out garden beds. Physical work was a stress reliever this time of month. Kate had her period so there was a self-imposed no contact rule in the bedroom.

He could rely on Kate. His wife's body ran like clockwork. Five days was the average length of her monthly cycle, and she always came out the other end hot and bothered. The countdown began Thursday, so Tuesday was now his favorite day of the week.

When Kate arrived home from Sharon's house, Danny's hard work was rewarded. She walked around the yard with a wide grin, making plans for new plantings and flowers.

"Next week, I'll take the truck and a wheelbarrow to the nursery and scoop our own wood mulch. We won't have to pay a delivery charge this year," she said smiling excitedly.

"Well, I guess the truck is already paying for itself then." Danny turned his ball cap around and pulled Kate in for a sloppy kiss.

"I'm gonna run inside and change," Kate said. "I want to help."

"Don't bother, Trouble," he said. "Take it easy this afternoon. Tonight, we're going out to dinner and a movie. Just the two of us. Peter is babysitting."

"Really?" she said clasping her hands together. Kate's eyes glistened with happiness. It was astonishingly easy to please his wife.

"All your favorites, baby. Sushi first and then you pick the movie. I promise I won't complain."

"Yay," she cheered as she pranced into the house. "I'm lovin' Daddy's guilt trip."

Of course, it was obvious. Danny was a simple man with simple motives and Kate couldn't resist pointing them out. She wasn't going to let the Natalie Bell-Charles debacle slide by without some serious ribbing.

"Guilt trip?" Peter asked. "Is that why I'm babysitting? Because of the blonde lady from the train?"

Danny lifted his eyebrows and shook his head. "Let it be a lesson to ya, Pete. Don't mess around unless you're willing to pay the price."

"But you were just talking, Dad," Pete reminded him.

Danny stared down into his son's eyes—gray, like his own—and was reminded of how much Peter resembled him. For once, he had the kid's undivided attention, so he decided not to waste it.

"It felt nice having a good-looking woman flirt with me. Mom didn't like it, just like I wouldn't like it if a guy flirted with her. It was a stupid thing to let happen, and I want Mom to forget about it. So I'm kissing up. That's why you're being forced to babysit."

"What will you do on Monday?" he asked. "What if that blonde lady tries to talk to you again?"

Danny laughed remembering Kate's performance at the train station and slapped his son on the shoulder. "Do you really think she will?"

Peter laughed too. "I'd like to see it if she tries. Yesterday was totally awesome. I've never seen Mom go thermonuclear."

"Son, you have no idea," Danny scoffed. "Your mother was just getting started. I've seen Mom make grown men cry. She gets scary really fast."

"But Mom doesn't scare you," Peter said smiling.

Danny shook his head. "That's where you're wrong, Pete. Mom scares me silly."

Picking up his shovel, Danny began hacking away at a patch of overgrown day lilies. He already emailed Natalie Bell-Charles his apologies. She expressed her own regrets and hoped she hadn't caused him too much trouble. He intended to break it off, but he couldn't figure out how to phrase it.

Danny felt like a jerk making assumptions about Natalie's intentions even though he was ninety-five percent sure she wanted to fuck him. So he kept stewing on it. Composing simple sentences in his head, he couldn't quite get the words of an appropriate email together. The day lilies bore the brunt of his frustration as Peter's question haunted his thoughts.

If Natalie Bell-Charles had enough courage to show her face at the train station, he would have to ignore her. He cringed. Danny didn't like the idea of giving Natalie the cold shoulder. Maybe he should meet her for lunch, give her a proper good-bye, end on friendly note.

The smartphone in his pocket was becoming a nagging reminder of unfinished business. Danny tossed his shovel to the ground and stomped into the house. He hastily hit the power button on his phone and slid it into his briefcase. Monday. Danny would sit at his desk at work and calmly decide how to handle final contact.

Monday, he would deal with Natalie Bell-Charles.

CHAPTER 50

A PROPOSAL

He waited inside his new car. It was late for a run. The sun high in the sky. The streets and sidewalks crowded. She wanted to opt out of Sundays. Kathryn rose early with her family and went to church. But after a successful negotiation, their jog was rescheduled. Time and place didn't matter. Unlike Kathryn, he was free. His wife and children were attending church services in Kentucky.

When she came over the hill towing her yellow dog, he almost laughed. Kathryn the fox. Bushy tailed and bright eyed, she stopped short. The lips of her pouty mouth fell open in disbelief. Stooping her shoulders, she peered into the windshield.

Joy welled in his chest. Fun. Kathryn was simply too much fun. Throwing open the door, he climbed out of the vehicle.

"Jeff," she stuttered. "I can't believe you did it."

He stroked the hood of the car as she jogged to meet him. Her white T-shirt spelled *Hockey Mom* in bold red letters across her chest. Probably a gift from one of her children. Or perhaps the idiot husband thought it was funny. Labeling Kathryn as an overburdened, car-pooling, middle-class suburbanite would be something the ingrate would enjoy. He should have been disgusted. But the

269

T-shirt made her more endearing. Sweet. Lovely. And enchanting. Kathryn did Hockey Moms justice.

"You may not have the garage space, but I certainly do," he teased when she stepped next to his side.

Kathryn leaned into the open window of the driver's side door and glanced around the interior. Eyes shining. Smiling. It was glorious. He made Kathryn smile. What a relief. It was agony knowing she was in pain. Vulnerable. The lumberjack husband's rough hands bruising her radiant skin. Intolerable. Being apart unacceptable.

Kathryn's current state of indecision was torture to them both. Like the Porsche, he was prepared to out-perform his rival. He had created a plan of action. Forcing Kathryn into deep water was tricky. But the only remedy to her miserable condition.

"It's beautiful," Kathryn said.

Her voice hinted at sadness. How intriguing. The inner workings of her mind still so fascinating.

"Not nearly as beautiful as you, my fox," he murmured.

He ran a finger along her cheekbone. Kathryn stared. Unblinkingly, the pupils of her eyes widened. The tip of his finger burned. He longed to take her somewhere private. Out of the sun. Into the shadows.

"Would you like to go for a spin?" he asked seductively.

The key dangled from his index finger. Kathryn shook her head reluctantly and gazed down at Marigold. He didn't care. The dog could squeeze in the back.

"I can't, Jeff," she sighed. "My son, Peter, is right behind me." She glanced over his shoulder. "He caught me running out the backdoor. He was lacing up his in-line skates when I left the house. I couldn't think of an excuse."

Frowning, she bit her bottom lip. Expecting a temper tantrum, he guessed.

"Another time then," he said, smiling slightly. He climbed back into the Porsche and slammed the door.

"I'm sorry," she said. The relief was visible on her face.

It was pleasing. Knowing he exceeded Kathryn's expectations. Her son made his forecasted appearance. Peter glided elegantly down the sidewalk in skates.

"Before you go," he began.

Reaching an arm through the open window, he laid a hand loosely on her elbow. They froze. Like lightening. His skin seared with electric heat. She felt it too.

"I've got a proposal," he said quickly. "It troubles me. This situation…I know it's very difficult for you. I've got business in the Cayman Islands, and I'd like to extend an invitation to you.…"

Kathryn shook her head wildly. Tendrils of caramel-colored hair fell into her eyes.

"Kathryn," he said firmly. "Let me finish before you refuse. If you should decide to join me, we would leave early Thursday evening by private jet from Naperville's airport—9:00 p.m. For three nights, I have reserved the use of my partner's beachside condominium. We would return home late Sunday night."

"It's impossible, Jeff," she hissed. "I can't get away. Danny would never allow it."

"I have every confidence in your ability to manufacture a cover story," he replied smoothly. "A conference. A sick friend. An unforeseen family obligation. A desperate need for alone time. You know better than I which would be the most convincing."

As he rattled off excuses, Kathryn's attention moved away. Her son. She gave the boy a wave before turning her fake smile on him.

"I can't," she said—artificially sweet.

"You haven't heard what I'm offering in return for your company."

Kathryn's brow furrowed, and the fake smile dissolved into a frown. How fun. He enjoyed out-foxing her.

"Give me three nights in the Cayman Islands," he said. "After those three nights, I will say good-bye. Or not. It will be your choice, Kathryn. I promise."

Opening her stance, she welcomed her son into the conversation. "Peter, this is Mr. Dixon. We met last week at the Village Board Meeting."

Peter paid little attention to either one of them. He was gazing lustily at the shiny black sports car. The situation was humorous. The Porsche was just as seductive as the boy's wily mother. Peter extended a long arm and shook hands enthusiastically.

"Nice ride," Peter exclaimed.

"Thank you. It's last year's model, but I didn't want to wait. I bought it right off the lot."

Peter failed to make eye contact. The boy's eyes were busily admiring the smooth lines of the Porsche. It was too comical. Stifling laughter impossible. And Kathryn rolled her eyes.

"Peter," she said handing the boy the dog's leash. "Take Marigold. I've got some business to finish with Mr. Dixon. I'll catch up in minute."

Kathryn's tone snapped her son to attention. Peter met his eyes for the first time. Reaching into the vehicle, the boy offered a hand again. "It was nice meeting you, Mr. Dixon."

Polite and respectful. Of course. Peter was Kathryn's child. And she was an exceptionally good mother.

"Likewise, Peter," he said smiling up at the boy. "You definitely take after your father."

"You've met my Dad?" Peter asked.

"Not officially. But even from a distance, your resemblance to him is striking."

"I get that a lot," the boy pronounced proudly.

"I'm sure you do."

Peter skated away with the dog faithfully trailing along. Delightful. He hoped all Kathryn's introductions went as smoothly.

Exhaling loudly, she looked after her son. "Nice, Jeff."

"I thought that went well," he said defensively.

"I can't keep doing this," she cried. "Now my kids are involved. Please, I'm begging you...leave me alone."

"I'll see you tomorrow, Kathryn," he said as he turned the key in the ignition.

The engine purred. Like Kathryn. It was sleek. Sexy. And incredibly responsive to the slightest touch.

"Give my proposal some thought. It's the answer to your problem."

Shifting the car into gear, he glided away from the curb. He watched from his rearview mirror. She stood alone. Hands on her hips. Motionless in the middle of the street. Gazing at her feet. So sad.

272

Braking at a stop sign, his eyes rose expectantly to the rearview mirror. She was gone. Disturbing. Turning in his bucket seat, he searched. His heart's desire disappeared in a flash. Quintessentially fox-like but still unsettling.

Revving the powerful engine, he gloried in Kathryn's natural tendencies. The vixen loved the thrill. The danger. His aching heart brimmed with satisfaction. The truth his greatest ally.

Kathryn could not resist a challenge.

CHAPTER 51

PURPLE LILACS

Sleep was her only escape, and Kate was doing it soundly. It was the kind of slumber reserved for the dead. For seven consecutive hours, Kate's guilty conscience was wiped clean. But she could not stop the inevitable.

Daylight crept in through the cracks in her window shades, disturbed her peace, and stirred her awake. Her first conscious thought was of Jeff Dixon—waiting at the entrance to the jogging trail.

She lay in bed listening to Danny's slow breathing—mulling over her options. There were only three worth considering. The first was to tell the truth. The second was to go to the Cayman Islands. And the third was to do nothing. None of the three options produced a viable outcome, and she hesitated to consider a fourth.

Kate knew her problem had a solution. Pondering on it—dwelling on it—was not getting her any closer to acting on it. She needed to do something—and that something felt drastic—extreme—and possibly earth shattering. The consequences of her actions weighed heavily on her spirit. So heavily, it was difficult to push herself out of bed. But she did. Jeff Dixon was waiting.

Marigold watched while Kate got ready for their jog. Kate brushed her teeth, washed her face, and pulled her hair into a tight ponytail. Marigold stayed at her heels and was a comfort. A willing participant in Kate's deception, the dog embodied the virtues she desperately guarded but did not deserve—trust, loyalty, faith, and love. Danny. Danny was the first and only man to live in her heart. And she hated herself for not being strong enough to deserve him.

Kate cleansed her noxious spirit by breathing in the scented air of spring. There were still a few tilted daffodils dotting the landscape of the surrounding neighborhood. Kate's own spring flowers were spent. She had worked in her garden most of Sunday—turning down stems, tilling the soil, and planting seeds. The promise of summer made it impossible to regret the passage of spring, and all it cost Kate was a pair a dirty hands.

Of course, Jeff was there. Waiting next to his Porsche, he ran through a series of stretches as she made her approach. Kate quickened her jog—daring him to keep pace. He fell in step with her on the jogging trail. She tried to find her own rhythm—vary her stride—skip over footfalls—but it was too difficult. They were so close. Fighting her body's natural impulse was taking all her concentration, so she surrendered, deciding it was best to conserve her energy. It was invigorating—and so very unfair. Jogging side by side, they were the perfect match. Kate hated him, but she hated herself more.

They flew off the jogging trail and raced to the secluded end of the fishing pier. He was smiling widely—white teeth glinting in the bright light of the morning sun—as they paced breathlessly—cooling down—slowing their heart rates.

"You're in a good mood this morning," she said after catching her breath.

"And you're not?" he teased.

"I'm curious, Jeff—don't you have any feelings of loss?" Kate was careful to keep her tone non-judgmental.

"Are you speaking of Ainsley or of the children?"

Jeff lifted himself off the pier and sat on the wide railing. He took the ball cap off his head and ran a hand absentmindedly through his sweaty hair. It was distracting, and Kate struggled to remain focused. Leaning forward, he gripped the rail. Muscles rippled along his arm, and she flashed on the memory of his naked chest. Sculpted like a Roman statue, Jeff Dixon's body was divine. Kate dropped Marigold's leash, losing the battle to remain focused. She gazed into the black pools of Jeff's eyes and wished him dead.

"Kathryn?"

His mouth turned up ever so slightly at the corners. His cheeks were rosy pink beneath the dark stubble. Course. Stinging. Forbidden but so very tempting. Kate took a long step—her legs hollow. And reached for him.

Jeff landed on the pier with a resounding thud that rattled the boards beneath her feet. His arms caught her around the waist, and she fell into him. The kiss was all business—the games forgotten. Kate turned herself over to the needs of desire. Quench the thirst, satiate the hunger, fulfill the ache.

Jeff Dixon, she cursed as she tasted his mouth with her quick tongue—lapped up his musky scent. *Jeff Dixon,* she gasped as he pulled at her ponytail—ran gentle fingers through her hair—rubbed coarse whiskers against her neck. *Jeff Dixon,* she sighed as the molten blood coursed through her body—melted the ice cold tension of resistance.

"Jeff," she groaned.

He kissed her gently on the lips before running his hands along her face—down her neck—across her shoulders. His fingers skimmed the flesh of her arms. Grasping her hands firmly in his, he breathed in and out. Filling his lungs deliberately, he calmed his own raging desire.

"Kathryn," he whispered. "You mustn't pounce. My willpower cannot withstand the temptation, and we are out in the open. I can't fuck you here."

She pushed him away and turned her back. Clenching and unclenching her fists, she beat back the overwhelming urge to roar—to fight—to run. She jumped when he came from behind. Startled, her head flew up, and she scanned the park. Jeff was undeterred. Shushing softly, he wrapped his arms around her waist—buried his face into her hair—kissed the hollow curve at her neck. His purpose was to comfort, not seduce.

"Someone might see," she warned, searching the empty park.

"It's Monday," he whispered. "People sleep late on Mondays."

"Don't you worry?" she asked. "What if Ainsley is having you watched?"

"Why would she do that?" he laughed.

Kate pulled away to retrieve Marigold's leash. The dog was sitting still as a statue watching the tall grass surrounding the pond.

"The divorce," Kate said impatiently. "She could win a large settlement if she proves you were unfaithful."

"Kathryn," Jeff smiled. "Ainsley doesn't care about money. She never has. Her father secured her trust fund and family inheritance by forcing me to sign a rock solid prenuptial agreement. I'm the pauper in the marriage."

"The Porsche?" Kate asked, pointing aimlessly.

"Well," he laughed. "Comparatively speaking, I'm the pauper. I've managed to earn my own money."

"Oh," Kate said.

She was hoping she had at least one card in the game. Now it was gone. Jeff did not fear Ainsley's lawyers.

"And the children?" she asked. "What about them?"

"Of course, I am responsible for my financial share…not that it will be necessary. Their grandfather has already provided them with funds for their education and so forth," he shrugged. "It's really not that complicated. I'm meeting with an associate this morning and asking him to draw up a separation agreement. Ainsley needs to understand it's over. Official papers will help her with closure."

Kate shrunk away. She hated the way he spoke of his wife. It was as if he had no feelings for her at all.

"Aren't you the least bit sad? The least bit sorry about losing your family? Your children?" she pressed, too curious to let the subject die.

"I'll have visitation rights," he said casually. "But for now, I think it's best if I keep my distance. Get them used to my absence."

"Your absence?" Kate asked numbly.

"They are very young, Kathryn, and well looked after," he said assuredly. "I can't say I ever felt necessary in their lives. Maybe when they are older...like your children...it will be easier to relate to them. But for now, the best place for them is with their mother."

Kathryn peered into his eyes searching for something warm to hold onto. "I could never leave my boys, Jeff."

"Oh, Kathryn," he said, leaping to take her hand. "I did not mean to imply that I'm adverse to children in general. You couldn't abandon your boys. Of course not."

"Of course not," she repeated.

"Have you given thought to my proposal?" he asked.

"I have," she nodded.

They walked side by side towards the jogging trail. Kate was with Jeff, but she was also thinking of home. The boys and their breakfast—Danny and his newspaper—the full dishwasher—her grocery list.

"It won't work," she said, shaking her head. "Danny would be suspicious if I took off alone, and I don't want to involve anyone else in a lie."

"I'm sure if you tried, you could come up with an excuse," he said cheerfully.

They jogged through park at an easy pace. Their breath was even—the rhythm familiar. Kate stole glances at his chiseled profile. Jeff's ball cap was faded and fraying at the brim—an old favorite—Vanderbilt University. It was unsuitable attire for a high-paid attorney, but she imagined he wore it since graduating—perhaps even on campus. The idea of Jeff Dixon as a young law student sent chills up her spine. She could have been a law student. She could have sat next to him in class. They could have gotten that close.

"My answer is no," she said firmly as they rounded the path around the baseball diamonds. "It will make too much trouble at home."

"We've got a couple of days yet," he shrugged. "Think on it some more."

He was so positive—so persistent—so resolute.

"And if I don't?" she asked. "Will you leave for the Cayman Islands without me?"

"I would rather imagine the possibilities," he said enthusiastically. "My business won't consume much time. We can enjoy the beach, the sun, and the private balcony. Have you ever sunbathed in the nude?"

"No," Kate said with a curt laugh. "I can't say that I have."

"We will be alone, Kathryn," he said enticingly. "Think about what that could mean."

They slowed to a walk as they neared the entrance of the park. Kate knew what being alone meant, and she didn't trust herself to take the risk. Even if he kept his promise and said good-bye after their return home, she could not be sure that she was strong enough to turn him away. The prospect of three nights alone was terrifying.

Lilac bushes surrounded an unsightly equipment shed and their sweet fragrance drifted in the breeze. Kate lifted her nose instinctively and inhaled deeply. Jeff dashed over to the overgrown bushes. Sawing at the branches with a small pocket knife attached to his car keys, he managed to quickly pull together small bouquet. His eyes shined with childlike enthusiasm.

"For you, my fox," he said. "In the language of flowers, purple lilacs symbolize the first emotions of love."

Kate received the flowers with a cautious smile. "Thank you."

"Now," he said tugging her on the elbow. "Time for a spin."

"Jeff, no," she protested. "What about Marigold? I have to get back. Danny is awake by now."

The passenger door of the Porsche was already open, and he took away Marigold's leash. The traitor dog jumped in between the two bucket seats and situated herself comfortably in the hatch. Jeff shoved the keys in her hand and climbed into the passenger seat.

"Just around the block. It will only take a minute," he said.

Kate sighed in frustration but found herself hurrying around the hood of the black sports car. Jeff did not hear the word no.

She handed him the lilacs and slid into the luxurious leather of the low seat. Her body sunk into the contours of the car's interior.

It felt natural and snug. Inserting the key into the ignition was a strangely sensual experience and her excitement mounted when the powerful engine ignited with awe-inspiring ease.

She sat silently enjoying the thrum of the engine and moved automatically to the radio—flipping to her favorite country music station. Jeff startled her when he opened the sunroof. She'd forgotten to stay on guard. Immediately, she turned the radio off.

"I like country music," Jeff remarked.

"No you don't," she challenged.

"I went to law school in Nashville. I hung out in in country bars all the time."

"Yeah, right," Kate said smiling widely.

"What do I have to do to prove it?" he asked teasingly. "I know all the words to "Walk the Line." Would you like to hear them? I can two-step. Care to dance?"

"No, Jeff," she said, shifting the car into drive. "I believe you."

Jeff turned the music up as they rounded the corner. Lifting a lone lilac bud from the bunch gathered in his lap, he leaned over and tucked it behind her ear.

"Gorgeous," he said. "In the Caymans, I want you to wear flowers in your hair every day."

Again, the Cayman Islands. Kate let some pressure off the gas pedal. She glanced in his direction and caught him grinning out the window. Hair curled at the nape of his neck.

"Any other requests, Jeff?" she asked abruptly. "You seem to have put a lot of thought into the particularities of this fantasy trip."

"It's not fantasy," he retorted. "And yes, now that you mention it, I do have another request. A Brazilian wax. Have you ever considered getting one?"

"What?" she exclaimed.

"Yes," he answered calmly. "A Brazilian wax removes pubic hair."

"I know what it is, Jeff. And no, I've never considered it. I like my vagina the way it is. It works very well, and I don't like the idea of messing with it."

"That is very practical," he sighed. "And a point worth making."

Kate coasted to a stop close to Winfield Road's intersection and shifted the car into park.

"We should do some research on the internet before we schedule the spa appointment," Jeff added. "Brazilian waxes are fairly common. I'm sure there is a lot of information regarding the resulting sexual side effects."

Kate examined his eyes before they got out of the car and decided he was joking. His humor was disguised in the dryness of his delivery. It was very lawyerly, but nevertheless funny, so Kate laughed.

Marigold must have enjoyed the ride, because she didn't want to get out. After a little prodding, she leapt over the driver's seat and joined Kate on the street. Jeff was waiting on the sidewalk. One hand lay casually on the hood of car, and the other twirled her bouquet of lilacs.

"Can I have a kiss good-bye?" he asked, his mouth pulled up into a crooked smile and his raven eyes flashed with humor.

"In comparison with your other requests this morning, I would have to say that a kiss is somewhat anti-climatic," Kate teased.

She walked towards him hesitantly. Taking the lilacs from his hand, she kissed him lightly on the lips before stepping away. The kiss was innocent, but her body betrayed her. The muscles of her lower body clenched, and she squirmed—subtly pressing her thighs together in search of relief. Jeff smiled knowingly before tugging at her hand—holding her in place—he whispered in her ear as he brushed past.

"For the Cayman Islands, Kathryn, get a Brazilian. I'd like a naked pussy in the chaise lounge next to mine. When I go down on you, I don't want anything between my mouth and your clit."

Shock vacuumed the air out of her lungs. And then he was gone. Stunned, she stared after the taillights of the Porsche. Finally, she gasped. Marigold looked up with curious eyes.

Kate ripped at the lilac in her hair and threw it into the bushes with the gathered bunch in her hand. Disgusted, she channeled the desire pooling at her core into hatred. The emotions made an easy substitution.

Kate steered her feet towards home. Gazing up at the cloudless sky, she was grateful for the bright morning sun. It warmed her skin and added starch to her resolve. She had no time for self-pity. Kate dashed across the empty intersection with Marigold faithfully at her side and forced a smile. The smile was a lie but also necessary.

It masked the exhaustive battle raging inside her chest.

CHAPTER 52

CRAZY

He sat with his back to the window. The fingers of his left hand lay over the prepared file folder. His suit coat unbuttoned. Legs crossed. He preferred his coffee simple these days. Reminiscer of the time period when he was a penniless student. Black. Craig Haskins did not. The fancy, overpriced coffee took time. So he amused himself by watching his colleague flirt with the underage help.

Craig was a divorce attorney. Bald. Poor guy. Bad genes. But he was smart. Like him, Craig was a partner at the firm. The man couldn't bring in the same kind of money, but he was still very good.

Craig shuffled over to the wobbly bistro table with a foamy coffee and a leather portfolio. Angling his chair so the sun wasn't in his eyes, Craig finally sat down.

"I need a separation agreement." He avoided the pre-meeting niceties. Preferring to get right down business.

"I'm sorry, Jeff," Craig said. "I didn't realize you were having problems at home."

285

Craig was sincere. After all, a separation agreement was bad news. Keeping his face impassive, he slid the prepared file folder to Craig and took a sip of his coffee.

"My pre-nup," he said. "We should be able to avoid extended legal proceedings. All of Ainsley's assets are outlined in great detail."

"Do you want to fight it?" Craig asked as he scanned the marital contract. "Were you pressured to sign?"

"I just want to get through this with as little conflict as possible, Craig," he said shaking his head for emphasis. "I'm putting the house on the market. Ainsley's lawyers need notice. I don't expect to make any money off the sale, but I should get enough to cover the mortgage."

"Okay," Craig opened his portfolio and took a few short notes. "I'll tailor something to go along with the pre-nup."

"I included the names of the children. Their dates of birth. Social security numbers. And all of my insurance information. When you calculate child support, keep in mind that they will be residing in Kentucky. The cost of living is considerably lower than Chicago."

"Do you want to include a visitation schedule?" Craig asked.

"That's not necessary. Ainsley won't be difficult."

"Was this her idea, Jeff?" Craig asked. His eyes narrowed, and he tapped the pen on the paper. "Or was it yours?"

Taking a deep breath, he jumped. "I met another woman."

Craig dropped his pen and set himself back in his seat. His face wrinkled in disapproval. The reaction was anticipated. But Craig was his counsel. And needed to be made aware.

"Don't do it, Jeff. You're smarter than this," Craig shook his said. "How many times have we seen this scenario play out? You, yourself, make fun of guys who leave their wives for young, high-maintenance models. It never works out."

"I'm not doing that," he laughed. "She's not younger. And I've already done high maintenance. Ainsley was a full-time job."

"Ainsley is a gem. A real lady. And she's rich. What you're doing makes no fucking sense. As soon as her old man kicks the bucket, you'll be set for life."

Peering at Craig over the brim of his cup, he sipped his coffee. They stared at each other for a long moment.

"So it's love," Craig finally said.

"Yes," he agreed. "It's love."

"And is the love mutual?"

"She won't admit it," he shrugged. "Not yet. There are obstacles. She's married. Has three children. She's reluctant to hurt them. But, we can't be apart. It's inevitable."

"Shit, Jeff," Craig hissed. "You dumped Ainsley for a middle-aged mother of three who is reluctant to leave her husband?"

The smile crept across his face. Having a conversation about Kathryn was very satisfying. And justly so. She was in his every thought. Sharing was more than a relief. It was heavenly. As his lawyer, Craig could be trusted. But the man wasn't stupid. It didn't take long for the light bulb to go off.

"It's the sex, right?" Craig asked eagerly.

The smirk was unintentional. But automatic. And felt very right. "Craig," he said dryly. "After our first encounter, I spent two days worrying she was a figment of my imagination. Since then, she's exceeded every fantasy I've ever had."

"So she's great in bed," Craig replied after eyeing him suspiciously. "Is that really the foundation for a lasting relationship?"

"Actually," he corrected. "We don't fuck in a bed. She knows, like I do, that her marriage will be over once we do. I'm still working on getting her flat on her back. But it won't be long now."

The concept of sex outside of a bed threw the seasoned divorce attorney for a loop. Craig was stunned silent.

Again, the smirk was unintentional but automatic. And delightfully childish. "We met in the park. She is a jogger. Like me," he added for fun.

Craig readjusted himself in his chair. Eyes wide. The man rocked the table when he leaned his elbows on it. "You've been having sex in the park?" Craig asked in disbelief.

"I didn't know her name for weeks," he shrugged. "When I asked, she wouldn't tell me. Kathryn was afraid if we knew each other's names the intensity of our sexual connection would diminish. But it hasn't. If anything, it has grown."

Craig was concentrating very hard. Listening acutely. But not comprehending. It was as if Jeff was speaking in tongues. And in some measure, it was true. After all, to Craig and to every other person he knew, his reputation was rock solid. A reasonable man. A serious man. Not prone to romantic ramblings. Constructing an argument took only seconds. Leaning in, he locked onto Craig's befuddled gaze.

"This is not the first time I've been unfaithful, Craig. So trust my judgment. My connection with this woman is unique. When I draw fingers across Kathryn's flesh, it's as if I'm coaxing a blue flame. My fingertips burn. I can actually feel the heat rising to the surface of her skin. Hot shivers. Passion's flash point is always within reach. As a man, I've never felt so empowered. So in command. But at the same time, so utterly helpless. I'm completely defenseless against her."

"She comes with baggage," Craig reminded him reluctantly. "Three kids can douse the flames of passion pretty damn quick."

"If it was just sex, I wouldn't be sitting across from you right now. She's my equal in every way. Relating to her intellectually is just as stimulating as relating to her physically."

Craig rolled his eyes and snorted. Why was it so hard to believe? Sex and intelligence were not mutually exclusive. It was offensive. Kathryn was no simple housewife. Allowing her to be considered as such was unacceptable.

"She scored 174 on the LSATs, Craig. Name someone we know who has done that."

He got the man's attention. Craig's eyes narrowed as he sat back in his chair. Kathryn's LSAT scores were on record and accessed after a few well-placed phone calls. The scores were worthy of Harvard and Yale. Tragic and mystifying. The circumstances of her life choices remained a puzzle. Nevertheless. He was grateful. Whatever the reasons, the choices brought Kathryn to him.

"When you said *mother*, I assumed she was a housewife." Craig was apologetic. An elitist. Like most men in his profession, the divorce attorney was hyper-competitive. But at the very least, Kathryn's LSAT scores gave her some measure of the respect.

"She is," he replied sadly. "Kathryn never made it to law school. Married her college boyfriend. A jock. He commutes to Chicago on the train. The man is inadequate. No match for her intellectually. It's no wonder she strayed. The idiot husband is a bore."

"And sleeping with the woman you love," Craig added.

"True. I hate him. But, I've made a considerable effort to smother my jealousy. It's best if the marriage dies for reasons other than my interference. Kathryn is a very good mother. She will want her boys to maintain a relationship with their father. And I can concede to that. If the husband knows I was the catalyst for the destruction of his family, civil relations will be impossible. Kathryn's happiness is at stake, and I would never want to cause her unnecessary pain. So, I've resigned myself to the wings. Waiting for the marriage to die on its own."

"And how do you think that will happen, exactly?" Craig asked.

"There are other factors working against the marriage," he added. "The husband is a player. He's has a blonde he toys with on the side. Also, Kathryn is re-starting her career. That alone will succeed in driving a wedge between them. The husband is very possessive and won't like Kathryn spending time outside the home."

"I don't know, Jeff," Craig was still unconvinced. "I hope it ends well but experience tells me otherwise. You didn't ask for my advice, but I'm going to give it anyways. Re-consider. You cannot afford to make rash decisions especially when there are children involved. It's not too late. Reconcile with Ainsley. Save your family."

Lifting his coffee to lips, he gulped. Craig had fulfilled his role as counsel. Conversation over.

"Thank you, Craig," he said. "I appreciate the advice. But it is too late. I'm obsessed. Infatuated. Dangerously close to becoming pathological. And honestly, I don't care."

Rising from his seat, he buttoned his suit coat and waited for his colleague to situate the papers.

"Okay," Craig sighed—resigned now. "At least you know how crazy you sound. Most clients in your position delude themselves into thinking their actions are based in reason."

He laughed. Heartily.

"No, Craig," he said. "I'm done deluding myself. Done pretending I'm something I'm not. If Kathryn would agree, I would run away with her. I know it's unrealistic, but like I said, she's already exceeded every fantasy I've ever had. I've got my money stashed away. Prepared for the chance that Kathryn might be willing to start new somewhere else."

"Christ, Jeff," Craig snapped in alarm. "Do you really think that's a possibility?"

Laughing, he gave Craig's shoulder a friendly pat as they walked towards the door of the coffee shop.

"We're at a crossroads," he said. "I'm going to the Cayman's to finish up a client deal this weekend, and I'm taking her with me. Kathryn keeps a firm choke on her emotions. It makes her highly combustible. If I apply just the right amount of pressure, she might finally succumb and decide to end the marriage charade. The odds of Kathryn abandoning her children are very small. But…a man can dream."

"Now I know you're crazy," Craig scoffed.

It was a clean lob over the net. Irresistible. He smiled slyly before correcting his colleague.

"Crazy like a fox."

CHAPTER 53

BLOODY-MINDED

Living the lie wasn't difficult because daily life was relatively simple—rote—and she did her work on auto-pilot. At the very least, daily chores occupied her thoughts and kept her hands busy. Kate found herself humming as she applied eye makeup in her bathroom mirror.

Freshly showered, she dug through her closet and built an outfit—two hundred dollar jeans and red cowboy boots. Dressing up was part of her campaign against self-pity. Danny liked a bit of lace. For him, she left the top four buttons of her blouse open. The lacy undershirt peeked out at her cleavage.

She looked good, and it helped. The confident clack of her boots reinforced her determination. Jeff Dixon was going to the leave for the Cayman Islands without her. Every problem had a solution. Sooner or later—she hoped sooner—the solution would come to her.

Kate was conspicuous when she arrived at Joey's preschool. The truck was an attention grabber, but Marigold was over the top. The dog hung out the passenger window eagerly waiting for Joey to appear. Bursting out of the school's double doors, Joey whooped with glee before climbing into the truck.

"I've got to go to the grocery store, little man," Kate said as Joey tried to maneuver his way past a very happy Marigold. "We need milk, and Daddy wants me to make a deposit at the bank."

The Food Wise was small compared to the grocery stores on the edge of town. It specialized in customer service, and the community bank had a convenient location inside. Kate was willing to spend the extra twenty cents on milk for the sake of crossing the bank off her list.

"What about Marigold?" Joey asked.

He scratched the dog's belly absentmindedly. Marigold was astride his lap with her head poking out the window—her funny ears flapped in the wind.

"She'll be okay," Kate said assuredly. "We'll leave the windows open halfway."

Kate parked and hurried around the hood of the truck. Joey struggled with the heavy passenger door. He was tangled up with Marigold and using all his weight to shove at the door handle. Kate feared he would tumble onto the pavement, but Joey hated being treated like a baby. So she did not fuss.

"We'll be right back," Joey promised—kissing Marigold between the eyes.

Kate parked purposefully next to the entrance, so Marigold could a have a clear view through the automatic doors. True to form, the dog watched faithfully as they crossed the parking lot.

Avoiding the tables laden with colorful cupcakes and frosted donuts, Kate pulled Joey towards the dairy aisle. Her son skipped and his enthusiasm for the simple errand lent a genuine smile to Kate's otherwise placid face.

They were moving quickly towards the checkout line when Joey became transfixed by a display at the end of an aisle.

"Can I can get some sugar cereal?" he asked sweetly.

"No, Joey, come on. You know better than to ask."

She left him in front of the display and positioned herself in one of the two active checkout lines.

"Please, Momma," he begged. Picking out a box, he waved it. "Look, the lady on the box is smiling."

The checkout clerks laughed quietly. Joey's freckled face and pouty mouth were hard to resist.

"Joey, put it down."

Stubbornly, he clutched the box to his chest. "Uncle Walt eats sugar cereal, and he doesn't have rotten teeth."

Kate's line was moving, and she lost patience. They were center stage—performing the classic mother-child conflict scenario. The role was familiar but grated on Kate's nerves. Unwilling to let the scene play out to its normal conclusion, she improvised.

"If I buy the cereal, will you eat it with a piece of fruit and a scoop of cottage cheese?" she asked.

"Yes," Joey answered solemnly.

"And do you promise to brush teeth afterwards? No arguments?" she bargained.

"I promise," he answered.

Joey ran to meet his mother in line and got a dirty look when he shoved past the man standing behind her. Kate set her hands on Joey's shoulders and gave the rude man a disgusted glance. He didn't notice. He was too busy yammering on his cell phone.

Joey moved closer to the cheerful woman operating the cash register adjacent to their narrow aisle. He was fascinated with store clerks and coveted their position behind the counter. Venturing into forbidden territory, he put one foot on the cushioned black mat beneath the woman's sturdy shoes.

"Joey," Kate said redirecting his attention. "Give the lady the cereal."

Handing the clerk his box, Joey quickly hid behind Kate's legs. The clerk's wide grin made him suspicious. Joey didn't like being regarded as cute.

"Here ya go," the clerk winked.

Joey snatched the bag from her outstretched hand. "Thank you," he said shyly.

Kate smiled apologetically at the clerk and ran her debit card through the little black machine. While waiting for the machine to process her information, Kate's tangled thoughts crystallized. Her attention was captured by a pair of teenage boys. They entered the store slowly through the automatic doors. They were not dressed appropriately for the weather—hooded jackets.

The generic music playing on the store's sound system and the rude man's incessant yammering faded to the background. Quiet. She listened to the steady inflow of her breath—the rhythmic pumping of her heart muscle. Mind and body fused. Homogenized. Ready to spring, she focused. Kate watched.

One boy hung back. White. Poor complexion. Left earring. Hood up. Dirty brown hair. Slight—maybe 140 pounds. The boy glanced nervously around the store with his hands stuffed into the pockets of his baggy jacket.

His friend was murmuring to the bank teller. One hand in his pocket—twitching—the other gripped the edge of the counter—tense. Tall. Maybe 170 pounds. Scripted tattoo along the dark skin of his neck. Hispanic, maybe.

These boys were not making a deposit. Instinctively, Kate shielded Joey—pushing his little body behind her legs. The bank teller was frightened, and she moved hesitantly behind the counter.

The hooded boy made eye contact—dangerous—but still a child. Maybe seventeen years old. Kate knew she should look away but did not. Every instinct told her to focus. *Watch. Study.* His beady eyes darted across her body. The excitement was too much—his movements were jerky—and he paced. Shoes unlaced. Jeans rode low. Kate's eyes widened in horror. The boy pulled an ancient looking revolver out of his jacket pocket. Setting it beneath his lips, he blew Kate a kiss.

The clerk behind the cash register jumped and released an earsplitting screech. Kate's eyes never left the hooded boy. Her peripheral vision sensed the fear, the anxiety of the people around her, but she let the images run past—her vision tunneled—the hooded boy—the gun.

"Don't move," the hooded boy barked, his voice rough with tension. "Everybody chill."

His eyes darted again. Blind to details—he was looking for bold moves—sudden changes. The gun went beneath the folds of his jacket. The hooded boy's accomplice turned his back to the store—trusting his nervous friend to maintain control of the customers. *Unwise.*

The boy's eyes flew back to the bank counter continuously—craving a successful score—wishing to be gone. The whimpers of the people surrounding Kate barely registered. Joey's warm body was her only priority. She felt it, attached to her legs—*Joey.* Slowly, she edged backwards, away from the gun.

The hooded boy turned his back, and Kate moved. Joey read her signal and scrambled beneath the shelves of the neighboring cashier line. Following his instincts, he made himself small and fit snugly beneath the counter. Kate released a tight breath when the cashier repositioned herself—further shielding Joey from view. Stepping forward, Kate barricaded the checkout aisle with her body—legs apart, a discreet fighting stance.

As the hooded boy paced, Kate calculated an exit—three known—one next to the public bathrooms at the rear of the store—two at the front. Kate's eyes narrowed when the boy at the bank counter signaled. Avoiding eye contact with customers, the boy took the money and dashed for the automatic doors.

Instead of following his partner, the hooded boy walked slowly past the grocery checkout. Emboldened by his apparent success—his nerves quieted—he misread his circumstances. It wasn't over yet. Stopping, his gaze lingered on Kate's jeans.

"Were you eyeballin' me?" he asked, waving his gun at Kate.

It rattled. Empty. But maybe not.

"Cause rich bitches give me hard on," he sneered.

His blinks were rapid—strung out. Sirens wailed in the distance. Kate nodded in the direction of the door, encouraged him to run, but he did not. *Stupid.* He lurched and caught Kate's left wrist. He was quick—a surprise—and she stumbled forward.

"No," Kate growled.

Clenching—she unleashed counter measures—dropped her butt to the floor. She used her dead weight against him. But he was strong. The adrenalin added to his superman buzz. And the floor was slick. Her boots lent no traction. Kate slid across the polished surface.

"No," she screamed.

She fought against the warm clamp of his grip.

"You won't be screaming with my dick your mouth," he countered.

Kate's butt dragged. There was nothing to hold onto—so she pulled against him—struggled to throw her attacker off-balance—and she did. But he would not relent. The sirens fueled his urgency, and he dragged her towards the door. Inch by inch, she skittered away from Joey and towards bright daylight.

"The cops," she warned. "Let me go. Run."

The first set of automatic doors opened. He passed through, but she would not go, not against her will. Surprise registered in the roomy recesses of her brain. It was easy—the choice simple—she would die first. The hooded boy could not win.

His friend rammed the escape car to an abrupt stop. Silver. Honda. Hatchback. No hubcaps.

"Let her go, man," his friend called through the open passenger window. "We don't have time for that shit."

Standing in the vestibule between the two automatic doors, the boy's lock on Kate's wrist struck her as perverse. Contrary to his own survival, he refused to let go. *Madman. Lunatic.* Kate's muscles strained, keeping her body in the store. She grappled against the hooded boy's top position. Winning—she had stamina—he did not.

Pointing the gun, the boy stared into her eyes and threatened, "Get in the car."

Joey—his desperate pleas stabbed at Kate's heart—broke her fierce concentration. In one brief second, her assailant sensed her weakness and jerked her forward. Throwing a look backwards, she fell into a momentary panic. Joey was wrestling with the clerk, struggling against the woman's shielding arms. He was crying for Kate—*Momma.*

Setting Joey aside, Kate hardened her heart, turned a deaf ear, and re-focused. Her breathing evened and blood flowed easily through her veins. She felt all five fingers of the boy's hand wrapped around her wrist and imagined them broken. Unhinged. She readied her body.

"Let go of me," she raged.

The hooded boy moved tempestuously, like a feral animal, and he closed the distance between them. She could smell the steel of the ancient revolver as he waved it past her nose. Lurching, she swatted at the weapon. He jolted in shock and nearly lost the gun. Kate leapt for the door—gripped the aluminum edge with her right hand. She swallowed hard. The heels of her boots hit the track of the automatic sliding door—anchoring her weight—aiding her resistance.

The hooded boy's eyes flashed with fear. The smug taste of victory watered her mouth— bloody minded—she leered at the frightened boy.

"Run, you little prick," she warned.

"Let her go already." His partner was out of the car. Standing in front of the first set of automatic doors, he waved both arms in the direction of the approaching sirens. Running back to the driver's side, the partner slammed the car door—his tires squealed—and the hooded boy was left behind with only his gun.

Marigold lunged at the window of the truck. Her view unobstructed, the dog spotted Kate fighting within the door. *Vicious.* Marigold attacked the glass. Her snarls ripped across the parking lot. The vehicle rocked. The metal of the truck's cab shrieked. *Good girl.*

Panicked, the boy pointed the gun at Marigold. *Now.* Releasing her grip on the door. Kate clenched her fist. *Fight.* Her mind's eye found its target. Arcing her body, she sprung onto the balls of her feet—legs bent—her right fist launched into the softness of the boy's groin.

Kate rejoiced. The subject of her punishment cried in agony and released his grip on her left wrist—doubled over—helpless. In top position, she did not stop—would not stop until he was down, incapacitated, or dead. Gripping the sides of his hood, she closed in—clinch fighting. She slammed his face into her right knee. Blood spurted. *Yes.*

He screamed but would not go down. The gun was feeble— loose in his hand. The stiff nose of her boot landed behind his knee. Crumpled on the floor, he held his nose. More blood. One slight step backward, Kate let loose the flanks. Her eyes never left the gun as she swung her right leg into his gut—once, twice, three times. Finally, the gun hit the linoleum floor. Leaping over the boy, who was now curled in a fetal position, Kate kicked the weapon through the open door and across the parking lot.

Joey's cries were shrill—like javelins they pierced the wall surrounding her consciousness. Urgent. The clerk's pleading was desperate. Kate heard her son's tennis shoes squealing against the floor. *No.* Curled on the cold linoleum of the vestibule, her attacker's eyes were still open. *No.* She wouldn't allow him to lay eyes on her child.

Taking aim, she seethed hatred and kicked the boy in the head until he rolled away, away from Joey. The boy's hands covered his face—blind, crying, and pitiless. She abandoned the fight.

Kate turned and made for her son. Joey struggled against the store clerk's grasp crying *Momma.* Barreling at top speed, she ducked and ran into her son's outstretched arms. Picking him up, she fled. He weighed nothing.

Joey's tear-streaked face was pressed against her chest, his legs dangled across her right hip, and she broke for the back door— away from the hooded boy and away from the gun. She shot past the neatly lined shelves. *Surreal.* Jostling Joey's doll-like body, they escaped into the bright sunlight.

No direction but forward—she ran past the overflowing dumpster, through the rear alleyway, and across the adjacent neighborhood.

Kate held her son to her chest and never looked back.

CHAPTER 54

RE-GAINING POSSESSION

The silence must have bothered her. Natalie switched on the radio. The music added to his discomfort, and he stared—jaw tight—out the window of her car. Danny checked his phone again.

Kate had called twice but left no messages. She rarely used his cell number, but he had ignored her anyways. He was at lunch with Natalie Bell-Charles ending their "friendship," but regardless, Kate would not have approved. Danny hadn't answered the calls because talking to his wife in Natalie's presence had felt too much like betrayal. Danny rolled his eyes.

Betrayal was a small word in comparison to what he was doing now. Accepting a ride from Natalie seemed like the only option. He was desperate to get home. He followed her out of the restaurant, numb, empty. The phone call from his office was more than shocking—it was like electric paddles to his heart. Danny wasn't sure if it was still beating. *Kate was nearly abducted.*

"Shit," he hissed. His arm slapped against his leg, and he dialed again. "Fuck," he swore—voicemail.

"She's at the police station, Danny," Natalie said. "The call probably can't get through."

"She does this all the time," he snapped. "Katie never answers the phone. Never calls. It drives me frickin' nuts."

Staring out the window again, he tried to get air into his lungs. His chest was tight. He felt claustrophobic. *Kate was unhurt.* That's what his boss said. *Joey was fine.* The words replayed in his head, but they gave him no comfort. Reaching, he switched off the music.

He knew this would happen. He felt it in his bones. Something bad was coming at him, coming at his family. *Kate.* He needed to see her, to hold her.

"Shit," he inhaled sharply.

Natalie's hand touched his thigh. Startled, Danny slapped it away. It was the wrong thing to do. She cowered in her seat, hurt. But how could he care? His wife and kid were at the police station.

"I was trying to help," she sniffed.

Danny shook his head. He was tired of this, tired of Natalie. The guilt was going to kill him, to kill his family. And he was to blame. The universe was punishing him, tit for tat.

"I appreciate the ride, Natalie, and I feel like a real horse's ass telling you now, but I asked you to lunch for reason," he said. "I can't see you anymore. I can't talk to you anymore. And I can't e-mail you anymore."

"Okay," she said slowly.

"I'm a simple guy," he added in defense. "Risk averse. I don't want trouble. Kate...my wife...I'm sorry. We can't be friends."

"Danny," she said. "We didn't do anything wrong."

He kept his mouth shut. The only thing he had left to say to Natalie Bell-Charles was good-bye.

The drive was excruciating, especially the last fifteen minutes. They coasted through downtown Wheaton at thirty miles an hour. Four-way stops were pure hell. Danny fought the urge to jump out of the car and make a run for it. Thankfully, Natalie didn't park. She drove right up to the curb. Danny's hand was already on the door handle.

"Thanks," he said as he leapt out. "Good-bye."

Danny didn't bother to hide his urgency. He ran. He ran straight through the doors and up the stairs.

"My wife," he said to the uniformed cop behind the desk. "She was involved in a bank robbery."

The cop nodded and rose immediately. "Mr. Maller," she said. "Your wife and son are fine."

Fidgeting, he followed closely behind. The corridor was long and narrow, glass walls on either side. She wasn't there.

"Kate," he bellowed.

The officer leading him down the corridor threw him a backwards glance. He didn't care.

"Katie," he called again.

Then, her unsure voice, "Danny?"

He shoved past the officer. "Katie," he called again.

"That's my husband," Kate's voice trembled.

Finally, he caught sight of her. Sitting with her back to the open door, she was with three officers at a metal conference table. She shoved her chair, rising to meet him.

"Baby," he sighed.

Kate met his eyes and then crumpled inwards. Her whole body jostled when her knees failed. Sobbing, she reached one arm out to him. And then suddenly he had her crushed to his chest. Inhaling deeply, he filled his lungs. He could finally breathe. His heart was back where it belonged. *Kate.*

Danny moved to a chair when he realized she was shaking. Pulling her into his lap, he rubbed her back. The officers stood, and for the first time, Danny made eye contact. They were shocked, taken aback by Kate's emotional outburst.

"My son?" he asked.

"Joey is in the lunch room with Marigold," one officer answered.

"The fellas are looking after him," another added. "We want to adopt him. Make him our new mascot."

Danny smiled half-heartedly. "How is he?" he asked.

"He didn't see much, Mr. Maller," an officer answered. "He was hiding, but he did hear his mom struggling. The clerk managed to hold him back. Kept him out of harm's way."

"He's still ticked off at the clerk," another officer laughed. "Joe is quite the little tough guy."

"When he first got here, he was real quiet. We were concerned, but Mrs. Maller figured it out. He dropped his cereal at the store." The officers were obviously charmed by his youngest son, and Danny's immediate concerns were calmed.

Kate squirmed uncomfortably in his lap before curling up tighter, smaller, against his chest.

"Officer Dennis drove Joey back to the Food Wise in a squad car," another added. "Broke protocol and turned the siren on. Said lost sugar cereal was an emergency."

"Sugar cereal?" Danny asked, looking down at his wife. "I can't believe it. You bought Joey sugar cereal?"

Kate hid her face in his shirt and nodded. She wasn't crying anymore, but she wasn't strong enough to talk.

"Do you want us to go get him?"

Kate's head shook, and she choked on a sob.

"Not yet," Danny said quickly. "Joey shouldn't see Kate like this."

The officers moved awkwardly towards the door. "She was fine before…" one said defensively. "Honestly, Mr. Maller. Tough as nails."

"She is fine," Danny said, tightening his hold. "She just needs a minute."

They filed out of the office confused. Their first impression of his wife was shot out of the water. Kate was tough as nails. They weren't wrong. It was the shock. One good cry, and she would be all right. Kate stayed strong until she didn't have to. Danny knew what the officers did not. She was waiting for him.

"I got here as fast I could," he murmured into her hair.

"I'm sorry, Danny," she sniffed.

"It's okay," he reassured her. "I've gotcha now."

Kate rubbed her face into his shirt. "I love you."

"And I love Trouble."

In the quiet of the moment, he relaxed. His wife was safe in his arms, and then he remembered. Kate pushed away to look in his eyes.

"Did they catch the other kid?" he asked. "The one that got away?"

"Yes," she nodded. "They chased him down on the Eisenhower Expressway."

"I can't fucking believe this," he fumed. "In broad daylight, they start waving guns around."

Sighing, Kate loosened a bit and set her head on his shoulder.

"Well, I'll tell you right now, DuPage County better not fuck this one up. I want to see those kids screwed to a wall, or I swear to God, I'll show up at the courthouse and do it myself."

She stroked his chest. It was nearly impossible to hang onto the rage. Kate was safe. His kids were safe. Nothing else mattered.

"You've got blood all over you."

"My jeans are ruined," she complained. "I think I might have broken the little bastard's nose."

"Mama Bear Syndrome." Danny looked up to find the voice belonging to a gray-haired officer. "A woman with a child is a dangerous opponent," the officer added and then smiled affectionately at Kate.

Kate got up from Danny's lap and wiped the tears with the sleeve of her shirt. "Danny, this is Captain Terrance."

Captain Terrance held out his hand, and Danny rose to shake it.

"Thank you for taking care of my family," Danny said.

"Our pleasure," he smiled. "But, Mrs. Maller doesn't need much looking after. This woman can take care of herself."

Danny smiled and wrapped an arm protectively around Kate.

"She claims she never trained in self-defense," the Captain added doubtfully.

"She was raised on a farm. Has two brothers," he explained.

"Well you oughta thank those fellas for toughening her up," Captain Terrance laughed. "I just got off the phone with the hospital. Our young perpetrator has two cracked ribs, a broken nose, and fifteen stitches around the eye."

"It was the boots," Kate said defensively.

Captain Terrance eyed Kate's feet, "Maybe I should confiscate them as a deadly weapon," he deadpanned.

Kate looked up at Danny and clung tightly to his side, "Should I feel bad?"

"About what?" Danny asked his face crinkled in shock. "You were defending yourself."

"I know," she shrugged. "But I brought the attention on myself."

"Mrs. Maller," Officer Terrance interrupted. "You are not to blame for any of this."

"He said I was eyeballing him. I should have kept my eyes down," she answered.

"You're talking nonsense. You must be tired," Danny said. "Can I take her home now?"

"Yeah, we know where to find you if we need you," the Captain answered hesitantly. "I want to warn you, Mr. Maller. There was a joker inside the store with one of those fancy camera phones. The numb-nut didn't make a move to assist your wife but managed to catch the whole damn thing on video. And I can tell you straight up, his motives weren't to aid in the police investigation. He's got something else in mind. I'm afraid you've got a shit load of unwanted attention comin' your way."

Danny laid a hand on Kate's hip and directed her towards the door. It was time to collect his son and go home. He didn't give a goddamn about what came next. He'd handle it, lesson learned. He got distracted and lost his game. Danny fell out of position and got burned. After re-gaining possession, his guard was up, and he was ready. *Let them come.*

No one would ever succeed in separating Kate from him again.

CHAPTER 55

SAFETY NET

Local Chicago news was running footage of Kate and the bank robbery on a loop. Damage control was now Kate's main focus.

After speaking with her father, she unplugged the phone. He was coming for a visit. He was insistent, and in the end, Kate was glad. Joey was cheered by the prospect of Papa's visit. Kate lay in bed with her youngest son until he fell asleep.

Since they had stopped answering the phone, Molly walked over and knocked on the door to inform them that Kate made the cable news. Shocked by the intensity of the media storm, Kate snuggled into Danny for support as they watched the coverage.

The news was off limits while Joey was awake. He wasn't showing any outward signs of stress, but Kate planned to keep him home from school for the remainder of the week. The story was headlined as "Hockey Mom Fights Back." Peter and Billy watched the story with the same intensity as a hockey game. Completely engrossed, they erupted into cheers when Kate pummeled the hooded boy into the ground.

Naturally, their concerns were focused on their little brother. They both got very quiet when they glimpsed footage of Joey crying and wrenching away from the clerk, and then they both sighed in relief when Kate scooped him up and ran.

"I can't watch this anymore," Danny said, clicking off the television. "It's making me sick. I actually feel physically ill."

"I feel a little disgusted myself," Kate huffed. "I want to know who told them I was a hockey mom."

"Hockey always gets a bum rap," Danny complained. "Folks are making the assumption that violent moms have kids who play violent sports."

Kate punched Danny in the arm. "What are you saying? My act of self-defense is giving hockey a bad name?"

"No," Danny laughed. "I'm saying hockey is guilty by association."

"Yeah, Mom," Peter added. "Maybe you should take a break from the rink for awhile."

"Our reputations are on the line," Billy teased. "I don't want any bad calls being thrown at me because you're my mom."

"Okay," Kate said, rolling her eyes. "That's enough. I'm tired, and I want to go to bed."

Readying herself for sleep, she listened to Danny's solid footfalls as he checked and double-checked the locks on the doors and windows.

Marigold was a new addition to his routine. He let her out every night and patrolled the house while he waited for her to do her business. When they came back inside, Kate laughed to herself when she overheard Danny's version of baby talk. He loved the dog more than ever. Marigold was instrumental to Kate's escape, and the dog was receiving extra pats and praise in a show of appreciation from the man of the house.

It wasn't Danny's habit to come to bed so early, but he did. He was hovering, always keeping a hand on her. When he climbed into bed, he pulled her into a spoon.

"How are you?" he asked into the back of her neck.

"I'm fine, Danny, really. Just thinking about the television coverage. I can't believe what a big deal it has become."

"You're a hero," he laughed.

Kate rolled over. Pressing her face into his chest, she ran a hand along his tense shoulders. "If you are going to stay home tomorrow, I want there to be a reason other than you wanting to keep watch over us," Kate gave him a quick kiss on the lips. "Let's load up the wheelbarrow and get wood mulch from the nursery. We can work in the yard for the next couple of days."

"Put Joey to work," he agreed. "That's a great idea."

"My Dad should arrive around lunch," Kate yawned dramatically and rubbed her nose into the course hair on Danny's broad chest.

It was quiet. Kate listened to Danny's breathing. It was shallow—nervous and tense. So she held him closer—ran a hand tenderly along his back. Not being there when she needed him most was eating Danny up inside. Anytime someone praised Kate, he shrunk a little. It was grating on his manhood. And she wished it wasn't—wished the attention would go away and leave Danny in peace. But they were wishes and wishes were worthless. So Kate peppered him with kisses, stroked his back, feigned contentment—all in hopes of making him feel better.

"I have a confession," he said and then quickly added. "I went to lunch with Natalie. Only to say good-bye. I felt bad about the scene at the train station and wanted to smooth things over. She was with me when I got the news about the bank robbery, and she gave me a ride to the police station. I told her we can't be friends. It's done. Natalie Bell-Charles is gone. Out of our lives."

Kate took a deep breath and rolled away from him. Fuming, she stared at the ceiling.

"Trouble?" he asked through the dark. "I'm sorry."

Danny laid a hand on her shoulder. Jumping up, she threw her legs out of the bed and rigidly sat with her back to him.

"Why are you telling me this?" Kate seethed. "After the day I just had, what would possess you to lay something like Natalie Bell-Charles in my bed?"

Danny rolled over onto his back and threw his arms over his eyes. "I don't want anything to come between us. I wanted you to know the truth."

"The truth?" she snapped. "The truth is you are trying to make yourself feel better by unloading your shit on me. You are being incredibly selfish, Danny. That's the real truth."

"I'm sorry," he cried. "It's killing me, Katie. Say you forgive me. Please."

"Forgive you for what?"

Kate got off the bed and paced. Marigold watched her with eyes full of fear. The dog kept her head on her paws and remained very still. It was a reminder to Kate to keep her voice down. She didn't want the boys to hear them fighting—not today—not now.

"Forgive you for taking Natalie to lunch…or forgive you for not keeping the whole damn thing to yourself?" she whispered loudly.

"For both," Danny sat up in bed. "I thought you would want to know. I'm sorry."

"I don't want to know. Truly. Honestly. Don't," she hissed. "Your attraction to that woman is revolting. It's so beneath you, Danny. The next time you see her, please refrain from telling me about it."

"I'm not attracted. I swear to God there won't be a next time. I ended it. It's over."

"Good for you," she said hurrying back to the bed. "You finally did what you said you'd do weeks ago."

Kate pulled roughly at the blankets and curled into a ball. She wanted to punish him some more but knew it was wrong. Nothing Danny could ever do could possibly measure up to the devastating sins she herself committed against their marriage. Wincing, Kate tried hard not to think about the sins she was still willing to commit—today and tomorrow.

Danny wanted nothing but the truth between them. Exhaling loudly, Kate shoved her regret to the back of her thoughts—the truth was not welcome in her bed—those days were over. She was growing used to the company of lies.

After laying gingerly on his pillow, Danny moaned softly. He wasn't going to stop beating himself up until she forgave him.

"I don't like it, but I understand. You wanted to say good-bye—apologize for your role in her humiliation. You've always been that guy, Danny—you are way too nice. I forgive you. I'm just tired," she said impatiently. "It's been a really long day. Go to sleep."

Kate closed her eyes and waited. The cool sheets absorbed the warmth of their bodies and soon Danny was breathing heavily, twitching as he fell into deep slumber. Lying in bed—finally alone with her thoughts—Kate exhaled loudly.

Jeff Dixon. Sorting through a bag of mixed emotions, she listed her options—laid out a plan. In the dark, beneath the soft blankets of her bed, Kate weaved a tight safety net of lies. Tightrope walking required concentration and balance, and she was not about to do it free hand. The safety net of lies was a requirement. She could not perform the feat otherwise. The net was insurance. If Kate went down, she risked more than just her own life—her own happiness. This devastating knowledge had her double checking the knots—searching for gaps—and testing the slack.

Unlike Danny, she would get little sleep.

CHAPTER 56

THE REQUEST

His eyelids were heavy. Sleep disjointed. Interrupted by bouts of rousing consciousness. The television helped some. White noise. So when he heard soft knocking, he disregarded it. It was past midnight. It was the television. And he wrestled his thoughts back into slumber. But the knocking grew impatient. And he moaned. Clenched his eyes tighter.

The door bell. He jumped. Shocked his heart. The den. One in the morning. Restless night. His fox. A bank robbery. He searched for his eyeglasses. Stumbling towards the door he turned on the lights and squinted. Ainsley? Returning home? Kathryn? No. Kathryn belonged in the world of dreams.

Yanking open the door, he blinked into the night. Her silhouette. Like a ghost. Like an angel. Standing on his doorstep. He shook his head once. Kathryn? Was he still asleep? His bare feet were ice cold on the marble floor of the foyer. Not a dream. Reaching, he switched on the outside lamp. To wake up. To make sure he wasn't hallucinating. Before he could turn his attention back to the threshold, she was in the house.

"Turn out the light," she ordered as she wrapped her arms around his neck.

311

"Kathryn?"

The door shut. She pulled him towards it. Leaned against it. She kissed his mouth. Quick. Noisy. Urgent. Wet. Her breath in a pant. Heaven.

"I'm sorry," she whispered into his mouth. "I couldn't sleep. I snuck out."

Yes. Of course. Kathryn. The bank robbery. Her escape. The news. Pulling away, he looked into her hazel eyes. Ablaze. He ignored it. Set her desire aside.

"Are you hurt?" he asked, nearly fully alert.

Running his hands over her cotton nightshirt, he did a quick examination. She was in one piece. Still strong. Still Kathryn. Hair around her shoulders. Tousled. Messy. Gorgeous.

"What is it? Why are you here? Are you all right?"

Kathryn shook her head. Dismissing his concerns, she stepped out of his arms. Gardening clogs. She kicked them off next to the door. The nightshirt was oversized. Button down. Soft and worn thin. He could see the shadows of nipples beneath. And sweatpants. Red. The University of Wisconsin.

Like an aberration. She moved slowly across the foyer. Admiring the paintings. The chandelier. Running a hand along the polished wood of the newel post at the bottom of the staircase, she set one bare foot on the bottom step. He struggled with reality. She was there. Kathryn was in his house. And she was unhurt. Thank God Almighty.

She locked her eyes onto his. Exhaling stiffly, she licked her lips. "Take me to bed, Jeff," she breathed. "Please. No talking."

It was like a cloud-to-ground strike. The house shook as they bolted up the stairs. Hand in hand. Stride for stride. The lightning streamed into the master bedroom. There was a tussle. Their clothes ripped away. His eyeglasses hit the floor. Naked, she wrangled to be on top. In control. The fox. The vixen.

Breathing, he took her in. Slowed down. Tasted her with deep kisses. The only light was from the foyer. Distant and weak. The window shades were open. The night sky lit a back drop. Kathryn hummed. He could barely discern her breathy utterances. *Oh. Yes. Good. More.*

An over-current surrounded them like a second skin. He could feel it when he touched her. Electric. Conductive. His fingers only brushed the surface, and she shuddered. Gasped. *Yes. Oh. Good.* An undercurrent to her words. Hunger. Lust. Need. The atmosphere static charged. Waiting. Anticipating the clap of thunder.

Her mouth left his. Moved down his neck. His chest. Her body fused to his skin. She slid along the length of him. Drawing a path with her tongue. He understood the direction she was going. Watched as the top her head moved down. Her luxurious hair splayed across his flesh. Merciless, she wrapped her mouth around his erection and slammed it to the back of her throat. He was trapped. Kathryn held his weight by the hips. Pressing him into the depths of the thick bedding.

Reaching above his head, he searched for something to grasp. The headboard. Heavy and sturdy. He clenched. Struggling, he longed to see her. Look at her. But she was vicious. Working to devour. The sensation overwhelming. If he let her go, there would be nothing left. He would not waste it. This time alone. In bed. Naked.

"Kathryn," he managed to cry out. "Stop."

She groaned, ran a tongue along the base of his shaft, and leered at him. When she reached the tip, she licked sloppily before running her teeth ever so dangerously along his throbbing staff. On all fours. Her ass riding high. She was an animal. Carnal. Wild. He nearly gave into her. He nearly came. But he was determined.

He sat up. Pushed himself off the bed. And she whined. Impatient. So Kathryn. The fearsome creature thwarted. He threw her onto her back. Gazing into her eyes, he recognized himself. The spark of intelligence. The smoldering passion.

Following the same path as she, he started at her hot, wet mouth. The scented skin of her neck. Citrus. Her glorious mounds of flesh. Hard tits. So tempting. He bit cautiously. And she thrashed. Ripping at his hair, she cried. *More.* Kathryn liked it. Liked the bite. The thrill. So he lingered. Working the nipples. Pulling. Nibbling. Until she begged.

Moving downwards. He ran an ear along her belly. The sinewy muscles lean and taut. Nubile. A goddess. And finally, the coarse hair of her pussy. The rich smell of her. So potent. He drove his nose into her.

Kathryn writhed. Kicking at the bed, she moved until her head was lifted on the pillows. Pressed against the headboard. Shoving three fingers into her pussy, he watched as Kathryn threw her head from side to side. She fought.

"Spread your legs for me, my fox," he coaxed.

One hand on her knee. The other beneath a supple ass cheek. She whined. The noise of a scared child. And shook her head.

"Trust me," he murmured. The muscles in her legs relaxed. "Wider…that's a good girl."

Biting her lower lip, she exhaled through her nose and sunk. Sunk into the pillows. Surrender.

It was a dangerous business. Like playing with fire. His senses were on high alert. Judging the tension in her muscles. Listening to the hum of her breath. He was learning. Attune to Kathryn. She hissed. And cried. Her voice rose and fell. Husky seductress— whimpering girl. It was wet. Slippery. And crazy erotic. He relished the taste of her. Rich and sweet. So very savory. Kathryn's flavor was a sharp mix. Like tangy butter.

"Jeff," she called out. "No more. I can't." *Oh. Yes, you can. And you will.*

Straining against the mattress, her groans got louder and louder until finally, she shook. Rattling the headboard. And cursed. Words never uttered in his bed. So Kathryn. The fox. The vixen. She came. She climaxed into his mouth.

Her body softened. Pliable as she caught her breath. Eyes closed. Hair splayed across the pillow. Climbing between her legs, he kept his weight on his elbows and kissed her neck. Buried his face in her hair. So lovely.

"Jeff?" she gasped into the dark.

Subtly, she readjusted her weight so his erection glided in between her legs.

"Yes?" he asked.

Nudging with her hips, she sought it ought until it slid easily into the hot wetness between her legs. Heaven. Inside Kathryn.

Naked. In bed. She kissed his mouth. Groaning, she tasted the sex on his lips. Slurped it with her tongue.

"You're so good," she sighed.

He smiled. Pride welled in his chest. Kathryn was his. Flat on her back in his bed. He had achieved the impossible. The seduction of a fox.

He cringed in restraint when she moved beneath him. Wrapping her legs around his waist, she drew him closer. Their bodies hot enough to fuse sand into glass.

"May I ask you for something?" she whispered in his ear.

In one long penetration he drove deeper into her. Growling in her ear. Kathryn gasped. Clung to his back with strong fingers. The fox. So tricky. She knew when to ask a favor.

"Jeff?" she whined, persistent.

"What is it, my fox?" he asked. His voice was rough with yearning. Kathryn's body rocked beneath his. He was stiff with restraint. Ready to ravage. Take what he needed.

She sighed. Her body shuddered once and her hands moved to the sides of his face. Staring into his eyes, she kissed him softly on the lips.

"This is too much for me," she murmured. "You and me. This thing between us. I have to take care of my family now. Give me a week. Please, Jeff. A week to sort things out with the police, the press, my kids."

Moaning reluctantly, he collapsed into her neck. She was begging. And he could not refuse her. Patience. Kathryn was in his bed. One week was not so long.

"Jeff?" she pleaded. "Promise me one week. Please."

Nudging her hips, he moved inside her. Inside the depths of Kathryn. So hot. So wet.

"One week," he growled. "I promise."

And then he took her. Pounding into her flesh, he locked onto her eyes. Darkened with desire, he rode her. Rode Kathryn until she cried his name. For the second time, she writhed beneath him. Climaxing again. And he gloried at his victory. Her body was a mass of sweet tenderized flesh when he finished. Stiffening in climax, his own release was pained. Bitter sweet. One week. Kathryn's request.

"I can't stay," she said after their heavy breathing subsided.

Kathryn curled herself around his side. One leg thrown over his stomach. He wrapped a hand around her thigh. So soft. Like silk across steel.

"Are you going to give any interviews?" he asked.

His tone was businesslike. Lawyerly. His eyes on the ceiling.

"I'm not sure what to do, Jeff," she sighed. "We've had calls. So many calls. I've just been trying to deal with the kids. Reassure them that everything is okay. Danny is hovering. He is at a loss as well. All of us are a bit traumatized."

"Sit down and write a statement," he counseled. "Leave it on voicemail and screen your calls. Decide what you want to share and stick with it. With everyone. Your family. Your friends. Your neighbors. The press will be sniffing around. Looking for antidotes. Don't give them any."

"Do you think I should give an interview?" she asked.

Kathryn rolled on top. Straddling his hips, she ran her hands over his chest. Caramel-colored hair fell across her face. Reaching up, he tucked it behind her ears. Useless endeavor. There was no taming her wild mane.

"That's up to you, my fox," he shrugged. "Wait and see if there is a chance the hype will blow over. If not, an interview might be the only way to diffuse interest. Pick a major outlet. Stick with the same story. Don't embellish. And of course, shield your son."

"Of course," she repeated solemnly. "Thank you, Jeff."

He drew a finger along her jaw. "You're welcome."

"You won't send me a bill for the advice, will you?" she teased as she leapt off the bed.

He sat up. Kathryn scurried around the room collecting her clothes.

"I'll take it out in trade," he offered.

Smiling, she handed him his glasses before kissing him on the lips. "Stay," she said. "I'll walk myself out."

He shook his head and threw his legs over the side of the bed.

"No, Jeff," she said curtly. "Stay here. I don't want you to watch me leave."

"Why not?" he asked.

The inner workings of her mind were still a mystery.

"Just don't." Standing in the doorway, she waved. Her eyes sparked. "I will see you a week from today. 5:30. At the park," she said. "We'll jog."

He nodded. "Okay."

Kathryn turned her back and walked quickly down the narrow hallway. Lifting himself off the bed, he pulled on his pants and followed. She caught him. Standing at the top of the stairs, she pointed an accusatory finger.

"Jeff," she warned. "Stay. Don't watch me go."

He laughed and held two hands up in mock surrender.

"Good-bye." His voice was soft. Smiling. Full of affection.

"Good-bye," she said and dashed down the stairs.

Out of sight. He skidded down the hallway. Anxious for one last glance. All he caught was the soles of her ugly garden clogs and the toss of her hair. He ran to a window. Her headlights flashed across the house. The van. Kathryn chose the vehicle of dutiful mother as her getaway.

She stole one hour. Rolled away from her sleeping husband. Escaped into his welcoming arms. One triumphant hour.

They rollicked in deep water. Their passion pulled them under, but surely she took solace in their ability to kick their way to the surface. Treading water was worth the energy. And Kathryn was strong. Surely, she could see the possibilities. The adventure. The thrill of testing oneself in the dark, watery depths. The shallows could not hold the same appeal. Not for a woman like Kathryn. The vixen.

Overjoyed, he pumped his fist in the air. "Yes."

CHAPTER 57

A LITTLE BRUISED

Kate did not stir when he rose from bed. Danny stood over her for a long minute and watched as she breathed in and out. It was remarkable how unaffected she was by yesterday's events. Kate was strong, stronger than he was. He realized it on the way home from the police station.

Danny could not survive without her. Losing Kate would be catastrophic. He would never recover. It was a weakness, a profound vulnerability, and he was still working through the implications in his brain.

The boys were already awake. Danny could hear them upstairs. They were talking in excited tones. Billy and Peter were anxious to get to school and brag about their mom. Kate was a hero. Danny knew this already—guarded it like a secret—but now, thanks to the Internet, Kate's champion spirit was displayed for all the world to see.

Marigold barked softly from the bedroom when the doorbell rang. Like Danny, the dog was content to watch Kate sleep and reluctant to leave her side. Impatient, Danny yanked open the front door. Sharon was waiting on the porch. Kate's friend looked very professional in a cream-colored trench coat and high heels.

"I brought food," she said, holding up two shopping bags.

Danny ran a hand absentmindedly over his beard and watched as Sharon walked self-assuredly into his home. It was annoying opening the door to Sharon, but at least she had brought breakfast. He wouldn't have to feed the boys.

"How's our girl?" Sharon asked.

The high heeled shoes made a sharp noise on the wood floor filling the house with the sound of purpose. She set the bags on the counter and began unpacking the food containers.

"Kate is as tough as nails," he said borrowing the cop's analogy.

"Very true," she agreed.

Sharon untied her trench coat and threw it over a kitchen chair. The boys arrived in a flurry of activity, and she was in the center of it. Taking down plates, dishing out food, she joked lightheartedly with them about school, their mom, and the media attention their family was garnering. Sharon was a class act—a true friend—and Danny smiled at her in between bites of food.

After the boys were off to school, and Joey was situated in front of the television, she broached the subject. The subject Danny didn't want to think about let alone talk about. Any earlier affection he felt for Sharon vanished.

"I was hoping to talk to Kate personally, but I suppose you can give her the message."

Sharon never looked up from the kitchen sink. She was washing dishes and setting them in the rack to drip dry. Like Kate, she was a multi-tasker.

"Initially, I thought it was bad timing but after thinking about it, I feel like it's a good thing. Kate needs a distraction, a reason to get out of the house. I told her I wouldn't need her to start the new job until August, but the plant is in a bigger mess than I anticipated. I could use her right now."

Danny walked over to the kitchen chair and picked up Sharon's expensive coat.

"No, Sharon," he said simply. "Thanks for breakfast. I know Kate will appreciate it, and I'll be sure to tell her you dropped by."

Sharon set her hands on her hips and stared at him open mouthed. "No? Who the hell do you think you are, Danny Maller? Since when do you make Kate's decisions?"

"She's my wife. I won't have her traipsing around a factory floor while a bunch of union hacks check out her ass. I don't care if she's wearing steel-toed boots. It's not happening."

Sharon eyes tightened and her mouth twitched. "I'm gonna let that pass, Danny. I know you've been through a lot since yesterday. But you better get your head together. You won't be able to hole Kate up in this house forever. And God knows, our girl is capable of taking care of herself."

"Oh, I don't know about that," Kate said from down the hall.

Kate appeared and interrupted the standoff in the kitchen. She was sleepy, warm, and her hair was a mess, but she radiated a healthy glow. Danny had to blink twice before he could get a real look at her. She wore his robe. It was flannel and way too big. She could have wrapped it around her torso twice. It nearly dragged on the floor, and the sight of her was beyond cute. He had to fight the smile. He didn't want to break. Sharon was in the room.

"As soon as I saw Danny at the police station, I collapsed into a fit of tears." Kate shuffled quickly to his side and tucked herself under his arm. "I'd be a mess without him. He's my rock."

"A rock head," Sharon sneered. "He just tried to blow me off, Katie."

Kate looked up at him suspiciously.

"She wants you to start work right away," he said hesitantly. "I told her no."

"It's not as bad as he makes it sound," Sharon said in defense.

Sharon dropped the hands from her hips. Her eyes filled with emotion. "Can I at least have a hug or something?" she whined. "I've been so worried."

Kate was out from underneath his arm in a flash. The two friends clung to each other. It made him uncomfortable, so he went to pour himself some coffee.

"Are you okay...really?" Sharon whispered into Kate's hair.

"Yeah," Kate answered. "I'm really okay. Just a little bruised."

Danny slammed down his coffee cup when he saw Kate's arm. The little son-of-a-bitch had left a handprint on his wife. A shadowy purple bruise encompassed Kate's tiny wrist.

"Shit, Katie," Danny leapt to her side, shoving Sharon out of the way.

"Shh, Danny," Kate warned. Her eyes flew to the doorway leading to the family room. "I don't want any fuss. It's only a little sore. I'm fine."

Sharon took his wife by the elbow. They turned their backs on him and walked outside onto the deck. Danny followed behind like Marigold. If Sharon wanted privacy, she wasn't going to get any.

"The plant's in a mess, Katie," Sharon said as soon as they stepped foot outside. "I'm meeting with management this morning. News about the sale of the factory has trickled down to the workers, and they are freaking out. The rumors are flying. We can't afford to lose some of them. The kind of work they do is very specialized. The sale isn't complete until late July, but we need to work out a transition plan. I'd like to be in a position to say I've found someone to meditate between us and their crew."

"How soon?" Kate asked calmly.

"Two weeks," Sharon said. "The transition team will meet once a week. Wednesday. You'd meet with labor in the morning and management in the afternoon. I'll be there the first couple of weeks, but then I'll expect e-mail updates. You'll have to do some homework. I've got a pile of OSHA regulations and union agreements you'll need to sift through, but you can do that whenever. Just keep track of your time so you can bill us. After the sale, maybe late August, we would want to increase your hours. But we can talk about that later."

Kate stepped away from Sharon and looked up at the clouds chasing across the spring sky. She turned to Danny after a quiet moment, and he was heartened to see doubt in her eyes.

"Can I think about it?" she asked. "We've been through so much. I don't want to lay too much change on Joey. He may need me at home."

"Sure," Sharon said nodding. "We'll give it a week and then talk some more."

"Thank you, Sharon," Kate said walking into another hug.

Sharon squeezed Kate tight. "You deserve a day at the spa," she declared. "My treat. We'll call Molly. Book a couple massages, manicures, pedicures. It'll be fun."

"Spa?" Danny snorted.

Both women looked at him in surprise. It was like they had forgotten he was there.

"Katie doesn't go to the spa," he chuckled.

"Well, it's about time she started," Sharon snapped, giving him a dirty look.

"Painted fingernails creep me out," he said defensively. "It's unnatural."

Kate opened her mouth like she was going to say something but quickly snapped it shut. She was thinking the same thing he was, and he wished he kept his mouth shut. Natalie's fingernails were long and painted. He had imagined them racking across his back way too many times.

"Shut up, Dan," Sharon said as she directed Kate to a deck chair. "No one is asking you for an opinion."

Danny frowned and wondered when Sharon was going to leave.

"Sit down," she directed Kate. "I'll get you some coffee before I go."

Sharon swatted Danny's arm on her way back into the house. Looking at his feet, he made his way over to Kate and sat with a dramatic huff in the deck chair next to her.

"Spa," he said disgustedly. "Do you really want to do something like that?"

"It could be fun," Kate said, directing her comment at the sky. "Have you ever heard of a Brazilian wax?"

Danny sat straight up in his chair. He couldn't help it. His wife could still shock the hell out of him.

"Don't knock it, Coach," she teased. "You might want to think about pampering your wife a little bit. A naked pussy cat could be a lot of fun for you."

Danny snapped his mouth closed after he realized it was hanging open. Kate laughed the kind of laugh he loved. It sang through his veins and made his heart beat stronger. Reaching over, he ran fingers over Kate's bruised wrist. Kate rolled her hand over, palm up. She wiggled her fingers inviting him to take a hold, and he did. Kate's hand.

It was all he needed.

CHAPTER 58

POSITION IN THE SPOTLIGHT

Danny spent the rest of the morning trailing Kate around the house. She teased him mercilessly, but he didn't seem to care. Danny was content to carry her laundry basket. Outside in the bright sun, Kate hung wet rugs on the clothesline after Danny shook them out and handed them to her.

The phone rang, but Danny programmed their machine so it picked up after one ring. Following Jeff's advice, Kate wrote a statement and recorded it onto their voicemail message.

Hello, this is Kathryn Maller. Thank you for calling. If you are calling as a representative of the press, I have the following statement. I was acting out of self-defense. I merely reacted as any other mother would if she perceived her child to be in danger. We are overwhelmed with the well wishes of our neighbors and friends. We do not, however, wish to prolong our family's position in the spotlight. The sooner our lives return to normal, the sooner our household will return to a healthy environment for our children. Thank you again. Good-bye."

Kate set her hands on her hips and admired her work. It was very windy, and the rugs strained against their pins flapping like the colorful sails of a gypsy boat. Her hair whipped around her face blinding her—she had to pick the flying tendrils out of her mouth.

"Weren't you supposed to get a haircut?" Danny asked.

He took one long step and pulled the hair away from her face with thick fingers.

"Friday," she said—smiling into Danny's crinkly gray eyes. "Molly arranged it."

As if on cue, Molly stepped out of her back door carrying a basket. She waved nervously before walking across the yard. Marigold ran to greet her—eagerly sniffing the goodies in her basket. Danny set his arm across Kate's shoulders.

"Hi, Molly," he said.

"I made you lunch," Molly said holding up the basket.

Kate clicked her tongue and took the offering from her neighbor's outstretched arm. "You and Sharon are spoiling me."

Molly dismissed Kate with an impatient wave. "I cook when I'm upset. I made chicken salad, oatmeal cookies, and picked up some fresh bread from Nino's."

"Thank you, Molly," Danny said smiling gratefully. "Kate's dad is driving down from Wisconsin, and she was fretting about what to make him for lunch."

"I've got to go to the store," Kate sighed. "I left my milk behind yesterday."

"You're not going to the store without me," Danny said sternly.

Kate rolled her eyes dramatically at Molly. "He's starting to drive me crazy. He won't let me alone."

"I don't blame him, Kathryn," Molly said. "I can't understand how you can act like nothing happened. If I was you, I'd be in curled up in bed in a fetal position."

"It's over," Kate shrugged. "I don't think about it."

"Well, the rest of us aren't as resilient," Danny said, running a rough hand along her shoulders. "Some of us haven't quite gotten over it yet, so try to be a little understanding. I'll take you to the store after your dad gets here. He can stay with Joey."

"No," Kate shook her head. "If I'm gonna be stuck in the house with you for the next couple of days, we are going to accomplish something. I want you take my truck and the wheelbarrow to Bruss Nurseries. They give a discount to folks who scoop their own wood mulch. I can go to the store by myself. Lightning never strikes twice."

Danny crossed his arms and stubbornly shook his head.

"Make a list," Molly said. "I've got to go to the store anyways. I'll get you whatever you need."

Kate pursed her lips into a frown. She didn't like the way they working as a team against her.

"You can repay me by letting me borrow your truck," Molly added politically. "Our garden beds need wood mulch too. Tom won't be able to complain if we avoid the delivery charge."

Surrendering, Kate turned for the house to make her grocery list. Joey was on the floor with crayons drawing a welcome sign for his papa. Kate ruffled his hair as she stepped over him. He wasn't happy about missing school. They were both chaffing under all the attention. Neither one of them liked being fussed over.

Looking out the patio window, she caught Danny standing guard in the driveway—hands on his hips—Marigold standing alert next to him. Danny glared at the car traffic passing by their home. It couldn't last. He would get over it. Kate prided herself on being self-reliant. It was one of things Danny loved about her.

Taking a deep breath, she made her grocery list and worried about Molly's ability to pick out fresh produce. The whole situation felt ridiculous. But Kate vowed to be patient.

Escape was not an option.

CHAPTER 59

THE DRIVEWAY

He circled Kathryn's charming yellow house. Keeping an eye out. Judging. Like the television news crews, he was stalking the neighborhood. A Wheaton police cruiser took permanent residence on the corner. It was a subtle deterrent. But not to him.

His stomach flipped. Nerves. It made him chuckle. The idiot husband was in the driveway. Shoveling wood mulch out of the bed of Kathryn's decrepit pick up truck. Yard work. How droll.

The SUV was less conspicuous than Kathryn's Porsche. A practical choice. Coasting to a stop, he blocked the end of the driveway. He was stopping by. A courtesy call. Completely appropriate. Within the realm of social possibilities. He was, after all, officially acquainted with Mrs. Maller.

The husband tossed the shovel into the bed of the truck when the SUV shifted into park. In old jeans, work boots, and a University of Wisconsin ball cap, Kathryn's husband looked more like a longshoreman than a mechanical engineer. Shit. Daniel Maller was a mountain of a man. But at least, no longer armed with a shovel.

Taking a deep breath, he lifted the large envelope off his passenger seat and stepped out of the SUV. The husband was leery. His stance protective. But this was expected.

"Daniel Maller?" he began by holding out his hand.

Courteous. The husband maintained eye contact and reached half-heartedly for his hand. The circumference of the man's wrist was alarming. Tree-like arms. He imagined getting hit by Daniel Maller was a lot like getting sideswiped by a slab of lumber. He dared not remove his sunglasses. Cover.

"My name is Jeff Dixon," he began.

The husband stiffened. The cog recognized his name. The wily fox.

"I met Kathryn at the Village Board Meeting last week," he explained. "She is friendly with my wife, Ainsley. They had coffee."

"Yeah," the husband said off-handedly. "The garden project. I remember."

Smiling, he tried to put the husband at ease. "How is Kathryn?" he asked. "And your son? I'm sure the press has made the after-effects of the bank robbery that much more difficult."

The husband's brow furrowed as he scanned the street protectively. "Things have died down since the police parked a cruiser on the corner. No more television crews. We get the occasional curious neighbor walking by the house. It's annoying, but my son is oblivious to the extra attention. Kate just took Joey inside to get dinner started. He likes to help her in the kitchen."

Dinner? Kathryn was still cooking for the cog.

"Your wife is quite a trooper," he said smiling slightly. "Fighting off an attacker one day and making dinner for her family the next."

The husband smiled knowingly. "Kate is as tough as nails."

"Still, the woman deserves some rest and relaxation. Maybe an appointment at the spa. A massage, perhaps?"

He couldn't help but point it out. Daniel Maller was undeserving. An ingrate. A selfish fool.

The husband laughed. "That's the second time someone suggested Kate get a massage. I'm beginning to think it might be a good idea."

Seething, he was grateful he kept his sunglasses on. It hid his disgust. His profound disdain. Leaning against the SUV, he crossed his arms and peered up at the husband. He felt like David

330

to Daniel Maller's Goliath. With no slingshot, he armed himself with the only weapon in his arsenal. Words.

"I'm sure this is very difficult for you," he began softly. "Man's most primal instinct is to protect his mate. Lucky for you, Kathryn is competent at protecting herself."

The husband exhaled stiffly. Taking his hat off, he ran a hand through his hair before setting it back on his head. Squaring his shoulders, Daniel Maller smiled patiently.

"What can I do for you, Jeff?"

"You know," he said wagging a finger at the man's colossal body. "I didn't recognize you at first, but I certainly do now. I've seen you on the Metra. The 7:44 commuter train into the city. You sit next to Natalie."

The husband's stance shifted. Cautious, the ingrate threw a glance over his shoulder. "You know Natalie?"

Smiling tightly, he nodded at the ground. He was enjoying the husband's discomfort very much. And wanted to prolong it.

"I know lots of things." Tapping the stiff paper of the envelope with his fingers, he counted to ten silently in his head.

"Natalie is not the kind of woman a man easily forgets," he remarked snidely. "She's quite the cup of coffee in the morning. A real eye-opener. Wouldn't you agree, Dan?"

The husband could not hide his distaste for the sexist remarks. Fascinating. The jock did not engage in locker room talk outside of the locker room.

"I've got my hands full with Kate," the husband said, keeping his eyes on the black top of the driveway. "Natalie Bell-Charles doesn't sit next to me anymore."

Laughing, he kept his stance loose. Casual. Unlike Daniel Maller. He exuded confidence. The imbecile did not have a clue. He felt a twitch in his loins. His thoughts strayed. Kathryn writhing in sweet ecstasy. Rattling the headboard of his bed. Straining against the mattress. Keep the blonde. He would retain the prize.

"Oh," he said lightly. "I didn't realize the seat next to Natalie was vacant."

The husband became visibly agitated. Narrowing his eyes, Daniel Maller pointed at the overflowing wheelbarrow.

"I'm kinda busy here, Jeff. Is there a reason you stopped by?"

"As a matter of fact, there is," he said holding out the envelope. "Kathryn's name was dropped in passing at the office today. When I mentioned my acquaintance with her, it was suggested I swing by."

The husband received the envelope with careless fingers. No doubt intending to throw its contents in the trash.

"My firm would like to offer representation," he shrugged. "We've got offices throughout the country, including one in New York City and Los Angeles. A lawyer could be quite helpful to a family found in your precarious circumstances."

"Thanks," the husband said letting envelop dangle next to his leg. "I'll be sure to give this stuff to Kate."

The sound of a door opening, alerted both men's attention to the backyard. Marigold dashed around the corner of the house. Charging down the driveway, she dropped her head and wagged. Not just her tail. Her whole body wiggled in greeting. It was obvious. She recognized the visitor.

Reaching down, he confidently scratched the odd looking dog between the ears. She sat at his feet. The husband pursed his lips. Disconcerted. The idiot puzzled over the clue. The evidence right under his nose.

The sight of Kathryn was too much of a distraction. Daniel Maller's looming presence forgotten. He broke into a wide grin and pushed off the SUV. Standing erect. Cheerful anticipation. Kathryn was irresistibly cute. The farm girl.

The bib overalls rolled up over the ankles. The ugly garden clogs more fitting than the night before. She wore nothing but a tank top beneath the loose-fitting denim. Kathryn's wild mane was stuffed beneath the broad brim of a straw hat. Tendrils of caramel-colored hair fell along her long neck.

So sensual. So very natural. So incredibly comfortable in her own skin, Kathryn walked assuredly to the end of the driveway. Sharp eyes on the envelope dangling from the husband's fingers. He swallowed down a chuckle. The fox was alert. Ready to pounce.

"Whatchya got there, Coach," she asked playfully.

The husband looked down at the envelope. "Jeff brought this by. Thought we might be interested in a lawyer."

The envelope was out of the husband's hand before he could finish his explanation. Kathryn's deft fingers opened it in seconds. Her quick eyes scanned the contents and then just as quickly her attention landed on him. Glorious. Her hazel eyes hardened ever so slightly, but she smiled.

"That was very thoughtful, Jeff," she said. "How is your wife? And the kids?"

"Ainsley and the children are in Kentucky. Visiting family," he said.

His mouth twitched at her trickery. So cunning. So quick.

"Oh," she said nodding her head. "That must be hard for you. Being all alone in that big house."

"Not really," he said. "I'm at work for most of the day. Solitude never bothered me."

"Well, it was nice of you to drop this by," Kathryn said waving the envelope. "Thank you, but we couldn't possibly afford to retain your services. I've been handling inquiries."

"Surely, some professional advice would be helpful," he challenged. "And, the firm has offered to waive the retainer fee. It wouldn't cost you a dime. We have a bastion of media savvy lawyers in New York dying to consult with you."

"I'm not interested in courting the press," Kathryn said with a smile.

"Of course not, but you should consider doing at least one interview," he said taking one step towards her.

Closing the space. The husband's stare not entirely forgotten. But he could not help himself. So alluring. Their exchange exciting. He longed to engage every sense. Smell. Touch. Taste.

"The Internet is abuzz with video footage of your escape. Folks are clamoring for your story. That kind of interest doesn't die down on its own. An interview could diffuse the situation."

"Or...it could do the opposite," Kathryn countered. "It could create more buzz. I'm not interested, Jeff."

"What's the harm?" he asked seductively. "Really, Kathryn? Fifteen minutes of fame could generate a great deal of money for you and your family."

"And I suppose your firm would expect a percentage of the income generated by my fifteen minutes of fame?"

"Why yes," he said. "My motives are not entirely altruistic, but they are based in genuine concern for your well-being. The video of you and your young assailant was quite graphic. You kicked him while he was down. Not just once, but several times. As a lawyer, I can tell you with confidence that the ambulance chasers are aligning themselves with your attacker as we speak. A lawsuit is not entirely out of the question."

"Lawsuit?" the husband was alarmed.

"It's not a winnable case, Danny," Kathryn soothed the beast.

"That might be true," he conceded. "But you are failing to consider the high cost of fighting a frivolous suit. Courting the press might not appeal to you now, Kathryn, but they would be your greatest ally in garnering sympathy for your plight."

Fuming, Kathryn looked down at the envelope. She was clenching her jaw. Holding back.

"My advice is to meet with our team in New York," he suggested softly. "It would cost you nothing. There is a flight out of O'Hare Thursday evening. A three night stay at one of the city's finest hotels, and you could have this entire mess resolved in one weekend. My associates would oversee the interview. Negotiate the terms. Make sure the interview is taped with a major news outlet in a controlled setting. You can decide later if you wish to continue your association with our firm. Your choice. Nothing is written in stone."

Silence. She stared. Her gaze penetrating the shield of his sunglasses. Kathryn. So cunning. She saw through the subterfuge. The web of deceit. He was giving her an out. Tugging on a lifeline. Towing her into deep water. The air between them buzzed. Crackled with tension. With possibility.

"Katie?" the husband interrupted their silent interchange. "We couldn't possibly go to New York? What about Joey? This is way too soon."

Kathryn looked up at her husband with soft eyes. "I'd go alone, Danny. I couldn't leave without knowing the boys were safe. You could take them to Walt's. He already invited us for the weekend."

Throwing his hands up, the husband mumbled something unintelligible. It was amusing. Like watching a bull kick the dirt. Daniel Maller was ready to charge the red cape of a matador.

"No," the husband repeated. "You are not going to New York City alone."

Pacing back and forth, the cog kept his eyes on the blacktop. Kathryn frowned. She was displeased, so he fought the smile.

"No fucking way, Katie."

The bull-like husband took her by the elbows and shook. It was startling. Very disturbing. And the language offensive. The man was prone to violence. Left marks on Kathryn's skin. He longed to step in between them. Shove the raging giant away.

"Okay," she said mildly as she gently extricated herself from the husband's grasp. "I won't go. I have a hair appointment anyways. Molly prepared a file folder full of new styles and would kill me if I rescheduled."

"Haircut?" He didn't think to gauge his reaction. The thought was too offensive. Kathryn's hair. Her luxurious mane. *No fucking way.* Stepping closer, he wanted to model the husband's outrage and shake her by the elbows. "No. Very bad idea. No haircut."

The husband turned and laid an enormous hand on his chest. Shoving slightly, Daniel Maller forcibly put distance between Jeff and Kathryn. He was not sure how he got so close to her. Kathryn stirred dangerous emotions. Jeff stared. Kathryn the fox. His heart's desire. The fearsome creature.

"How is Katie's hair your business?" the husband asked.

The husband demanded his attention by stepping in between them. Hiding Kathryn from view with his gigantic body. Inhaling deeply, he calmed the shock and panic generated by the queer notion of a haircut. Utterly absurd. Completely intolerable.

"Cutting Kathryn's hair would be detrimental to media exposure," he said calmly. "The woman in the bank robbery video has long hair. Kathryn is recognizable. A haircut would be appropriate later. After the media storm passes. Not now. Not while photographers are still camped in your bushes."

"Well," Kathryn said politely. "Thanks for the advice. But Danny is right. I can't leave Joey. The timing is wrong."

335

The fox maneuvered herself around her husband's hulking body and offered a hand. The smile on her face sweet. But her hazel eyes burned. Her touch seared.

"Take a look at the information I've tucked inside the envelope," he said. "I've got the travel information listed on a separate sheet. If you change your mind, give my assistant a call. She can make the arrangements."

"I've got to get inside. Dinner is in the oven," she laughed slightly as he reluctantly released her hand. "Since Ainsley is away, I suppose the polite thing to do would be to invite you to stay for dinner, but we already have company. My dad. And he loves my lasagna. I'm sure I won't have enough."

Kathryn turned and headed back up the driveway. "Marigold," she called.

The dog remained. Looking up with devoted eyes. Waiting for a pat. Reaching down, he scratched the dog behind the ears once more. Satisfied. Marigold chased Kathryn up the driveway.

"She likes you," the husband said suspiciously.

"You think so?" he asked. "I didn't get that impression. The dinner invitation was empty. I'm afraid I might have offended her."

"Not my wife," Daniel Maller corrected. "The dog. Marigold. She likes you. Usually she is suspicious of strangers. Kate jogs in the park and found her. She was a stray."

"Yes," he laughed as he rounded the hood of the SUV. "I know. I recognize her floppy ears. I jog in the park, too."

He climbed quickly into the SUV. Revving the engine, he released the brake and lurched away from the curb. Examining his rear view mirror, he smirked. The husband stood frozen. Staring blindly. He could almost hear the wheels inside Daniel Maller's thick skull grinding.

Perhaps the husband wasn't quite the idiot after all.

CHAPTER 60

BETTER THAN ANYONE

Danny didn't eat his dinner. He pushed the food around his plate while Kate's dad led the conversation at the table. Kate forced herself to eat. She hoped the food would quiet the nerves trembling her stomach.

Danny was upset, stewing since she left Jeff Dixon alone with him in the driveway—an obvious mistake in judgment, but necessary at the time. She had to get away from Jeff. His raven eyes bore right into her soul—saw who she really was. It was too dangerous being close to him. And now she worried—worried Danny already knew, already witnessed too much.

When the conversation turned to Kate's new job, she jumped to temper her father's enthusiasm. Danny didn't need another reason to lose his temper.

"I'm not so sure about the job, Dad. The timing doesn't seem right. I feel badly, but I may turn Sharon down—tell her to find someone else. If I want to go back to work, I can easily find a part-time job around town. Something not so time-consuming."

Kate shoved away from the table and went to pour decaf coffee. Her dad would want a cup with Molly's oatmeal cookies.

"Whatever makes you happy, my dear," her father said. Opening his arms, he welcomed Joey onto his lap.

Both Danny and her dad set themselves back in their chairs as the older boys cleared the table for dessert.

"I thought you were excited about Mrs. Hilliard's job," Peter said, piling the plates on the counter.

"I was," Kate agreed. "But I'm worried about spending too much time outside of the house."

"Take the job," Danny said in a low tone.

Kate's heart stuttered. His voice was monotone—unfamiliar—scary. Danny stared out the patio door. "Your dad is right. You should do what makes you happy."

"I am happy," Kate said cheerfully.

She set the cookies on the table and slid the steaming cup of coffee in front of her dad. Danny kept his eyes on the backyard.

"No," he said assuredly. "You haven't been happy since Sharon showed up in town."

"That's not true." Kate set a hand on Danny's shoulder, but it was cold—like stone.

Her touch delivered no comfort—he remained rigid. Looking up into her eyes, he searched—his stare angry. He didn't believe her. Kate's father shifted in his seat and cleared his throat.

"Danny's gotta point, Kathryn," her father said. "Some girls would be content to stay at home, but I think your time is just about up. You've done your duty. Joey is a big boy. Ready for school. You gotta get yourself out. Find yourself a mountain to climb. Slay a couple dragons. Pick a couple fights. I'm surprised you lasted this long. A girl like you needs stimulation."

Danny rose from his seat abruptly and went to the refrigerator. Pulling out a beer, he ignored his family and turned for the front door. Kate whined softly before sitting in a kitchen chair.

"Leave him be, Kathryn," her dad said as he reached to pat her hand. "This business with the bank robbery has got him worked up. He's a good man. He'll work through it."

338

"It doesn't help when you say things that incite him, Dad," she whined. "Danny won't let me out of the house to go to the store. He certainly does not like the idea of me slaying dragons and starting fights."

Laughing, Dad reached for cookie. "He ain't stupid. Danny knows you better than anyone, my dear. I wasn't saying anything the man didn't already know."

Kate groaned. Her head collapsed on the table, and she hid her face in her arms. The boys laughed at their mother's dramatic display, but she wasn't playing.

Danny knew her better than anyone. It was true and not something she wanted to be reminded of.

CHAPTER 61

SIMPLE

The boys came out onto the porch to say goodnight, but Kate left him alone. It wasn't smart and very unlike her. The longer he was alone, the crazier he became.

He was working through it in his brain—remembering insignificant details, picking apart Kate's words, picking apart Jeff Dixon's words.

The police car was still stationed at the corner. His family was safe. Their home secure. But something else rattled in his gut. Something close to fear simmered inside his stomach, and as it did, it thickened into something close to insane rage. He fought for hours against it—tried to reason his way out of it—but there it was, lying in his lap. Jeff Dixon.

He left his empty beer bottles on the porch. The pictures on the foyer wall shook when he slammed the front door. He didn't bother to lock it. What was the point?

Standing over her, he watched as she breathed. Kate was awake and pretending to be asleep. He thought about wringing her neck but switched her reading lamp on instead. Kate blinked and set herself up on one elbow, her pouty mouth opened slightly in surprise.

"You fucked him, didn't you."

"Danny, who?" she asked sitting straight up. Kate was fully alert. "No."

"Just tell me the truth, Katie. I'm not fucking stupid."

She shook her head, eyes on the blankets. She struggled for words. "I know you're not stupid, Danny. I could never…"

She jumped when he laid a hand beneath her chin turning her face upwards. He held her still.

"Look me in the eyes. Tell me now. Tell me now how you could never fuck that little weasel, that lawyer prick, Dixon."

"No," Kate tried to shake her head again, but he held her tight, gripping her face. "I didn't Danny."

"I can see it in your eyes. You're lying to me."

Disgusted, he released her face and paced. He wanted too much to lay hands on her—to make her hurt, make her cry, make her confess. Clutching his ears, he roared. Trapped—he was trapped inside the walls of their bedroom. Their bed was a testament to the thousands of times he had laid down with her. The thousands of times she had seduced him, tested him. She had made him do it, made him cross the invisible line, made him want to hurt her, punish her, spank her. Kate asked for it. And now he knew why.

"How could you say that to me? What did I do? I don't understand. Why are you accusing me?"

"Shut up," he hissed. "The only thing I want to hear out of your mouth is the truth. Or is it too much of a stretch of you?"

"Oh God." Kate's cry was pained. *Good.* She should feel it too.

Whirling, he faced her, stared her down. She was cross-legged on the bed. Her face buried in her hands, shaking her head.

"When?" he demanded. "When did it start? In the park? At the Village Board Meeting? Or was it the night you came home late with that bullshit story? The night of the storm when he drove you home? You were alone with him. I know you, Kate. I know how you love it. Did you go down on him in that fancy SUV? Did you suck Dixon's cock?"

"No," she whined. "Danny, stop."

"That's why he came sniffing around again. You're too good, Kate. Too goddamn good at being a whore. You were a whore before I met you, and you're a whore now."

"Okay," she pleaded, holding her hands over her ears. Her whole body was tense with fear. Or was it pain? "I'll tell you. If I tell you, will you stop? Please, Danny. No more."

His heart wrenched inside his chest. Gulping, he tried to get air. *Kate. No.* He didn't want to hear it, not anymore. It hurt too damn much. He set himself on the edge of the overstuffed chair in the corner. Elbows on his knees, he folded his hands and stared at his red knuckles. He'd endure it, the agony. If got to be too much, he'd run.

"The night of the Village Board Meeting," she began. "We debated. It got heated, but I won. No question, I had the stronger argument. He followed me and Sharon out into the parking lot. He asked me about my schooling. He was very complimentary. Gave me his card and invited me to phone him. He wanted to talk about the garden. Sharon saw the whole thing, Danny. She was waiting by the truck. You can ask her. I wouldn't have believed it, if she hadn't confirmed it. He was coming onto me."

"Did he touch you?"

"Yes," she sighed. "Once when he shook my hand, and once when he fingered the necklace I was wearing. The one Joey made me for Mother's Day."

"Fuck." Danny leapt to his feet.

"I'm sorry. Please, Danny. It was an accident."

"What? What was an accident? Tell me."

"I liked it," she cried. "The verbal combat. I encouraged him. It was exciting."

"Did you fuck him? That night you were alone?"

"No," she shook her head wildly. "But, I knew I'd allowed the verbal sparring to go too far. He said he was leaving his wife. Said his marriage was over. It was horrible. Danny, his wife, Ainsley, she's so sweet. So innocent. I felt like I might have had a hand in hurting her. Like, I let him think he had a chance at something with me."

"Did he make a move on you? Did the little prick touch you?"

"No. You were on the porch," she was still pleading, holding her hands out to him. Desperate. His wife was desperate. "It stopped him cold. You scared him, Danny. He asked how tall you were."

"I knew it. I knew it that night. But you lied, Kate. You tricked me into believing I was delusional. You said I was projecting my guilt."

"I couldn't tell you," she whined.

"Why? Don't I have a right to know when a man makes a move on my own goddamn wife?"

"Look at you," she accused. "I knew you would react this way. I was afraid you'd storm over to his house and start a fight. But I couldn't let you. His wife, Ainsley. Danny, I couldn't do that to her."

"And the park? What about that?"

"What about the park?" she asked, confused.

"He told me he jogs in the park. He recognized Marigold. Knew she was stray."

"Lots of people jog in the park. I'm sure lots of people have seen Marigold."

Marigold lifted her head off her paws and cocked her head at Kate. Looking past him, Kate stared at the wall, remembering.

"I saw him outside of the park once. I was with Peter and Marigold, but he wasn't jogging. He was in his car. I was on foot. We talked about the garden. He told me he withdrew his complaint. Said it was Ainsley who had the objection to the site. Not him."

"You told him about Natalie. He knew her name. Was that why you fucked him? Revenge."

Kate shook her head. "No. I didn't even know Natalie's name until last Friday. How could I have told him? I never fucked him, Danny. It never got that far. I wouldn't."

Confused, he paced. She had explained it away, all of it. Jeff Dixon came onto her. The little fucker made a play for his wife and then had the balls to drive up to his house. Jeff Dixon still wanted her. He was trying to get Kate away from him.

"New York," he seethed.

"Yes," Kate said quickly. "The deal was too good to be true. I threw it in the garbage. I told him no. You heard me, Danny. You were standing right there. Did I do or say anything to encourage him? Remember, I asked about his wife."

"Shit," he mumbled. He stared down at his hands. They were shaking. For Christ's sake, he was shaking.

Kate got up from the bed and approached him slowly. She stopped at the end of the bed, hesitant to get too close. She was barefoot, wearing one of his old T-shirts as pajamas, shivering. Kate was cold. Danny took two long steps and grasped her neck with both hands. Tilting her head, he stared into her scared eyes.

"You didn't fuck him?"

"No," she didn't blink, didn't hesitate, and he wanted so much to believe her.

Danny slid his hands over her shoulders and down her arms. Yanking at the T-shirt, he laid his cold hands over her breasts. *Mine.* Gently he cupped them, weighed them in his palms. Slowly, he tightened his grasp, increasing pressure.

"Did he touch your tits?"

"No," she gasped.

He couldn't really look at her—not yet—so he took her apart, focused on her body not her face, his wife. Kate knew exactly what to say and knew how to say it. Hunching, he wrapped his left arm around her, held her close and let his right hand drag down her stomach, reached two fingers in between her legs. *Mine.* She cried and bit her lip. Her whole body winced.

"Did he spread your legs? Kate, did he put his fingers inside you?"

She locked onto his wrist, tugged at it, but it only made him delve deeper. Groaning, he wanted to hurt her. He hated himself for the way he wanted her—he wanted her still, wanted to fuck her.

"Stop it, Danny." Her voice was unsure. Very un-Kate. She shoved until he released her. "You're hurting me."

Kate turned her back and strode into the bathroom.

"Isn't that what you like?" he seethed and chased after. "How many times have you asked me to make it hurt?"

"Enough," she shouted. Shrill. Scared. Naked. "Stop it. Now. Danny."

Kate shuffled on a robe and backed against the sink, her stance defensive, her fists clenched. He laughed—as if she could hurt him anymore than she already had.

"Mom?"

There bedroom door cracked open, and Kate flew past. A blur—she ran to their son. Billy. *The kids—they were Kate's top priority.* He listened from the bathroom as she quieted Billy's fears.

"Why are you yelling?" Billy asked. "You never yell."

"I yell all the time," Kate laughed awkwardly.

"Not at Dad," he said. "Are you all right? You sounded scared."

"Go to bed, Bill," Danny snapped from the bathroom.

"I'm sorry we woke you," she sighed. "It's just a fight. Married people fight all the time. We'll hash it all out and make up. Don't worry."

"Are you sure you're okay?" he asked again.

"Yes. Daddy is upset but that's all. I'm okay."

"Why is Dad upset? Are you fighting about the lady from the train?"

Danny turned on his heels and marched into the bedroom. His son was standing in the doorway. Kate's hand was on Billy's arm, soothing him, mothering him.

"Go to bed," Danny repeated. "This is none of your business."

Kate tore her gaze away from Billy. The hair whipped across her face. She cut Danny with her eyes, warning him. She shielded their son and drew tight lips across her teeth. She wasn't scared anymore, she was pissed.

Waving his arms in frustration, he stomped back into the bathroom. Kate reassured Billy again. Her offer to tuck him into bed was declined, and then she waited by the door, listening to his footsteps as they crossed the wood floor. Danny heard her sigh in relief. Billy was in bed. He charged back into the bedroom. Kate blocked the door.

"Where are you going?" she asked, tightening her grip on the door handle.

"I'm going to go find that lawyer prick and beat the shit out of him."

She moved so fast he barely caught her. Kate's arms wrapped around his neck. She clung to him, pleading. "No. You can't. Danny, please. The boys. They'll hear you leave. Billy is already afraid."

It happened very fast. Begging, she let the robe slip away and rubbed her body up the length of his, making it impossible to think. Kate undid his belt and unzipped his fly. She tore at his clothes.

"I can smell it on you," he murmured as she knelt before him.

He groaned and stumbled backwards when she went down on his cock. "Dixon could smell it, too. You wanted to fuck him…suck his cock."

She released him then. Looking up at him, she sunk her hands into his ass cheeks, rubbed her face along his cock. He groaned again, but this time it escaped from a place deep inside Danny's chest. She was so fucking sexy. And it was all her fault. Her fucking fault for making him want her so much. Need her so much.

"No, Danny. I only want you." Her voice was low, husky, full of longing.

Laying a hand on her shoulder, he shoved her onto her back. Dropping to his knees, he pushed two fingers into her pussy. Of course—she was wet. Kate was always ready.

"Did Dixon make you this wet," he asked.

"Danny, please."

He growled at the writhing body beneath his hand. *Kate. Mine.* Rolling her over onto her stomach, he slapped her ass, making her cry. She kicked and moved away. *No.* Gripping her by the hips, he pulled her up onto her knees. She was so wet. He could feel it, smell it. Kate was bad, and he knew it. Danny knew it from the very beginning, and he hated her, hated himself for wanting her. *Kate.*

Danny wanted to fuck her ass—wanted to make her scream, to rip her apart, to make her hurt. But he didn't. He couldn't; he wanted it too much. Instead, he held her in place with a tight grip and pounded his cock into her sopping wet pussy.

Kate bucked and tossed her head. She gratefully took his abuse, whining she pled for more. *Please…please…please.* Her ass smacked against his tense stomach with every penetration. His pace was deliberate, punishing. He took her to the brink and her whines became high in pitch. *Danny…Danny…Danny.*

Slick with sweat, he laid down his fear, released his need, gave in to his overwhelming desire to possess her. *Kate.* Climaxing, he clawed at her hips.

"Mine," he uttered as his cum spilled into the hot, wet depths of Kate.

She sighed, welcoming his release. She breathed and relaxed. Danny left her wasted body on the floor, stumbled to the bed and collapsed into the pillows. Closing his eyes, he tried not to listen to her familiar movements—cleaning herself, getting ready for sleep. Her tiny footsteps shuffling across the thick carpet. Carefully, she climbed into bed next to him and laid a warm hand along his back.

"I'm sorry, Danny."

"You should have told me sooner," he mumbled into his pillow.

"I know."

Rolling onto his side, he searched. And he found her—his wife—peering lovingly at him through the darkness. Kate loved him still. He pushed the hair away from her face.

"I could never forgive you, Katie. Just the possibility of you wanting to fuck another man—it's too much for me."

"I know, Danny. Don't think about it. Don't let it come between us."

No. Danny pulled her into his chest, kissed the top of her head. *Never.* He wouldn't let the lawyer prick weasel his way in. Closing his eyes, he prayed for sleep. He needed rest, sweet slumber.

Instinctively, his arms tightened around Kate as he experienced one sudden clear thought. It rang like a bell in his head. He was resigned with new knowledge. It helped relax his tense muscles. It slowed his racing thoughts. *Simple.*

If Jeff Dixon came sniffing around again, he'd kill him.

CHAPTER 62

TIGHTROPE WALKING

Billy gave his father suspicious sideway glances all through breakfast. Danny was not saying much—his gray eyes were darker than usual—but he was going through the motions. He drank his coffee, read his paper, and got showered. Kate managed to get the boys off to school without any fuss.

After some gentle encouragement, Danny took Marigold and Joey for a walk at a nearby forest preserve. He finally left her alone—alone with her dad anyways. She could have taken off then—slipped to the store without an escort—gone for a jog in the park—but she didn't. Kate gritted her teeth and went about the business of keeping house. She felt better if she was moving forward—accomplishing even the smallest of tasks.

Kate striped the sheets off the beds and began to sort through the mountain of dirty linens piled in her basement laundry room. She could hear his footsteps overhead. Marigold was skittering at his heels, and they both immediately sought her out.

"Katie?" he called.

"Down here, Coach," she shouted, her voice nearly drowned out by the whirling washing machine.

He stood on the staircase a bit out of breath and gave her a good once over. His gray eyes were brighter now. The exercise and fresh air had alleviated the stress. Marigold nudged her eagerly with a wet nose, and Kate set her chore down to give her a kiss.

"You sure do a lot of laundry."

"Towels on Monday, rugs on Tuesday, sheets on Wednesday," she recited. "Where's Joey?"

"I left him outside. Your dad was on the deck," he replied. "Joey wanted to skateboard a bit."

Kate nodded—Danny hovered.

"Could you do me a favor?" she asked.

"Sure."

"I stripped the beds," she said. "As long as I have you here, I want to take advantage of your muscle. Could you flip the mattresses? I'll make them up when you're done."

Danny spun on his heels and shot up the stairs. Marigold eagerly chased after him. At least, he was anxious to be of some use. Playing bodyguard couldn't be very fun.

Danny finished his task too soon. He walked up behind her—suspiciously eyeing the legal pad on the kitchen counter. Kate was listening to voicemail messages and listing out names and phone numbers.

"I thought I should create some kind of log," she explained. "Just in case we decide on granting an interview. There was a producer from one of the cable networks. She called twice and sounded nice. Said she was a mother of a boy Joey's age."

Danny held his breath—his gray eyes grew cloudy again. But she didn't have time to placate him. Kate spied Molly through the glass of the sliding patio door. Her neighbor was running towards their house—waving her arms wildly—her face distraught. Molly was yelling at someone—someone in their driveway.

"Danny," Kate said, pointing out the window.

He was out the patio door before she could set her pencil down. His footsteps thundered across the deck. Marigold ran excitedly after him. When Kate got outside, her dad was blinking himself awake—caught mid-doze in a deck chair. Molly stood frozen at their property line, and Danny—Danny was yelling in the face of a young man holding an expensive-looking camera.

"Joey?" she called desperately.

Her son was hidden from view—cowering behind his father—Marigold standing sentry at his side. When he heard his mother's voice, he bolted. Joey ran across the driveway and leapt into her open arms.

"He was nice," Joey whimpered into her neck. "I thought it was okay."

Shouting questions, Danny towered over the reporter. Curse words fired across the yard. They were harsh, angry words too ugly for a bright spring day in their Chicago suburb. Whimpering again, Joey held hands over his ears and clenched his eyes shut.

After calling an anxious Marigold, Kate rushed into the house, deposited Joey in her father's arms, and dashed for the front door.

"I'm going for the police. They're still parked on the corner."

Kate ran out of the house waving her arms. The cop spotted her immediately. He turned on his lights and sped down their street. Kate met him in the driveway and was grateful to see it was a familiar face. It was Officer Dennis. The cop who fussed over Joey and made him smile after the bank robbery.

"There was a reporter in the yard," she explained. "He was talking to Joey."

Officer Dennis put one hand on his holster and ran towards the commotion. Danny was done intimidating the young reporter with words. He was shaking him—shaking the reporter senseless as he spit profanities.

Officer Dennis interceded immediately—his eyes only on Danny. It was obvious who the threat was, and it wasn't the trespasser. Molly was nervous—confused at what might be required of her, but also obviously desperate to get away from Danny's violent display. She waved with a slight shrug of her shoulders and walked briskly back into her house.

Kate tried to soothe her husband—stroked his arm—set herself between him and Officer Dennis, but there was no calming him. Danny had more than enough anger to spare and laid a generous portion of his abuse on the police.

"Mr. Maller, you need to calm yourself down," Officer Dennis warned.

"And you need to do your goddamn job," Danny shouted.

Straining against Kate's imposing body, he waved his arms. She was using all her leg strength—planting her running shoes into the driveway, she held him back. Kate willingly put herself in the path of Danny's fury.

"What the fuck? Were you taking a nap? How did this guy get on my property? I want that fucking camera. He was taking pictures of my kid."

Officer Dennis showed incredible restraint. He never responded back. Instead, he took the reporter by the elbow and escorted him down the driveway. Danny was not letting up. He fought against Kate as Officer Dennis stuffed the reporter into the backseat of the police cruiser.

Hurling insults, Danny questioned the competence of the Wheaton police department. The police department that took care of Kate and Joey—brought them lunch—made her tea. In horror, Kate covered Danny's mouth with her palm, and he swatted. His elbow came down hard on her shoulder, and she lost her footing. Her ankle twisted, and her knee hit the black top of the driveway.

Kate didn't stay down long. Danny had top position, but he was vulnerable—apologetic, he stooped to help her. Instinctively, Kate fisted her right hand and jumped to her feet. She punched Danny in the gut, injuring herself in the process. When he didn't flinch, she cried out in frustration.

"What the hell is wrong with you? Stop it, Danny. Stop it right now."

Danny stared down at her, his eyes cloudy. Kate stared back—too furious to trust herself, she held her tongue. Searching through a cluster of emotions, she calmed herself down. It was not the time to abandon reason and discipline. Closing her eyes to her husband's frozen form, she breathed.

352

Danny insisted on staying close to her, but the longer he did, the more volatile he became. It was the excuse she was looking for, and she took it. Kate pulled out her safety net of lies, double checked the security of the knots, and began to mentally fill in the gaps with a few necessary deceits.

"Where's Joe?" he asked meekly.

Kate opened her eyes. Danny was suddenly pitiful. His mental anguish weakened his proud posture. His shoulders stooped, and he ran a hand absentmindedly over his beard.

Kate glanced at the police cruiser as it backed out of their driveway. She waved apologetically at Officer Dennis. Nodding once, he gave her a solemn look and drove away.

"He's inside with my dad. Away from the windows, I hope."

Kate turned her back on Danny and searched for a task to keep her nervous hands busy. Impatiently, she began picking up the yard. It was strewn with Marigold's tennis balls. Danny shuffled behind.

"I'm sorry, Trouble. Did I hurt you? I lost my temper."

"I want you to take the boys to Wisconsin," she said curtly. "I'm going to call that news producer in New York and arrange an interview. If I start with a major venue, maybe interest will die down quicker. I can negotiate my own terms with the network. I don't need a lawyer."

"No," he said mildly. "Katie, please. I'll go with you. We'll send the boys with your dad. Walt and Rosemary can watch over them."

Kate walked into the garage and dumped the tennis balls into a bucket. She turned to face him. It was decided.

"I'm going alone, Dan, and I am not asking your permission. You're scaring me, and you're scaring the kids. I think you need to get away from me for a while."

Danny growled. His hands balled into fists and his eyes narrowed. Inside the garage—away from the bright sun—her husband morphed into someone else. Hulking, he loomed over her. He fought fear with anger. It was his mental defense.

"Jeff Dixon," he seethed. "You're going to New York with that lawyer prick."

Kate moved fast—took an offensive position. She had to stop his train of thought, and she had to stop it convincingly. Gripping the baseball bat leaning against the ball bucket, she swung, missing on purpose. Danny backed away instantly.

"You want to do it again, Danny?" she asked in a low tone. "I forgave you once, but I won't a second time. Call me a whore. I dare you."

Kate loosened her grip on the bat, relaxed her fingers into the grip. It felt very natural. Her muscle memory already had her in correct wind up position. She played baseball too many times with her brothers. The bat was a perfect weapon in her hands. Danny was confused—her stance was shocking.

"Do it, Dan," she taunted. Taking a sidestep, Kate lined up her swing.

Clinch fighting did not work on Danny. He was too strong. It was like trying to kick a hole in the solid rock beneath her feet. The bat kept him at a distance. She couldn't afford to get too close. She would lose. Inhaling deeply, she shifted her weight—steeled her backbone. "I know you want to. I know it's on the tip of your tongue. Call me a whore and see what happens."

Danny covered his face with his hands and collapsed against the car parked in the garage. Instead of putting the bat down, Kate waved it, used it for emphasis as she paced across the cold cement of the garage floor.

"This is not about the lawyer prick. This isn't even about the bank robbery. This is about you and me, Dan. We've been together for nearly twenty years. Never in all that time have I given you reason to question my faithfulness. It's not enough that I've devoted my adult life to you. You cannot forgive the countless boys I fucked before you."

Danny moaned, shook his head, and tried feebly to make her stop. But she didn't. Kate let it roll. Pacing, her words hit below the belt. There was no time for gentle persuasion. He had to let her go.

"I will always be the girl who showed up at your house party with a condom in her pocket. That's who I am to you. The girl who lifted her skirt and begged to be fucked."

"Stop it, Kate," he begged. "Please, you can't expect me to let you go to New York alone. For Christ's sake, you were nearly kidnapped."

"Let me go, Danny. I am not a woman who needs to be looked after. Don't try to change who I am. You won't like the end result. Go to Wisconsin with the boys. It will be good practice for you. I won't live in your shadow anymore."

He stared at her blankly—gray eyes wide with surprise—his mouth partially open.

"Don't be so shocked," she said, tossing the bat back into the bucket. "You know who I am. Sides of my personality have been in remission. Laying dormant while I played house. But they were never gone, Danny. I'm sorry, but I'm done pretending to be something I'm not. These last couple weeks have been a revelation. I'm going to clean up this mess. You can't stop me. I'm going to New York alone."

Kate said the words, but she didn't hear them. Her mind was already listing the tasks she needed to complete before packing her suitcase and meeting Jeff Dixon at the Naperville Airport. Turning her back, she left Danny behind. Hurting him was her only way out, and she could not feel bad about it. There was no time.

Kate was already tightrope walking—her confidence balanced on the edge of a knife, her only direction forward, and her urge to look backwards dangerous. So she pushed, moving farther away from Danny. Trusting her safety net, she focused on a glimmering spot in the distance.

Failing was unthinkable. She would make it across the tightrope, and she would do it alone.

CHAPTER 63

DEPENDABLE

Danny was living on reserved air, and he didn't have much left. Breathing through his nose his intakes were sharp and shallow. Kate ignored his pleas. Told him to shut up when he got too pesky and slept on the edge of their mattress. She avoided even accidental physical contact.

The boys were suspicious, especially Billy. They wanted to know why their mom was going away. But Kate explained everything carefully and quieted their fears. Danny nodded in agreement as she told the boys her plans at dinner. He couldn't speak. His words came out wrong. Kate wasn't listening anyways. She was like a machine. In and out of the house, she went on countless errands, made phone calls inside the privacy of their bedroom. And lists, she made lots of lists.

Near panic, Danny stood in the doorway of Joey's bedroom and listened to her say good-bye. Kate gave him a stuffed yellow dog with a personally recorded message tucked inside its belly. It was her voice reminding Joey that his momma loved him. Danny wasn't looking forward to a similar message.

Trailing her down the stairs, he couldn't help but notice the way she scanned the house. Inspecting every corner, Kate seemed unsatisfied, reluctant to leave—like she was forgetting something.

"Order a pizza for dinner tonight. The potpies are for Wisconsin," she said, pointing to the food cooling on the counter. "And don't forget, Dan, Joey will need to bring his security blanket. Let him have it as much as he wants. Please make an effort to be sweet to him. Give him extra kisses. Tuck him in with a story."

"You don't have to tell me to be sweet," Danny griped.

"He's going to miss me," she retorted. "That's all I meant to imply."

Kate picked up her suitcase and glanced around the kitchen again. Reaching, Danny took the suitcase away. His hand brushed against hers, and she quickly released her grip. *Why was she avoiding his touch?*

"I sent a note to school excusing Billy and Peter from school tomorrow, but I also asked the teachers to give them makeup homework. They should do it tonight or on the ride to Wisconsin. Don't give them electronics until all the work is done. Don't take their word for it. You'll have to check."

She was still giving instructions as she walked out the backdoor. Marigold pranced at her heels. The dog didn't know Kate was leaving without her. And Danny was envious, envious of the animal's ignorance. Kate swung open the truck's door and stood blocking the seat and forbidding Marigold from jumping in.

"And please, take care of my dog," she pleaded. "Marigold has never been to the farm. I'm afraid she will run off to look for me."

Marigold sat at Danny's feet and looked up at him with glassy yellow eyes. "Marigold and I understand each other. We'll get along just fine."

His words sounded dead, mute, detached. Kate pursed her lips and nodded. She wasn't going to forgive him anytime soon. It was hard to believe she stayed mad this long. Inhaling deeply, his lungs failed to expand. The air was empty, lacking oxygen. Kate nodded at her suitcase. She wanted him to let go of it. Moving his heavy feet, he approached the bed of the truck and stopped.

"Maybe you should take my car," he said.

"No," Kate said, shaking her head once. "I like my truck."

"Then give me a minute to take the wheelbarrow out of the back."

"Danny, no," she said curtly.

She ripped the suitcase out of his hand and threw it into the bed of the truck.

"I have to get going," she said dismissively. "Sharon said if I get to O'Hare early enough, I might be able to catch an earlier flight to New York by getting on standby. She does it all the time."

"It will only take a minute, Kate," he said evenly.

"I don't care," she said with a shrug. "Leave it, Danny. And apologize to Tom and Molly. They can use the truck to get wood mulch when I get back."

Sighing did nothing to release the tightness in his chest. "I wish you would let me help you," he snapped.

"You are helping me," she snapped back. "You are taking care of the kids."

"Will you call?"

"Of course," she said. "I'll call to say good night to the boys. And I'll leave my cell phone on just in case they want to talk to me."

"How long are you gonna stay mad at me, Trouble?" he asked meekly. "I am sorry, you know. I haven't thrown any temper tantrums in the last twenty-four hours. Don't I get points for that?"

The tension around Kate's mouth eased, and she gave him the tiniest hint of a smile. For the first time, his panic subsided enough so he could really look at her. She was dressed in a new outfit. Green, it complimented her eyes. It looked soft and comfortable, like something a rich woman would wear to yoga class but more stylish. It made her look very lean.

"I've never seen that outfit before," he said. "It looks pretty on you."

Surprised, Kate looked down at her clothes. "Thank you. I bought it yesterday."

Tugging on the waistband, she shrugged. "Elastic waist. Molly said it was good for travel. Wrinkle resistant."

"It's new, then?"

"Don't worry," she said snidely. "I paid cash from my household fund. I didn't use the debit card."

"Katie," he exclaimed. "That's not what I meant."

She brushed quickly past. He didn't have time to make a grab for her. Climbing into the truck, she left the driver side door open as she turned the key in the ignition. No kiss goodbye, then. Kate was going to leave with no reassurances. Not one kind word.

"Please be careful," he said, pleading with his eyes.

"I promise," she answered.

"I love Trouble."

Kate looked at him for a long moment, like she was deciding something. So he jumped. Danny took two long steps and wrapped his arms around her waist. Because she was sitting inside the cab of the truck, they were nearly the same height, and he took advantage. His right hand moved to the back of her neck. Holding her in place, he kissed her full lips, tasted her with the tip of his tongue. Danny kissed his wife like it was the last time. *Mine,* he repeated silently in his head, hoping his message came through but knowing it did not. Kate didn't reject him, but she wasn't responding to his touch, at least, not in a way he was used to.

"It's only because I love you too much," he whispered into her ear. "I can't help it. I want you all to myself."

Kate kissed him quickly on the cheek before shoving him out of the truck. Slamming the door, she kept her eyes on the windshield and shifted into reverse. His arms were heavy. In search of something to hold onto, he dropped a knee and wrapped loose arms around the dog. Marigold's ears went back, and she circled before settling in between his legs. The dog sat pressed against Danny, and they watched their favorite person in the world back out of the driveway.

"She'll be back, girl," Danny whispered into the dog's ear.

"Take care of my boys," Kate called out before shifting the truck into drive. "Danny, I'm depending on you."

The boys—they were Kate's top priority.

"Don't worry, Trouble," he said, feigning confidence. "I'm nothing if not dependable."

Nodding once, Kate smiled an emotionless smile and drove away. The tightness in his chest turned into sharp, jagged pains. Kate was gone. He had driven her away, sent her running off to New York City—alone. Danny knew she didn't have to go. She could have taped an interview with the cable network via satellite at one of Chicago's local affiliates, but Kate wanted distance. His wife didn't want to be with him.

Danny buried his face into the thick fur of Marigold's neck. Kate's scent lingered. Marigold was loyal, faithful, and completely devoted, and for this, she was rewarded with Kate's hugs and kisses. Danny could do that. He was crazy jealous, but he possessed the same qualities as Marigold. He was loyal, faithful, and devoted. Kate couldn't withhold her hugs and kisses forever.

Rising to his feet, he righted his shoulders and gazed down at Kate's dog. Danny would do his job—take care of the boys, take care of Marigold, read and re-read the list of instructions she left behind. Kate was counting on him.

And he wouldn't let her down again.

CHAPTER 64

THE CATCH

Jitters. Not nerves. Anxiety. He was anxious to see her. Shifting his weight, he curled and uncurled his toes. Waggled his fingers. They were tingly. Like a drug addict, he was anticipating his next hit. Kathryn.

Grinning, he laid a heavy foot on the accelerator. The Porsche sped down the empty highway. Kathryn surrendered. Willingly ventured out of the shallows and waded into deep water. Called his office to accept his invitation. Reminded him of his promise to honor her choice. And hung up. Short and very, very sweet.

The Cayman Islands. He wanted her naked. On her back. Caramel-colored hair fanned across white linens. Heaven. After three days alone, he would own her. She would choose him. No doubt. His heart's desire. Kathryn. His promise to honor her choice was bait. Enticing her to bite. He knew returning to the cog husband would be painful. Absolute torture. Kathryn. So sharp. So cunning. Definitely not built for bourgeois living.

Driving west into the outskirts of Naperville, he witnessed the red sun fall. The sky was every shade of happy. Purple, pink, orange, yellow. Only the occasional farmhouse dotted the horizon.

The airport was out of the way. Secluded. Private. Off an abandoned highway. And it was growing darker. Twilight.

Removing his sunglasses, he squinted into the dusky horizon. Kathryn's decrepit blue truck. It was parked across from the airport's chain link fence. Next to a field of thorny bushes and leggy trees.

Kathryn sat on the open tailgate. Her ankles crossed. Chin resting on raised knees. She was casual. Watching. Waiting. For him. His heart grew. Filled the empty cavity in his chest. Smiling, he crossed the highway's center line. Coasted to a stop on the gravel embankment. And locked eyes. She returned his smile before sliding off the tailgate.

Kathryn wore dewy green from head to toe. An outfit suitable for travel. Very becoming. The thin fabric hugged her clean lines. Accented her sculpted frame. Running shoes. Very practical. He had packed his own. Hoping they would jog together on the beach. She wore her hair in a new style. Pulled away from her face, it was wound into a messy bun. Deceivingly delicate. Long neck. Pinked cheeks. Wide eyes. Like a ballerina.

In slow motion, he swung open the car door. Unfolded his body. Righted his shoulders. Put one foot in front of the other. Kathryn's open arms. Eyes ablaze. Fervor bolted. Cross lightning. The distance between them flashed over. She purred beneath his kiss. Fused. He took in her scent. Ran hands over the soft fabric of her shirt. Reaching, he longed to undo her hair. Let loose her wild mane. But she caught his hands.

Warm despite the cool breeze. Her sturdy fingers wrapped around his wrists. Hazel eyes locked. Their gold flecks danced in the dim of twilight. Kathryn guided his hands. First her breasts. She tossed her head. Exposed her neck while he ran thumbs over her nipples. Braille reading. She wore lace. A lacy bra. Underwire boost. He coaxed. Hardened the tips. Moaning, she moved his hands slowly. Over the curve of her hips. Until finally, she let them rest. Cupping her runner's ass, he did another search. No panties. He groaned before diving for her open lips.

"Jeff," she whispered, pained. "Why are you so irresistible?"

Again, she breathed his name. Jeff. And again. Jeff. Yes. Dear God. Thank you. So hot. Impossible to contain. Their coupling unwitnessed. Their reunion private. Heaven.

"Kathryn," he answered. "My fox."

The wind blew through them. Instinctively, he turned. Blocking. Shielding her from the chill. Maintaining their heat. Kathryn clung to him. Breathing heavily, she buried her face into the collar of his shirt. Like a scared child. She whimpered. Stroking her back, he tried to soothe. Waited for his own thundering heart to quiet.

Growing comfortable, he relaxed his grip. Alone at last. No car traffic. No people for miles. The lights of the airport blinked in the distance. Past the chain-link fence. Down a long, narrow paved drive. The small, exclusive airport was a hidden gem. A politician's pet project.

"I apologize," he said into the wind. "Did you wait long? I was hoping to beat you here."

"I knew I was early," she shrugged. "That's why I waited outside. I was intimidated by the gate. The airport seems far off the highway. And lonely. I wanted to drive in with you."

Standing on her tiptoes, she nudged her nose beneath his ear. Delivered a soft kiss. He shivered involuntarily. Electric. His blood stirred.

"Jeff, you are dangerous," she whispered. "You make me forget. I can't help myself."

He chuckled. Yes. He felt it too.

"Three nights, Kathryn," he promised. "You and me. Together. It will be complete bliss. Worth every sacrifice. You will see. I promise. Your soul answers to mine. The perfect match."

"I believe you," Kathryn said as she stepped out of his embrace. "I cannot deny it anymore."

Her eyes hardened ever so slightly before she looked away. Looked into the distance. Darkness loomed. He checked his watch. Anxious again. He wanted Kathryn safely strapped into the private plane. A lovers' rendezvous.

"Are you ready to go, my fox?" he asked gently.

Reaching, he took her hand and stroked her fingers softly with his thumb. Kathryn's attention was still off in the distance. Gently, he tugged. Luring her back into deep water.

"Kathryn? Just follow me. I will show you where to park. The flight crew is probably ready. Sometimes they allow an early takeoff."

"Flight crew?" she asked.

"Yes," he teased. "The crew comes with the plane. Package deal."

She looked down at their joined hands. "Can I show you something first?" she asked shyly.

"Of course," he answered giving her a reassuring squeeze.

Kathryn released his hand. Backing up, she leaned ever so slightly against her open tailgate. Her hands went to the waistband of her pants. Lifting at her shirt, she revealed her belly button.

"I did something," she said.

Her smile was wicked. The excitement made him fidget, so he stuffed his hands into the front pockets of his khakis. The fox. So tricky. She had a surprise.

"The last time we were together," she began slowly and then moaned. Pressed her thighs together. "You were so good."

He nodded curtly. His house. His bed. Kathryn flat on her back. Spread wide. Rattling the headboard. He could still taste her on his tongue. Mouth watering.

"I wanted to do something. Something for you." She pulled hesitantly on the elastic waistband of her pants. It slid easily over her hips. Revealing more skin. Yes. The Brazilian.

"I'm glad I did it," she said in a low tone.

Naughty. She was teasing. Moving too slow.

"I did it for you, Jeff, but I like it. It's very pleasing to the eye."

Reaching into the soft confines of her pants, she rubbed with her right hand. Moaning. He held his breath. Watching Kathryn pleasure herself. Wanton. Brazen. It was complete rapture.

"And so soft," she moaned before meeting his gaze. "Like velvet."

"Yes," he hissed. "Show me. I want to see."

Right now. On the tailgate. He was rock hard. Ready to explode. Kathryn and her naked pussy. Smiling seductively, she pulled out her hand. Drew fingers under her nose. Took in her own scent. He groaned. Drawn to her, he moved closer.

"Not yet. Close your eyes and turn around," she ordered.

He shook his head. But she was serious. Frowning.

"I've already spoiled the surprise, Jeff. I couldn't wait. Don't ruin my fun. Close your eyes and turn around. I'll tell you when I'm ready."

Nodding impatiently, he agreed to play her game. Turning his back, he closed his eyes and waited. Envisioning her spread on the open tailgate, he tried very hard not to squirm. Almost desperate. Ready to unleash his desire.

Kathryn the fox. The inner workings of her mind were such a mystery. Longing. He wanted to understand. Wanted to know her. Own her. Still, she eluded him. Surprised him. Kathryn was hard to catch.

But so worth the chase.

CHAPTER 65

ESCAPE

The shrill cry of a seabird woke her before the sun could have a chance. Sneaking out wasn't easy, but Kate craved solitude. She wasn't used to so much togetherness. The empty beach was too tempting. The crashing waves were rhythmic and soothing.

Jogging on wet sand challenged her endurance. Kate was already winded, but stubbornly, she pushed her body forward. Her exercise regiment accompanied her on her travels. Her disciplined routine kept her from dwelling in the past, forced her to focus on the present, the future. Breathing salted air in through her nose, out through her mouth, she kept her eyes forward. The beach was endless. She didn't have to stop—didn't want to stop—not yet.

The breaking sun reflected off the water, and the light was blinding. Kate pulled the brim of Jeff's hat over her eyes. It bore his alma mater's emblem, Vanderbilt University, and it was his favorite. Jeff wore it on damp mornings—his dark curls peeked out from underneath. In the park, the hat always hit the ground first—carelessly discarded by Kate's impatience. Possessively, she tugged at the frayed brim.

Slowing to a walk, she let her eyes drop to the sand. The physical memory of Jeff's silky dark hair made her fingers twitch.

She loved his hair almost as much as his eyes. In their glassy raven depths, she recognized herself.

Gasping, Kate doubled over with the shock of self-realization. Jeff. She should not want him—still—so very much. Kate tried to focus on the present, to forget the past, but the memories cranked and crept into her consciousness.

The air was too heavy—her lungs burned, her chest heaved, her body was exhausted. Finally, she gave in—stopped fighting—and collapsed onto the sand. Gazing at the horizon, she caught her breath and watched the pink sky turn blue. Pelicans flew over the surf hunting for their breakfast.

Gliding effortlessly, one enormous bird spied its prey and hovered. Eyes glued, it plunge-dove into the ocean. Kate cringed. The splash was noisy, familiar. Hanging her head, she closed her eyes—the splash. The memory was emotionally intense—jolting to her heart. The size and scope of the splash was startling—unanticipated.

She likened her jagged memories to post-traumatic stress disorder. Most of the memory clips were mashed up—blurry—but others ran on a highlight reel. Clear flashes assaulted her consciousness. Rolling over and over, they were vivid. Brief clips flickered like a mental run-through. Kate bit her lip—shook her head. She should have said goodbye. It was her greatest regret.

She should have laid eyes on Jeff Dixon's beautiful face one last time before dumping his lifeless body into the dark water of Naperville's quarry.

The sounds of a murder rang in her ears. On a loop. They sounded off. The hollow thump of the metal baseball bat as it made contact with the back of Jeff's head—the rip of duck tape—the crunch of the stiff blue tarp.

The blood in her veins went cold. It was a chemical reaction. Like that night, like the day of the bank robbery, her surroundings became pristine—clear as bell, her senses raw, her pulse steady.

Flashes. Lightning. Kate glimpsed the scene. The black Porsche loomed in the darkness—abandoned—emptied. She took evidence—his wallet, his glasses, his keys, his phone—all stuffed into the compartments of her backpack.

Despite her planning, the quarry proved to be the most hazardous—the most physically daunting. The wheelbarrow was weighed down with Jeff's body. Kate struggled against ruts, rocks, and exposed roots. Sheer determination got her to the cliff's edge—the deepest point of the quarry, the longest drop. She had scouted the perfect dumping point earlier that morning and left cinder blocks, chains, and calipers under a clumpy bush.

The sky was clear, and the starlight gave her some advantage, but the surrounding woods were dark, foreboding. Kate's flashlight kept the shadows at bay—guided the rim of her wheelbarrow as she made slow progress to the quarry.

The memory burned, and she rubbed her temples. As she felt her way along the length of Jeff's body—knees, waist, neck—fastening three chains around the crunchy tarp—Jeff moaned more than once. The sounds were muffled—his mouth duct taped, his head bagged, his body wrapped—but she heard him nevertheless. Kate heard Jeff moan just before she rolled his mummified body over the cliff. The splash was so loud she stood frozen, too afraid to move.

Alone on the edge of the cliff, Kate shone her flashlight on the broken water. The cinderblocks sunk hard and fast, taking Jeff for a ride to the bottom. She waited—staring—and witnessed Jeff Dixon's disappearance. She watched until the dark water grew still. Kate waited until the surface of the water reflected light like Jeff's glassy black eyes. She didn't cry. Discipline and reason kept her emotions in check.

Kate had committed her crime of passion in the park when she cheated on Danny over and over with a dangerous stranger. The evening she flew to New York was the other side of the coin. The momentum of passion swung back violently turning Kate into a cold executioner. The murder was premeditated and calculated.

It was so easy it scared her. Every move was scripted—pre-determined. She covered her tracks on her drive to O'Hare Airport. Depositing contaminated evidence, she exited the freeway frequently and made use of public trash cans and rusty dumpsters.

She took Jeff's suitcase to New York. The taped television interviews fleshed out her alibi. New York was crowded. Jeff's belongings were easily absorbed into the city's trash every time she left the ho-tel—out to eat, shopping, sightseeing. Little by little, pieces of Jeff disappeared—all but one. Kate kept the hat. Smiling to herself, she gave the brim another tug. Jeff would have appreciated the gesture.

After a long exhale, Kate forced her tired legs to stand. The sun was up, but the light was still weak. Florida's summer heat was tolerable in the early morning. Her eyes flew away from the hori-zon, drawn to the familiar sound of jogging footfalls. The breath caught in her chest and her heart skipped a beat at the sight of him.

The jogger was streamlined and sleek. Shirtless, his tanned skin glistened with sweat. She couldn't help but leer at the corded muscles of his shoulders and chest. Lean, trim, and completely masculine—so much like Jeff. Overwhelmed with desire, she let her admiring gaze linger too long. The jogger slowed. Out of breath, he set his hands on his hips and smiled.

"Good morning," he said breathlessly.

The voice was deep and inviting, but his eyes were light blue—friendly—flirtatious. Zip. Nada. He did nothing for her. This was not the jogger she longed for.

"Good morning," she answered briskly.

"I've seen you before," he said. "On the beach. Jogging."

Kate smiled politely before trying to brush her hands and legs clean of sand.

"Do you live in Sanibel? Or are you vacationing?" he asked conversationally.

"Vacationing," she answered mutely. "My husband rented a house. Our three boys love the beach."

The jogger's eyebrows rose in shock. "I must say, you certainly don't look like a mother of three."

Kate shrugged her shoulders before striding away, but he caught her lightly by the elbow.

"My name is Trent Long."

Kate froze and stood staring at his outstretched hand. "No thank you, Trent," she finally answered. "I'm in a hurry to get back to my husband."

Kate pulled the brim of Jeff's hat over her eyes and ran away. Her shoes had left a trail of identifiable footprints, and she ran over them. Tracing her way back to Danny, she was decidedly untired. Kate felt the sand shift beneath her feet, and she dug—sunk the soles of her shoes deeper—harder and harder. She pounded the beach. *Danny.*

Kate was completely out of breath when she reached the threshold of their sun-bleached rental. Kicking her beaten shoes off, she stealthy unlocked the door and slipped into the air conditioned bungalow. It was quiet. Everyone was still in bed.

She removed Jeff's hat and opened the tiny hall closet. Standing on her tip toes, she zipped the hat into a compartment of her backpack. It was her habit to put Jeff away. Safely hidden, the hat only came out for early morning jogs.

"Trouble," Danny called sleepily from the master bedroom. "Is that you?"

Kate jumped at the sound of his voice but quickly recovered. Carefully, she closed the closet door.

Still slightly out of breath, she slid her socked feet across the cool ceramic tile and crept into their bedroom. Leaning against the door, she smiled at her husband. The blinds were drawn, but the morning light penetrated the slants. Twisted in the sheets, Danny's body weighed down the soft mattress, and the entire bed creaked when he rolled over.

Kate leapt at him before he could focus. His laugh made her giddy, and she pinned him down while covering his face with kisses.

"You stink," he complained.

Kate straddled his hips and pulled her sticky wet running tank over her head. Danny's hands moved to her naked breasts. Kate ran her hands over the bristle of his morning stubble. Danny shaved his beard after she got her hair cut. He liked her funky new hair style but griped about the way it made her look younger than him.

"You look tired, Coach," Kate teased as she pinched his cheeks pink. "Maybe you should go back to sleep."

Danny swatted her away. "You really put me through the wringer last night."

"Me," she laughed. "You've got to be kidding. You were an animal."

Smiling shyly, Danny ran tender hands down her torso and over her hips. "Show me. I want to see it again."

Kate leapt off the bed. Eager to please, she shimmied off her running shorts. Turning her back, she set her hand on her hip and tossed her head over her shoulder.

"How does it look?" she asked.

Danny drew a finger lightly over her left ass cheek. "It's still a little red," he said, pursing his lips. "Does it hurt?"

"Not anymore."

Danny leaned back onto the pillows and stared half-smiling. "You surprised the hell out of me, Katie," he sighed. "It's the perfect gift. My name tattooed on the best piece of ass in town."

"You asked for it," Kate reminded.

He laughed. "I was only joking. I didn't expect you to actually do it."

"It makes me feel sexy," she said. "And no one but you will ever see."

"That's why I love it," he murmured.

Kate dove for her side of the bed and curled her body around his. Grateful, she set her ear to his heart. Danny's love had one condition. It was not a sacrifice. Faithfulness was all he required. Danny made her different. Danny made her good.

Closing her eyes, she disciplined her urge to revisit her mistakes. It wasn't easy. Jeff Dixon was gone. Kate did what was necessary to protect her family. Dwelling in the past served no purpose. Instead, Kate appreciated the present.

Because of Sharon, she was gaining the respect of new colleagues. The job was a chess match between management and labor, and Kate's sharp mind was engaged as gamekeeper. Working was fun and added hours away from home were welcome. Her substantial new paycheck secured their sons' future, and the boys were happy and safe. Every day the they grew closer to manhood. Danny was the ultimate role model, and Kate loved him. More importantly, she loved herself when she was with him.

"You're not falling asleep are you?" Danny asked as he rolled on top of her.

The bed frame groaned when the weight shifted. They sunk into a deep hole at the center of the mattress.

"We're gonna break this bed," Kate laughed.

"I don't care," Danny said as he dramatically fell on her. "They can bill me for the damages."

Kate smiled into his crinkly gray eyes and vowed to remember. Danny was the best thing about her.

"I love you," she swore solemnly.

"And I love Trouble," he answered immediately.

Laughing, she threw her hands over her head. Exposing her neck, she invited his kisses.

"Danny Maller," she sighed comfortably. "Your love for trouble makes me a very fortunate woman."

Danny's hands moved possessively over her body. His breathing grew heavy. Discipline and reason kept her from veering wildly off the path. But there were times—moments—especially while making love to Danny—when she lost control, and Jeff Dixon's raven eyes flashed in her mind's eye.

Kate's heart stuttered. She heard his voice murmuring her name. *Kathryn. My fox.* She gasped, writhed deceivingly beneath Danny's roaming hands.

She hoped Jeff Dixon's invisible power would fade with time, but it did not. Jeff said compartmentalizing feelings was dangerous. Sooner or later, he said, the opposing needs and desires collide. She planned to prove him wrong. Kate couldn't let him go—not totally—and she accepted it as weakness and learned to cope. In the hall closet, stuffed in the bottom of a dark backpack, Jeff secretly lurked.

Tomorrow, they would escape together. Tomorrow, they would go for a jog.

ACKNOWLEDGEMENTS

Taking on a project of this magnitude does not happen without sacrifice. Every minute I spent in my fictional world was one minute taken away from my family. Thank you to my children (Jack, Annie, Claire, Nina) and my husband for supporting me in my pursuit of a dream.

My friend, sister-in-law, and marketing diva, Karla Jo, pushed and pushed and gave much needed words of encouragement when the job of publishing *The Jogger* became too much. Thank you for believing in me.

Thank you to Jimmy. I love you. You are the provider of my happiness and the muse of my imagination. Thank heavens, you are mine, mine, mine. Forever, baby.

And to my mother, Ann Spencer. I've never written a word she didn't believe was brilliant. She is my biggest fan and alpha reader. Thank you, Mama, for teaching me to love books.